For Love or Country

For Love or Country

Book 2
The MacGregor Legacy

Jennifer Hudson Taylor

Abingdon fiction
a novel approach to faith

For Love or Country

ISBN-13: 978-1-4267-3385-7

Published by Abingdon Press, P.O. Box 801, Nashville, TN 37202

www.abingdonpress.com

Published in association with Hartline Literary Agency

Library of Congress Cataloging-in-Publication Data

Library of Congress Cataloging-in-Publication Data

Taylor, Jennifer Hudson.
  For love or country / Jennifer Hudson Taylor.
    pages cm. — (The MacGregor legacy series ; book 2)
  ISBN 978-1-4267-3385-7 (trade pbk. : alk. paper) 1. North Carolina—History—Revolution,
1775-1783—Fiction. I. Title.
  PS3620.A9465F66 2014
  813'.6—dc23

                                                                2014010209

Scripture quotations from The Authorized (King James) Version.
Rights in the Authorized Version in the United Kingdom are vested
in the Crown. Reproduced by permission of the Crown's patentee,
Cambridge University Press.

Printed in the United States of America

1 2 3 4 5 6 7 8 9 10 / 19 18 17 16 15 14

*To all the heroes who have fought for our freedom
and our country*

Acknowledgments

To everyone who helped make this book possible, and you know who you are, thank you!

Dear Readers,

As I was writing *For Love or Country*, I did a lot of historical research on the Revolutionary War in North Carolina, and specifically in Wilmington. I thought it would be helpful to discuss which characters existed in real life. The Tuscarora Indians really lived in the swamps in the Wilmington area, but the specific characters in the book are fictional.

Major James H. Craig was a real British officer who held control over Wilmington in 1781. The two Continental soldiers who were prisoners at the Burgwin House were real, General John Ashe and Cornelius Harnett. The events in the book regarding Cornelius being paraded around the town, beaten, and locked outside in a blockhouse in the cold are true.

Major James H. Craig issued a proclamation demanding that local residents give their allegiance to the crown. The Battle of Guilford Courthouse is real and reenactments take place each year in my hometown of Greensboro. The tunnels beneath Wilmington are real and date back to before the Revolutionary War, including beneath the Burgwin House, which really was built over a former jail.

I hope you enjoy *For Love or Country*.

All my best,
Jennifer Hudson Taylor
February 2014

If my people, which are called by my name,
shall humble themselves, and pray,
and seek my face, and turn from their wicked ways;
then will I hear from heaven, and will forgive their sin,
and will heal their land.

2 Chronicles 7:14 KJV

1

$\mathcal{T}$yra MacGregor did not want the Christmas feast to end. She leaned back in her wooden chair and peered at her family gathered around the long dining table, laughing and talking in jovial spirits. It had been a miracle her father, Lieutenant Malcolm MacGregor, and her elder brothers, Callum and Scott, were given a few days off from the Continental Army to spend Christmas with them. This time when they left, they would be taking her younger brother, Alec, now that he had turned ten and five. Tyra blinked back sudden tears as a searing ache twisted her insides.

"Lauren, this was a delicious meal." Da leaned over and gave their mother a kiss on her rosy cheek. They shared an intimate glance of love and devotion. Tears sprang to her mother's blue eyes. Tyra looked away, unable to witness the emotional exchange as the back of her own throat constricted.

"I did not prepare it alone, Malcolm." Mama's voice carried down the long table. "Tyra's cooking skills have greatly improved since ye've been away at war."

"Indeed?" Her father lifted a russet eyebrow, as the corners of his mouth curled in an approving grin. A full beard and thick mustache layered with gray specks in his reddish-golden whiskers branded its mark into her memory. "Then I daresay, well done, lass."

"Thank ye, Da." Tyra forced a tender smile to hide her fearful worry. Thinking of her gift to them, genuine joy crept into the muscles of her tense face. "And now I have a surprise for you all."

"Dessert?" Kirk's voice cracked as he shoved his empty plate aside. At ten and three, her youngest brother often suffered the embarrassment of his tones vibrating from his throat. He rubbed his hands. "I thought I smelled a sweet treat earlier."

Tyra took his empty plate and placed it on top of hers, biting her bottom lip to keep from blurting out the answer. She whirled and stepped toward Alec.

"No, leave mine." Alec threw a hand out to protect his unfinished plate. "I intend to eat every bite." He glanced at their father and older brother, Scott. "I do not know when I might have the blessing of another home-cooked meal after this day."

Tyra paused, her gaze meeting Alec's brown eyes. Her heart thumped against her ribs in an attempt to stomp down the rising grief welling inside her. Even though she was only ten and seven, she believed Alec was too young for war. She didn't care if other lads his age had already signed up these past five years. Many of them were gone from this world. The knowledge alone made her want to drop the plates and wrap her arms around him and beg Alec to stay. Others who had enlisted at his age continued to survive like her older brother, Scott. They had grown into fine young men, accustomed to the ways of war, always fighting for their freedom.

"I wanna go!" Kirk plopped his elbow on the table and set his chin on his palm. A disgruntled expression marred his forehead. "I am not much younger than Alec."

"Hold yer tongue." Mama's blue eyes were like the crystal frost outside as late evening approached. She toyed with the wrist of her cream-colored blouse, her dark blond hair coiled into a French bun. "'Tis bad enough I must part with three sons and a husband. They can at least leave me one son."

Tyra gulped, hating the tide of emotion threatening their last moments together. She carried the plates from the dining room to the kitchen where she placed them on the table. As she pulled out the dessert plates, her mother entered. She wiped at her eyes and took a deep breath. At five feet and eleven inches, Tyra towered over her mother by at least five inches, but she didn't let it stop her as she threw a comforting arm around her mother's shoulders.

"Mama, do not worry. God will keep them safe." Tyra hoped her voice sounded more certain than she felt. "Da, Callum, and Scott have been safe these past few years. We must have faith for Alec as well."

"Of course, ye're quite right." Mama grabbed the extra plates and gave her a grateful smile as she reached up and cupped Tyra's cheek. Thin lines framed the corners of her mother's eyes, but she still looked young at two scores and one. "I am thankful I have ye here to remind me, lass." She motioned to the dessert tray and waved Tyra forward. "Now on with ye, they are waiting."

Tyra hurried to the dining room and set the tray before her father. "I hope you all saved room for my cinnamon gingerbread cake. 'Tis a small Christmas gift I want to give each of you."

"Then we shall cherish it." Her father rewarded her with a wide grin, reaching for the small plate with eager anticipation. He grabbed a fork and carved out a bite. With slow precision, he slid it into his mouth as he watched Tyra and chewed. He nodded in appreciation. "Mmm, quite good."

"Thank you, Da." Tyra said, pleased her father liked it. "Now, the rest of you must try it."

"I am ready." Kirk leaned up on his elbows against the dining table and drummed his hands on the surface. He beat out a ditty of "Free America." "See? I could be a drummer. Plenty of boys my age have enlisted."

"Well, ye shall not be one of them," Mama said, as she set a plate by Alec and Scott. "Mind yer manners, lad."

Tyra cut slices for each of them before carving a slice for herself. She enjoyed the sweet taste of the moist cake on her tongue. With the British blockade along the coast, they had learned to do without certain supplies and cooking ingredients. Sugar was rare, but the Tuscarora Indians who lived in the nearby swamp provided them with honey. She had been able to barter for it over the past couple of months to save what little sugar they had left in anticipation of their upcoming Christmas feast.

"Someone has been making you into a fine cook while we have been gone." Callum sat back with a satisfied grin and pushed his empty plate aside. "'Tis good to be home again, all of us together one more time. I will cherish this fond memory in the months to come." His brown eyes glistened in the candlelight as he blinked back moisture and looked away. When he had first arrived yesterday, she had hardly recognized him with a full beard and mustache. She was glad he had shaved it off. He now looked more like the brother she remembered with the exception of his somber mood. Tyra could only imagine what horrible images lurked in his mind from the war. He no longer acted like a young vibrant man of only a score of years to his credit, but a seasoned man who had seen too much of life.

Tyra glanced at Scott to see if he shared the same sentiment as Callum. Scott cleared his throat and looked down, hiding his blue-eyed gaze. His blond hair looked darker than she remembered, most definitely longer, tied back in a ribbon at his neck like her father.

Always the charmer in their family, Scott had changed as well. He was more pensive and quiet than she had ever known him to be. At ten and eight, he had only been serving for three years, unlike her father and Callum.

"Mama is a patient teacher," Tyra said, breaking the silence. She glanced at her mother, knowing herself to be a difficult pupil with her unladylike qualities and lack of interest in domestic skills. She and her mother had set aside their differences and worked together while the men were away from their rice plantation at The MacGregor Quest. Tyra taught her mother to shoot a rifle and a pistol, while she made more of an effort to wear constricting gowns and assisted with more household chores—like cooking.

"Tyra has turned out to be quite a teacher herself." Mama winked at her as she took a bite of her cake. "There has been too much strife in Wilmington of late between the Whigs and the Tories, so I decided the boys should receive their education here under Tyra's guidance."

"Aye, she is more like a growling bear," Kirk grumbled, reaching for another slice of cake.

"No!" Tyra snatched the plate from his grasp, covering its contents with a protective hand. "The rest is for Da and our brothers. I wanted them to have at least one more slice to remind them of home whence they leave on the morrow."

Kirk gave her a scowl, but sat back without another protest. He glanced at his father and brothers, his green eyes wide with concern. Tyra knew he felt the same fear as she—that it might be the last time they were all together. Most of his childhood had been stolen by the War of Independence. Soon they would welcome the year of seventeen eighty-one.

"Let us retire to the parlor." Mama stood with a smile. It brightened the dark room lit only by a few candles which made shadows dance upon the paneled walls. Even the fruit painting by a local artist hung on the wall in darkness. A slight chill hovered at the glass windows of the dining room with no fire to warm them. "Kirk, go build us a warm fire in the parlor." Her brother hurried to carry out their father's bidding.

Frantic beating on the front door sent alarm through Tyra as she exchanged worried glances with the rest of the family. Who would dare interrupt their Christmas? Most of their neighbors would be at home celebrating with their own families. "Lieutenant MacGregor! I have new orders for you." A man's voice called through the door. More knocking followed.

"Wait here. I shall only be a moment." Da's boots clicked across the wooden floor as he left the dining room and entered the foyer. The sound of him unlocking the latch and sliding it back grated on Tyra's nerves. The hinges creaked and low voices conversed. A few moments later, he closed the door and walked back into the dining room. Tyra held her breath.

"I am sorry," Da said, standing at the threshold. "General Greene has gained new information and is calling all the troops back to service. We must leave now."

"Can it not wait till the morn when ye had already planned to leave?" Disappointment carried in Mama's tone. Her chin trembled as she lifted fingers to her lips as if to still the motion. Her gaze slid to each son and lingered on the three eldest. "I had hoped to have a wee bit more time."

"Me too, my love, but 'tis not to be." Da took a deep breath of regret. "Leaving now will make the difference of eight hours of travel."

"When will ye sleep?" Mama asked.

"War does not always give us time to sleep." Callum stood to his feet. Scott and Alec followed his example. "Da, I shall prepare the horses."

"Excellent." He motioned to Scott. "Pack us some food."

"I shall help." Tyra launched into action, standing to her feet. Her head swirled in denial as her legs moved of their own accord. The back of her throat went dry, while it seemed as if stones churned in her stomach. The moment she had dreaded was now upon them.

❧

Captain Donahue Morgan bristled as the hairs upon his neck and arms rose, crawling over his flesh. They were being watched and their red uniforms were like a bull's target. He held up his hand to signal the four soldiers following his lead. Their mounts slowed to a stop. Hugh listened as he gazed into the layered forest of green pine needles and bare branches of oak and poplar trees. The earthy scent of fresh pine and melted snow drifted through the air. No sound of human life caught his notice, but winter birds sang and flew above them. Wiry bushes dotted the thick woods full of dark shadows where anyone could be crouched in hiding, waiting to ambush them.

The only map in his possession wasn't drawn to scale, so he feared they might have wandered off the path to Wilmington. The drawing lacked significant landmarks and could have been more insightful. His superior officer had given it to him when he commissioned Hugh to find two of their ranking officers and negotiate their freedom from the rebel Continentals. Hugh could not fail. One of them was Colonel Neil Morgan, his elder brother.

A shiver of foreboding slithered up his spine and branched over his neck and shoulders. If Hugh had learned anything during his time in the colonies, it was the fact these blasted rebels did not fight fair like an upstanding British soldier, full of honor and courage. Instead, they would take cover behind rocks and trees, picking off His Majesty's Royal Army one by one like the red-skinned savages he had heard about.

"Get ready," Hugh unsheathed his sword from his side. "We are not alone." He kept his voice low as he continued to watch the woods around them. Hugh saw and heard nothing that would alert him to danger, but surviving the last three ambushes in South Carolina with his full regiment had given him enough experience to trust his instincts.

The birds above flew away. Eerie silence followed. Hugh tensed. The sound of a rushing wind sailed by him. A low thud hit the man behind him and a gut-wrenching moan wrestled from him. Hugh twisted to see his comrade clutch the arrow in his chest, a look of shock and then pain carved his expression into a memory of guilt and it would not soon leave Hugh. His friend paled and fell from his horse.

"Go!" Hugh urged his mount forward. Arrows whistled past them from every direction. They were surrounded and outnumbered. Strangely dressed men left the cover of the trees with loud shrilling sounds which vibrated through Hugh's head. He maneuvered his horse around one dark-skinned man who met his gaze, lifted his bow and arrow, and took aim. On instinct, Hugh dropped his head and tried to crouch his large frame behind his horse's mighty neck. As

Hugh raced by the Indian, pain sliced into his left side. It felt like someone had branded him with the end of a red-hot iron poker, fresh from a burning fire.

Air gushed from Hugh's lungs as another fallen comrade landed in the dirt behind him. The man's horse neighed and reared up on its hind legs, his hooves pounding thin air. Hugh raced on, eager to escape the same fate. He could not fail in this mission. Who else would rescue his brother? Clenching his teeth against the increasing pain in his side, Hugh blinked to clear his vision and leaned forward with determination.

More shrieks and warrior cries bounced through the forest, and they followed him. As near as he could tell, most of the Indians were on foot. Two of them climbed upon the horses of his two fallen comrades and chased after Hugh and his last remaining friend. They knew the layout of the land better than Hugh, and it showed as they caught up with them. Hugh ducked and leaned to the left and right to avoid the large tree branches, but he couldn't miss the sting of some of the smaller ones as they slashed across his face and neck. A cut above his eyes poured blood into his blurry vision. With each breath, his heart continued striking against the inside of his chest like a fist that wouldn't stop.

"Argh! They got me, Hugh!" Miles called to him.

"Just hang on and keep going." Hugh glanced over his shoulder. The movement twisted the arrow still lanced into his side and caused a wave of dizziness to wash over him.

Something pierced his left thigh, stinging his flesh. Shock reverberated through his system as he glanced down to see another arrow had hit his leg. Warm blood oozed over his breeches, soaking and discoloring the white material. Hugh struggled to stay seated as his energy evaporated, and his remaining strength drained with his life's blood. The jarring of his winded horse pushed both arrows deeper. Hugh groaned from the pain and almost lost consciousness.

The two Indians closed in on him from the front, and Hugh couldn't find the strength to guide his horse in another direction.

Instead, the animal slowed to a trot, then walked, until he stopped altogether. The Indians grabbed the reins and pulled Hugh down. Hugh grabbed his side as he landed on his right hip and gritted his teeth in agony.

A moment later, Miles landed beside him. Blood now soaked his shirt beneath the opening of his red coat. His pale face was testament to how much blood he had already lost. Hugh hoped their end would be swift and merciful. The thought of more torture was enough to make him pray for death. Instead, he sat still and held his head up when he could find the strength. He would not be a coward. If he had to die, he wanted it to be with honor.

"I am Red Fox," said the man who had stared at Hugh and shot him in the side. "You on MacGregor land. They fight redcoats." He pointed at them. "You enemy. We take you to War Woman." He bent and broke the long stem of the arrow sticking out of Hugh's thigh and side. Red Fox moved over and did the same for Miles.

"A woman?" Hugh blinked with a weary sigh. His body swayed one way and then the other, his head numb from a loss of blood. "Dying . . . by the hand . . . of a woman . . ." Hugh took a deep breath to gather what little strength he had left. "Has no honor." His head rolled back on his shoulders and his blurry vision saw a mixture of colors and light. "Kill us now."

✑❤

The next morning Tyra slid the latch back and swung open the side kitchen door. The rising sun cast an orange-pink glow across the slanted gray clouds. The frigid air promised another cold day, but it didn't look like more snow would fall. As much as she enjoyed the rare snow, she rubbed her hands in a silent thank-you to the Almighty. Harsh weather would make things harder on her father and brothers.

With The MacGregor Quest plantation located southeast of Wilmington, their homestead overlooked the road and a semicircle dirt drive. On the other side, lay the Cape Fear River, shimmering like diamonds when the sun's rays angled upon the surface of the water. The swampy woods served as their only neighbors on the right and on the left their rice fields extended for several acres beyond the stables. Tyra followed the familiar path to the well on the swampy side. Patches of snow still lingered where their house shaded the ground. A thick white frost covered the rest.

As she walked toward the well, her black boots crunched against the stiff white frost layering the grass like thick pie crust. She breathed in the crisp air, allowing it to cleanse her lungs. Winter was here, so they kept the doors and windows closed and the hearths burning, but at times it almost stifled them.

The sound of men's voices carried in the breeze. Tyra paused and tilted her head to hear better. A horse snorted. It sounded like they were on the other side of the house by the swamp. She rushed back to the house and entered through the front door to keep from alarming her mother who was no doubt still in the kitchen.

Hurrying down the hall, Tyra tried to keep her footsteps light. She opened her father's study and reached above the hearth to lift the rifle from where it hung on the wall. A quick search in the desk drawer revealed a pouch containing round bullets and gunpowder. Tyra loaded the rifle as her father had shown her and slipped out of the study. She rushed down the hall and out the front door, determined to meet the men before they reached the house. Lifting the hem of her brown skirt, Tyra ran down the porch steps, hoping she wouldn't trip. She rounded the corner and lifted the rifle, taking aim.

"War Woman, we bring you redcoats!" Red Fox called out. He led two horses carrying wounded British soldiers. Both men looked unconscious as they lay over the back of each horse with broken arrows sticking out of them. Tyra's gaze scanned the somber expression of the other ten Tuscarora Indians surrounding them. She lowered her rifle in stark confusion. "They on MacGregor Land. Redcoats enemy to MacGregor."

"What happened?" The words slipped from Tyra's mouth before she could halt them. She hoped her tone did not sound like an accusation. Would this deed now bring British wrath down upon their heads? They had heard rumors the British were heading toward Wilmington. She had to find a way to protect her mother and Kirk. How could she make this right?

"We bring them for justice." Red Fox continued walking toward her. Tyra knew him to be a fair man, but he did not always understand the white man's ways. She wished her father was here to speak for her.

"You found them on MacGregor land?" Fear iced up Tyra's spine, but she stiffened to keep from shivering. Fear would not aid her now. Instead, she hoped to draw strength from the Lord and the wits He gave her just as her mother had always done. She lifted her chin and met his gaze. "Were there more of them?"

"We killed two others." Red Fox turned to glance back at the wounded men and nodded his dark head toward them. "These two live. We bring them to War Woman. You decide fate."

"What were they doing?" she asked.

"Riding to your house. Your father and brothers gone. We stop them." He pointed to one of the men with an arrow in his side and thigh. "This one must be leader."

"What did you do with the others?" Tyra accepted the reins of the two horses he handed over to her. "I have heard more redcoats are coming. I do not want your tribe to be in danger." Tyra thought of his wife and daughter, a close friend from childhood. "Their army has too many soldiers, many more than the small tribe you have left in the swamps."

"We will bury them as your people do." He nodded his head to the two wounded men. "How will you judge them?"

"I shall try and get them to talk. I cannot fight hundreds of soldiers when they come, but if I save their lives, the new soldiers may give my family mercy."

Red Fox laughed and exchanged doubtful glances with his friends. "Few white men understand mercy. Your father and brothers rare."

Tyra swallowed at the memory of their smiling faces at the Christmas feast. A hollow spot formed in her throat. She gripped the reins tight in her hand. "You speak the truth, but I must try. I am only one woman. I cannot fight hundreds of soldiers."

"War Woman fight with wisdom." Red Fox pointed to his own head. "If you need us, you find us in swamp."

"Indeed, I will." Tyra nodded.

Red Fox motioned to his men, and they followed him back to the woods.

A groan caught Tyra's attention. She looked over to see the one with two arrows grimacing in his semi-conscious state. If she didn't hurry, he would soon awaken and the pain would be unbearable.

Tyra led the horses to the front of the house where it would be easier to carry them inside. Indecision wrestled in her heart. How would she get them down and drag them inside without causing them further damage and pain? She couldn't leave them like this to die.

2

$\mathcal{H}$ugh woke to a searing headache and the enticing aroma of bacon and strong coffee. He blinked as gray light filtered through the curtained windows. Blue walls surrounded him with a cold hearth on the far side, a dresser and a wash basin on the other. His thigh throbbed like a ball of fire branding through his skin.

Where was he? Nothing about this chamber looked familiar. Memories of savages attacking him and his men came to mind. He had lost two men in the struggle, but he hoped Miles still lived. Hugh had passed out from exhaustion and a loss of blood, and couldn't remember anything else. If only he had the energy to drag himself from bed and leave the comfort of this chamber to learn more. As captain, he was in charge. It was his duty to see to the well-being of his men.

Even the slightest movement to sit up cost him more discomfort than he could bear. He gritted his teeth and reached down. Bandages were wrapped around his leg. Someone had taken the time to remove the arrowheads from his torn flesh and repair the wounds. Surely, no rebels would have done such a thing for a wounded British soldier. He must be among friends—Tories who were still loyal to the king. Hugh relaxed against the goose-feather pillows.

Footsteps echoed down the hall drawing near to the door. A knock sounded on the other side. He braced himself wondering what matronly woman would soon cross the threshold. In spite of his pain, Hugh forced a smile, determined to properly thank the people who had saved his life.

"Come in," he called, wincing from the sharp stab shooting through his side.

The knob turned, clicked, and the hinges creaked as the door opened. Instead of a middle-aged woman, a young female strode in carrying a silver tray of food. Her strides were purposeful and deliberate. Wavy hair flowed down her back in vibrant shades of red and auburn. The sides were pinned up by silver combs. Amazed, Hugh lost his voice as she turned piercing green eyes upon him. Her expression didn't hold the welcoming warmth he had hoped to find. She paused.

"Good. I see you are awake." She glanced down at the tray and back at him with a lift of a red eyebrow. "I assume you are hungry?"

Hugh managed a slight nod, since his throat remained unusually dry. Was she as tall as she appeared? Perhaps his sense of perception was off from lying flat on his back.

She carried the tray to a table by the bed. A revolver lay on the far corner of the tray just out of his reach. Alarm slammed through him. Why would a respectable woman carry around such a weapon in her own home?

"Your eyes do not deceive you Captain Donahue Morgan. It is a revolver." Her wide eyes met his gaze. "And I assure you, I know how to use it. The Indians do not call me War Woman for naught."

War Woman? He coughed and cleared his throat. A burst of pain sliced through his side, clamping down on his flesh in a squeezing pinch.

"Now, can you feed yourself or do I need to do it as well?" She cocked her head as if he were an inconvenient child.

He cleared his parched throat and swallowed. "I can manage." He motioned to the tray. "If you would be so kind as to bring my breakfast to me . . . without the revolver, of course."

"Of course." She snapped, removing the gun and setting the tray over his lap. A whiff of honey teased his nose. Too bad her character wasn't as sweet as the aroma surrounding her. Up close, he noticed a few dotted freckles across her creamy complexion. Her oval face drew a silhouette full of mystery and intrigue.

Was there a measure of disdain in her tone or had he imagined it? Perhaps someone else in her family had saved him and brought him in out of the cold against her approval. Hugh picked up the steaming cup of coffee. As dry as his throat was, he would have preferred a glass of water, but this would do. If he complained, she might decide to use the revolver on him.

He swallowed the warm brew, welcoming the soothing refreshment it brought, jolting the rest of him. With his throat feeling better, he met her gaze as he set down his cup. "I am afraid you have an unfair advantage. You know my name, where I am, and have a weapon. I am wounded, without my weapons, and completely at your mercy. Who should I thank for saving my life?"

"My name is Tyra MacGregor." She gestured around the chamber with a sad smile. "This property is The MacGregor Quest, my parents' rice plantation—or what is left of it."

"Miss MacGregor, I am in your debt."

"You say it now, Captain Morgan, but I fear I must beg your forgiveness. I read through your letters. By the time I found them in your pocket, there was so much blood on them. I tried to read a few lines to determine if they were worth salvaging. My curiosity got the best of me. 'Tis a fault I have not quite overcome. I was curious to know what kind of man we had brought into our home."

"I suppose there is no harm . . . this time." He waved a hand in dismissal. "After all, there were no details to be kept from a Tory family such as yourselves. His Majesty would be pleased to know you have saved and cared so well for his British soldiers."

"You presume too much, Captain." Her tone grew defensive. "I saved you out of Christian charity and naught else. I have heard a British troop is marching toward Wilmington, and I had hoped you might grant my mother and I, and my brother, a bit of mercy. I will not have you believe a lie." She crossed her arms and tilted her head, and her radiant hair fell over her shoulder. "Besides, all the townspeople know which side my father and brothers fight on. You will no doubt soon discover all the rebels in the area."

"And is it why you brought a revolver in here?" Hugh asked, disbelief coloring his original image of her.

"No." Her cheeks grew a shade darker. "'Tis because you are a man. Were you a rebel or a Tory, I would do what is necessary to protect myself."

"I see." A new respect for her blossomed. Too bad she wasn't a Tory. Disappointment filled his chest as he watched her cross her arms.

"I assume Colonel Neil Morgan is a relative?" she asked. It was a piece of information she no doubt picked up from his bloody letters.

"He is my elder brother," Hugh said, pushing away the annoying concern continuing to haunt him since his brother's imprisonment.

"I hope you find him . . . in good health." Her voice faded as she turned from Hugh, grabbing the revolver from the table and securing it in a pouch hanging from the belt on her waist. Why hadn't he noticed it before? She walked toward the window where she pulled back the navy drapes.

Hugh finished chewing his bacon and took a bite of porridge. It was warm and smooth going down his throat. It pooled in his stomach like balm on a wound. He was famished. Hugh took another bite and swallowed. Was it true British troops were on the way? Perhaps he could join up with them and convince the commanding officer to spare a few men for his commission. He glanced over at the woman staring out the window. It was brave to save the life of one's enemy and honesty was something he valued. "Tell me about yourself."

"I do not wish to bore you." She didn't turn around. "While you recover, you will be cared for by myself, and my mother, Lauren MacGregor. Kirk, my younger brother will assist you in relieving yourself. He is ten and three."

"Miss MacGregor, thank you for saving my life and for all your care." Relief poured through him knowing he would not have to be humiliated at having two women assist him to the chamber pot—especially by a woman as radiant as she. While her stark beauty was enough to stir an attraction in him, her bold mystery appealed to him even more. He sensed she had much more depth and grit than most of the women he knew back home. None of them carried around a revolver. And how did she manage to thwart the savages? More silence filled the room as he ate.

"Well, I shall leave you to eat in peace." She turned from the window.

"Wait." Hugh wiped his mouth with a napkin as she paused by the foot of his bed. "What about my comrade, Miles Carter? Those savages managed to kill two of my men, but I thought perhaps he might have survived."

"I am sorry." Her gaze dropped to the floor, and she rubbed her palms together in distress. "We tried to save him, but he passed away late last night. Now that I know his name, I shall have my brother carve his name on a wooden cross. We will give him a proper Christian burial this morning."

Hugh didn't respond. A deep ache buried inside as he processed the news of another loss. The back of his throat throbbed with pressure and anger shot through him. Had they tried everything? She had admitted to being a rebel. "How do I know you tried everything and did not merely let him die?"

"Then why save you?" She leaned forward. "Those savages you referred to are our friends. Around here, if you trespass on someone's land, you risk getting shot. The Tuscaroras have taken it upon themselves to protect us and our land while my father and brothers are away fighting for our freedom."

"You speak treason!"

"Then I suppose you shall have to get better before you can do aught about it." She strode across the chamber and slammed the door behind her.

Tyra stood outside Captain Morgan's chamber and waited for the door to stop vibrating in its frame. It wasn't often her temper got the best of her, but Captain Morgan had an arrogance about him and it grated on her nerves. It didn't matter that his English sounded like honey nearly stealing her breath. Accusing her of treason was beyond ridiculous, especially since she had never set foot on England's soil or swore any allegiance to England's king. She was born an American colonist, and as far as she was concerned, she was American.

"What did he do?" Kirk rushed from the kitchen with a piece of bread in his hand. "It sounds as if you wanna kill him, not save him."

"He is British and 'tis enough." Tyra snapped, breaking into a brisk pace toward the kitchen. "As soon as you finish breaking your fast, we need firewood brought into the house for all the hearths."

"Red Fox came back with other British soldiers. They are dead." Kirk followed her. "What will we do with 'em?"

"Bury them, as is proper." Tyra entered the kitchen to see her mother kneading dough for more bread. She had tied a light blue apron around her dark green gown. It was covered in white flour as she pounded the dough. She looked up and smiled.

"Lass, ye might want to slam fewer doors if ye plan to appeal to his mercy on our behalf for saving his life."

"I am sorry, Mama. I was at least civil to the man." Tyra strode over and poured a cup of water from the bucket and drained it dry. "It does vex me he is in your and Da's master chamber as if he was the king himself, especially after he accused me of treason."

"Treason?" Her mother paused, giving her a sharp look. "Tyra, what did ye say to provoke him?"

"I told you she had to do something." Kirk grinned and pointed at her as if he had figured out the answer to a puzzle.

"I told him the truth." Tyra crossed her arms and turned to face her mother as she looked down at her. "He thought I saved his life because we are loyal subjects to his high and mighty king. I could not, in good conscience, allow him to believe such a lie. Not when my father and brothers are risking their lives fighting against such tyranny." Tyra took a deep breath to calm her racing heart. Just the mere subject raised her patriotic heart and duty to her country. In spite of how women were viewed to be emotional supporters and contribute as best as they could from the homefront, Tyra longed to be joining her brothers on the front lines of the war. If she truly believed in their freedom as they did, why should her sacrifice be less than theirs?

"So he knows we are rebels?" Her mother asked, wiping her hands on her apron in distress. "What was his response? Will he be merciful?"

Tyra dropped her gaze, now feeling guilty she had not held her tongue or temper in check. Had she put all of them in danger? Was Captain Morgan a forgiving man or a tyrant? She had not even bothered to determine his character before she blurted everything out to him.

"Tyra, what are ye not telling me, lass?" Mama prompted, watching her with suspicion.

"Honest, Mama, I did naught to cause him to be unmerciful unless he already has a tendency to be that way." Tyra walked to the doorway. "I shall go outside and begin digging the graves for the other British soldiers. I will take the wagon to the other side of the woods away from the swamp."

"No need," Kirk said. "Red Fox is still outside with a few men. He wanted to speak to you. He said he will help you dispose of the bodies the white man's way." Kirk scratched the side of his brown head. "I think he might be worried you are mad at him for killing them."

"Any time a man takes the life of another, he ought to feel a wee bit of remorse," Mama said, rolling out the dough with a roller. "I have never understood how men could be so cold-hearted. It goes to show the Tuscaroras have not lost their human nature after all the wars and murder they have endured."

"They have always been good to us," Kirk said, walking toward Tyra. "I shall go with you."

"Nay." Mama shook her head and pointed to the northeast side of the house. "First, go to Captain Morgan's chamber and assist the man with his personal needs. 'Tisn't proper yer sister and I would have to do it if there is a male here in the house. And be respectful. We still might need an advocate in the British Army afore all is over."

Tyra strode from the kitchen, down the hall, and out the front door. She gasped as the frigid air clawed into her lungs, forcing a tight cough from her. Red Fox stood from where he had been sitting on the front porch steps. The others lounging around the yard merely looked up.

"We have the other red coats." He cupped his hands and blew warm air on his fingers. "War Woman saved the life of their leader. Are you angry we killed MacGregor enemy?"

"No." She shook her head. "We thank you for protecting our family. I saved their leader because hundreds more redcoats are coming, and I hoped they might have mercy on my mother and brother since we saved his life."

"Have we caused War Woman trouble?" Red Fox scratched the side of his temple as he tilted his head. "Your father told us to look out for you."

"We will be fine, but once we bury these redcoats, you and all the Tuscaroras must go into hiding." Tyra pointed toward the woods with the hidden swamp. "Their leader knows you killed his men and may seek revenge against you when the other redcoats arrive. They will outnumber your warriors and will have guns and cannons."

"The Tuscaroras know how to survive and hide. Do not worry." Red Fox motioned to his men. They gathered around. "Tell us what we must do for a white man's burial."

Tyra explained how deep they would need to dig each grave, the wooden crosses they would craft with the names, and the prayer she would say. "There is a wagon in the barn. Put them in it and take them to the edge of the property. I do not want them anywhere near the house."

"Tyra!" Kirk hurried toward her with a twisted frown on his smooth face. "Captain Morgan is demanding to see you."

☙

Hugh lay upon the bed enduring the pain eating at his flesh and trying to recover from the humiliation of leaning upon a young lad to tend to his personal needs. He took a deep breath and winced from the effort. When would Miss MacGregor return? She was the only person who could make his pain diminish from the challenging conversation and wit in which she distracted him. Ever since her departure, a visit from her brother and mother had not induced the same effects upon his countenance.

He wished the window was closer, for then he would at least have a decent view. Mrs. MacGregor had come and collected his empty plate and glass. While here, she had pulled back the drapes to tease him with a bit of sunlight. Somewhere out there Miss MacGregor might be on her way back. He listened for the front door, but the sound of it opening never came.

After a while, a chill set into his body and a sweat broke out drenching his clothes. A ringing tortured his ears as he listened for the door to open with Miss MacGregor's presence. Each hour passed in disappointment until he fell into a fitful sleep. His head ached and burned like fire, and his eyelids were so heavy he couldn't find the energy to open them.

After dreaming of a raging battle where he saw his brother taken by the ragtag rebels, Hugh heard a woman calling his name. Her voice sounded familiar and endearing. Someone lifted his head. Cool liquid touched his lips and dribbled down his chin.

"Good, Captain Morgan. Drink a bit more," she coaxed.

Miss MacGregor's voice. When had she returned? Hugh forced his weary eyes open. A dim candle burned on the table by the bed, but it was enough light to see an angel with flowing red hair falling in waves around her shoulders. She leaned over him with a look of concern. Her brow wrinkled as she bit her bottom lip and lifted the cup to his mouth. He opened his mouth to ask a question, but she poured water inside. Hugh closed his mouth to gulp down the liquid. He choked. Miss MacGregor leaned him up and pounded his back.

"There now, I daresay, you shall be all right." Her hair fell onto his face as the fragrance of sweet honey filled the air around her. It was a refreshing change from the stuffy chamber. "'Tis good to have you back. The fever made you take leave of your senses for several hours."

"Fever?" Had he been ill? He lifted an eyebrow in question, too weak and weary to do more.

"Indeed." She nodded sitting back down. "You have been running a temperature since evening. 'Tis now three o'clock in the morning."

"Really?" Hugh yawned, fighting the onset of drowsiness. "I thought I had merely dozed off and took a short nap, while I waited for your return. Did Kirk not tell you I asked for you?"

"He did." She nodded, flipping her wayward hair over her shoulder and drawing her shawl tight around her. "But I am not one of your soldiers to drop what I am doing and come running at your beck and call. Instead, I thought it more of my duty to see your men receive a proper Christian burial."

"Forgive me, Miss MacGregor, but I had hoped to attend their funeral." Hugh glanced down at the foot of his bed. "'Tis one of the reasons I had asked for you."

"Well, in spite of your noble intentions, you were not in any condition to do so." She relaxed against the back of the wooden chair and smiled at him. "When you are well enough, I will be pleased to show you their graves. I am sorry we did not have a minister to preside over them, but I prayed for their souls and for their grieving families. I read Scripture. 'Tis better than anything I could have said even if I had known them."

"Pray tell, what did you read?" Hugh struggled to clear the mire from his brain and concentrate on what she was saying. The woman wasn't afraid to shoot a gun, bury dead men, or act in place of a minister. Yet, she had taken excellent care of him, a man who could cause much hardship for her family as her enemy. She had asked for mercy. Was it not why she had chosen to save him—to care for him? Miss MacGregor may be the War Woman to the local savages, but to him she was a woman of mystery and intrigue.

"First Thessalonians 4, *For the Lord himself will descend from heaven with a cry of command, with the voice of an archangel, and with the sound of the trumpet of God. And the dead in Christ will rise first. Then we who are alive, who are left, will be caught up together with them in the clouds to meet the Lord in the air.*" A rosy glow filled her smooth cheeks as she glanced away. "I was not sure what would be proper, I thought something with hope and promise would be best."

"Quite an unusual choice. I must admit, you are full of surprises. I would have expected a few verses from Psalms." He ran a hand through his unruly hair as a yawn interrupted his speech. "I must beg your pardon for keeping you up so late. 'Tisn't my intention to rob you of your rest."

"Too late, but I will gladly forgive you for an exchange of mercy for my family," Tyra said.

"It remains to be seen." Hugh awarded her with a grin as he rolled to his uninjured side and closed his eyes.

3

$\mathcal{K}$irk burst through the front door and hurried into the parlor where Tyra read the *Cape Fear Mercury* and her mother sewed a pair of socks for one of the boys. The fire blazed as he gasped for breath, leaning over his knees. He glanced up at them with red cheeks from the biting cold outside.

"Goodness, lad, ye need to calm down afore ye cause yerself the pneumonia in this brisk weather," Mama said with a severe expression meant to scold him. "At least give yerself time to catch yer breath."

"Darren an' I went to town to buy some feed for his Pa." Kirk paused to take a few more harried breaths. "Redcoats were marching through town on Front Street, so many of 'em they took up the whole street, an' part of Market Street."

"Was it really so many?" Tyra set down the newspaper and exchanged a concerned glance with her mother. She touched a finger to her chin. "I wonder if it means they were just passing through on their march or if they have a particular place in mind."

"We overheard some men talking an' they said the major plans to occupy the Burgwin House. He sent a scout ahead and ordered the family to remove themselves," Kirk said.

"Are ye sure?" Mama asked, her sewing now discarded on her lap. She searched Kirk's expression for further clarity.

"I know what I heard." Kirk nodded, as he walked over to the fire and rubbed his hands to gain a bit of warmth. "Some of the soldiers are setting up tents around the Episcopal Church and holding meetings there."

"But where is our army? Did they not meet any resistance at all?" Tyra stood, folded her arms and paced across the parlor. Her heels clicked against the hardwood floor as she paused in front of the window and stared out at the overcast sky. It had been three weeks since her father and brothers departed. Captain Morgan had survived an infectious fever, but now he was mending and the British Army had arrived, she feared he would turn her family over to his superiors.

They had enjoyed civil conversations over the last few days. To her surprise, Captain Morgan had even attempted to tease her a couple of times. His recovery was taking longer than she would have preferred, but it couldn't be helped. It would be another week before she could take out his stitches. Until then, she feared they would have to endure his company a while longer.

"Well, I suppose Wilmington is now occupied." Mama resumed her sewing and pricked her finger. "Ouch!" She shook her hand as unshed tears filled her eyes. "I hate to think how long it might be afore we see yer da and brothers again. I daresay, the colonials shan't come around while the British are here."

"I have not thought of it." Disappointment speared Tyra's chest. She turned from the window and strode to where her mother sat. Placing a comforting hand on her shoulder, she bent forward. "We shall be strong and have faith the war will end soon and they shall come home safely to us."

"Indeed." Mama covered her hand with her own. Over the years, Mama had always been the one to comfort her, but these days she often returned the favor. Having a husband and three sons at war took its toll on her, but the special bond her parents shared between each other had always fascinated Tyra. Their relationship shared a unique love and warmth she had not witnessed among other married couples. Tyra had always dreamed of a marriage like theirs. It was a gift too many lacked.

"Miss MacGregor!" A familiar voice called from the chamber on the other side of the parlor across the foyer. Tyra lifted her eyes to the ceiling in frustration, letting out an unladylike sigh. "Why does he never call upon the two of you?"

"At least you do not have the duties I normally have," Kirk twisted his mouth in disgust and wrinkled his nose.

"In the last few days Captain Morgan has been able to take care of his personal needs on his own." Tyra whispered as she stood to her feet. She could not hide the teasing smile tugging at her lips. "I will be sure to call you if your services are needed."

His green eyes narrowed and his lips twisted as he shook his head. "'Twould be fine by me if I never see another chamber pot again."

Tyra strode from the parlor and across the foyer. Her booted heels announced her arrival at Captain Morgan's door. She knocked and waited until he bid her permission to enter. Gripping the brass knob, Tyra forced a jovial smile as she peered around the door. Dim light cast a slight glow. The warm hearth had grown cold several hours ago.

Captain Morgan sat up in bed propped against the carved wooden headboard. His black hair looked as if he had tried to comb it to the side with his fingers. A dark, scruffy beard had formed on his jaw. Guilt ripped through her because she had not offered him a blade to shave. The boundary lines continued to blur as to what was appropriate and what went beyond the Christian care of a man who was her enemy. After all, if he came face to face with her father or one of her brothers, would he not be compelled to try and kill or take them prisoner? A war of indecision wrestled within her pounding heart.

"How may I help you, Captain?" she asked, forcing herself to meet his intense gaze. Something about him intrigued her curiosity. Under more pleasant circumstances, she had no doubt she would have liked Captain Morgan. He was polite, respectful, and full of intelligent conversation, but his current position and power overwhelmed her with fear for her family. What would he do to them once he was well, now that his superior had taken control of the town?

"I did not mean to intrude on your conversation, but I could not help overhearing that British forces are marching through Wilmington as we speak and setting up headquarters?" He lifted a dark brown eyebrow, and she could almost feel the excitement he tried to contain. Resentment spiraled inside her.

"Indeed. It is what my brother has witnessed. He can be a bit animated at times." Unease trembled through Tyra, but she kept her expression passive. "I imagine you would like to return to them?" She searched her mind for a way to carry him outside to the wagon bed. He wasn't yet strong enough to ride a horse by himself or walk too far.

"As much as I would like to own up to my independence, reality screams at me when I stand to bear pressure upon my leg." He tilted his head and regarded her with a peculiar expression as an easy grin spread across his face, revealing a row of healthy teeth. "Besides, the Army's physician is not nearly as beautiful as my nurse here."

Tyra blinked in disbelief, knowing color rose up to her face like a wave of heat. Already aware of his handsome features, Tyra wasn't about to encourage him. What was the point when he would soon be leaving and they were opposing enemies? She said nothing as she waited for him to reveal his purpose in calling for her.

"I would be much obliged if you would have Kirk take a letter for me, so I can inform my superior of my whereabouts and the excellent care you have provided." He scratched at the whiskers on his chin. "Perhaps they will send out a wagon bed to take me back to headquarters. I would not want to trouble your family any longer than necessary."

Concern for her brother's safety formed in her belly. She had heard stories of young boys being impressed into the British Navy and Army. Somehow, she had to keep Kirk as far away from the British headquarters as possible. "I need to visit the post office and the general store. I shall go myself and deliver your letter."

"Alone?" Captain Morgan shifted to sit up, his lips forming a thin line. "Miss MacGregor, I realize I have no right to impose my will on you, but I wish you would not go into town alone." He shook his head. "'Tis too dangerous."

"I fear it might be even more dangerous for my brother. I shall bring you quill, ink, and paper to compose your letter. In the meantime, I will be ready to leave within the hour." She walked to the door, opened it, and paused. "I should be perfectly safe among your gentlemen officers. 'Tisn't likely they will try to impress a woman among their numbers, but I am not convinced where an innocent lad is concerned."

Hugh stared at the closed door behind Miss MacGregor's departure. Frustration filled him at his limitations. He longed to be up taking part in their conversations, learning more about the MacGregors, particularly Miss MacGregor. She was not as forthcoming in answering his questions as he would like, yet the woman certainly knew her own mind. How could he convince her not to go alone? Memories of some of the debauched behavior of the soldiers in his regiment came to mind. As soon as their superior officers turned their heads or gave them the night off, they would head to the taverns to find the first willing wench available. He wouldn't trust any of them around Miss MacGregor.

Flipping back the covers, Hugh swung his legs over the side and scooted to the edge of the bed. His feet hit the cool wooden floor and his legs shook as he bent his knees and pushed himself up. His injured leg trembled even more, but his strong leg held him steady. Taking a deep breath, Hugh wrapped the blanket around him and took a step forward. He limped upon his bad leg as a searing pain etched through his side. Hugh gritted his teeth and dragged himself to the door, determined to reach Mrs. MacGregor before her daughter returned downstairs.

He made it to the door of the parlor and leaned against the threshold frame. He hated how much he needed their support. Mrs. MacGregor looked up with a startled expression, her blue eyes widened. "Captain, are ye sure ye should be up and about?"

"I realize it may not be any of my business, but Miss MacGregor intends to take a letter of mine to my superior officer. I suggested the lad take it, but she fears he will be impressed into the British Army and insists on going herself." Hugh tipped his head back to make sure Miss MacGregor wasn't yet coming down the stairs. "At the risk of being too forward, please do not allow her to go alone. 'Tis too dangerous. Do not misunderstand me. There are good men in our service, but as with any place there are bad ones as well."

"She has always been a headstrong lass, to be sure." Mrs. MacGregor nodded, setting her sewing aside and rising to her feet. She walked toward him and took his arm to lead him back to his chamber. "I thank ye for the warning, and your meaning is quite clear. I shall accompany her, and we will stop by our neighbor's house to see if Mr. Simmons will escort us into town, considering the circumstances."

Hugh breathed a sigh of relief, unsure of when Miss MacGregor's welfare had become so important to him. How could he help it? She had not only saved his life, but spent countless hours in his company reading the Bible to him, giving him news of the war and of town, feeding him, and staying up late to care for him throughout the night when he had a raging fever.

"I think it will be a wise alternative, and I daresay, 'twill not offend Miss MacGregor's independent spirit." He chuckled, not wanting anything to change her bold personality. "Thank you for being so understanding."

"Sounds like ye've come to understand my daughter quite well in the past fortnight," Mrs. MacGregor said.

Footsteps sounded on the stairs as Hugh entered his chamber and hobbled back to his bed.

"Captain, why are you out of bed?" Miss MacGregor's voice carried across the chamber in her usual forthright manner. He paused like a child in the midst of a naughty act. She set the quill, ink, and paper on the table by the bed. Turning to look at him, she placed her hands on her hips. Few women stood tall enough to meet him at eye level, but Miss MacGregor claimed the honor.

"The exercise is good for me." He offered her a teasing grin. "How else am I to rebuild my strength?"

With a frown making her lips look pouty, she leaned forward, pressed her hand against his chest, and pushed him. Hugh stepped backward until his knees pressed against the bed. He lost his balance and stumbled onto the bed. He prayed the rope under the mattress would hold his weight from such force as he grunted and glanced up at her in surprised confusion. She pressed her fingers against her lips as if she couldn't believe what she had done, but a budding smile toyed at the corners of her mouth.

"Tyra!" Mrs. MacGregor stood at the foot of the bed. "What are ye doing, lass?"

"Captain Morgan is not ready to be up and about. If he is, he could make the trip into town to deliver his letter himself." Miss MacGregor looked from her mother back at Hugh. Her eyes were full of fire, and it stirred his blood in a way that made his head swim like a dizzy fish. He was right to go to her mother in an effort to try to protect her. With such bold courage, she might provoke the wrong soldier in town.

"Apologize, Tyra," her mother said. "I helped Captain Morgan back to his chamber myself. I assure ye, lass, he is not ready to travel on his own and has done naught to deserve yer ire."

Miss MacGregor stepped back from him, the smile in her expression faded to hurt betrayal as she stared at her mother. She blinked and gripped her stomach. Regret filled Hugh with a desire to make her smile again.

"No, 'tis all right." Hugh shook his head and pulled the covers around him as he lay where he belonged. "Miss MacGregor is only concerned for my welfare. After saving my life, I am quite grateful for her judgment."

"Captain, I appreciate your mercy," Mrs. MacGregor said. She turned her gaze back to her daughter. "Lass, ready yerself. I shall be going with ye to town. I would like to stop by the Simmons place on the way."

"But are they expecting us?" Miss MacGregor asked.

"Nay, but that is the beauty of it." Mrs. MacGregor's smile widened as she gripped her hands together in front of her. "They shall be pleasantly surprised."

Tyra sat on the wagon bench, freezing in the cold while her mother went inside to ask Mr. Simmons to escort them into town. Her teeth chattered as she rubbed her hands inside her muff and snuggled deeper into her brown cloak wishing they would hurry. In truth, she had no idea why her mother insisted on requesting his escort unless it was the presence of the British. Over the past few years since their men folk were at war, she and her mother had gone to Wilmington many times by themselves until today.

The front door opened and laughter followed with dim candlelight. Mr. Simmons and her mother walked toward Tyra. His gray hair inched beneath his black hat, but his shaggy beard and mustache hid his expression. He assisted her mother as she climbed onto the wagon and settled beside Tyra and walked around to the other side. Mr. Simmons hoisted himself like a young agile man and took the reins in hand. He clicked his tongue, snapped the reins upon the two horses, and off they rolled onto the path ahead.

A drafty breeze made her nose feel frostbitten and her cheeks frozen, but the rest of her was protected by having Mr. Simmons on one side and her mother on the other. Once they arrived in Wilmington, Tyra was shocked by all the redcoats in sight and the white tents encamped in various places along Front Street. For once, her brother had not exaggerated. Mr. Simmons kept his gaze focused ahead of them as they came to the corner of Queens Street and tried to make a right turn. Several redcoats formed a line in front of them and blocked their passing.

"Halt! Who goes there?" a man called in a stern British accent. He strode toward Mr. Simmons carrying a rifle and wearing a black tricorn hat. At least his brown hair was tied back in a ribbon rather than those ridiculous white wigs the British insisted on wearing. "State your name and purpose," he demanded.

"My name is Mr. Simmons." Their neighbor pulled back on the reins to stop the horses before further action could be carried out against them. "We seek the officer in charge. We have a letter for him from Captain Donahue Morgan. He has charged us to deliver it into the hands of no other but his commanding officer."

"And where is this captain?" The soldier narrowed his eyes in suspicion as other redcoats came forward and checked their wagon bed and underneath. "Why did he not come himself instead of sending an old man and two women in his place?"

"He is lying in our house, sir," Mama said. "Recovering from an injury that my daughter stitched herself." The man's blue-eyed gaze slid to Tyra, but he kept his expression unreadable. "At the moment, he is unable to come, but when he heard of the arrival of your troops, he bid us to bring a letter to your commanding officer, so he would be aware of his existence. We asked our neighbor, Mr. Simmons to escort us here." She nodded toward their neighbor.

"Why should I believe you?" He lifted an eyebrow.

"As you pointed out, how dangerous could one old man and two women be?" Mr. Simmons asked.

"Our superior officer in charge is Major James Craig. He has set up temporary headquarters at St. James Episcopal Church on Third Street." The soldier lowered his rifle and motioned for the others to move back and let them pass.

Mr. Simmons called to the horses, snapped the reins, and they continued. Few people were out and about like they were on Front Street. A curtain pulled back to watch them pass at one house. Tyra supposed it was Mrs. Baker. Her husband and sons were off fighting the British as were Mr. Simmons's three sons. Most of their rebel friends were staying indoors. The few who had ventured out to take a walk were known Tories.

They took a left onto Third Street where the two Hatfield sisters were taking a leisurely stroll. As professed Tories, neither of them had anything to fear now that their precious British had seized the town. They both smiled with vengeful delight and turned their noses up at them as they passed by. One was a year older than Tyra and the other was a year younger. No doubt, both of them would soon be setting their caps for a couple of unlucky souls in redcoats.

The stone church came into view, and Tyra's breath caught. White tents were set up all around the grounds, and redcoats were everywhere. Even though her family didn't attend this church, anger burned through her that the redcoats had so little respect for God's holy place. At least, the graveyard had been left in peace. They went through another round of questions and were searched a second time. After passing inspection, the soldiers gave them permission to leave the wagon and commanded them to follow one of them inside.

In the sanctuary, Tyra blinked, allowing her eyes to adjust to the dim light. Candelabras hung between the painted glass windows and the wooden pews that had been moved to make room for makeshift tables. Maps were rolled out on the tabletops and men wearing redcoats and white breeches with black boots were gathered in discussions. Upon their entrance, the officers' voices faded and pointed gazes targeted their direction.

"Sir, these people have a letter from one of our injured captains." The soldier they followed stopped before an older gentleman with white hair and saluted him.

"What injured captain? I am quite aware of all my injured officers, and no one has received any injuries upon arriving in Wilmington." The major's cold gaze speared Mr. Simmons, her mother, and then rested on Tyra. "Who has this letter?"

"I have it, sir." Tyra stepped forward. She pulled the folded letter from her reticule and handed it to him.

He snatched it, turned, and broke the seal. As he read, he paced. His boots clicked against the hard floor and stopped. He scratched the side of his white head. "Miss MacGregor, it appears you have saved the life of one of His Royal Majesty's officers, and we are grateful for the care and sacrifice you have made." Major Craig raised a finger at them. "Do any of you know where the Indians are hiding who did this to Captain Morgan and his men?"

"No, sir. They hide in the swamps and never stay in one place," Tyra said. "They are like nomads."

"Well, no matter." Major Craig grasped his hands behind him and paced again. "If they are in the area, we shall find them. I intend to discover every hidden enemy against the king. And when I do, they will suffer the consequences."

Fear slithered up Tyra's spine as she exchanged a worried glance with her mother. Would he imprison innocent women and children as well? The man couldn't be trusted, and she wanted nothing more than to escape the discomfort of this place.

"Sir, what should we tell Captain Morgan when we return home?" Tyra asked.

"You shall tell him naught." Major Craig turned dark eyes upon her and strode toward her. His mouth curled into a wicked grin as he regarded her with eyes as black as onyx. "I am sending a couple of my men back with you. They shall report my commands to him, as well as report back to me all they learn of this Captain Donahue Morgan. In the meantime, I shall write to his superior officer in South Carolina and dispatch a messenger to confirm his story." He snapped his fingers and motioned two men forward. "No need to concern yourself further, Miss MacGregor. I am now in charge."

4

$\mathscr{H}$ugh wished he had the energy and health so he could pace his worry away. Instead, he was forced to lie in bed and fret over how his commanding officer might receive Miss MacGregor and her mother. He prayed the man would not discover their loyalty to the Continental cause. The thought of something unpleasant happening to them soured his stomach.

After several hours, wagon wheels rolled up to the front of the house. Anxious nerves tightened in Hugh's gut as he tried to push himself up on his elbow. The door swung open, and Kirk rushed in. "Redcoats came with 'em! What does it mean?" His wide eyes searched Hugh's for answers. "Is my mother and sister in trouble?"

"Look through the window and tell me what you see," Hugh pointed to the right.

Kirk strode over and pulled back the drapes. "A redcoat is at the reins on the wagon, sitting by my sister. Mama is on the other side of her." He bent lower as if trying to see through an obstacle. "An' two are on horseback."

"Only three?" Hugh asked.

"Yes, sir." Kirk nodded his brown head. "Is it a good sign there are only a few of 'em?"

"Indeed." Hugh motioned to Kirk. "Come here, lad." Hugh waited until Kirk leaned over. "I realize you are proud of your family's loyalties, but for the moment, do not divulge your loyalty to the Continentals. It is up to us to keep your mother and sister safe. Understood?"

"You will not turn us in, then?" Kirk asked, as the front door opened and muffled voices carried through the air.

"On the contrary, I shall protect your family as best as I can." Hugh hated the burning in the back of his throat. In truth, he had no idea if he could do anything at all, but he had to try. "Miss MacGregor saved my life. I owe her the same."

A knock sounded at the chamber door. He nodded to Kirk who went to open it. Miss MacGregor and her mother walked in and stood on the left, while the three soldiers gathered around the bed on the other side. They glanced at Hugh's redcoat lying on a nearby chair. The royal crown and stripes on the shoulder were proudly displayed. His sheathed sword lay across it within easy reach. The eldest soldier cleared his throat and saluted Hugh. The other two followed his example.

"Gentlemen, thank you for coming." Hugh nodded toward them. "I assume our commanding officer issued new orders for me?"

"Indeed, sir. My name is Private Benjamin Truitt," said the elder soldier. Hugh judged him to be about five and twenty, as his brown eyes burned with an intense fire each time they strayed in Miss MacGregor's direction, but she seemed oblivious as she watched Hugh. "Major James H. Craig ordered us to come here and see the extent of your wounds. We are to give him an estimate of when you will be able to report for duty, as well as about the family and supplies here. Our army is in need of all possible livestock and food. One of us will remain behind to attend you, Captain."

"Very well." Hugh turned to Mrs. MacGregor and her daughter. "Would you mind providing a little refreshment for these soldiers, while I show them my wounds?"

"Is it necessary?" Miss MacGregor stepped forward. She reached out to touch his arm, but paused, as if realizing how inappropriate the action would be. "He has only recently recovered from an infection.

At one point, I feared we would be forced to burn the infection out of the wound, but he began to improve."

"I am sorry, miss." Private Truitt set his hat on top of Hugh's red coat. "We must follow orders."

"Fine, but for the record, I am the one who cared for him and stitched him up. If something is not satisfactory, I am to blame, not my mother." Anger poured from Miss MacGregor's tone as she stormed from the chamber.

"I shall put on a pot of tea," Mrs. MacGregor said with a quick bow. Her cheeks darkened, and she ushered Kirk out of the chamber.

Hugh was quite amused by Miss MacGregor's boldness. Why did it vex her to leave? Was she hoping to learn something of value for the Continentals? Or did she merely dislike the idea of leaving the enemy in her home without proper supervision?

Private Truitt turned to Hugh. "What kind of wounds have you suffered, sir?"

"Indians shot me with arrows, here," he pointed to his side. "And here." he pulled back the covers and gestured to this thigh. Miss MacGregor had cut through his breeches in an effort to tend his leg. It left a gaping hole, but he was thankful to have something to wear.

"I shall send for clean breeches before you are required to leave the premises." Private Truitt wrinkled his nose. Hugh glanced down at the dried blood on the once white material and knew a moment of humility. "Looks deep." Private Truitt cleared his throat in discomfort. "But clean and the stitches are tight and sturdy."

"Yes, Miss MacGregor did a fine job. The cut goes through the muscle to the bone," Hugh said. "When she pulled the arrow out, the wide part of the stone ripped through my flesh. It made stitching it even more difficult."

"When does she anticipate taking out the stitches?" Private Truitt asked.

"I believe Miss MacGregor intends to remove the stitches in a few days," Hugh said. "They have given me every possible comfort."

"Every comfort but a decent bath." Private Truitt flipped the cover back over Hugh and straightened. "What sort of people are they? Where is Mr. MacGregor?"

"I was sick with an infectious fever and slept most of the first week I was here. Since they leave me to myself in this chamber most of the time, we have had few discussions." Hugh met his gaze, determined Private Truitt wouldn't have a reason to suspect him of hiding anything to protect the MacGregors. "I assume he may be away at war. I cannot imagine the MacGregors saving the life of a British soldier if they hold aught against the crown."

"Perhaps it is precisely what they wish us to think." Private Truitt turned to the two soldiers who remained. "According to Major Craig's orders, check the barns, stables, and fields and keep a log of every animal. Do not forget the storage of wheat, grain, flour, sugar, and salt, anything our troops could use." He gave Hugh a devious grin. "If they are truly loyal to the crown, they will not complain of contributing their share. I am appalled they would allow a wounded British officer to go so long without a decent bath." He motioned for the soldiers to go.

"I was too ill to even think of it." Hugh waved his hand to make light of the matter. The last thing he wanted was to cause problems for the MacGregor family. The sooner they left the better. It was selfish of him to stay because he wanted to be near Miss MacGregor. If he left with the soldiers now, he could spare the family from divulging their loyalty to the Continentals. "I am sure Mrs. MacGregor would not mind us borrowing her wagon so I could have a place to lie down when we return to headquarters."

"That will not be necessary. After seeing the condition of your injury, I shall remain here with you for the duration." Private Truitt walked to the door. "In fact, I intend to order the MacGregors to prepare your bath now. This oversight shall be remedied right away."

Tyra's nerves gnawed on her insides like a rat caught in a bin full of grain. To break their fast, her mother had made biscuits while she cooked the eggs and bacon. The smell of freshly brewed coffee floated in the kitchen, but they were now short on what sugar they had been saving. The two British soldiers left yesterday with their wagon loaded. They took bags of flour, salt, sugar, four caged chickens, and tied a cow to the back. At least her father and brothers had taken the extra horses or the British would have taken those as well. The redcoats left them with only one horse, and she supposed she should be grateful. They had Captain Morgan to thank. He had talked them into leaving it here.

When Private Truitt ordered a bath for Captain Morgan, Tyra felt chastised she had not offered him the opportunity before now. Any movement had been difficult for him and a hint of pride swelled in his words whenever she or her mother needed to help him. With Kirk as the only male around to assist him, Tyra thought it best to spare him, but now she wondered if she had been wrong. Private Truitt had made no effort to hide his disappointment.

She wished the man had returned to town with the others. Now she and her family were stuck not only serving Captain Morgan, but Private Truitt under his watchful scrutiny. Every word, action, and behavior could spark unwanted questions, especially where Kirk was concerned. The lad was at an awkward age, lacking in judgment.

"Mrs. MacGregor, this smells delicious." Private Truitt arrived in the kitchen with Captain Morgan leaning on his arm. "We thank you for the fine care you are giving us."

"Yer verra welcome, gentlemen." She nodded as she set a plate of biscuits on the table. "'Tis the least we can do."

"Not if your husband and sons are sacrificing their lives with the Tory militia," Private Truitt said. "You are doing quite much."

Tyra stiffened as she whirled to meet his gaze, standing several inches taller than the soldier, even in his black boots. Captain Morgan must have seen the fire in her eyes, for he tried to take a step on his injured leg and swayed. The motion caught Private Truitt's attention as he bent to further assist his captain. "If you will simply lead me to a chair, I think I can manage to eat breakfast this morning with everyone." He met Tyra's gaze over the soldier and winked at her. Relief flowed through Tyra as her cheeks warmed. With the simple and deliberate act, Captain Hugh managed to spare her the need of answering while distracting Private Truitt.

"Of course, sir." Private Truitt helped him limp to the nearest chair at the table. "I shall begin working on a walking stick for you today."

"That would be splendid. The more independent I can be, the better," Captain Morgan rubbed his hands as he gazed at the plate of bacon and scrambled eggs. "Indeed, this does smell inviting."

"Captain, would you like a glass of milk or a cup of warm coffee?" Mama asked, pausing to look over her shoulder.

"Coffee, please. Ever since I have been away from the mother country, I have developed a keen taste for strong coffee." His gaze slid to Tyra's, but she turned back to the counter to grab a bowl of grits her mother had boiled earlier. Why did he keep trying to protect them? Was he not putting himself at risk with his own superiors? The man thoroughly confused her. She could feel his gray eyes always watching her. At first it had disturbed her, but now as she was coming to know Captain Morgan, she couldn't help glowing under his appreciative gaze, and she knew it was wrong.

"I had planned to remove your stitches in a couple of days, Captain Morgan." Tyra poured a cup of coffee for herself and her mother. She sat across from him. Her brother was seated to her right and unusually quiet this morning. He drank his milk in silence as he listened to them. "Will it still be sufficient or do you need me to remove them sooner?"

"No, it should be fine. I thought I would wait until one of the other men return with a pair of breeches. I prefer to arrive looking like a proper captain." He cleared his throat and looked down at his empty plate. "Thank you for the loan of your father's clothes."

"You are quite welcome. He has no need of them at the moment." Tyra set a biscuit on her plate and scooped out a portion of eggs before passing them to her brother.

"Mrs. MacGregor, which regiment is your husband serving under?" Private Truitt asked, as he dropped three pieces of bacon onto his plate. "We have been in contact with all the local Tory militia. I may have some news for you if I were to know with whom he is serving."

"He is not with the Tories," Kirk said, his breathing hard and his eyes wide and too innocent for his own good. "My father and brothers are Continentals."

Dread pinched Tyra's gut as her mother clutched her stomach with an open mouth and a shocked expression. Captain Morgan paused, not taking the bite he was about to eat and masking his reaction to perfection. He lowered his fork, his gaze traveling from her brother to Tyra.

Tyra cleared her throat as she kicked her brother under the table, hoping to hush him before he caused them all to be slammed into the brig. Would the British harm innocent women and mouthy lads? She had no idea. The rumors circulating over the last few years were enough to make her insides melt with worry. She wanted to believe God would protect them, but she imagined many soldiers felt the same way and now lay cold in their graves. God had given men free will. To what extent did it flow?

"Indeed?" Private Truitt asked, raising an eyebrow. He turned to Captain Morgan. "Was this something you were aware of?"

"I was beginning to suspect it, but since Miss MacGregor had saved my life, and I was in her care, I wanted to wait until I was better to confront them about it." Captain Morgan met his gaze and didn't flinch when Private Truitt scoffed.

"Captain, you had every opportunity to confront them yesterday when the others were here." He pointed to Tyra. "Or perhaps you have come to favor Miss MacGregor and hoped to leave before they were discovered?"

"Careful, private, you do rank beneath me." Captain Morgan's stern tone reprimanded him. "We are at war with Continental men, not innocent women and children. Whatever enemies might lurk around me, I am a gentleman in His Majesty's Royal Army, and I will conduct myself in a manner as befits the king. Regardless of what the men in this family have done, Mrs. MacGregor and her daughter have saved my life and taken me into their home. They have willingly given to the British Crown most of their goods. Their actions have been the opposite of traitorous."

"Forgive me, sir, but you must be aware that women and lads of this one's age are capable of passing on pertinent information to the right people fighting against us." He tilted his head and twisted his lips. "I meant no disrespect to the king."

"Private Truitt," Tyra said. "We are but lowly women who cannot hold jobs to support our families while our men are away at war, or hold political positions, or even voice an opinion or have a vote in what our husbands and grown sons do, whether or not we agree or disagree with them. 'Tis our responsibility to love our men and lend a helping hand to those in need as Christian charity dictates. We have no opinion that counts for either side."

⚘

Once Private Truitt took himself off to find a sturdy piece of oak to carve Hugh a walking stick, Hugh breathed a sigh of relief. Prolonged silence filled the house, and he wondered where Miss MacGregor and her mother had disappeared. He pushed himself up from his chair where he had been sitting by the window in his chamber and limped into the foyer.

Footsteps came toward him from the parlor, and Miss MacGregor appeared with her red hair falling from the pins at the crown of her head. Her green eyes were wild and worried. "Oh, 'tis you. I thought Private Truitt may have returned—all too soon." Her gaze traveled down to his injured leg. "Why are you up and about?"

"I wanted to talk to you," Hugh said, hoping his strength didn't fail him lest he fall to the floor like a weak ninny.

"What about?" She blinked at him in expectation.

"About naught in particular." Hugh managed a grin as he struggled to hold onto his dignity. "Has it not occurred to you I am as much relieved by Truitt's temporary departure as you?"

"I am sorry, no such thing had occurred to me." As if remembering her manners, she strode toward him and took his arm at the elbow. "Allow me to help you into the parlor."

As usual, the smell of honey surrounded him when Miss MacGregor came near. He closed his eyes and basked in the scent of her and the warmth of her nearness. The woman had a way of making him forget the army, they were enemies, and a war raged around them. Her presence stirred his compassion, brought a peace he could not explain, and a desire for her attention that ate at his independent nature.

"Miss MacGregor, why do you always smell of honey?" he asked as they entered the parlor, and she led him to a Chippendale chair with carved feet and arms like claws. She sat on a settee by double windows across from the wide hearth. Green drapes matched the settee.

"I suppose it might be because I am the beekeeper of the family." She awarded him with a genuine smile as he took his seat and stared up at her in surprise, reluctant to part from her. "Your fellow comrades may have taken the last of our sugar, but I have something else to work just as well."

"Honey in my tea is something I have never considered . . . until now." He noticed a smudge of black ink on her right middle finger and wondered if she had been writing a letter. Hugh glanced over at the closed oak desk with slanted carved top. "You are full of surprises. I would have never guessed you kept honeybees, but then again it is hard to imagine you facing Indians with a rifle all on your own."

"I thought you were unconscious when you first arrived here?" She tilted her head in question and turned a shade darker as if embarrassed, but a slow smile lifted the corners of her pink lips. "My father and brothers taught me how to shoot. Mama never liked the idea of me learning, but once they left for the war, she realized how valuable such a skill would be."

"Speaking of your mother, where is she this afternoon?" Hugh asked.

"I am afraid she took to her bed with the headache." Miss MacGregor frowned in concern.

The front door opened and closed as hurried footsteps pounded the foyer. Kirk appeared and stopped short in front of his sister. "Tyra, I finished my chores in the barn and wanted to ask Mama if I could go visit Darren."

Tyra . . . Hugh longed to call her by her given name, but such familiarity would not be appropriate even though he had now been staying with them for a couple of weeks. He would think of her as Tyra, even if he could not call her by the blessed name.

"Mama is not feeling well," Tyra said, relaxing her shoulders and resting against the back of the settee. "You may go this afternoon, but be back in time for supper and be careful. I do not want you going back into town now that the British soldiers have arrived."

"Thank you." Kirk grinned and disappeared from the parlor.

The lad's eagerness brought back memories of his own childhood, as well as his immature behavior and the lectures he and Neil had to endure from their father. Kirk's loyalty and admiration of his father and brothers was commendable, but his actions and careless words could cause serious harm to not only himself, but his sister and mother. Considerable pain lanced across his chest at the thought. The lad needed some stern guidance before he caused further trouble.

"Did you ever talk to Kirk about his blunder this morning, revealing your Continental connections?" Hugh asked.

"No, but I intend to discuss with him the seriousness of staying out of the way of the British and bringing as little attention to our family as possible." She linked her hands in her lap and pinned him with a stare meant to chastise him. "No need to concern yourself with Kirk's discipline, Captain Morgan. What he said was the truth and 'twas stated in a polite manner. He did no wrong."

"But he could unknowingly cause further hardship for you and your mother. Even though what he said is true, some of my comrades—the ones with a weaker character—could have still taken exception and twisted his words to mean something he did not intend." Hugh's thigh began to ache and he rubbed his hand beside the stitches to ease the tense muscle. "Do you understand my meaning? We are at war, and your family is considered an enemy to the king, traitors. Even though you are not men and do not wear a soldier's uniform, you are still dangerous by any information you could obtain and give to your father and brothers. Make no mistake, your brother is young, but there are other lads his age already in service. I implore you to speak to him."

"Are you saying your countrymen are dishonest in character?" She crossed her feet at the ankles as a slow smile crossed her lips. "My, my, captain, I am surprised you would admit such a thing."

"I will always be as truthful as possible under the disagreeable circumstances." He continued to rub his leg and tried to ignore the small pain now jabbing at his side. He shifted, hoping to ease it, but the movement deepened his discomfort. Confound it all, he should be healing faster than this. "There is not an army on the face of this earth without a few souls of questionable character, including ours."

"I am not afraid." Tyra leaned forward and lowered her tone with meaning. His heart danced at the sultry tone she did not mean to imply and once again his admiration for her courage spiked. The woman's innocence could be misleading to some, especially since she was completely unaware of her own appeal. And her size and boldness could be quite an intimidation, if he was a lesser man.

"You should be," he said, wishing he had the energy to match her animated conversation. How could he make her understand the seriousness of their grave situation? Not only did Kirk worry him, but Tyra herself was a constant concern. If he had not interfered and gone to her mother, she would have ridden into town alone and right into the midst of the hornet's nest. He thought of her bees and grinned at the analogy, but she was used to it, was she not?

"Are you suggesting, Captain, that I should be afraid of all the men in your army with the exception of yourself?" She lifted a red eyebrow in skepticism with a grin of distrust. The knowledge wounded him, but he could not blame her. "Did I not hear you say you were waiting until you are better to confront us about our loyalties to the Continental? What, pray tell, were you truly planning?" She shook her head as her lips thinned in a straight line. "Forgive me, Captain, but I do not trust you either. Do you think me so gullible as to believe you would turn your back on your king and country, and risk all you have worked for in gaining the rank of captain to protect two women and a young lad you have only recently met? The notion is not only silly, but laughable, and you insult my intelligence, sir."

Before he could respond, the front door opened, allowing a blast of cold air to breeze into the parlor from the foyer. Private Truitt walked in with a questionable frown carrying a sturdy piece of oak to make a walking stick and an Indian arrow.

5

$\mathcal{T}$he next morning two British soldiers returned with a pair of white breeches and a letter for Captain Morgan, as well as a letter for Tyra. To her relief, they did not stay. She closed the front door behind them and leaned against it, pulling her gray shawl tight around her.

"Tyra, ye must read it. We need to know what it says." Mama strode toward where Tyra leaned against the door. "Goodness, they brought a draft inside. Kirk, build a warm fire in the parlor." She gripped Tyra's arm. "Let us go rest."

Captain Morgan took his letter and limped to his chamber where he closed the door, leaving them alone with Private Truitt. Tyra thought back to what Captain Morgan had said yesterday and wondered if he longed to escape the insufferable man as much as they did. She allowed her mother to lead her into the parlor as she clutched the letter in her hand. Neither of them spared a glance in Private Truitt's direction.

"I suppose I shall go out on the front porch and finish carving the captain's cane," Private Truitt said. Footsteps carried him across the foyer. The sound of the door opening and closing gave Tyra a blessed peace.

She and her mother sat on the settee while Kirk laid another log on the glowing fire. Knowing the suspense ate at her mother and brother, Tyra broke the seal and unfolded the letter. She cleared her throat and read aloud, "Dear Miss MacGregor, Captain Morgan has written me about the diligent care and sacrifice you made in saving his life. On behalf of his Royal Majesty, I would like to take this opportunity to thank you and to show my sincere appreciation. As you may have heard, my men are in the process of moving my personal items to the Burgwin House where I will set up a more permanent residence for our duration in Wilmington. It would be my sincerest pleasure to invite you and Captain Morgan to dine with me this evening. I am in great anticipation to meet you both. Sincerely, Major James H. Craig."

Stunned silence followed as each of them pondered the letter. The fire now crackled and popped as a wave of heat poured from the hearth. Tyra welcomed the warmth since the words she had read left her confused and cold. She didn't want to dine with the insufferable British. They had torn her country apart, divided families, and it would be a direct insult to her father and brothers.

"You plan to actually go?" Kirk was the first to break the silence. "'Tis too dangerous, Tyra. You have spent plenty of time lecturing me on why I should stay away and those same reasons extend to you, and more so, since you are a girl." His wide eyes blinked in concern.

"I am not afraid. I merely have no wish to walk into the lion's den," Tyra said. "The thought turns my stomach to know those men could be fighting against my da and brothers."

"As much as it pains me to say it, ye must go, lass." Mama covered Tyra's hand with her own and tightened her grip for a dose of encouragement. "To refuse would be a great insult to Major Craig, and we cannot afford it. We must trust he is a good man. Ye shall be going with Captain Morgan. I believe we have witnessed enough of his character to know he is an honorable man. And ye know God will not forsake ye."

"I know." Tyra nodded. "I will go to my chamber and prepare myself. I need time to think and pray." Tyra stood and stepped around her brother. "This must have been what Queen Esther felt like before she was queen." The favored Bible story came to mind as she walked across the room.

Several hours later, Tyra rode in the family carriage with Captain Morgan. Private Truitt drove them since they no longer had a regular driver. Most of their men servants had joined the war and abandoned them when her father and brothers left. They arrived early so Captain Morgan could have a private discussion with Major Craig and receive his orders, as well as learn of new war developments. To her displeasure, Private Truitt had been charged with her care.

They continued down Front Street and passed Castle and Church Streets until they turned right onto Market Street. Tyra stared out the window paying little attention to the civilians walking or riding wagons or those on horseback. Redcoats and merchants drew a crowd of spectators. An older man had been stripped of decent clothing in the biting cold, tossed on the back of a horse like a sack of potatoes, and paraded around while redcoats mocked and laughed at him. From the side of his face, she could tell he had been beaten.

"What is the meaning of treating a poor soul like that?" Tyra demanded. She pointed out the window in horror. Her heart pounded against her ribs at the injustice.

Captain Morgan leaned forward and bent his head to peer out the same side. "I would imagine he is a Continental prisoner."

"Even so, must they humiliate him and expose him to the cold?" Images came to mind of her father and brothers being beaten and treated in a similar manner. The unwanted thoughts pinched her heart. "Do you approve of such behavior?" she demanded, searching his handsome face as he swallowed in discomfort.

"Miss MacGregor, most likely, he is not just any prisoner of war. He must be a ranking officer for them to make such a public example of him." He sighed and sat back, a look of disgust now claiming his features. "No doubt, the Continentals do similar things with the British officers they capture."

"You did not answer my question, Captain Morgan." Tyra allowed her biting tone to thin the air. She hardened her heart against him, determined not to soften against a man who would condone such behavior—war or no war. "Whether he be a Continental or a British officer, 'tis inhumane. I would not treat an animal in such a manner."

"'Tisn't what I have heard about you. I heard the Indians talking before I lost complete consciousness." Captain Morgan leaned forward and grabbed her wrist, "Why do the Indians call you War Woman? Is it because you are so gentle and perfect? Or were you forced to be uncivilized?"

"'Tis because I am accurate with a pistol." Tyra jerked away from him as they rolled to a stop in front of a large white house she had always known as the Burgwin House. "Your assumption is quite accurate. I killed a man who tried to take my life. I understand war better than you think, Captain Morgan." She pointed out the window. "But these foolhardy redcoats are no longer in danger from this poor soul."

☙

Feeling properly chastised, Hugh stepped from the carriage and offered his arm to Tyra as Private Truitt drove the wagon around to the side of the house to see to the horses. She slapped it away, lifted her pert nose, and descended all on her own. The sound of her skirts swished by as her boots crunched the pebbles in the dirt road. He closed his eyes to inhale her honeyed scent. The woman had a way of distracting him from things like meeting his new superior officer, which should be uppermost on his mind. Instead, he was more concerned by Tyra questioning his character.

He took a deep breath as he leaned on his new cane and watched her forge ahead of him across the dirt path. She stomped up the steps leading to the front porch as if she knew this place. Perhaps she did since she was a native of Wilmington. Hugh grinned at Tyra's impertinent behavior toward him. Would she continue to be so haughty once she came face to face with Major Craig? Under normal circumstances, she would amuse him, but war changed everything.

Once he made it up the steps at a much slower pace, Hugh nodded to the two soldiers standing guard on each side of the front entrance. Noticing his rank on his red uniform, both men saluted him. Hugh ignored his throbbing leg and reached around Tyra to tap the iron knocker against the heavy oak door. A few moments later, it opened and the hinges creaked as another young soldier appeared.

"I am Captain Donahue Morgan with Miss Tyra MacGregor," Hugh said.

"Come in, Major Craig is expecting you both." The man stepped back and opened the door wider. "You may leave your hats and coats on the rack." He pointed to a wooden stand with upturned arms in the corner of the foyer by a set of wide stairs leading into a hallway. Hugh had no intention of removing his red uniform coat, but he stepped forward to assist Tyra with her dark brown cloak. At first, she looked as if she would refuse, but she glanced at the other soldier and relented with a sigh. She pulled back the hood, unbuttoned it at the neck, and lifted it from her shoulders. With a glint in her beautiful green eyes, she handed it to Hugh.

"Miss MacGregor, I have been instructed to ask you to wait in the parlor," the soldier extended his arm toward a large open archway as he nodded in its direction. He turned back to Hugh. "Captain Morgan, I am to bring you to the study."

They walked past the staircase, their boots clicking against the hard pinewood floor. Hugh's cane broke up the rhythm of their steps like an awkward third leg. The soldier paused by an open door and cleared his throat to announce their presence. "Sir, I have brought Captain Donahue Morgan."

"Good. Show him in." An authoritative voice carried into the hall where Hugh waited. More pain shot through his thigh, but he tried to ignore the discomfort. A chance to sit down would be most welcome as soon as he could manage it. The soldier stepped out into the hall and waved Hugh inside the study.

"Close the door behind you," the major said.

Hugh did as requested and turned to salute his commanding officer. "Captain Donahue Morgan reporting back to duty, sir."

"I appreciate your recent letter explaining what happened to your men in the Indian attack. You are fortunate Miss MacGregor has cared for you." Major Craig stood from his desk and walked toward a chair in front of the warm hearth where a small fire burned. "Please have a seat." He motioned to a dark green upholstered chair across from him. "In your letter, you stated Lord Cornwallis commissioned you in South Carolina to undertake the charge of freeing an officer captured by the Continentals. Why were you given this responsibility, and who is this officer?"

"I was given the responsibility because I requested it." Hugh lowered himself on the cushioned seat with relief. "They have three officers, and one of them is Colonel Neil Morgan, my elder brother."

"I see." Major Craig linked his fingertips and studied Hugh. "And are you close to this brother?"

"As close as any two brothers can be, sir," Hugh said, hoping he could soon set out to find his brother and set him free. If their roles were reversed, Neil would never give up. He was relentless. Even as a prisoner of war, Hugh had no doubt his brother was busy collecting valuable information from the enemy. He never let an opportunity pass him by. His dark brown eyes and black hair came to mind, and Hugh experienced a moment of nostalgia.

"In the meantime, while you are healing, I thought it might be best for you to remain with the MacGregors." Major Craig said, crossing his legs. "I have inquired about them and discovered they are traitors. Even though Miss MacGregor saved your life, I fear she cannot be trusted. I have not only invited her here to thank her, but to assess her character."

"And what is to be my role in the MacGregor household?" Hugh asked, suspicion and concern kindling inside him.

"To learn what you can and report any valuable information to me. I have stationed a few of my officers at questionable households around the city." He drummed his fingers on the wooden arm of his chair. "I intend to ferret out any rebellion. In fact, we just captured Cornelius Harnett. One of his own servants gave him up at his plantation in Onslow County. Once we finish making an example of him, we shall put him in the open blockhouse."

"And how long will you keep him there? He will not last long in the elements if you want to use him as leverage against the enemy," Hugh said, wishing he could convince Major Craig not to torture the man in such a way. "Do you think it could stir up the local Patriots?"

"I hope so and 'tis one of my strategies. He is a native of Wilmington and a local hero who has built the leadership against us. Bringing him down like this will take away some of their momentum and destroy their hope."

"Speaking of the Patriots, I really doubt the MacGregors know anything of value. Since I have been among them, they rarely talk about the war, and I have seen no evidence of them receiving or sending letters to their loved ones. There is no way they could be gaining new information since today is the first day Miss MacGregor has been to town and no visitors have paid a call to the house."

"The Tories tell me Miss MacGregor has been quite vocal about her loyalties to the Patriots and there is some talk she is even known as the War Woman among the Indians. 'Tis unlikely a woman would have such a reputation without some cause. I want you to find out what it is. Seduce her if you must . . . she is, after all, . . . a woman."

✐❦

After waiting almost thirty minutes in the parlor, Tyra began to fidget. She browsed the contents of the room, viewing the portraits on the buff-colored walls, the pianoforte in the corner, and paused, holding out her hands near the waning fire in the hearth. Brass candles stood tall on each end of the mantle. A mirror with a gilded frame hung over the center.

Booted footsteps drew near. Tyra gripped her hands tight, hoping it would be Hugh rather than Major Craig. A cold shiver crept up her spine, and she sensed he possessed a bad character. Everything inside Tyra warned her not to trust him.

"Miss MacGregor, would you accompany me to the dining room?" Hugh's voice floated across the room. Grateful he had returned for her after all, Tyra turned and offered him a genuine smile. He strode toward her and lowered his voice. "Be careful around Major Craig. The Tories have told him about your family's loyalty to the Patriots and that the Indians call you War Woman."

"What does this mean?" She tilted her head as he gripped her hands. "Is my family in danger?"

"Not at the moment." He tightened his warm grip around her fingers. "I shall be returning to The MacGregor Quest with you. I have been assigned to watch over you. British officers will be stationed at all homes where Patriots are known to reside."

"You mean to spy on us and report any suspicious activity." She snatched her hands away and stepped back, glaring at him with suspicion. "I may be a woman, Captain, but I am no fool."

"I never took you for one." He gripped her shoulders and forced her to face him. "But I can promise you this, as your protector, I can ensure you and your mother will be treated with the utmost respect, but I cannot guarantee the same treatment from other fellow officers assigned to your Patriot friends." He gave her a gentle shake. "Do you understand what I am trying to tell you?"

"Yes, I understand you are an honorable man." She nodded. "And you intend to prove it, or I shall be forced to become the War Woman once again."

"Is that so?" He grinned with a slight chuckle as his eyes sparked with interest, raising a brow. He turned, stepped in line beside her, and offered his elbow. "Shall we go in to dinner before our prolonged absence is noticed?"

"Indeed." Tyra nodded, slipping her hand around his strong arm. "I am quite ready. You may lead me into the lion's den."

"Guard your words carefully," he said. "I imagine Major Craig will try to gauge your every expression and trick you into saying more than you intend. He would like naught more than to learn the secrets of the Patriots."

They stepped into the hallway and passed painted portraits of men and women before entering the dining room on the right. Conversations carried around the oblong table. The shiny silverware sparkled in the candlelight spaced down the middle of the table. Major Craig sat at the head and gave them a welcoming smile as Hugh escorted her to the empty seat beside his superior. Tyra imagined a cold indifference beneath the facade he displayed. His white hair reminded her of a powdered herring, if there was such a thing.

Hugh pulled out the wooden chair for Tyra and motioned for her to sit in the space by Major Craig. She gritted her teeth and tried to conceal her dislike as she settled on the upholstered cushioned seat. Hugh walked around and sat across from her, meeting her gaze. Somehow his expression gave her reassurance. She took a deep breath and lifted her chin.

"I was not aware we were now cavorting with the enemy." Miss Kelly Gordon glanced at Tyra from across the right side of the table. As children they had attended the same school and even played together as friends, but once the war broke out and their families took opposing sides, Tyra assumed they would now be forever divided.

"The enemy?" Hugh turned to Kelly sitting on his right. "This courageous lady saved my life. Regardless of her family's choices, I would not call her an enemy. I would stake my life on it . . . again." He winked at Tyra with a grin in an attempt to lighten the mood.

All conversation grew silent, and the gazes around the table turned toward Hugh. He met each eye with unflinching dignity and held his head up, his back straight, and showed a confidence she had only imagined in storybooks. As long as she lived, Tyra would not forget this moment, and she prayed God would remind her if she was tempted to forget—even for a moment.

"Do not worry about the Patriots." Major Craig's strong voice carried down the table. "We are well aware of where loyalties lie in the city of Wilmington." He gestured toward Tyra. "But as gentlemen officers of His Royal Military, we are honor-bound to reward good deeds on behalf of His Majesty. Therefore, Miss MacGregor is an honored guest."

"Thank you, sir." Tyra looked into his dark eyes, hoping to judge the thoughts he didn't speak aloud. When his stoic expression revealed nothing but a dangerous distrust that made her uneasy, Hugh's warning came back to her remembrance. Her gaze traveled around the table at other British officers. Their expressions were a mixture of curiosity, interest, distrust, and contempt.

"I must confess, it feels strange to be referred to as an enemy by people I have known all my life, especially those I went to school with as a child." Tyra shifted her gaze toward Kelly, who looked down at her plate in shame. "I did what was right in helping Captain Morgan, and I would do it again."

"Well, in this case, anyone who defends His Majesty's soldiers is a friend to us." Mrs. Isobel Gordon said, glancing at her daughter from the corner of her eye.

"I daresay," said a British officer beside her. "The next time I am on the battlefield, I would do well to have Miss MacGregor by my side." Laughter erupted in the dining room.

"Indeed." Major Craig rested his elbows on the table and gave her a pointed look as he linked his fingers. "I believe it would be a boon to have the War Woman around. I, for one, would be most interested in seeing what she is capable of."

Fear slithered through Tyra like a boa constrictor tightening the noose around her neck. His tone was almost a direct challenge. Did he intend to provoke her?

6

*H*ugh faked a chuckle trying to ignore the fear of betrayal in Tyra's wounded green eyes. It had to be hard to have longtime friends turn against one's family. His family never had many friends to lose. Their poverty and his father's drunken behavior made sure of it.

He needed to distract everyone's attention from her and lighten the mood in the room. Servants came in and served the first course of potato soup, starting with Major Craig. While he was distracted, Hugh seized the opportunity to steer the conversation from the MacGregors' loyalty to the Patriots.

"What kind of fool would think of Miss MacGregor as the War Woman?" Hugh lifted his glass, meeting the gazes around the table. "I daresay, those Indians have quite lost their minds. I am tempted to hunt them down for what they did to my men."

"And I share in your sentiment, lad, but I already gave you your orders." Major Craig nodded in Tyra's direction. "Your responsibility is clear. However, if we do come upon any savages, we shall finish them off."

Tyra gasped and leaned back in her seat like a rigid pole made of iron. Her expression paled in stark comparison to the bold red hair framing her face in thin curls. The rest had been swept up in combs and piled on top of her head in a lovely way making him want to stare. Instead, he forced his gaze away, hoping she realized he had no serious intention of pursuing her Indian friends.

"And I will take my orders with the utmost attention, I assure you." Hugh leaned back as a servant placed a bowl of potato soup before him. He would have to be careful not to show how much interest and care he felt toward Tyra MacGregor. Otherwise, Major Craig might be tempted to station him elsewhere. In spite of his growing attachment to her, Hugh could not afford to fail in the attempt to rescue his brother. Eventually, he would have to move on and carry out his plans to rescue his brother as soon as he could convince Major Craig to give the order.

The conversation turned to other pleasantries as they finished their soup and the main course of roast pork, stewed vegetables, and buttered bread was served. He wondered how much of their meal had been stolen from nearby farms and plantations. His stomach churned, and he had to swallow down the angry thoughts. War had always been a harsh reality for the civilians caught in the midst of it. None of this was any surprise to him, so why did he have an inconvenient conscience all of a sudden?

His gaze strayed to Tyra as she sipped from her cup. The glow from the candlelight masked her light freckles into her smooth marble skin. Her dark lips curled into a smile and her green eyes lit like lanterns at a tale Sergeant McAlister shared about some pirates on the high seas.

Without warning, her knowing gaze flicked to Hugh and his heart raced as if being caught at something he should not have been doing. She blinked pensive eyes at him as she studied him in an open manner. The woman was direct. Such bold courage was considered an advantage for a man, but could be a curse for a woman. If it wasn't for the time he had spent in her company to know how innocent she was, he could have mistaken her manners. A less honorable man might not have the discipline to rein in his thoughts on her. It was another reason he feared her being in the company of his fellow soldiers for too long. The sooner he got her home, the better.

"Miss MacGregor, you have lived here on the coast your whole life. Have there been any pirates to scavenge your shores here?" Sergeant McAlister turned to Tyra. He smiled at her through his trimmed beard and mustache as if he doted on her. "I understand you live outside Wilmington, closer to the sea."

"Indeed, I do." Tyra nodded as she set down her glass and folded her hands in her lap. "I am afraid to disappoint you, sir. Most of the pirate days were before my time. The elder folks in these parts tell tall tales about how the fearsome Blackbeard roamed the Carolina coast and spent time living on Ocracoke Island. He anchored the Queen Anne's Revenge off the shores for weeks at a time."

"Do you suppose there might be buried treasure around here?" Corporal Jackson asked, as he leaned forward, his brown eyes beaming. Unlike the sergeant, he had no beard, only a thin brown mustache making him look even younger than his score and one year. "I am sure he had to store it all somewhere, and he would not have wanted to share most of the bounty with his men."

"People have been talking about buried treasure for years and naught has been found." Mrs. Gordon waved a hand in the air as if to dismiss the subject. "Not as much as a single map has been discovered."

"True. Lots of disappointed hopes have been dashed on the idea of finding Blackbeard's treasure," Tyra said, covering a yawn. "Please forgive me, I am growing quite weary."

"But the night is still young," Major Craig said. "I intend for us to retire to the drawing room and play a few games and have a glass of port."

"What a delightful idea!" Kelly brightened. "Shall we play a game of whist?"

"I shall be fine," Tyra said, ignoring Kelly. "All I need are a few moments to freshen up. It has been a long time since I have visited this house. Is there a water closet?" She lifted an eyebrow as she regarded Major Craig from her angled profile.

"There is a water closet with a wash basin and towel down the hall toward the back of the house, but the facilities are actually outside. You will need to go down the back stairs to the first floor," Major Craig said, as Tyra rose from her chair. "One of my servants will attend you."

"No need." She waved his concern away. "I am used to functioning without a servant for every minute detail. I am sure I will manage on my own, thank you." She bowed into a brief curtsy and retreated to the open threshold.

Hugh watched her, wondering if she was all right.

❧

Tyra lifted her chin, straightened her back, and walked out of the dining room before Major Craig could think of a reason to stop her. She had heard from her neighbor, Mr. Simmons, the British were keeping Patriot prisoners in cells below the house. It was well-known the house had been built over the foundation of a former jail. If she could figure out the layout of the rooms on each floor, the knowledge might prove helpful for the Patriot supporters brave enough to attempt a rescue.

She committed to memory each room she passed and came to a set of stairs at the back. It looked as if the plain, wooden steps led down to the servant quarters. The temptation to follow them gnawed at her until she realized it would be necessary to go downstairs in order to visit the outdoor facility. It could certainly serve as a proper excuse if she were caught. The opportunity would also afford her the ability to seek the entrance to the secret tunnels existing beneath the house and leading to other parts of Wilmington.

Childhood rumors were filled with such stories about the underground tunnels and the so-called ghosts who haunted them. Tyra assumed they were simple, make-believe stories until her father confirmed their existence. He had used them once to visit her mother's father after he was jailed for killing his son, an accident from which he never quite recovered.

As she descended the steps, she prayed her weight would not cause the boards to creak and draw attention. The steps led into a brick layered hallway with a rounded arch. A lit lantern hung on an iron peg encased into the wall. The brick floor did not provide a smooth surface, and Tyra had to lift her skirts to ensure her steps were stable. Men's voices carried from the end where she witnessed black iron bars. A guard in a redcoat sat in a wooden chair where he leaned back against the wall slumbering.

Tyra kept to the shadows so no one would notice her. She didn't want to give the Patriots false hope, since she didn't know if she could do anything to release them. The damp cold seeped into her bones, so she could only imagine what these men must be enduring without proper winter clothing. She inched her way along the wall, hoping she didn't come into contact with any disease-carrying rodent. If only she had spent more time here as a child, she might know where to begin looking for the small door in the floor.

Footsteps sounded down the hall as two maids approached carrying a large tray each. Tyra held her breath and pressed herself even further into the shadows, praying she wouldn't be noticed. As they passed the single light, Tyra could see they both wore gray service gowns and their hair was pulled back into a bun at the crown. The first tray was filled with about ten small plates of crusty bread, while the second had tiny bowls Tyra assumed might be soup. No appetizing aroma accompanied the food. Instead, the dank musty smell mixed with old urine filled the place with a nasty stench.

The guard woke at their approach and the low murmur of his conversation with the maids echoed through the brick walls, giving Tyra the momentary distraction she needed to sneak back upstairs. She inched her back toward the stairs. Footsteps appeared on the steps, and Tyra was forced to crouch low. Her fingers crawled over the brick floor to a wooden door by her feet.

"Hey! Have any of you seen a young woman slip down here?" A man's voice called. He paused on the lower steps, but didn't come all the way down. "There seems to be some concern she might have gotten lost."

"Of course not," the guard replied with a chuckle. "I cannot imagine she would want to be down here for any reason." A set of keys jingled from the guard's hip as he stood and stretched.

"Aye, what a nasty place this is." One of the maids giggled beside him. "Ye know those sort of women would faint at the sights an' smells down 'ere." She walked over to the first cell. "Not strong as me."

"Ye can slide it through the bars and set it on the floor," the guard said.

"Just following orders." The man on the steps mumbled as he carried himself back upstairs.

Now they were looking for her, and Tyra realized she would have to hurry. She slid her hands along the wooden door where her fingers came across a metal latch. Could it be the entrance to one of the tunnels? It would make too much noise if she tried to open it. Suppressing the temptation, she took a deep breath and let it out slowly as she made her way along the wall to the steps. While they were busy sliding food under the bars of another cell, Tyra hurried up the stairs.

As soon as she returned home, she would sketch the layout of the house and the location of the tunnel door. If the Patriots intended to free the prisoners, the tunnels would be the best way to sneak in and escape without notice. Once upstairs, she took note of the time on the grandfather clock. It was eight-thirty. Now she knew what time they fed the prisoners. A plan began to form in her mind. She may not be able to fight in the war as a soldier, but she could certainly do her part as a spy.

Hugh felt a cold draft as he flipped the cover off his exposed thigh. He had been hardly conscious when Tyra sewed in the stitches, but now that she was about to remove them, a sudden discomfort settled around him. Perhaps he should have insisted the army surgeon do this. Doubt pressed him as she laid some metal scissors and tweezers on the table by his bed.

Since returning last night, Tyra had settled into a strange silence, and he longed to know her thoughts. As she broke her fast, she had eaten in silence until her mother and brother asked about their trip into town. Tyra gave vague answers. Hugh filled in details where he could.

"Do you need my assistance?" Private Truitt asked, standing at the foot of the bed with his hands linked behind his back.

"No, I shall be fine." Tyra shook her head, towering over him. She wore an apron over her blue gown. Her fiery red hair was pulled back and twisted into brass combs with a rose emblem. Soft curls hung around her ears. Even now she had a way of distracting Hugh. At times like this, it was hard to imagine her as the War Woman. Even if others couldn't see it, he recognized a softness betraying her caring nature and compassion. She had taken him in knowing he was the enemy, not knowing what kind of character he possessed or the harm he could bring to her and her family.

"Captain Morgan, I would like for ye to drink this." Mrs. MacGregor sailed into the chamber carrying a cup. She wore a dark green gown that swished as she walked toward him. Slipping a hand behind his head, she tipped the container toward his mouth.

"But what is it?" He asked, eyeing her with suspicion. The smell of strong drink overpowered the honey scent of Tyra nearby on the other side. He wrinkled his nose in distaste, knowing the liquid would soon leave a trail of fire down his throat and into his stomach.

"Just a wee bit o'my husband's homemade Scottish whiskey. We save it for times like these to dull the senses and ease the pain." With surprising force, she once again lifted his head and tilted the cup to his lips. Hugh was forced to sip or let the contents dribble down the side of his mouth and chin. He swallowed the burning fire and took a deep breath to cool his mouth. The liquid jolted every dormant sensation in his body as it pooled in the pit of his stomach like hot springs. A few minutes later, she tipped it again and he swallowed the liquid fire. He burped.

Tyra's lips twisted into a wry grin before she burst into laughter. "I thought you could handle a bit of strong drink." She gripped his arm. "Removing the stitches will not hurt as much as putting them in."

"I know." He covered her hand and gazed into her green eyes. "I am ready. I do not need more whiskey. I never cared for it." He turned to her mother. "But, thank you, Mrs. MacGregor."

"Aye, lad. 'Tis the least I could do." She stepped back. "My Malcolm would chide me for trying to ease his pain. Such a strong man, he is. And took great pride in it." Mrs. MacGregor turned to stare out the window, but it would take a simpleton to miss the longing in her voice when she mentioned her husband.

"'Tis time." Tyra picked up a small pair of scissors. She eased the tip under the first stitch and snipped it. With careful precision, she eased her way down the whole row of stitches. Each movement pinched his skin like a mild irritation annoying him. She took a set of tweezers and pulled out the thread. His thigh continued to sting until Tyra turned her attention to the wound at his side, and it took his breath away. Hugh gritted his teeth as she pulled the thread through his skin. For some reason, this part of his body was more tender.

Tyra cleaned both areas and dried them. Her touch was gentle, as if taking great care to keep from causing him further pain.

"Captain Morgan, you are healing quite nicely," Tyra said. "I am pleased with the results. I hope I did not cause you too much discomfort."

"Not at all." He shook his head. "In fact, I am most thankful."

"Mama!" Kirk raced into Hugh's chamber and rolled to a stop. "Aunt Carleen and Uncle Ollie just arrived."

"And why would they be coming here?" Private Truitt backed toward the window and glanced out the curtains. His mouth puckered into a frown as he shook his head. "A man and woman are leaving a carriage. They are wearing plain clothes."

"My aunt and uncle are Quakers," Tyra said, tucking the scissors and tweezers away into a cloth pouch. She fastened the button closed and glanced over at Hugh. "They do not believe in war and pose no threat against the king's army. Please allow us to welcome them in peace."

"We will welcome them," Hugh said, meeting her probing green eyes. "But I cannot guarantee they are as innocent as you claim. They will be watched and under the same scrutiny as yourselves."

"What do you mean?" Tyra demanded, stepping forward and leaning over him. "You know the men in our family fight in this war, but the Bates family has done naught to deserve such speculation."

"Perhaps." Hugh nodded in agreement. "But Quakers are known to defy the king. They will not bow to him or confess their allegiance. Through their direct disobedience, they are considered enemies to the King of England as if they had signed up for the Patriot cause." Hugh sat up straight, determined to right his clothing and prepare to meet their new arrivals. "This is why they will be searched, questioned, and detained before we allow you to talk to them." Hugh turned to Private Truitt and pointed to the chamber door. "You know your orders."

7

While Hugh and Truitt questioned Tyra's aunt and uncle, she escaped upstairs and retrieved a letter she had written to her father. She hurried down the stairs and slipped out the kitchen back door. While most kitchens were a separate building from the main house in case of fire, her father had constructed their kitchen of all stone and brick. In his mind if such houses were fine in Scotland, they would be fine here.

Tyra gathered her cloak tight around her and fastened the button at her neck as she strode toward the woods. Increasing her pace, Tyra disappeared into the shaded path toward the swamp.

Fallen twigs snapped under her boots as the path twisted and wound around a curve. The white sky served as a background against the brown branches above. The woods smelled of thick dirt and tree bark, but the further she walked, a musty odor came from the swamp. Birds chirped and their feathers fluttered as they danced from tree to tree. The thick oak tree they had always used to leave messages for the Tuscaroras came into view.

She bent to place her letter inside the hollow hole in the tree trunk, careful to set a heavy rock on it. Tyra closed her eyes. *"Lord, please don't let it rain or the swamp to rise before they come and get it."*

Unable to dally any longer in case her absence was missed, Tyra hurried back to the house. The cold air filled her lungs, but she didn't dare pause to catch her breath. Tyra made her way to the well and drew some water so she would have an excuse as to why she was outside. The door creaked as she stepped inside.

"There ye are." Her mother hung a pot over a fire in the hearth. "Glad ye had the foresight to bring in some more water. I am making some tea for everyone."

"Is the inquisition still taking place?" Tyra asked, carrying the bucket over to the counter and setting it down.

"Aye." Mama nodded as she took out teacups and saucers from the cupboard. "I would wager they are now regretting their trip here. I cannot imagine what would make them come here knowing the redcoats are everywhere, watching everything, and everyone."

Footsteps came down the hall, and Hugh appeared. He stood and crossed his arms as he surveyed them. "They have answered our questions to satisfaction. Tyra, I am sorry." Hugh stepped toward her, a look of remorse on his face as he sighed in frustration.

"'Tis Miss MacGregor to you." Tyra straightened to her full height, angry he would betray her kindness like this and berate her family. "I imagine you have scared my aunt and uncle to death. They are innocent and cannot imagine the horrors of the kind of wars you have fought." She touched her palm to her forehead. "I can only imagine what they must be thinking right now."

"We are at war." He chuckled. "Surely, they are not so naïve. They knew the moment they set out on this trip they were taking a risk." He stepped closer and lowered his voice. "It is well known all traitorous households are being monitored by British soldiers."

"We understand yer meaning, Captain Morgan," Mama said. "Please join us in the parlor. Tyra and I will serve tea in a moment."

"Indeed, and we would appreciate it if you could make our relatives feel a bit more welcome in the meantime." Tyra glared at him. "I would have thought those who represent His Royal Majesty would have more hospitable qualities."

Hugh's eyes widened in disappointment. He glanced at the floor and rubbed his mustache. "In spite of what you might think of me,

I am only following orders. As long as you do as I say, I can protect you—all of you." He gestured to her mother before turning and disappearing down the hall.

"He has more audacity than anyone I know of." Tyra balled her fists and slammed them on the wooden counter. "The pride brimming in him is most exasperating."

"Tyra, ye must control yer temper, lass." Mama set the tea in the cups. "'Twould be in our best interest if we earn his friendship and trust. He could be here for a long while." Mama turned and cupped her cheek, giving her a tender smile. "I am not saying ye need to trust him yerself. Remember, be as wise as a serpent and harmless as a dove."

"From the Book of Matthew." Tyra recognized the familiar verse as she reached for a container of honey to replace the sugar the redcoats had taken. It was hard for her to be wise at times, especially when her temper taunted her. With her size, she could hardly represent a dove, more like an ostrich. The image wasn't comforting. She hated being so much taller than most men and next to other women, she felt like one of the Amazon women in a mythical story she had read. She brushed her hair out of her eyes. "I shall try to behave. I promise."

"Good. I believe Captain Morgan is a decent man, in spite of being British." Mama pulled the pot of boiling water from the hearth and poured it in each cup. Steam floated up between them. "It could be worse. We could be saddled with one of those other redcoats who lack manners. God is looking out for us, lass. Keep that in mind." Mama tilted her head in a knowing nod.

"I will." Tyra poured a bit of honey in each cup and stirred, while her mother pulled out a silver tray. They arranged the cups and saucers for equal balance. Mama pulled some biscuits warming on simmering coals and set them on a platter in the middle. "Well, this should do it."

Tyra removed her apron, picked up the tray, and followed her mother down the hall to the parlor. As they approached, voices carried into the hallway. At least everyone appeared to be having a civil conversation. If her aunt and uncle were displeased with the questioning, they did not show it.

Aunt Carleen and Uncle Ollie were on the settee by the window, and her cousin Rebecca occupied a Chippendale chair by the hearth where Private Truitt stirred the growing fire. Captain Morgan stood from another chair across the room upon their entrance. Kirk stood leaning against the wall. His hesitant and questioning gaze met Tyra's. Was he worried she was angry? Remembering her promise to her mother, she forced a smile before turning to greet her aunt and uncle.

"I am so glad thee is safe." Aunt Carleen stood and pulled her into a tight embrace. She smelled of fresh air and mint. "I wanted to come and see for myself how everyone is getting along." Leaning back, she reached up and cupped Tyra's cheek. Her hazel eyes were warm as she assessed Tyra and frowned. "Thee looks tired, child. I pray thee has not been up to any tricks while my brother and the lads have been away?" She lifted a brown eyebrow.

"Of course not," Mama said, as she set the tray on a table beside Captain Morgan and served him the first cup of tea. "Tyra is growing out of her childish pursuits and behaving herself like a young lady these days."

"I always feared Malcolm encouraged thee too much to be like one of the lads." She sighed. "I suppose there was still too much of the highlands in him."

"True. My Malcolm was always a highlander at heart." Mama brought her aunt a cup of tea. "I apologize, but we no longer have any sugar. We are using Tyra's honey."

"'Twill be fine, I am sure." Aunt Carleen smiled and sat.

"Good to see thee again." Uncle Ollie wrapped his arms around Tyra and stepped back, looking up at her. "My goodness, but I think thee has grown another inch."

It was true. The last time they had seen each other, they were eye level. She looked down at the floor, knowing her face heated with shame. "I keep growing and I would like naught more than to shrink to the normal size of a woman, like Becky." She gestured to her cousin with a smile. "Now there is a bonny lass if I ever did see one and perfect in character."

Becky rose to greet her, wearing a simple blue gown, her sandy brown hair curled in all the right places. Her hazel eyes lit with mirth when they joined hands. "Becky is quiet, speaks only when spoken to, always has a word of wisdom upon her tongue, and never shows anger. Me?" She pointed a thumb to her chest as she turned to look at the others in the room. "I am loud, always sharing my opinions, and temperamental. Regardless, at the rate I am growing, only a tree will be taller than me by the time I am done. What man will want to wed a woman taller than himself?"

"Nonsense." Captain Morgan said. "At age ten and seven, you will not grow much more, and you have yet to reach my height. And if I may say so, I have witnessed some first-rate qualities in you any American colonist would be a fool to ignore."

"Such as?" Uncle Ollie asked, his tone laced with suspicion as he eyed the captain.

"Miss MacGregor can patch a man's wounds better than any physician I have known. She is full of encouragement when his head is filled with fever. And when the British came and took their goods, she did not waste time weeping over it, she offered her special-made honey as a substitute and immediately set out to think of other viable solutions. What man would not want such a woman by his side?" He smiled and looked around the room. "She has strength of character."

"Thank ye, Captain Morgan," Mama said, giving Tyra a meaningful look. "I have been telling the lass these same things for months. Perhaps she will be willing to hear it from someone else for a change."

"I do have one request," Captain Morgan said, turning his attention back to Tyra. "I would like to see a demonstration of the War Woman."

Still recovering from Hugh's unexpected flattery, Tyra stared at him in utter confusion. His gray eyes absorbed through her like transparent glass. Could he see how much she wanted to be admired like other girls her age? Had he somehow discovered her vulnerability and now attempted to trap her in a web of deceit and manipulation? Well, she wouldn't succumb to his overtures. She could not afford to trust a man who was not only their enemy, but who had been ordered to watch her every move and report her actions back to the major.

It was as if everyone else in the parlor faded into obscurity as she tried to conjure an appropriate response. She could not risk encouraging him. Tyra let go of her cousin and walked toward a wooden chair by the wall beside the green settee where her aunt and uncle sat. She folded her hands in her lap and shook her head. "I am sorry, Captain, but I could not give such a demonstration. I promised my mother I would retire my War Woman pursuits to childhood fantasy and be the young lady she is trying to make of me."

Mama gave her a smile of approval as she settled in a chair across from Tyra. "Indeed, Captain. Please do not tempt my daughter further. It has taken me years to convince her to retire the weapons her father should have never given her." Mrs. MacGregor's gaze slid to the floor and she grew pensive. "Malcolm always did have a soft spot for the lass. She could convince him to concede to things none of the rest of us could. I think the lads often resented it, but then they were just as guilty."

"I think if I were to have such a daughter, I might be the same way." Hugh sat back and crossed his booted foot over his knee. "There was only my brother and myself, so we never had a sister to pamper or protect."

"Believe me, sir, I was never pampered," Tyra said. "Da made me work hard, fight hard, and earn my rewards just like my brothers." Tyra turned to her visiting relatives. "Enough about me. What news have you brought us?"

Her uncle cleared his throat with a quick glance at Hugh before turning to Mama. "The Patriot leader, John Ashe, has been captured. He is being held in a cell at the Burgwin House."

"At least he was not beaten, paraded around town, and left out in a blockhouse to freeze to death." Tyra didn't bother hiding the hard edge in her voice. "Do you know if Mr. Harnett is still outside or has he been brought into a cell as he should have been with the rest of the prisoners?"

"I am afraid he is still outside, exposed to the elements," Uncle Ollie said. "And as for Mr. Ashe, I am quite certain he was beaten as well. 'Tis the way of things in times of war."

"But it does not make it right." Tyra let her tone drip with contempt.

"Tyra, my dear, I believe ye need a wee bit o'tea." Mama poured steaming tea into a cup and brought it over. "Here ye go, lass. Drink up." She leaned close and mouthed the word, "hush."

"I declare, but we shall run out of firewood if we do not take an ax to some logs soon," Private Truitt said. He stood and walked over to Kirk. "Why not help me, lad? Between the two of us, we could finish before we freeze."

"Aye." Kirk nodded, pushing himself from the wall. "It gets boring when they all sit around and talk." Private Truitt grinned and slapped a hand on his shoulder, leading Kirk into the hallway like old chums.

Hugh made no effort to join them, and Tyra assumed he intended to make sure they had no privacy with their relatives. He didn't trust them, which meant she should not trust him. The knowledge stung with reality, but she would accept it. She turned to look out the window as she sipped hot tea. The winter grass had turned brown with patches of green and the tree limbs were bare. White clouds filled the sky, hiding the sun as if it no longer existed. The cup warmed her hands as she gripped it tight.

"Captain Morgan, since some time has passed and Mr. Harnett has sufficiently suffered from the weather, may he be taken inside with the rest of the prisoners?" Tyra asked. She glanced in his direction and held her breath, hoping to appeal to his compassion. His gray eyes blinked. Tyra recognized the same sensitive expression he had shown when he had thanked her for saving his life.

"When next I go to town and report to Major Craig, I shall inquire about the matter." He finished the rest of his tea and leaned over to set his cup on the tray. "I give you my word."

"It will be kind of thee, Captain Morgan," Aunt Carleen said. She turned her attention to Mama. "Lauren, I had hoped thee might have some news from my brother or from one of thy lads?"

"Nay, I have not." Mama shook her head. "'Tis quite disappointing. I must rely on news printed in the *Cape Fear Mercury*, but of course, 'tis only general news. Never anything specific to my Malcolm and the lads."

"Did thee have a good Christmas?" Becky asked, her smile lighting up with enthusiasm. Quakers didn't celebrate Christmas the way they did with elaborate decorations, gift-giving, and feasts. To them, each day was a gift from God and no day was any more special than any other. Still, Tyra knew her young cousins were always curious about their Christmas celebrations.

"Indeed, we did." Tyra nodded, unsure if she should mention her father and brothers had visited them in front of the captain. Even though it was well into February, Tyra had no idea how far away they had traveled. What if the captain took it into his head to search for them and they were still nearby? She could not forgive herself for such a misjudgment.

"Thee can tell me about it on the way to the outhouse." Becky stood and glanced around the room. "Please, excuse us."

Tyra stood and followed her into the hallway, and she described their Christmas feast. Once they were outside, Tyra told Becky about the surprise visit of her father and brothers, and the tearful goodbye to Alec. The sound of Private Truitt and Kirk chopping wood on the other side of the house let her know it was safe to continue their discussion. Once they reached the outhouse, Tyra touched her cousin's elbow.

"Please, I need you to get a message to Mr. Saunders in town." Tyra whispered. "Could you do this for me?"

"Yes, what is it?" Becky asked.

"Tell him I will try and make it to the next Whig meeting, but he should not be alarmed if I cannot. Let him know I am being watched carefully by Captain Morgan, and I cannot take unnecessary risks."

"Is that all?" Becky nodded in agreement.

"There is more. Tell him I believe I found the tunnel door leading into the prison cells in the basement of the Burgwin House. 'Twill be difficult, but an escape may be possible using the tunnels."

Two days later, Hugh rode into town to report to Major Craig as ordered. Private Truitt was allowed to remain behind to keep an eye on the traitorous Americans, as the MacGregors were called in the letter he had received. The impolite reference to the MacGregors annoyed him more than he wanted to admit. It could only mean one thing. He had come to form an attachment to the MacGregors, specifically Tyra.

A pair of wide green eyes framed in a smooth pale face with a tangled mass of fiery red hair came to mind. She occupied his thoughts as soon as he arose each morning and was the last thought before he closed his eyes each night, providing he could actually sleep. How would he be able to stay objective under the circumstances? Or worse, how would he be able to protect her from the British Army?

Hugh was led through the Burgwin House and outside to the back. Major Craig stood wearing a black overcoat and pulled on a pair of black gloves. Another man stood beside him, a couple of inches shorter than Hugh. Soldiers were mounted on horses outside the stables.

"Sir, Captain Donahue Morgan is here to see you." The soldier who had led him out here saluted his superior.

"Thank you, Private." Major Craig waved him toward the stables. "Prepare to mount up. We shall be leaving shortly." He shoved his other hand into his glove and stepped back as he nodded toward the man beside him. "Captain Morgan, I would like for you to meet Captain Gordon."

Hugh shook hands with the brown-headed fellow near his own age. Captain Gordon grinned, displaying a thin mustache catching Hugh's attention. His sparkling brown eyes gave Hugh an aura of mistrust and suspicion. Two horses were brought forward.

"Captain Morgan, you may join us for our evening ride," Major Craig said. "We shall ride out those gates onto Third Street toward New Bern Road. We will be crossing the bridge over the swamp. Go collect your horse and meet us on Third. By the time my fifteen other men are mounted and ready, I am sure you will be waiting on us."

"Yes, sir." Hugh turned on his heel and headed back through the house and out the front door. He found his horse tethered to the tree where he had left him. Mounting up, Hugh took the reins in his hands and guided his horse around the corner to Third Street. As he approached, Major Craig and Captain Gordon led a parade of men onto the dirt street.

"Captain Morgan!" Major Craig grinned and tipped his fingers to his bicorn hat. "What news have you for me? How are the MacGregors?"

Hugh maneuvered his horse beside the major and sighed, wishing he knew what the man wanted to know. "Thank you for inviting me, sir. To answer your question, the MacGregor family is fine. Miss MacGregor removed my stitches a few days ago. I am healing quite nicely and will soon be ready to carry out my mission from General Lord Cornwallis to free the prisoners in Hillsborough."

"Yes, well, has Mrs. MacGregor or her daughter had any contact with Mr. MacGregor or the other lads?" Major Craig asked.

"No, sir. Not so much as a letter," Hugh said. "Nor have I seen any further evidence of the Tuscarora Indians."

"Is that a fact?" Major Craig asked, glancing at him sideways. "I really want to know what Miss MacGregor is capable of and if she could potentially be a problem. Only then will I consider the possibility of allowing you the opportunity to travel to Hillsborough to free your brother. You have your orders, Captain, and I have mine."

"But sir, I have no reason to suspect Miss MacGregor of anything that could be considered treason, other than the fact she happens to be the daughter of a Patriot."

"Captain, I understand she saved your life when she did not have to, but try not to allow it to cloud your judgment." Major Craig's tone lowered to a warning. "It could prove to be costly for you—possibly fatal. Do you understand?"

"Yes, sir." Hugh clenched his teeth to keep from protesting further. Who could have aroused Major Craig's suspicions against Tyra? He thought back to the dinner the other night and recalled at how Miss Gordon and Mrs. Gordon seemed to enjoy patronizing her as the enemy until Major Craig set them straight. Hugh leaned forward and glanced at the man on the other side of the major.

"Captain Gordon, are you any relation to Mrs. Isobel Gordon or Miss Kelly Gordon?" Hugh asked.

"We are cousins." Captain Gordon grinned at him. "They came here to the colonies about ten years ago, but my side of the family still lives in Staffordshire."

"I see." Hugh nodded, taking in this new piece of information.

"Captain Gordon arrived yesterday from General Lord Cornwallis," Major Craig said. "He brought me an update. The general is on the other side of Hillsborough tracking General Greene. He plans to attack sometime soon."

"What are our orders?" Hugh asked, keeping his horse even with the major as they reached the bridge over the swamp. Captain Gordon dropped back to allow them enough room to cross two men abreast. Their horses clip-clopped across the wooden bridge, and his horse snorted. The murky smell of the swamp reached his senses, and he wrinkled his nose.

"We are to wait in Wilmington for further orders. In the meantime, we will take our daily ride as we always do each evening. And when we return, we shall have a glass of port."

"But sir, if you take to riding out at the same time each day and go the same route, could it not be a temptation for the enemy to try and ambush you?" Hugh asked.

8

A scream ripped through the air as Hugh arrived back at The MacGregor Quest. It sounded like Tyra near the stables. He rounded the corner where three horses were tied to a nearby post. A man wearing a redcoat stumbled and fell at the entrance.

"The wench stole my bloody sword!" he yelled, scrambling back to his feet.

"Did you expect me to lie still while you all attack me and have your way?" Tyra's hysterical voice echoed. Swords clashed as Hugh slowed his horse to a stop. He dismounted and unsheathed his sword from his side. Tyra chased the men out of the stables, wielding a sword with as much talent as any trained man. She fought two men and kicked the other one from whom she stole the sword back into the dirt. "Stay down or I shall run you through with your own blade."

Anger shot up Hugh's spine and boiled in his temples at the sight of Tyra's ripped blouse. One man swung his sword high in an arc, while the other came at Tyra from the side. She kicked him in the knee, ducked, and swung her sword in time to meet the other coming down on her neck. They clanged in unison as the third one reached his feet and ran at her. Hugh rushed at him and slung the man down to the ground. Tyra lunged at the second man with her sword and outmaneuvered him until his sword flew into the air. She pressed the blade against his throat.

"Tyra, no!" Hugh shouted. She paused, drawing a slight nick at the soldier's neck producing a line of red. "What is going on here?" Hugh demanded, looking around at his fellow soldiers. "Am I to assume the three of you were attacking this lady?"

"She is no lady, only a tyrant American," said the only man still holding a sword in his hand. One paused and stepped back, while the other crawled to his knees. Tyra gasped and lowered the sword. Her lips were tight and thin with a grim expression. Her green eyes sparkled with unshed tears as she met his gaze. She trembled with uncontrolled anger. He feared she might be out of her mind with fright and determined to take revenge, but if she hurt one of the soldiers, Major Craig would see her pay for it. Hugh couldn't allow her to take the chance.

"Tyra, drop the sword. I shall deal with these men." Hugh walked toward her, approaching at a cautious pace. "If you do them harm, I cannot protect you from Major Craig."

"Is it all right for them to try and violate me?" She swung at the man nearest her. He jumped out of her path.

"No, of course not, and I will see they are punished, but I do not wish you to suffer for trying to defend yourself."

"Punished?" The man with the sword stepped forward. Tyra tensed and braced herself. "This wild wench went crazy when we started asking questions. We were only doing what Major Craig ordered."

"I doubt he ordered the three of you to rape an innocent woman." Hugh strode to the man and held out his hand. "Give me your weapon. I am the commanding officer in charge here. If you disobey, I shall have you court-martialed." He motioned toward the house. "Wait for me inside the house. I have taken over the study as my office."

To his relief, the men did as he requested. They wore frowns of disapproval and glared at him, but it was worth it to ensure Tyra's safety. With the way his heart pounded against his chest, he feared he would have done anything to protect her, even defend her against his fellow countrymen. He waited as they stomped away and disappeared inside.

"Come here." Hugh turned to Tyra and motioned her toward him.

"No." She shook her head as tears spilled over her lashes. The sword fell from her hand and thumped to the ground. "My mother cannot know," she whispered. "Please do not tell her." She sniffled and her trembling fingers worked unsuccessfully to button her blouse. It was no use; half the buttons were torn from the fabric. He doubted she could see the damage since the tears gathering in her eyes were so thick.

Hugh strode to her and gathered her in his arms, hoping she would allow him the opportunity to comfort her. Instead of pushing him away as he feared, she collapsed in his arms and sobbed against his chest. He pulled her tight against him and stroked her long hair down her back. No doubt, it had come untangled from her usual coil in the skirmish she had with the men. After a few minutes, her sobs subsided and she sniffed.

"You must think me weak," she said through watery tears.

"Never."

"I tried to fight them off, but they took me by surprise while I was grooming the animals."

"And you did an excellent job." He kissed the top of her head. "Now I know why they call you the War Woman. You have earned the name." She continued to tremble. He realized her cloak had been ripped from her. Hugh stepped back to unbutton his coat, shrugged out of it, and placed it on her shoulders.

"I cannot wear a despicable redcoat!" She slapped it away.

"You are freezing." He looked around. "Where is your cloak?"

"They ripped it with their swords." She looked down at herself and gathered her blouse closed in her fist. "You do not imagine I ended up like this any other way, do you?"

"Tyra, I realize my coat is an abomination to you, and rightly so." He cupped her face between his hands. "But you are freezing and you need to properly cover yourself. 'Tis all I have to offer you. Please

. . . accept it." He hoped she could see the pleading in his eyes. She stared at him for a moment and, with a sigh, jerked it from his hands. He slipped an arm around her shoulder and gathered her close. "And remember, they did not get away with what they intended."

"Why did they come?" she asked. Wounded green eyes peered up at him, and his chest tightened as if a stack of bricks lay upon him. "Major Craig has ordered you and Truitt to spy on us. Why would he send more men in your place knowing you were gone?"

"I do not know." He pulled her close to his side in a protective manner. "But I intend to find out."

⁓

Knowing her mother would be busy entertaining the British soldiers until Hugh arrived, Tyra entered the house from the back door through the kitchen. She didn't want to be humiliated all over again by running into them in her present condition, nor did she want to be caught by her family wearing a redcoat. It would raise suspicion and require an explanation. The other day she had overheard her mother praying for her father and brothers. Mama had enough on her mind to worry her.

She wrapped her arms round her chest and hurried up the back staircase, keeping as quiet as possible. Inside her chamber, Tyra closed the door and shrugged out of the redcoat dropping it on the trunk at the foot of her bed. She shivered and rubbed her hands over her upper arms. Glancing at the dark fireplace, Tyra crossed the room and grabbed a log and set it in the grate. Her cold fingers trembled as she fumbled to build a fire. A few moments later, blue-orange flames flickered and sparked, catching hold of the bark.

Tyra crouched low and held her hands out, seeking what warmth she could. Once her fingers were thawed enough to feel again, she worked on unbuttoning the remaining buttons of her blouse. She rummaged through a trunk under the window and found another white blouse. Tyra moved back to the warmth of the growing fire as she slipped it on and buttoned it.

For several moments, she sat staring into the fire. The warm glow now comforted her face and body as she leaned forward. The whole thing didn't make sense. The men came into the stables demanding to know why she was the War Woman. They fired a number of questions at her. Where were the Indians? How was she spying for the Patriots? How had she cuckolded Captain Morgan?

She refused to be taunted by them, but they kept coming, crowding around her. One of them grabbed her by the cloak and jerked her around. She hit him in the jaw. Angered, he shoved her back against the stall door and pressed his body against her as the others drew their swords and ripped her cloak from her. Tyra screamed, but he covered her mouth. She bit him while the other two laughed. Feeling the hilt of his sword jab into her side, Tyra bit his nasty hand and took advantage of the moment to draw his sword against him.

If Captain Morgan hadn't come when he did, someone would have gotten hurt. Most likely, she would have hanged from a noose because she had determined in her heart, she would not let them have her. The whole ordeal brought back memories of when she had been forced to defend herself against the outlaw Indians. She glanced at her Bible lying on top of her desk against the cream-colored wall. Like before, she needed comfort.

She went over to retrieve the book and brought it back to where she curled by the fire on the floor. Flipping to Ecclesiastes, chapter three, she read, *"To everything there is a season, a time for every purpose under heaven. A time to be born and a time to die. A time to plant, and a time to pluck that which is planted. A time to heal and a time to kill."* Her voice faded as tears of gratitude filled her eyes. The page grew blurry as warm liquid crawled down her face and dropped, staining the page with a dark wet spot. She swallowed and took a deep breath to ease the back of her aching throat.

"Lord, thank you for bringing Captain Morgan in time. I do not ever want to be in the position of taking another person's life in order to save my own." Thoughts of the compromising position her father and brothers now faced on a daily basis filled her with remorse and fear. So many lives were being lost and wasted on the battlefields across this great land—and all because a king wanted to oppress and dominate his subjects—to bring tyranny against the people.

Was freedom worth fighting for? Worth dying for? When she had been forced to defend herself—to kill or be killed—she had chosen to kill. It had earned her the name of War Woman like a badge of honor, but she didn't feel honorable. The name only stood to remind her of what she had done—something she wished she had never been put into the position of doing. Today she had fought with the same tenacity, knowing she would have killed again to save herself.

Did it make her a bad person? Even though she had prayed for forgiveness, Tyra often prayed her decision two years ago had fallen into the time frame described in Ecclesiastes. Her father had taught them the commandment to not kill referred to outright murder the way Cain had killed his brother Abel in the Book of Genesis. War and self-defense fell under the reference in Ecclesiastes.

Sounds of footsteps and men's voices carried from below. Tyra closed the Bible and set it back on her desk. She wondered how Hugh would handle the three men, especially since Major Craig, his superior, had sent them. At least, she knew Hugh wasn't part of the conspiracy, but now she had a concern for his welfare. What game was Major Craig playing?

She left her chamber and descended the hall staircase as the three soldiers walked out the front door. It slammed, shaking the framed timbers.

"Goodness, it sounds like someone is displeased," Tyra said, as she descended the stairs, noticing no one else was about.

"They should be." Hugh turned around and walked toward her, concern in his gray eyes. He cupped her cheek. "Are you all right?"

"Yes, but what did you say to them?"

"I told them that Major Craig sent them here to ask questions and get answers. He is too much of a gentleman and honorable for anyone to believe he would stoop to the level of having them rape an innocent girl."

"Do you really believe he is a gentleman and honorable?" she asked, lowering her voice with doubt. "And why would Major Craig not trust what you report back to him."

"No, in all honesty, I do not believe he is honorable." He shook his head, his palm growing warm on her cheek. "But they cannot know my opinion. My hope is Major Craig will at least want to appear to be honorable." His thumb circled her jaw making her tingle. "I suppose he may suspect I have developed a fondness for you. I am most relieved those blokes did not hurt you." He grinned. "But now, I know why you are called the War Woman." He touched the tip of her nose.

✐

Then next morning Hugh called Private Truitt into the study. The man arrived and stood at the threshold as if waiting for permission to enter. Hugh waved him in. He strode to the front of the desk and saluted him. While he had carried out Hugh's orders as requested and seemed to have a soft spot for Kirk, Hugh wasn't convinced of his loyalty. He stood with his hands linked behind him.

"We went hunting since Mrs. MacGregor offered to make rabbit stew," he said.

"There was an incident," Hugh said. "Major Craig sent three soldiers to question Miss MacGregor, but they attacked her in the stables and would have had their way with her if I had not arrived in time. Today, I have to ride into town and see Major Craig. I want you to stay here at the house and make sure naught untoward happens." Hugh looked him in the eye. "Do you understand?"

"I thought our orders are to watch the MacGregors and report traitorous activity, not protect them." His dark eyes burned with rebellion.

"Are you refusing this order?" Hugh asked. "If you are, I promise, there will be consequences."

"No, sir." He dropped his gaze.

"I shall endeavor to forget it as long as no harm comes to Miss MacGregor or her family while they are in your care."

"I understand, sir."

"Good." Hugh nodded toward the door. "You may go."

After he walked out, Hugh shrugged into his black overcoat and placed his hat on his head. He strode into the hallway and out the front door to the stables. As he saddled his horse, footsteps approached with the sound of a swishing skirt. He turned to see Tyra approaching. She wore a blue cloak and a purple skirt with a lavender blouse.

"Captain Morgan, I would like to go to town with you," Tyra said.

"Absolutely not." Hugh fastened the saddle in place and pulled down the stirrup. "We still do not know why Major Craig ordered me to town and sent those men out here to question you in my absence. He wanted me out of the way for some reason, and I need to discover why. Without this knowledge we have no idea how much danger you could be in."

"Staying here did me no good. I cannot hide away forever. We need supplies."

"But leaving will put you at even more risk than staying here. Make a list, and I will pick up the supplies you need." Hugh turned to face her, leaning an elbow on the saddle. "I know I have no right to ask this of you, but please trust me."

"I cannot promise to trust you, but I will do as you ask . . . this time." She reached into her skirt pocket, pulled out a folded piece of paper, and handed it to him. "I have already prepared a list. We have credit at the store."

Hugh accepted the list and slipped it inside his jacket pocket. He would not put it on their bill, not when he and Truitt had been eating their fair share around there. After what the army did in taking their supplies, replenishing them was the least he could do. He mounted his horse and leaned down. "Tyra, go back inside. Let Truitt fetch water from the well—at least while I am gone." He guided his horse around her and rode out of the stables.

By the time he arrived in Wilmington at the Burgwin House, his face was chapped from the biting wind. He longed for a warm fire and rubbed his hands together, blowing warmth on them as a soldier led him to the study.

"Sir, Captain Morgan is here to see you." The soldier in front of him stopped in the doorway.

"Good. Show him in," came the familiar voice, gruff and commanding.

The soldier stepped aside, and Hugh strode forward in a salute. Major Craig leaned over a map of North Carolina with Captain Gordon, Corporal Jackson, and Sergeant McAlister. A roaring fire blazed in the hearth. Each man had a glass of brandy in his hand. They were in full uniform except for their black tricorn hats. A five-prong candelabra sat at the center of the table to afford more light. Little natural light filtered through the side window.

Hugh had hoped to speak to Major Craig alone. He didn't feel comfortable approaching the subject of what happened to Tyra in front of these men. The major might take exception if he felt Hugh questioned his judgment. In the meantime, he would have to bide his time and continue to earn their trust if he wanted to learn what he could.

"Captain Morgan, we were just discussing the Patriot defeat on the other side of Hillsborough." Major Craig pointed to a spot on the map. "A little skirmish happened on March 2 at some place called Clapp's Mill." He met Hugh's gaze. "Did you not say you had a brother imprisoned nearby?"

"Indeed, I did." Hugh gripped his hands behind his back. Hope for his brother lifted in his chest. "Have you heard anything about the nearby prison?"

"No, but take heart, my good man," Major Craig slapped him on the arm. "We know it was a victory for our side and our men are getting close. I may not have to send you there, after all. I shall wait and see what we hear in the next week or so."

"Lord Cornwallis and General Greene keep playing cat and mouse, and soon enough there will be a major battle between them," Sergeant McAlister said.

"Is it not what we have been hoping for?" Captain Gordon lifted his glass, and they all drank.

"Would you like a glass, Captain Morgan?" Major Craig asked.

"No, thank you, sir." He shook his head.

They continued to discuss other strategies until the men departed to start their drills with the troops. Hugh approached the major where he stood staring out the window. "Sir, I wanted to talk to you about the three men you sent out to question the MacGregors yesterday."

"Yes, I was wondering when you would ask me about it." He turned away from the window and faced Hugh, his expression hard. "After observing you with Miss MacGregor at dinner, I grew suspicious of your attachment to her." He sighed with dissatisfaction. "But a lot of good it did me. They returned with less information than you have given me."

Relief filled Hugh as he realized he would not have to divulge what happened to Tyra. He stepped forward and met his superior's gaze. "Sir, I have not reported anything because I do not have anything to report."

9

While Hugh was gone, Tyra paced the house, sewed new buttons back onto her blouse, read a chapter in Daniel Defoe's *Robinson Crusoe*, and glanced out the window numerous times to see if Hugh had returned. What did those three barbaric soldiers tell Major Craig? Could Hugh have walked into a trap? She couldn't stop worrying for him, especially since he took a chance at protecting her against his fellow soldiers.

"Tyra, how many times are ye going to look out the window, lass?" Mama glanced up from her sewing and peered at Tyra from the corner of her eye. As usual, they were both in the parlor, while Kirk and Truitt were outside chopping more firewood. "If I did not know better, I would guess ye've set yer cap for Captain Morgan."

"Of course not!" Tyra bristled, shutting the blue curtains and stepping away from the window. She strolled toward the burning hearth and rested her hand on the mantle. "I have no plans to set my cap for anyone. How could I when he is fighting for our enemy?"

"Aye, but ye no longer refer to Captain Morgan as the enemy." Mama paused with her needle and thread in the air. "I think ye see him differently than ye did before."

Tyra stared into the fire, unable to meet her mother's gaze as tension tightened the muscles at the back of her neck. Mama knew her too well. If Tyra turned around, she would see the truth in her expression. Guilt tugged at her heart until the burden made her chest feel like she was about to crumble under the pressure.

"I did not save his life for any harm to come to him," Tyra said, closing her eyes against the gruesome image of Hugh being thrown into a dirty prison cell or worse, whipped across the back. *God, please keep Hugh safe!*

"I cannot imagine why it would," Mama said. "Seems to me only us Patriots have aught to worry about." Rare sarcasm laced her mother's tone.

"True. It does seem that way." Tyra pressed the heel of her palm against her forehead, a slight headache nagging her troubled mind. She needed to find something substantial to do to occupy her wandering mind. If only she had not promised to stay inside. A long, vigorous ride would be quite refreshing.

"Lass, yer face is flushed." Mama's voice penetrated her thoughts. "Tell me what is weighing so heavily on yer mind. And do not tell me 'tis naught." Mama shook a finger at her. "For I know better. Has Captain Morgan made any inappropriate overtures?"

"No." Tyra shook her head realizing she would have to tell her mother everything to keep her from suspecting the worst of Hugh. She walked to a nearby chair and sank into it. "I should have told you, but I did not want to worry you."

"Tell me what?" Mama set aside her sewing and scooted to the edge of her seat.

"Yesterday, when I went out to feed the horse and clean out the stables, three soldiers tried to attack me. I fought them off as best as I could, but Captain Morgan arrived in time to stop them. Major Craig had sent them, and today Captain Morgan went into town to find out why. So naturally, I am a bit concerned for his welfare."

"Why did ye not tell me, lass?" Mama blinked, processing the whole ordeal as if she couldn't believe it. "How long were ye planning to wait?"

"I did not want you to worry," Tyra said, her heart pinching at the pain and disbelief on her mother's face. Tyra left her chair and dropped to her knees in front of Mama. Tyra took her mother's hands into her own and peered up into her watery blue eyes. "You have enough to worry about with Da and my brothers being away at war. I did not wish to add to your burden."

"Tyra ye've misjudged my humble nature as a state of weakness, but I assure ye, lass, I am much stronger than ye think." Mama squeezed her hands and lifted a finger to brush a strand of red hair from Tyra's forehead. "I fear I have tried to protect ye from my past too much and concentrated on bringing ye up to be a proper young lady. But yer bold nature has caused ye to think of me differently than I intended."

"What do you mean? I respect and love you. I always have." Pain sliced through her heart and tears sprang to her eyes. "You must believe me."

"Aye, I do." Mama reached out and gripped Tyra's shoulder. "Tyra, the most humble person can have a strong will and spirit. Muscle and brawn will only get a person as far as physical endurance will allow, but the spirit, now there is where God can use a willing heart far beyond what the eyes can see."

"Watch and pray, that ye enter not into temptation: the spirit indeed is willing, but the flesh is weak." Tyra repeated a verse she had memorized from the Book of Matthew. "I know what God's word says about the flesh being weak."

"Indeed, ye know what it says, but do ye understand it, lass?" Mama looked away, her gaze staring off into the distance, as if her mind had escaped to some other place.

"Mama?"

"Tyra, I am going to share a wee bit o'my past to help ye understand what I mean. As ye know, twenty and one years ago, I landed on the shores of Charles Town and became an indentured servant. What ye do not know is the son of my owners took a liking to me and his parents were less than pleased. The owner sold me to a brothel."

"A brothel?" Tyra sat back in stunned silence as all sorts of images conjured in her mind, and she tried to imagine her sweet-tempered mother in such a place—among such vile people. Her mother had served the Lord from the time she was a young child, even against her own father's wishes. How could God allow such a thing to happen to someone who had been so faithful to Him?

"Aye, against my will, and to my utter despair." Mama nodded. "I was chaste and they wanted to prepare me for the auction, so I would go to the highest bidder. I was starved for days, stripped naked and humiliated, and beaten in the body to break my will to do their bidding. They cracked my ribs, bruised my insides, but left my face intact so I would still be appealing to would-be buyers."

"Did they . . ." Tyra couldn't bring herself to ask the worst.

"Nay." Mama smiled. "Yer father found me in time along with a pastor we had met on the ship from Scotland and a petition was formed by concerned citizens. God did not cause it, but He allowed my plight to occur in order to save other girls besides myself. My point is, they tried to break my spirit and my will, but they did not succeed. I am not weak as ye imagine, lass. I do not need yer protection, but what I do need is for ye to always be honest with me. As yer mother, 'tis my responsibility to help guide ye in this dark world."

Shameful tears filled Tyra's eyes, and her chest ached with guilt. For a few moments, she couldn't speak. She gulped down her tears and took a deep breath. "Mama, I am sorry. Please forgive me."

"'Tis all right, lass." Mama reached up and wiped her tears away with the pad of her thumbs. "Now, is there aught else ye might want to confess?"

"Aye, but you will not like it," Tyra said. She went over to the window to make sure Private Truitt was still occupied outside. Satisfied he was quite preoccupied, she went back to her mother. "I have joined the Whig Party, and I have been helping them gain valuable information they can use to further the Patriot cause. I need a reason to get back into the Burgwin House."

ℒ❦

Over the next week, Major Craig put Hugh in charge of one hundred twenty-five men. Hugh established a routine of going into town each morning to train them, learning news of the war from Major Craig, and answering questions about the MacGregors. To his relief, he had no suspicious activity to report. Tyra seemed pleased the three men who attacked her kept the incident to themselves, not wanting anyone to know a woman bested them. They were both relieved Major Craig had not reprimanded Captain Morgan for defending her. She had no idea he was prepared to do much worse to his fellow countrymen should any of them try to harm her again.

He sat at the desk in the study and pulled out his journal, flipping to the first empty page toward the middle. Hugh picked up a feathered quill and dipped the tip in black ink. At the far right he wrote the date, March 13, 1781. For the next few minutes, he wrote about Cornelius Harnett's failing condition where Major Craig still kept him out in the elements. The man's hollowed eyes and pale skin hanging on his bones were a sorry sight, but the wracking cough he had developed made one's stomach churn. While other people had appealed for Harnett's release, today Hugh had asked Major Craig to give him mercy. His superior officer had refused. On the way home, Hugh prayed for his soul and for God to ease his discomfort.

"I brought you some warm coffee." Tyra appeared at the open doorway. "Black just the way you like it."

"Thank you." Hugh waved her inside the study. At his gesture, she strode over and set the cup and saucer by his elbow on the desk. A log on the fire crackled. They both glanced in its direction. "I built a warm fire. Will you join me?"

"I did not mean to disturb you." She gathered her brown shawl around her shoulders and smiled.

"Nonsense. I have been so busy in Wilmington this week, we have had little time to talk." He missed their morning conversations when breaking his fast. Lately, he took to departing by dawn.

"'Tis to be expected now that you have healed from your wounds," she said, lowering herself in a chair by the fire. "How are the men taking to their new commanding officer?"

"Very well." He grinned, rubbing his new goatee beard. "Especially three unsuspecting soldiers who had the nerve to attack a certain young lady. Now I know where they are and what they should be doing most hours of the day."

"They are most deserving of it, I must say." The corners of Tyra's lovely mouth lifted into a bright smile that warmed his insides. "I shall endeavor to feel safe and secure here at The MacGregor Quest."

"Such a peculiar name," he said. "I have been meaning to ask you about it, but I always get distracted. What does it mean?"

"The way my da explained it, is he came here to the American colonies with the intention of using my mother as revenge against her father." Tyra twisted a red curl at her ear that had fallen from the security of a pearl comb. "Instead, he fell in love with my mother, and God turned what was intended for evil into good."

"So the quest was for revenge?" Hugh asked, watching her fascinating green eyes as they glistened in the glowing firelight.

"No, you are missing the point. The MacGregors have always been on a quest for freedom. They wanted a chance to make their own way without being chained to rules made by the upper class to keep the lower class in their place. They wanted their God-given right to freedom, and they fought for it in the Scottish Jacobite War, and they are fighting for it now in this war." Tyra tilted her head as she regarded him with hesitation. "This land represents what we could not have in Scotland, so he named it The MacGregor Quest in honor of God granting him this gift of freedom and the land to provide for his family."

"I see." He saw more than he wanted. It was hard to call such a noble cause an act of treason. He and his brother had not come from a titled family with land and wealth. It was one of the reasons they both had purchased a commission in the army from their savings. What else were they to do but work for someone else? A career in His

Majesty's Army would bring respect and honor no other skilled position would provide. It also afforded them the opportunity to make a small fortune if they survived long enough.

Where were his boundaries with this woman? She had him feeling empathy for their cause, a temptation he had never before felt. He could not listen to this and not point out the flawed logic. "This land grant was provided by the King of England—the very king he is now fighting against."

"True." She nodded. "But you asked." She scooted to the edge of her seat, licking her bottom lip. "Do you believe our Creator God is superior over any earthly king?"

"Of course."

"Why?" Unprepared for her response with another question, Hugh stared at her, wondering if she was trying to debate him.

"Because earthly kings are mortal beings." He waved his hand in the air. "They live and die like any man."

"Exactly." Tyra slapped her lap. "So why should any of us bow before anyone other than God himself? The persecution against people like the Quakers is immoral. How does one tell an earthly king that his law is wrong without being imprisoned, hung, or beheaded?"

Hugh searched his mind for a reasonable response, but nothing seemed appropriate to such logic. He glanced at her smooth neck and gulped at the thought of a thick rope around it. "Tyra, we never had this conversation. Promise you will never share these thoughts with anyone else. You do not know who can be trusted."

❦

A few days later, Tyra sat at a spinning wheel in the workroom next to the study. Kirk had sheared a couple of sheep the British missed in the far pasture. He left enough wool to keep them from freezing, enough to enable her to make some new socks. When she had entered the study the other night, she noticed Hugh had a hole in the heel of his right sock. He had removed his boots, not expecting her to bring him a cup of warm tea before retiring for the night.

If she couldn't make warm socks for her father and brothers, the least she could do was make sure Hugh's feet were warm, especially when he worked so hard to keep her family out of the clutches of Major Craig. No one knew what she planned, and it was the way she wanted it. Even though her feelings for Hugh continued to grow deeper, she needed to keep her distance so her mother and brother wouldn't feel as if she betrayed her father and brothers. She feared her mother already suspected.

The front door opened and closed. Footsteps echoed through the foyer and down the hall, coming closer. Tyra recognized the familiar gait belonging to Hugh. Her breath caught in her throat and her pulse quickened. She squashed the temptation to leave her tasks and rush to him—as if he had returned home to her after a long day at work.

"Miss MacGregor!" He called out to her. Tyra stopped spinning the wheel as he called her name a second time. Something in his tone delivered a sense of urgency. She rose, went to the door, and peered out into the hall. His black boots clicked against the hardwood floor. His redcoat looked dark brown in the shadows, but his concerned frown could not be mistaken.

Fear clawed up her neck as a feeling of foreboding came over her. She rushed to him, knowing something had happened. His gray eyes met hers, stealing her heart. He reached out to her, but dropped his hands to his sides as her mother appeared from the foyer.

"I have just learned a major battle has occurred at Guilford Courthouse toward the middle of the state between General Lord Cornwallis and the Patriot General Greene. 'Twas a bloody battle, and we lost a quarter of our men. While I cannot be certain, 'tis most likely your father and brothers were among them."

The news stunned Tyra into a momentary stupor. Various scenarios ran through her mind as she tried to imagine the actual disaster. It was as if her body floated into a state of numbness. She stepped back in disbelief.

"How many did the Continentals lose?" Mama rushed into the foyer from the parlor. Anxiety filled her deep blue eyes as her chin trembled. Hugh turned to her.

"I am sorry, but I do not know," he said. "We believe the Continental Army outnumbered our own forces by two to one. At the risk of sounding callous, we emerged as the victor, so I would imagine the Continentals suffered great losses." He removed his black tricorn hat and looked down at it. "I do not wish to upset either of you, but I am sure the news will soon be in the papers and the topic of conversation around town. I thought it best to inform you myself."

"Please, tell us as much as you can." Unshed tears filled Mama's eyes, but she lifted her chin and kept her composure.

"Yes, we both want to know." Tyra walked to her mother's side and linked arms with her. She met Hugh's clouded gray eyes and found empathy. While she appreciated his consideration, her allegiance belonged to her family. Right now, she would do all she could to give her mother support and encouragement.

"A messenger arrived earlier from Lord Cornwallis," Hugh said. "Both generals were forced to retreat and leave the dead and mortally wounded on the fields. Quakers at New Garden were trying to treat and save those they could on both sides. The Quakers are burying the dead together in mass graves."

"Such devastation." Tyra clutched her sour stomach with her free hand. "I can only imagine what they must be enduring."

"Aye." Mama nodded. "And my own husband and sons could be among them."

"Do not think on it, Mama" Tyra covered the top of her cold hand with her own. "We must hope and pray for the best."

"Of course." She nodded with a restless sigh. "But not knowing is going to be the hardest part."

"I know, but I believe we would know in our spirits if something had happened to one of them." Tyra glanced up at Hugh. "Thank you for telling us."

"You are welcome. There is one other thing." He lifted a finger. "Lord Cornwallis is marching his troops toward Wilmington. There will be over fourteen hundred men arriving in a few days. They are worn out, hundreds are wounded, starved, and wearing rags at this point. You may be required to give more goods and supplies."

"Will you be leaving us, Captain Morgan?" Tyra asked, fearful she would be forced to defend herself and her family once again.

"I hope not. Right now we have been commanded to prepare for their arrival." He leaned close and lowered his voice. "I will do my best to ensure your safety."

"I have come to believe it, sir." Tyra tugged on her mother's arm. "Come, Mama, let us remove to the parlor, and I will make a pot of tea."

Tyra spent the rest of the afternoon keeping her mother company until she slipped into the kitchen to cook dinner. She missed having household staff to do certain chores, but after her father and brothers left for war, their field workers volunteered to fight in the war as well.

She gave everyone a heavy dose of chamomile tea, including Captain Morgan and Private Truitt. Once everyone retired for the night, Tyra dressed in a pair of Alec's breeches. He was closer to her size than her other brothers. She pulled on a thick overcoat and borrowed a hat from Alec. To keep anyone from hearing her footsteps, Tyra made her way downstairs in a pair of thick socks she had sewn for herself. She carried her boots in her arms, thankful she had thought to oil the door hinges earlier. Outside, she pressed her feet into the boots and laced them up. Grabbing the lantern she had set on the back porch, Tyra waited until she reached the woods to light it.

The silver half-moon provided an angle of light through the leafless trees. It was so cold she could breathe gray smoke into the darkness. If she wanted to reach the Tuscarora camp and be back before daylight, she would have to hurry without getting lost in the dark. She had never attempted to find them at night.

10

$\mathcal{H}$ugh emerged from his chamber to the fresh aroma of brewing coffee that intensified as he descended the stairs. Soft footsteps and busy sounds came from the kitchen. He entered to see Mrs. MacGregor hard at work rolling out dough for biscuits. She wore a brown apron over her clothes.

"Good morning, sir." She glanced up with a bright smile. Her blond hair was piled upon the crown of her head as usual. "I hope to have a warm-cooked meal to break yer fast before ye leave this morn."

"Where is Miss MacGregor?" he asked. "Is she not usually up by now assisting you?"

"Indeed, but maybe she needs a wee bit o'rest." She used the round edge of a cup to carve out perfect round dough shaped in a circle. "I figured I would let her sleep some more."

"In that case, how could I help?" He pointed outside. "I could gather some eggs. Back home I used to get them for my mother."

"I already got them earlier." Mrs. MacGregor chuckled as she shook her head. "I wish my lads were as eager to help as ye. Why not relax with a cup of warm coffee while I prepare the meal? I imagine ye'll be plenty busy preparing for Lord Cornwallis's arrival."

"Indeed." Hugh grabbed a clean mug from one of the cupboards and poured a steaming cup of coffee. "I hope we will know more in the next day or two."

He walked back to the wooden table and sat down. A rooster crowed outside. Now Tyra should wake up. Hugh sat back and sipped the black liquid with a little more satisfaction than before. A few moments later, Private Truitt joined them. Kirk appeared a while later, rubbing his sleepy eyes and blinking.

By the time they finished eating, Tyra still had not shown. An uneasy feeling now lingered in his gut. Truitt tossed down the rest of his coffee and looked at Hugh. "Sir, I shall go saddle our horses."

Once he had disappeared, Hugh glanced at Mrs. MacGregor and then Kirk. "Perhaps someone should go up and check on Miss MacGregor. 'Twould ease my mind to know she is not sick before I leave."

"I shall go wake her up," Kirk said with a mischievous grin. "I bet she is just being lazy, hoping I will do her chores for her."

"Nonsense," Mrs. MacGregor chided with a stern look meant to reprimand him. "Since when have ye known yer sister to do such a thing?"

Dropping his chin, Kirk shot from the table and hurried upstairs. Hugh sat in silence as Mrs. MacGregor gathered the dirty plates with a worried frown and dumped them in a wash bucket. She returned to the table for the coffee cups.

"Mama, Tyra left. No one has slept in her bed all night." Kirk's teasing tone had changed to one of concern as he scratched his eyebrow in puzzlement. "I cannot understand it."

"Did you know anything about this?" Hugh rose to his feet and met Mrs. MacGregor's gaze.

"Nay, I assumed she was tired is all." She pressed her fingers to her lips and glanced at her son. "Did she leave a note?"

"I checked her desk and there was naught." He shook his brown head. "We got to go look for her."

"Kirk, go to the stables and see if she took a horse. Let Private Truitt know and tell him to saddle another horse for you. If we have to go out into the wilderness to find her, we will need you since you know the area better than we." The lad nodded and disappeared down the hall.

"Mrs. MacGregor, do you have any idea where she might have gone? Did she say aught yesterday?" Fear for Tyra's safety continued to build inside him, and he had to control his growing anxiety.

"Nay. I am just as baffled as ye." She followed him to the door. "Where are ye going, lad?"

"Checking the doors to make sure there is no sign of forced entry. I am surprised none of us heard anything." He scratched the side of his head, thinking back to how tired he had been the night before. Even his memory of going to his chamber to retire for the night escaped him. "Although, as I think about it, I slept deep and hard almost as if I had a couple of drinks."

"When you went out this morning, was the door bolted from the inside?" he asked.

Mrs. MacGregor blinked as she stared at the door and bit her bottom lip. "I cannot remember sliding the bolt back, but it does not mean I did not. When I first woke this morn, I was not as alert as usual. Like ye, I slept soundly last night." She touched his arm and gulped. "Captain, those British soldiers will not come back for her, will they?"

"I hope not. Can ye think of anywhere she might have gone?" he asked.

"She may have tried to find the Tuscarora Indians. They move their camp around, and she would have had to search for them." Mrs. MacGregor placed her palm over her chest and took a deep breath. "My Tyra is headstrong. Her da and brothers taught her well how to defend herself, but I still worry if she is outnumbered."

The front door swung open and Kirk rushed inside, breathing heavy. "She took no horse. I told Private Truitt, and he has the horses saddled and ready to go."

"Very good, Kirk." Hugh turned to Mrs. MacGregor. "Stay here in case she returns before we do. I will do my best to find her and bring her back home safely."

When he did find her, she would have some explaining to do. In the meantime, he would have to concentrate on keeping his wits about him as his fraying nerves crumbled at the fearful images of what might have happened to her lurked in the back of his mind. He swallowed the rising panic and strode out of the house, putting all his military training at the forefront, determined to succeed on this new mission.

❦

Tyra woke with a start as her Indian friends built a new fire in the middle of the longhouse where they lived and had invited her to stay. Last night one of their guards found her wandering in the woods. He recognized her and brought her to their swamp village where she was greeted with delighted surprise.

To her relief, Red Fox had found her letter in the tree weeks ago, before the Battle at Guilford Courthouse. He and his brother traveled to Hillsborough, but they could not find her father and brothers. They learned from a young boy that General Greene had taken his army across the Dan River and into Virginia. They continued north until they caught up with the army and some soldiers led them to her father. Once she was settled by the fire, Red Fox handed her a letter from her father.

Tyra broke the seal and unfolded the letter, using the firelight to read it. She had to tilt it at an angle to see it better.

Dear Tyra,

It is good to hear from you. Your brothers and I are still under the command of General Nathanael Greene. Alec is doing fine and adjusting to soldier life as well as Callum and Scott in spite of his young age. We are staying warm with the blankets you and your mother provided. Our feet are in better condition with the new socks you have made for us. Food has been scarce at times, but we are well fed when we are allowed to take the time to hunt in the wilderness.

We heard the British took over the occupation of Wilmington, and I wondered if you and your mother would receive our letters. It was clever of you to smuggle a letter through the Tuscaroras. They are resourceful, used to hiding, and not drawing attention to themselves.

Receiving your letter gave the boys and I comfort in knowing you, your mother, and Kirk are well. I want you to be careful with the British soldiers in our home. Trust no one and do what they say to keep from drawing their ire. Remember all I have taught you. If you feel in danger, leave and go to the Tuscarora Indians until the war is over.

As for your request, I have inquired about Colonel Neil Morgan. He has been taken prisoner in Hillsborough and is still alive and in good health. Since he is a British officer, the Patriots hope to exchange him for one of our own officers. Tyra, use this knowledge wisely and do not take unnecessary risks. Your safety comes first above the cause. Our family has already sacrificed and given much to this war. We do not need to give our women as well. I could not bear it if anything were to happen to any of you.

Write me back and let us know all is well. Give Kirk our love and tell him I am proud of him. I have enclosed another private letter to your mother.

Love,

Da

"Would like water?" White Cloud's voice broke Tyra's thoughts of her father's letter. A wooden cup appeared in front of her. Tyra glanced up at the soft brown eyes peering at her in concern. White Cloud had always shown her such kindness. She was Red Fox's wife and mother of their two children, a five-year-old boy and an eight-year-old girl.

"Yes, thank you." Tyra accepted the cup and drank the cool spring water. She hadn't realized how thirsty she was until the smooth liquid quenched her parched throat.

"You sleep well?" A long black braid fell over her shoulder as she lifted a dark eyebrow.

"I did." Tyra patted the fur pallet where she sat. "This is very comfortable and warm. I am sorry I fell asleep by the fire."

"We glad you safe." White Cloud touched her arm in a reassuring grip. "I make food."

"No, I need to get back before I am missed," Tyra said, rising to her knees and then to her feet. A sudden panic sliced through her stomach. "The British will be suspicious if they notice I am gone. Thank you for taking care of me and for all you have done to help my family."

"You welcome. I get Red Fox take you back." White Cloud disappeared outside the door of the longhouse. Tyra glanced over at their children in the corner who were eating what looked like porridge from a bowl. She smiled at them as she finished drinking her water and waited on their parents to return. The longhouse was filled with several other Indian families. Some were still sleeping on their fur pallets, while others were stirring and starting their day.

A moment later, Red Fox came inside, wearing a heavy coat of furs and a thick beaver hat. He ran his hands together as if trying to drive the chill from his fingers. He coughed and cleared his throat as he looked at Tyra. "White Cloud says you go home."

"Yes," Tyra nodded, pulling her cloak back on. "I am concerned the redcoats will think I am spying and will question my family in my absence."

"Then we must go," he said. "After redcoats came, we moved the village far away. Soon the sun will be up, and it will be bright when we get you home."

Tyra hugged White Cloud goodbye, as well as the children. She thanked other villagers before stepping outside with Red Fox. He swung her up onto his horse and mounted behind her. It felt strange to be sitting bareback on a horse. Reaching around her for the reins, Red Fox guided the horse through an invisible path to keep them on solid ground around the mud and swampy bog areas. At times, a patch of moss and green vegetation looked like solid ground, but when they passed, she realized it was a puddle.

"Tyra, now that a big battle has happened, two men will go to New Garden Quakers. We find out if Malcolm MacGregor and sons are wounded or dead. A Quaker will write letter and I leave it in tree."

"Red Fox, I do not know how I can ever repay you," she said.

"Your father saved our village from white people many times."

They rode in silence as the sun rose and brightened. Tyra worried too much time had passed and her disappearance had already been noticed. Her breath caught at the sound of someone calling her name. "Red Fox, set me down here, and I will go to them alone. I do not want them to track you and follow you back to the village."

Tyra could feel each heartbeat pressing into her ears as he set her down. Once she landed on her feet, she covered his hand and looked up at the concern in his eyes. "Thank you so much. Please . . . go before they find you."

With a brief nod, he turned his horse and headed back. Tyra continued on. Her boots squashed with each step into the mud, which looked as black as coal. At least eight inches from the bottom hem of her skirt was filthy. She lifted the material as she sloshed through the thick mire.

"Tyra!" Kirk called out to her. Judging by his tone, he sounded worried. Since Captain Morgan and Private Truitt were probably with him, she couldn't respond. She needed to give Red Fox more time to make his escape. Instead, she would try to follow the sound of his voice.

❧

With each passing minute without Tyra being found, blood pumped through Hugh's temples with mounting pressure. Since there were no signs of forced entry and the bolt on the door was not locked, he could only assume she had not been taken. Small comfort compared to all the things that could happen to her in the wild. What could be so important she would risk her own safety?

Kirk assured him Tyra could take care of herself. She knew the layout of the woods in the swamp. As their search grew into an hour and then two, Kirk began showing signs of increased concern as well, calling for her more often and raising his voice. If they didn't find her in the next hour, Hugh would send for hunting dogs.

They now walked in mud two to three inches deep. Hugh had abandoned his horse and walked on foot with Private Truitt and Kirk. Someone approached him from the left side making noises in the brush. He turned to see Private Truitt walking toward him. "Sir, do you believe she would come out this far in all this muck?"

"Honestly, I do not know," Hugh said. "Miss MacGregor is not like any woman I have ever known."

"True." Private Truitt nodded as he walked beside him. He moved a limb out of the way. Their boots continued to squish as they walked in the thick mud. "I cannot say I have known many women who have earned the title War Woman."

Hugh thought back to the day Tyra had fought the three soldiers who had attacked her. She had fought with strength, courage, and strategy. She could use a sword. What other weapons had she learned to use? Whatever they were, he prayed she had taken one with her.

"I hope she has not come across any alligators," Private Truitt said.

The thought of a scaly creature with vicious teeth came to mind. His stomach spiked into a spasm, and the base of his neck sent a wave of fear throughout his body. What good would a weapon be if she came across an alligator?

"We have to find her," Hugh said. He continued marching forward, listening for any sound or sign that she was out there. So far, when they called out to her, the only answers were from birds.

"Tyra, where are you?" Kirk's voice grew desperate. "This is not funny!"

"I am coming!" The sound of her voice sucked the air out of Hugh. He whirled toward the direction and broke out into a run. Mud splattered everywhere, but he didn't care. All he could concentrate on was getting to Tyra. He needed to see her for himself to know she was unharmed. He ducked and dodged tree limbs, bushes, and briars. His breath came in short gasps as he pushed himself harder.

"What were you thinking, Tyra?" Kirk asked, reaching her first.

Swinging around a large tree, Hugh saw Kirk face his sister with his fists on his hips like an angry father. Tyra stood over him by at least a couple of inches. The lad had grown taller in the last couple of months. The situation would have been comical if it had not been so dire.

Tyra's fiery hair had fallen around her shoulders and down her back in disarray. A speck of dirt was on the left side of her jaw and the right side of her cheek. Even though she appeared to be fine, the hem of her blue skirt looked ruined with wet mud staining several inches from the hem up. As he approached, he breathed heavy from his exertion.

"I am of the same mind, Tyra." Hugh said. "What were you thinking?" Torn between pulling her in his arms, never letting her go, and throttling her, Hugh clenched his teeth and allowed his feet to take root. He braced himself and took a deep breath to clear his mind. Of all things, he needed to be level-headed and not do or say anything he would later regret.

"Hugh, I promise, when we are home, I will confess where I have been and why I went there." Her bold green eyes met his and something in her expression spoke volumes beyond his comprehension. A peace settled over him and for some reason he trusted her. He prayed he wouldn't regret this decision.

"Indeed, you will." He grabbed her cold hand and tugged her along beside him. She wasn't getting out of his sight. He didn't care he was supposed to report to Major Craig this morning for further orders. Marching her past Private Truitt, intense anger filled him as the sting of relief eased the panic inside him. Kirk and Truitt followed in silence and he was grateful.

Once they reached the site where he left his horse tethered to a tree, Hugh lifted her up into the saddle and mounted behind her. Kirk and Truitt mounted their horses. He reached his arms around her to grab the reins. Her close proximity brought a warmth and comfort to him he hadn't felt in a long time. Tyra leaned back against his chest. The action was not a burden as it should have been, but a relief. He couldn't explain why she meant so much to him. All he knew is he would do whatever it took to keep her safe—even betray his own countrymen. And he would do this, not knowing if she would do the same for him. What a fool he had become.

Hugh tightened his arms around Tyra. How could he convince her to trust him? To tell him everything as she claimed she would? Once they reached the stables, he commanded Private Truitt to see to their horses. He grabbed Tyra by the waist and lifted her down. She gasped at his abrupt force, but didn't resist in the kind of struggle he knew she was capable.

"I shall be taking Tyra into my study to question her," Hugh said to Kirk and Truitt. "See we are not interrupted." He gave Truitt his full attention. "When you finish with the horses, come inside and wait in the parlor with Mrs. MacGregor and Kirk. Once I finish interrogating her, I will inform you of what is to be done, and I shall report the details to Major Craig."

"Yes, sir." Private Truitt saluted him.

Hugh grabbed Tyra by the arm and hauled her from the stables to the house. Upon their entry, Mrs. MacGregor was upon them. She threw her arms around Tyra as worried tears of relief crawled down her face. She cupped Tyra's cheek. "Lass, what have ye done?"

"I am sorry, Mama." A measure of guilt flickered in Tyra's eyes. Hugh took a bit of satisfaction in knowing Mrs. MacGregor had not been part of Tyra's scheme, whatever it was.

"Mrs. MacGregor, I will be taking Tyra into the study for questioning. Please do not disturb us." Hugh pulled Tyra from her mother's grip and hauled her down the hall and into the study as promised. He slammed the door closed behind them.

Once they were alone, Hugh stalked her. She backed up with a fearful expression until her back was against the wall. He imagined all sorts of dangers which might have befallen her. Unable to resist, Hugh grabbed her in a fierce hug and pulled her close. He could feel the warmth of her body against him and her rapid heartbeat next to his. Unwilling to deny the attraction between them and the gravitational pull she had on him, Hugh basked in the moment. He dropped his chin and gazed into her wide green eyes. It was his undoing. Hugh lowered himself until he touched her lips. She was soft and warm, all he had imagined she would be. Just like the scent following her everywhere, Tyra tasted of honey. When he needed to breathe again, he lifted his head and gulped fresh air.

"Tyra, please do not ever scare me like this again," Hugh whispered against her lips. "I do not understand what is happening between us, but in spite of this war and our countries, I could never consider you my enemy. When I am apart from you, I now feel like I am severed." He leaned his forehead against hers and took a deep breath, hoping she would embrace his feelings and not cast him away.

11

Shock vibrated through Tyra as Hugh's forehead pressed against hers. She thought he had intended to box her ears, but he had kissed her instead. His warm breath heated her face and raised her pulse. He cupped her cheek and pressed his lips against hers in another tantalizing kiss. Breaking away from her, he wrapped his arms around her in a tight embrace as if he never wanted to let her go. He made her feel cherished and valued.

"I feared something might have happened to you." He relaxed his hold as he stroked her hair. "Tell me why you went out in the middle of the night into a swamp at the risk to your health, safety, and reputation. I want to understand."

Tyra laid her head upon his chest. The wool on his redcoat was rough against her cheek, but she wanted to stay right here against him for as long as he would let her. His heart drummed against her ear as if he were on a march. She closed her eyes, hating for the moment to end. What would he think of her when he learned what she had done? Would the news of what she had learned about his brother make a difference?

"When you dragged me in here, I thought you might try to throttle me." She said, stalling before telling him everything.

"I freely admit the thought did cross my mind." He chuckled, pulling back to meet her gaze. His gray eyes lit with a smile. "I was torn between it and smothering you with thankful kisses. I settled on the latter." He leaned forward and placed a kiss on the tip of her nose.

"I must admit I prefer the choice you made," she said. "Only because I dislike being throttled."

"Is that so?" He lifted a black eyebrow, his smile fading into a serious expression. "Now, tell me why you did it?" He stepped back and crossed his arms over his chest as he waited with a calm demeanor, ready to judge.

"A month ago, I sent a letter to Red Fox, the Tuscarora Indian who brought you here." She linked her hands in front of her. This felt worse than confessing to her father when she was a child. Hugh was a man she had romantic feelings for in spite of the fact that she should not, and she wanted him to respect and think highly of her. Even though he spared her the humiliation of having to confess in front of everyone else, his opinion was fast becoming as important to her as her family's. "The letter was to my father. Since Major Craig is watching all the known Patriot families and has been known to have his soldiers read incoming and outgoing mail, I did not trust sending a letter through the regular carrier who passes through Wilmington."

"The Indians are now running courier service?" Hugh gave her a skeptical look as if he didn't believe her. Disappointment filled his expression as he blinked and rubbed his eyebrows, pinching the bridge of his nose. Her anxiety increased as she searched her brain for the right words that would help him understand.

"No, but they are great at being loyal to their friends, traveling hundreds of miles without being noticed, and discovering pertinent information because people think Indians are insignificant." She rubbed her hands together and lifted her chin. "They respect my father and were willing to help me. Red Fox and his brother traveled until they found my father and gave him my letter. My letter was more than updates about our family. I told him how the British troops had taken over Wilmington, and I asked him about your brother, Colonel Neil Morgan."

"What did you say?" Hugh asked, his voice rising. "Am I supposed to believe this is why you risked your life to go out there?"

"There is more." She shook her head and scratched her chin. "After you told me about the huge battle at Guilford Courthouse, we needed to know if my da and brothers are still alive. We could not wait months knowing naught. I knew Red Fox could find out for me, and that is why I took the risk."

"I see." Hugh turned and strode toward the window. He stared outside in silence.

Tyra pulled the letter out of a pouch White Cloud had given her. She walked over and reached around Hugh to hand it to him. "You might want to read this. 'Tis the letter Red Fox brought back from my father. It has information about your brother. He is alive, Hugh."

He accepted the letter and unfolded it. While he read, Tyra waited and stared down at the floor. A few moments later, he turned and looked at her. "How do I know if this is true?" He held up the letter and shook it. "Why would your father give you this information about my brother, a colonel from the very enemy he has spent the last five years fighting?"

"Because he trusts me to do the right thing," Tyra said. "I have done no wrong. I have not betrayed you or my family. I merely found out what I could . . . your brother is alive, and so are my father and brothers." She lifted her hands in surrender. "Is it something I should be punished for?"

"Tyra, you have caused more trouble than you realize." Hugh massaged the back of his neck. "Major Craig will want to know why I am not at my post in Wilmington this morning. Private Truitt is well aware of the fact you disappeared, and we had to spend time searching for you. I must provide a convincing story, but something to keep you from being whipped or imprisoned."

"What do you suggest?" she asked, hoping the sacrifice he required of her would be bearable.

Unable to trust himself to be near Tyra, Hugh gestured to a nearby chair. He needed to keep a level head, and the last few moments alone with her had tested him beyond his endurance. Without a word, she followed his suggestion and sat. A breath of relief escaped her, almost as if she needed to be off her feet.

Puzzled, Hugh sat beside her and leaned sideways, bracing his elbows on his knees and linking his hands in the middle.

"Tyra, I cannot hide the fact you ran off in the middle of the night. Private Truitt will wonder how I intend to handle this." Hugh rubbed the back of his neck and looked away. "I do not want to punish you, but I have to give the appearance I am doing something about this. Otherwise, my commanding officers will question my judgment and reason for being here."

"What do you mean?" Dread pooled in the pit of Tyra's stomach. Images of all sorts of tortures slashed through her mind. In a feat of determination, Tyra clamped down on the rising panic quivering in her heart. "After such fine displays of affection, you would punish me?" Tyra lifted her hand, itching to strike him, but something stalled her. Betrayal lanced through her like a spear. Not wanting him to see her reaction, Tyra stood and walked across the room, wrapping her arms around herself.

"Tyra, please. You must understand." His voice followed her across the room, but she lifted a hand to stop him.

"Do not come near me," she said, her tone forceful and harsh.

"I have the dilemma of Private Truitt knowing what has happened, and he could go to Major Craig at any time. If they suspect I have developed feelings for you, they could remove me from here and send someone in my place. Would you prefer that?" Concern filled his tone, but she refused to turn around. Instead, she stared into the dark fireplace, realizing for the first time how cold the room felt. She rubbed her arms up and down.

"My concern is for your safety. Another soldier could be a tyrant. Believe me, I have seen them at their worst."

Hot tears filled her eyes as she blinked them away. She was a fool to think she and Hugh could be anything other than enemies. "What kind of punishment do you intend to inflict on me?"

"Inflict?" In spite of her request, Hugh stepped close and gripped her shoulders from behind. "Tyra, you misunderstood me. I have no intention of inflicting any kind of pain. I could not bear it. My thoughts were to keep you secluded in your chamber for a week—naught more." His warm hand gently squeezed her shoulders. "Although we shall call it imprisonment in your chamber to appease Major Craig."

"Are you sure it will be enough to satisfy your superior officers?" Tyra refused to mask the sarcasm in her biting tone.

"I wish I could make you understand," Hugh said.

"I understand perfectly well." Tyra stepped away to put a bit of distance between them so she could think more clearly. "You say you do not want to do this, but as you have so aptly insinuated, we all have responsibilities, and duty must come first." She met his gaze and squared her shoulders. "So you see, I do understand. Like you, I must do what is necessary to protect my family. You and I were born into different worlds and those two worlds are at war."

"Tyra, I realize you are angry, but I do not want to quarrel with you and make the obstacles against us even harder." He bent toward her as he lowered his voice, coaxing her. "This war will not last forever. If we hold fast, perhaps one day we could be together." He caressed the back of his knuckles against her cheek. "I always thought you a woman of faith."

"I AM a woman of faith, but I am also realistic." Anger flared inside her as she jerked away from his touch. How dare he question her faith? He presumed to know so much about her when it was clear he knew little. She placed her wrists against each other and held them up as if surrendering to him. "'Tis time for you to do what you must. Escort me to my prison, please."

"Nonsense," Hugh said, rolling his eyes with a disbelieving shake of his head. "It does not have to be this way between us."

"On the contrary," Tyra said, ignoring the jolting ache in her heavy chest. "We must give the perception we are enemies as everyone believes us to be." Tyra shoved past him and strode through the door.

Hugh followed as she stormed past Truitt, Kirk, and her mother. He gave them a brief nod, unable to address their concerned expressions and the questions swirling in their wide eyes. He hurried after Tyra, climbing two steps at a time, hoping to catch her before she could lock him out of her chamber. He wasn't finished with her.

Full of momentum, he charged inside and nearly collided with Tyra where she stood waiting with her hands on her hips, a glaring expression marring her smooth features. She tapped her toe against the wooden floor. "Am I to be locked in here inside my chamber the whole time?"

"If not, would your confinement be something others would believe?" he asked, hoping to reason with her and make things between them right again.

"Why do I get the feeling you are secretly enjoying this all too well?" Her green eyes narrowed as if he was the target at archery practice.

"I must admit 'twill be nice not having to worry about your safety or what you might be getting yourself into." He leaned forward, the scent of the outdoors and wood smoke clung to her hair. She must have been hovering over a fire to keep warm all night. He longed to reach out and touch her, but he sensed she would slap him by the fiery look lingering in her expression.

"I want you to know I have been the perfect lady since father left this past Christmas." She pursed her lips into a straight line. Tyra walked over to her bed and sat on the edge. She stared up at him, while folding her hands in her lap as if she was content and had all the time in the world. Her green eyes held a cold glint that was not there before. "Will I be able to see and talk to Mama and Kirk?"

"Yes, they may visit you, but Private Truitt will stand guard outside your room," Hugh said. Regret filled him as he questioned his decision, and wrestled with the temptation to change his mind. He looked around her chamber to avoid her accusing eyes.

It was the first time he had a chance to view her chamber. She kept it tidy with the wooden floorboards swept clean of dust. Floral blue curtains were drawn back to allow light through the panes. The walls were a light cream color, the simple mantle left bare with the exception of candelabras at each corner. She had an armoire and a desk across the room. A chest sat at the foot of her bed and another was under the window by the wall.

"There is one thing I still do not understand." He paced across the floor, memorizing every detail as if it could tell him more about her. "How did you manage to escape without any of us hearing you leave?"

"I slipped a heavy dose of chamomile in everyone's tea." He whirled to see her smiling. "I can be resourceful when I need to be."

Hugh had no doubt.

✐

After Hugh left Tyra's chamber, he gave specific instructions to Private Truitt and explained his decision on Tyra's punishment to her mother and brother. He left Truitt in a chair out in the hallway by her chamber door. A moment later, he stepped out on the porch with Tyra's mother.

"Captain Morgan, I would like to thank ye for not making it worse on her." Mrs. MacGregor's blue eyes held a measure of gratitude as she smiled up at him. For the most part, her skin was still smooth and the beauty of her youth visible, but today worry lines framed her eyes and forehead. "Our Tyra is a strong-willed lass and has tried our patience often, but she means no harm."

"Mrs. MacGregor, I shall do my best to protect her and keep her safe. The British army can be unforgiving at times, so we must be careful." He shook his head, gripping his tricorn hat. "Part of the responsibility lies on her shoulders to not draw attention to herself and to behave in a way to not rouse suspicion. My ability to protect her from Major Craig is limited. He is my superior officer, and while I have not been under his command for long, I sense he can be quite ruthless when necessary."

"I understand." Mrs. MacGregor nodded and her chin trembled, but she didn't break eye contact. "While you are away today, I shall talk to her." She let out a deep sigh. "And pray."

"It would be wise," Hugh said, trying to ignore the disappointment threatening to dampen his spirits. "I fear she is too angry with me to listen to reason right now. Good day." He bowed his head, placed his hat upon his hand, and descended the porch steps as he pulled on his gloves.

Hugh strode to the barn and saddled his horse. He kept his movements brisk to fight against the cold air nipping at his flesh. At least it wasn't as cold here as it often was back home in England. He led the animal out into the yard and mounted up. He turned to look at the white MacGregor house and imagined Tyra standing on the porch waving to him.

Pain sliced through his chest. He and his brother had joined the Royal Army to escape the poverty in which they had grown up. The military had provided a way to travel, educate himself, and do all the things he could have never imagined on a farmer's salary or working a labor position for someone else. He had never longed for a family of his own, a place to settle, or a deeper relationship with anyone beyond the family he had known and the few friends he had made. Women were always acquaintances and nothing more. He had always preferred it this way. Until now.

Tyra MacGregor was changing him.

He nudged his horse forward and rode down the drive and onto the long road leading northwest into Wilmington. Less than an hour later, he arrived at the Burgwin House on the corner of Market Street. A half-loaded wagon was parked on the side of the road by the house.

"Secure those trunks with another rope," Major Craig ordered two soldiers. He turned at the sound of Hugh's boots crunching the gravel. "Ah, there you are, Captain Morgan. I thought I would see you earlier this morning."

Hugh wanted to ask what was going on with the wagon and all the extra soldiers around the premise, but instead, he launched into the story of what had happened with Tyra. He omitted what he could and concentrated on the details of the punishment he had implemented. Major Craig listened as two soldiers deposited chairs in the wagon. He pressed the toe of his boot into the gravel and made a half circle. After Hugh finished speaking, Major Craig stood in silence and crossed his arms, placing his finger on his chin in thought.

"This letter Miss MacGregor was trying to send, are you certain it is merely a letter to find out if her father and brothers survived and naught more?" Major Craig turned dark eyes upon Hugh, reminding him of a looming storm cloud.

"Yes sir, as I mentioned, Miss MacGregor was only concerned about her father and brothers." Hugh stood in a soldier stance with his feet shoulder width apart and his hands linked behind his back.

"Her father and brothers have been at war for five years. Why would she be so concerned now?" Major Craig asked.

"I believe it may be my fault, sir," Hugh said. "I told them about the bloody battle at Guilford Court House."

A soldier brought out two more wooden chairs and placed them in the wagon. Sergeant McAlister marched by with a group of soldiers and saluted Major Craig and Hugh. No doubt, they were conducting the afternoon patrol through Wilmington. On the other side of the Burgwin House, swords clashed as men trained.

"They would have heard about it eventually." Major Craig tilted his head and pinned dark eyes on Hugh. "Why did Miss MacGregor not use the regular postal system?"

"I would imagine it is because several Patriot letters have been confiscated by the troops." Hugh took a deep breath in discomfort. Now came the moment when the major would analyze what Hugh had told him and decide if he could be trusted.

"It would indicate Miss MacGregor had something to hide." Major Craig twisted his lips into a frown as he pondered the situation further.

"I am as certain as I can be under the circumstances," Hugh said. "It is possible Miss MacGregor enclosed a letter to a lover with her letter to her family." The mere thought turned Hugh's stomach sour, but he needed to distract Major Craig's attention from suspecting her of spy activities.

"True, but I have not trusted the woman since I met her." Major Craig's tone turned bitter. "There is something about her I distrust." He lifted a finger. "In fact, after her house arrest is over, I would like for you to give Miss MacGregor a little bit of freedom. It is my experience if a person betrays another, their actions will eventually give them up."

"Yes, sir." An uneasy feeling entered Hugh's gut. Tyra was too headstrong for her own good. Even if she was innocent of spying, he feared her daring behavior could still cause her trouble.

Major Craig walked around the wagon, pulling and tugging on the rope to make sure everything was tight and secure. His white powdered wig was pulled back, tied in a red ribbon behind his neck, and it moved with each jerking motion he made. With a nod of approval, he turned to his men waiting for further orders and said, "Well done, soldiers."

"Sir, I cannot help but notice all the activity today," Hugh said. "Do we have new orders?"

"Indeed, I have recently learned Lord Cornwallis will be here within the hour. He has requested the best house in Wilmington, which means I must vacate the premises." He pointed north. "I will be moving into the Mitchell House."

"Where will we keep fourteen hundred new men?" Hugh asked.

"They will camp out all over Wilmington while the officers take over housing as needed." Major Craig came over to stand in front of him. "After the Battle of Guilford Courthouse our soldiers are tired, hungry, and in the worst of conditions. Lord Cornwallis is hoping to not only rest them, but to stock up on new supplies."

"I see." Hugh turned and looked his commanding officer in the eye. "What are my orders, sir?"

"You are to oversee a place for all the men to sleep when they arrive, a system with medical attention and food. I have Captain Blake overseeing their training and weaponry." Major Craig turned and walked toward the back of the Burgwin House. Hugh fell into step beside him. The blockhouse was now empty.

"What happened to Harnett?" Hugh asked.

"The man finally got what he deserved," Major Craig said. "He contracted some kind of illness. The Tories felt sorry for him and asked for his release. I let him go free three days ago."

"How is he now?"

"Dead."

12

This confinement was killing her. Tyra had always been active, running and playing outside during childhood, trying her best to keep up with her brothers. Staying inside the walls of her chamber for a week made her feel like she might suffocate under a lake of water.

For the first few hours of her confinement, she read her Bible and prayed, wrote letters to her aunt Blair in Charles Town and to her cousin Rebecca. She considered trying to sketch the view of the east fields from her window, but she didn't have drawing talent and the prospect bored her. She paced and mentally fumed at Hugh until her mother brought a tray of hot food for dinner.

Private Truitt insisted on inspecting the tray and would not allow them to close the door to have any privacy. He sat in a wooden chair out in the hallway within hearing distance. While she ate boiled potatoes and a buttered slice of bread, her mother talked about Kirk's exploits of the day. They discussed how the rice fields suffered without her father and brothers. They would have another year of no crops. Her mother didn't say it aloud, but Tyra knew their savings were getting low.

Tyra knew her mother made idle conversation to keep from raising private Truitt's suspicions. In spite of her mother's controlled efforts, Tyra wanted to rant and rave at the injustice of how Patriots were being treated during the British occupation of Wilmington.

Specifically, she longed to confide in her mother at the confusion she felt between her feelings for Hugh, his tender kisses, his obligation to the Royal Army, and her obligation to her family and the Continental cause for their freedom.

By the time she finished her meal, Tyra could no longer hold back her questions. She set her tray on the desk and went back to sit on the edge of the bed beside her mother. She cleared her throat, hoping to set a nonchalant tone. "Has Captain Morgan not yet returned?" she asked, glancing at the dark sky outside her window. "When did he say he would return?"

"Tyra, were ye hoping to appeal to Captain Morgan's conscience?" Mama asked. "He does not strike me as the sort of man who would change his mind so easy. In spite of him being a captain in the British Army, the punishment he gave ye is no worse than what ye've endured from your own father at times. I am afraid ye may eventually push him too far and anger him."

"But that is the point, Mama," Tyra said. "He is not my father nor my husband. I am not a soldier to be ordered about. In spite of this awful war, honorable men treat women and children with decorum."

"Aye, but it is why I believe yer punishment is fair. Lass, I want ye to remember he is still an officer of the army occupying this town. 'Tis too dangerous to keep pushing him. I sincerely believe Captain Morgan has tried to be accommodating to our family as much as his limitations will allow." Mama touched her shoulder. "'Tis only for three more days. Surely, ye can manage?"

"Yes, not for my sake, but for you and Kirk." Tyra chuckled with sarcasm. "It amazes me, just like Da he knew exactly what would be the hardest on me. I could have probably endured some other unpleasant chore much better than being confined in pure idleness."

"I would imagine he thought it a better punishment for a woman than any other alternative," Mama said.

"I know, but he is the most exasperating man." Her mind clouded over, and her heart ached with confusion. She wasn't sure she could trust her own judgment anymore. What was she thinking kissing him? The knowledge that her father and brothers could end up facing Hugh in the heat of battle and that they would be obligated to kill the other, filled her with sorrow. After all her family had done in making sacrifices and risking their lives for freedom, she did not want them to feel as if she had betrayed them.

Tears stung her eyes, and she looked away to keep her mother from seeing them. She clenched her teeth with determination. Somehow, she would have to train herself to overcome this dangerous attraction and affection she had developed for Hugh. Winning this conflicting battle within herself was detrimental to her state of mind.

"*Lord help me.*" Her heart's prayer came out as a whisper.

"Tyra, he is the best person to call on in times of trouble and where matters of the heart are concerned." Mama covered her hand and gave her a gentle squeeze. "God knows what is best. Allow him to lead you through this."

Tyra wanted to deny she was wrestling with a matter of the heart, but she refrained for fear of lying.

Approaching footsteps sounded in the hall, and Kirk greeted Private Truitt. A moment later, he arrived in her chamber with a slight grin on his face. His black boots were coated with thick mud where he had been outside. At least the mud was dry and would only leave pieces of crumbling clay in her floor.

"You really did it this time, Tyra," he said. "After scaring us like that you are getting what you deserve. If I had pulled a stunt like that, Captain Morgan probably would have put me in the cellar."

"Kirk, 'tis enough," Mama said. "Do not antagonize yer sister. She is going through enough at the moment." Her voice held a tone of warning. She rose to her feet with a reluctant sigh and walked over to the desk where she pulled a piece of paper from under Tyra's empty plate. "I brought some Bible verses I hoped might be helpful."

Tyra accepted the paper to keep from upsetting her mother, but she feared they would not hold the answers to her conflicting emotions.

"We shall leave ye in peace now." Mama pointed behind her. "Kirk, grab the tray and come."

Tyra studied the Bible verses her mother left behind. The one in Proverbs stood out to her. *Trust in the Lord with all your heart, and lean not on your own understanding. In all your ways acknowledge him, and he shall direct your paths.* She paused, realizing how little she had prayed in the last few weeks. Growing up she had always felt safe and believed God would protect her in any circumstance, but war had changed her. War was unstable, evil, and it destroyed a person's faith. She had come to depend on things she could see, touch, and what she knew. At times, it felt like God had abandoned them. She couldn't understand all the killing and destruction, but understood it was necessary in order to survive when attacked. How could she come to trust God with what she couldn't understand? It seemed so hard.

After reading more encouraging Scriptures, Tyra went to her desk and pulled out paper, quill, and ink to write a letter to Mr. Simmons in the Whig party. When she finished, she waved the letter through the air to help it dry. She needed to put it away before someone came in and discovered it. The lives of the prisoners at the Burgwin House depended on her success.

The fire in the hearth had smoldered. Tyra poked her head out the door and asked Truitt for more logs. Carrying the candle from her desk to the table by her bedside, she settled down and took up sewing. Soon she would have a new set of gloves for Alec.

A few moments later, a door opened and closed downstairs. Tyra assumed it was Private Truitt bringing the logs. She snuggled under her blanket looking forward to more warmth in her chamber. Footsteps climbed the stairs and approached her door. A bold knock followed.

"Come in," she called.

Hugh walked in carrying a load of logs. He grinned at the surprised look she couldn't hide. A new warmth glowed in her heart as if the fire had been rekindled in her chamber. The anger she had felt earlier in the morning was gone.

"I was not who you were expecting, was I?" Hugh asked.

"'Tis late." Tyra scrambled to sit up straight as she pulled the quilt up to her chin. Hugh suppressed a grin. At least she was speaking to him after he forced her to stay in her chamber all day. "You are usually home before now. Where is Private Truitt?"

"Were you worried about me?" The way she referred to this house as his home as well as hers filled him with an unexpected tenderness and longing. Hugh set the spare logs in the large basket by the hearth and placed two small logs on the iron grate over simmering coals. At least the coals were still hot enough to build a larger fire without having to spend a lot of time rubbing flint and steel together. He dusted his hands and glanced at Tyra.

"Not in the least." She lifted her chin like a defiant child. He grinned, sensing she tried too hard to show an attitude of indifference. Of course, at ten and seven, Tyra was still young. At times, it was hard to remember six years separated them. Though many girls her age married, some were committed to men much older than himself.

His thoughts were going too far down the wrong path. He shook his head and concentrated on the earlier question she had asked. "As for Truitt, he has been here all day, so I thought I would give him a break." He turned back to building the fire and stirred the coals to stoke the tiny flames. More sparks caught the bark on the new logs. "I have some news I thought you might be interested in."

"What news?" she asked, her tone changing to curiosity. He knew her interest would be piqued and grinned.

"Lord Cornwallis arrived in Wilmington today with over fourteen hundred men. They took a severe beating at Guilford Courthouse, more so than I originally realized. They are in need of supplies, food, clothing, and anything residents can spare."

"So it is why you are late?" Tyra bit her bottom lip as she looked down at the floor. He sensed something else was on her mind, but wasn't sure if she would tell him. "In spite of what you must think of me, I am sorry they are in such a sorry state." She sighed and dropped her head back on her shoulders and looked up at the ceiling. "I am so tired of this war."

Hugh studied her profile. The tears that sprang in her eyes reminded him of her compassion, the part of her which decided to save his life before she knew him. "I believe you, Tyra." He hated the thought of being her enemy. How could he ever consider himself as such? It was impossible.

He could feel his loyalty to his nation slipping as his feelings for her continued to grow. As a soldier, he had been trained to serve God, king, country, and then family. As he studied Tyra, he couldn't imagine putting his country, before her, and she was not even family. Yet, the idea of her being part of his family appealed to him more than he wanted to admit. What was right? At one time he thought he had his priorities straight, but now he wasn't so sure.

"Major Craig has moved out of the Burgwin House and has taken residence at the Mitchell House. Lord Cornwallis has taken over the Burgwin House, and the headquarters will remain there." Hugh stirred the flames one more time before setting the poker aside. He turned to stand. "Now as troops are covering all of Wilmington, tensions will be high. Residents will be expected to give more and things will change."

"What kind of things?" she asked.

"'Twill be much harder on the Patriots and your family." He walked toward her. "Now, more than ever, I need you to be on your best behavior. Do naught to cause more harm to you or your family." Fear twisted in his gut, knowing how independent and courageous she could be. "Promise me, Tyra."

She didn't answer as she considered what he had said in silence. He waited, but he could see the hesitation in her eyes. An eerie sensation raced up his spine. Was she already planning something? Or worse, had she already done something? He loved the spirited determination in her and admired her for it, but he didn't want it to be the end of her.

"Tyra, will you not promise me you will behave?" he asked, wondering how he could keep her locked up here for her own safety. Since Major Craig wanted him to give her more freedom, he feared his superior officer was right, she would cause her own demise. He stepped closer, hating the troubled ache in the back of his throat and the pressure gnawing at his heart. "I know you are a woman of your word. Promise me."

"No, I will do what I must to protect myself and my family." She gulped. "You must know me well enough by now to know I believe in the cause my family is fighting for. How can I believe as they do and be willing to do any less?" Her eyes pleaded for understanding.

At the moment, it was as if Hugh's heart collapsed to his stomach. He admired her conviction and respected her all the more. What man would not want such a woman by his side? Someone who would stick by him through anything and be there when the worst was over. Would his king do that for him? Would his country? No. Only God, and now, perhaps a godly woman like Tyra. He closed his eyes, but she wasn't standing beside him. She was against him.

"Tell me, Hugh." She leaned forward, her voice growing more determined. "What are you fighting for? King and country? A commission to fulfill?"

"I signed my name and gave my word," he said, feeling uncomfortable at having his personal decisions being questioned. Why did his reasons seem less convincing compared to hers? "I never break my word."

"I know, which is why, I could never give you my heart, but I do care about you." Unshed tears filled her eyes and they sparkled like green orbs. "'Tis why I asked my father about your brother. I know how it feels to wonder if a brother is alive and well. I wanted to help you, but I also know in my heart that if you were ordered to shoot me, you would feel obligated to do so."

His throat constricted as indecision wrestled inside him. For the first time in his life, he didn't even know himself. Hugh looked down at the floor, feeling guilt-ridden. An image of a shot being fired upon Tyra and blood spilling from her chest sent a panic of unrest throughout his trembling body. He wouldn't be able to live with himself. If he defied such orders, he could be executed. It was an image which didn't fill him with as much distress. She was wrong. He wouldn't be able to go through with the order.

"Your silence is answer enough," she said, sorrow in her tone.

Hugh couldn't meet her gaze. She would see the truth in his eyes, and if she knew the vulnerable state she had placed him in, would she take advantage of him? He wasn't ready to admit how deeply she affected him. He needed to change the topic.

"I have some more bad news. I discovered Harnett died. The Tories finally took pity upon him and asked Major Craig to release him a couple of days before he passed away."

He ventured a glance in her direction. A myriad of emotions ranged across her face. Shock. Anger. Sorrow. He could tell she was trying to sort through her feelings. More tears welled in her eyes and finally dropped, crawling down her smooth cheeks.

"I had hoped someone would have had compassion on him much sooner. I shall pray for his family. Thank you for telling me." Her lips twisted into a frown, and she looked up with a hard expression. "Major Craig is a cruel man. While your brother and other British officers are being treated humanely in Hillsborough, our officers are being tortured like vicious animals." She wiped the tears from her face. "I would like to be alone now." She rolled over and turned her back, dismissing him.

Mama's steady steps came down the hall and stopped outside Tyra's door. "Private Truitt, I want to thank ye for letting Kirk escort me to town. I am afraid our trip was in vain. Yer comrades have stripped the stores in town. There is naught left on the shelves. Whenever I run out of the last of my flour, I will not be able to make any more bread or biscuits. I am sorry."

"There is naught?" Private Truitt asked as if he didn't believe her.

"Nay." Mama sighed in defeat. "Lord Cornwallis has his troops everywhere, and I am sorry to say they are in such a ragged state. They have set up a makeshift hospital at the Episcopal Church. 'Tis so sad. We heard them screaming in pain as we passed on the road."

"Well, I suppose I could appeal to Captain Morgan and see if he will bring us some food home. If all the store shelves are empty, the food must be stored somewhere for the soldiers. Have no fear, Mrs. MacGregor, Captain Morgan will be able to get his hands on something for us."

"Thank ye, sir," Mama said. "In the meantime, Kirk shall go out this afternoon and try to find some deer. He is a good shot with a rifle. On the morrow, he can go with our neighbor, Mr. Simmons and his son, on the boat to cast nets for fish. No need to take away from the soldiers in need. Many of them look near starved to death."

"I did not know the lad was a hunter and a fisherman," Private Truitt said, an air of pride in his tone as if Kirk was his own son. Tyra gritted her teeth and tried to ignore his puffed-up attitude. Kirk had a father who had already taught him what he needed to know. He didn't need some stuffy British officer taking over the role. She was torn between being grateful or suspicious that Private Truitt only wanted to win over Kirk's trust to press him for information about their family. These days she couldn't trust anyone. Her painful conversation with Hugh came to mind.

"Aye, all my sons have developed many skills in order to survive here in the colony, thanks to my husband, Malcolm." Tyra smiled to herself, knowing her mother had just made it clear as to whom she gave credit to Kirk's skills. "Of course, I would need yer permission to allow him to go, especially since Captain Morgan is not here."

"Yes, he may go. I have no wish to starve myself or take more from the troops as you have so aptly pointed out." He coughed and cleared his throat. "I would go myself, but my orders are to stay here and guard Miss MacGregor and make sure she behaves."

"I understand, sir. Now if ye excuse me, I shall visit my daughter."

As Mama walked in wearing her blue day gown and a smile of triumph, Tyra's spirits lifted. "I hope ye're doing well today, lass," she said, speaking loud enough for Private Truitt to hear. She bent to retrieve a piece of paper from inside her stockings and handed it to Tyra.

"I am fine, Mama. I read the Scriptures you gave me, and I feel much better." Tyra accepted the piece of paper and unfolded it. Her mother had delivered her letter and sketch drawing to their neighbor Mr. Simmons. Since her artwork left much to be desired, she hoped her little sketch of the Burgwin House dungeon would be clear enough for the Whig party to understand as they planned the escape for the Patriot prisoners. Tyra nodded with a smile to thank her mother and let her know all was well.

"I brought ye the town paper," Mama said. "I thought ye would enjoy catching up on the news."

"Yes, thank you." Mama handed her the *Cape Fear Mercury* with a piece of beef jerky inside it. Tyra lifted her eyebrows in question.

"Ye may have heard me telling Private Truitt we do not have any food. We will have to wait for yer brother to catch us a deer. Then 'twill take me several hours to skin it, prepare it, and cook it." Mama pointed at the beef jerky and placed a finger over her lips. Tyra realized she had hidden food for the three of them she wasn't planning to share with the British. "I am sorry ye will have to wait so long to eat."

"'Tisn't your fault. When I am free in the next couple of days I will be able to help ye." Tyra smiled and bit her bottom lip. "I know where there might be some turtles, and I will be able to make turtle soup."

"Lass, I know I have always given ye a hard time about being too much like yer brothers." Mama cupped her cheek and tilted her head, a look of love and admiration in her blue eyes. "But ye've shown so much courage, and yer skills will help save us now that things are getting worse. I am so thankful to have ye as my daughter and proud of ye. I was wrong. Any man would be blessed to have ye just the way ye are."

Unexpected tears filled Tyra's eyes. All the confrontations between them had made her long for this day. She had often wished she could be more like her mother, rather than the awkward giant she had become. Overwhelmed with gratitude, Tyra wiped her eyes. "Thank you," she whispered.

A knock sounded on the front door below.

"I got it!" Kirk called.

"I have a message for Private Truitt from Captain Morgan." A man's voice echoed up to the second floor.

"Send him up Kirk," Private Truitt said.

Tyra exchanged a questioning glance with her mother. What could be happening now?

13

*O*ver the next couple of days, Hugh spent all his time taking orders from Major Craig and assisting the troops under Cornwallis as they marched into Wilmington. In many ways, he was grateful Tyra was still locked in her chamber and unable to cause any trouble.

As he rode through the streets of Wilmington, he hated to see the devastation of his fellow comrades. Tents lined the streets, and men huddled around campfires to keep warm. Dirt, blood, and soil covered their faces, necks, arms and hands, as well as what was left of their tattered clothing. Many hobbled around on leg wounds or blisters from marching in worn out boots with holes and the soles half gone.

Several women had brought blankets, and Hugh ordered one of his men to hand them out. A young soldier hobbled over to Hugh where he stood on the corner of Church and Second Streets. Brown whiskers had begun growing into a goatee beard on his chin. His hazel eyes were full of pain and dark brown hair hung in strands around his ears and neck. Three holes were on the arms of his redcoat. Dried blood soaked the thigh of what used to be his white pants.

"Everywhere I go, men are still talking about the Battle at Guilford Courthouse," Hugh said.

"The courthouse is gone." His voice was gruff, as if raw. "The Continentals had three lines of defense, and Cornwallis charged us to break through the middle. 'Twas a bloodbath." He rubbed his face with soiled hands. "The crisis of the battle occurred between the hill where the courthouse stood and the south woods. Cornwallis came down from his post and rode his white horse in a full gallop. Narrowly missing being captured by William Washington, he rode to the artillery and ordered grapeshot fire upon the mass of men, killing both British and Continentals." He swallowed with difficulty and paused. "We survivors saw it, and those who did not, are now hearing about it. The next time we go into battle, will Cornwallis do the same thing to the rest of us? There is not a man under his command who cannot help wondering."

"Sounds awful." Hugh stood beside his comrade with a listening ear. Now was not the time to talk about strategic warfare or to point out the strategy had worked in breaking up the American lines— even at the cost of his own men. Few officers would have had the guts to do what Lord Cornwallis did. His ability to make such difficult decisions was one of the reasons so many respected him.

They talked for a few more minutes and then a friend called out to him and they parted ways. Hugh headed down Church Street toward Front Street. There was not a street in Wilmington without soldiers camping along the road. Several soldiers had split up in groups to ride out to nearby towns to seek food and supplies. They took whatever they could from families along the way, even the MacGregors had lost what wasn't taken the first time their plantation was raided.

Even though Hugh had been indirectly under the command of Lord Cornwallis in South Carolina, he never had the privilege of meeting him in person, and it was an honor. He had heard so many glowing reports about him, but when the man had arrived, he looked tired and older than Hugh had expected. Cornwallis had white hair and wore it tied in a ribbon at the back of his neck. Lord Cornwallis spent the first few days writing letters to his superiors and other commanding officers. He and Major Craig consulted each other for strategy ideas. In the evening, Lord Cornwallis ate a good dinner, had a glass of wine during a game of chess or cards, and rested to take his mind off his troubles.

One evening, Hugh was invited to dinner at the Burgwin House with the rest of the officers. Even though he considered it an honor, he longed to be home at the MacGregor house enjoying Tyra's company, as well as her mother's and brother's.

During a game of Whist, the topic of conversation turned to Hillsborough. Hugh looked up from his cards and over at Major Craig for a sign he could ask about his brother. With a slight nod, Major Craig turned to Lord Cornwallis sitting beside him. "We have some officers being held prisoner in Hillsborough and one of them is Colonel Neil Morgan, Captain Morgan's brother," Major Craig said. "In fact, he was on his way there to rescue them when he and his men were ambushed by the local Tuscarora Indians. He was the only one to survive, but was severely wounded. He has since recovered and is ready to finish what he started. I am certain Captain Morgan would be more than happy to lead a mission to Hillsborough."

"Indeed, I am most eager to get my brother out of there," Hugh said.

"I will keep it in mind, gentleman." Lord Cornwallis nodded as he tossed his cards face down. "Let us finish this game another time. I have something I would like to show you in the study."

Each man dropped his cards and stood with a glass of port in hand. They followed Lord Cornwallis down the hall to his study. The layout of the room was the same as Major Craig left it. The only difference was a long table in the middle of the room with at least four maps rolled out. Paperweights were at the corners. One map was of the North and South Carolina colonies, another covered the colonies of Virginia and Maryland, and one additional consisted of the New England colonies. The last map was a street layout of Wilmington.

"Bring more candles," Cornwallis said. "We need light."

℘

After they learned Captain Morgan would not be returning for the night, Kirk went out hunting, while Mrs. MacGregor worked on chores downstairs. Private Truitt settled back in his chair outside her chamber. Tyra threw another log into the fireplace and sat on the floor to watch it burn.

A strange feeling came over her, and she sensed she was no longer alone. Tyra twisted around to see Private Truitt standing in the doorway watching her. His arms were crossed over his chest, and his dazed expression made her uncomfortable. Icy fear slithered up her back in spite of the fact she sat next to a burning fire.

"Private Truitt, you scared me." Tyra laid a hand on her chest and attempted a nervous smile. "Did you need something?"

"Just a little company." His lips twisted into a wry grin as his eyes preyed upon her as if she was a feast. Alarm gathered in the pit of her stomach and swirled like troubled waters causing a wave of nausea to overwhelm her. She recognized the looks. The same expression her attackers had held in the barn before Hugh had arrived. Lust.

"I have been watching you these past few days, and a deprived man can only take so much." He licked his lips and tilted his head with a cocky grin. "Since Captain Morgan will not be returning tonight, I thought you and I would have a little fun."

Her heart dropped at the reminder that Hugh would not be coming to her rescue this time—not as though she needed rescuing. She could handle Private Truitt on her own, but what worried her were the consequences if she wounded him—or worse. It was common knowledge she would receive no fair trial, and the British Army would only be interested in vengeance against a Patriot family.

Tyra scrambled to her feet. Remaining on the floor would give her no advantage. Even though she towered over him by several inches, she needed to be on sure footing if her struggle became physical. Over the years, she had learned from wrestling with her brothers the strength in her arms was no fair match for theirs. She depended on wit, speed, and skill.

"I much preferred you on the floor by the fire where you were." He chuckled, stalking toward her. The glint in his eyes made her feel like a sweetmeat at a banquet table. Still, she had to try and reason with him.

"I am sorry, but I am exhausted and would like to retire for the night." Tyra lifted up her palm to stop him. "Please leave."

"Oh, I do not think so," he shook his head and laughed, his dark mustache twitching. "Do you realize how long I have been waiting for an opportunity like this?" He kept coming, slow and steady, as if enjoying the control of his intimidation all too well. "Captain Morgan spent so much time around here with you I began to believe he might have eyes for you himself."

"He did not approve of those British soldiers who tried to attack me in the barn. What makes you think he will allow you to get away with this?" she asked, glancing over at her bed where she had hidden both a sword and a loaded revolver underneath. She tried to assess how quickly she could get past him to her weapons.

"Do not think you will make it by me." He followed her gaze. A moment of confusion clouded his expression as he glanced behind him toward the bed and then the door. "Captain Morgan knows as well as I do soldiers are not punished for taking our satisfaction where and when we can. Major Craig will not allow the captain to punish me too severely. Our superior officers tend to look the other way since we never know from one day to the next if it will be our last. 'Tis the least they can do for us." He shrugged. "And besides, no one will much care about a traitorous wench from the colonies."

Tyra realized he had spent a great deal of time thinking about this to justify his actions. To her disappointment, Private Truitt intended to have his way. He would pursue her, and she would have to fight him as best as she could. *Lord, please help me.*

His expression shifted to determination as he took a deep breath and locked his jaw. Truitt lunged for her, but she anticipated the attack and lifted her leg and slammed it into his middle. He staggered backward, bending over and groaning in pain. Tyra sprinted around him, heading for her weapons. He recovered enough to reach out and grab her foot.

She tripped and fell on her knee. Pain jarred up through her thigh and into her abdomen. Leaning on her elbow for momentum, Tyra kicked at his face with her other booted foot. He turned and she only managed to bruise his jaw, but she had the satisfaction of seeing his neck snap back. Still, he held onto her ankle, his fingertips gouging though her pantaloons and into her flesh.

Tyra reached under the bed, but the revolver was too far. He slammed a fist into her stomach, and she curled inward as her breath left her body. She lay gasping for air. Determined to fight for her life, Tyra forced herself up on her uninjured knee and balled both fists. She slammed her right into his temple and swung with her left, landing her knuckles against his jaw. Knowing she would have to take advantage of her speed and the essence of surprise, she swung another right into his neck and another left into his stomach when he raised his hands to block his face.

With her foot finally free, she kicked him in the forehead. He lost his balance and fell back on his knees, leaving him vulnerable to her foot once again. Tyra brought up her aching leg and kicked him in the crotch. Her goal was to make sure he wouldn't have the ability to take advantage of her. He doubled over. Tyra crawled under the bed and reached for the revolver, her fingers sliding over the dust gathered on the floorboards. Stirring it caused her to sneeze.

"Tyra?" Mama called. "What is all the noise?" Footsteps hurried up the stairs.

This time, Tyra's fingertips touched the cold surface of the gun, and she curled her fingers around it until her palm rested against the handle.

"I am going to kill you, wench!" Truitt sputtered through the blood dripping from his nose. Breathing heavy, he charged at her.

Tyra whipped out the revolver and pointed it at him between the eyes as she cocked the trigger. "I would not advise it!"

He stopped less than two feet away, lifting his hands. A mixture of indecision and rage filled his expression. Tyra kept her eyes trained on him as her mother and Kirk ran into the chamber.

"Tyra, what are ye doing, lass?" She approached with slow caution. "What happened?"

"He tried to rape me, Mama." Tears filled Tyra's eyes as relief and anger mounted inside her. "I have a good mind to put a bullet through his head anyway." She shook the gun at him as she stood to her feet. Her swollen knee caused her to limp. "Kirk, go get some rope. I intend to see Private Truitt does not sleep in comfort tonight."

"Are you going to hang 'im?" Kirk asked.

"Now!" Tyra screamed, as hot tears slipped down her cheeks. Kirk jumped and hurried out of her chamber and downstairs.

"Tyra, I know he deserves it, but do not shoot him, lass. He is not worth the trouble of what it will cost ye with the British Army." Mama walked toward her. Tyra wanted nothing more than to weep in her mother's arms and be consoled as she had as a child, but she couldn't let her guard down—not until she finished with Private Truitt.

⁂

"Our efforts in North and South Carolina colonies have been unsuccessful in moving this campaign forward," said Lord Cornwallis as Captain Blake set a lit candle on the table to afford more light. "The only real thing we have accomplished is a few skirmishes here and there. I thought it was high time to go on the offensive. In order to do so, I had to destroy our extra supplies so we could march quickly and catch up to the Continental Army." He pointed to the middle of the North Carolina map. "Guilford seemed to be the best place to make a stand. "

"But sir, it appears by all accounts we were victorious in this battle," Major Craig said.

"Yes, but at what cost?" Cornwallis looked at him before sipping more port from his glass. "Now I have no supplies, over four hundred wounded men, and the rest of my army is hungry and severely worn out."

"Sir, we have loyal connections in Charles Town where we could appeal for supplies," Hugh said. "I know a few merchants who may be able to spare some goods, specifically new boots."

"Excellent. Write them and we shall send a messenger. I cannot afford to wait on the mail system," Cornwallis said. He turned and glanced at the rest of his officers, pointing to the Virginia map. "In the meantime, I have been studying the landscape of Virginia, and I believe we can wage a better strategic campaign there by combining forces with General William Phillips and Benedict Arnold."

"Will you abandon the campaign in the Carolinas?" Major Craig asked.

"Certainly not," Cornwallis said. "I intend to keep you in charge right here." He pointed to the floor. "We have control of Wilmington, and I want it to stay that way. If reinforcements and supplies arrive by sea as I have long hoped, you will be in a position to receive them without any conflict from the Continentals."

"Sir, what about the rest of North Carolina?" Captain Blake asked. "Will we be waging any new campaigns here?"

"I would like to get our imprisoned officers back from Hillsborough," Cornwallis said. "Based on what you know about the landscape and the Continentals in the area, what are your thoughts? Do you think this is a possible feat?"

"Yes, but we do not know if our officers are still alive or what condition they may be in," Sergeant McAllister said.

"True," Major Craig said, nodding and leaning his palms against the table in agreement.

"Sir, I may have some helpful inside information as you make a decision," Hugh said. He did not want to reveal his close relationship with Tyra, but nor could he allow them to go on thinking there was no point in an attempt to rescue his brother and the other officers. As long as they were alive, it was their responsibility to try and save them. He would do everything in his power to make sure they attempted to rescue them. "In questioning Miss MacGregor, I discovered she sent a letter to her father and brothers through her Indian friends. She asked about my brother and the prisoners in Hillsborough. Her father responded in a return letter saying they were definitely being held and they were still alive."

"Why did you withhold all this information, Captain?" Major Craig asked, his dark eyes simmered like coal. He took a swallow of his port and continued to stare at Hugh as if assessing him. "How do we know Miss MacGregor did not give away pertinent information to our cause? Do you expect us to believe she was merely asking on behalf of your brother and the officers? There had to be a reason behind what she did."

"I confiscated the letter she had in her possession and read it for myself. There was no indication she gave him any other information." Discomfort rocked Hugh's confidence, but he held his own and continued to stare at Major Craig to let him know he had nothing to hide. "It was not my intention to withhold information, sir. We were interrupted after you saw to the loading of your wagon." Hugh pressed his fingertips on the table and leaned forward. "Colonel Morgan is my brother after all, and no one wants to see him free more than me, so withholding information would not be in my best interest."

"Gentleman, we are on the same team here," Cornwallis said. All eyes turned from Hugh back to his lordship. The tension in the room thickened. Cornwallis turned to Hugh. "Are you sure this was the real letter she received and not a second one to mislead you?"

"Yes, sir. I took it from her as soon as we found her. She had no time to hide anything, and she had naught else," Hugh said.

"If that is the case, then you may pursue a strategy to free our men," Cornwallis said. He unfolded his arms, walked to the other side of the table, and pointed to the Virginia map. "I have already written to Sir Henry Clinton that I will be marching to Richmond in a few weeks after my troops have rested and had time to heal from their wounds. Hopefully, our combined forces will be a good match for General Washington. 'Tis time that we change strategies, since we are getting nowhere in the Carolinas."

"We have heard General Greene has moved into South Carolina," Captain Blake said. "Should we pursue him?"

"We will not pursue an attack on the offensive, but if you see an opportunity where we may be effective, I expect you to take it," Cornwallis said. "In the meantime, we will replenish our supplies from Charles Town, while I and my men rest." He turned to Hugh. "Captain Morgan, please contact your friends in Charles Town and request assistance on my behalf. My men are in need of new boots, coats, and weaponry."

14

*I*t was a brisk morning with white frost over the crisp brown grass. The sun slanted over the pink sky as Hugh's senses awakened from slumber. The fresh cold air was enough to freeze a person's lungs. As soldiers emerged from their tents, they built small fires that glowed in the lingering fog.

The smell of burning wood and coffee drifted in the air, teasing him until his mouth watered. His stomach rumbled with hunger at the thought of a hot plate of food waiting on him at headquarters.

As he walked down the dirt street, his boots crunched the gravel and two soldiers drinking cups of coffee straightened at attention. They must have recognized the rank on his uniform as they lifted their hands and saluted him.

"Captain Morgan!" a voice called from down the street.

Hugh turned. Kirk ran toward him, out of breath. Alarm ripped through Hugh's gut. His first thought was of Tyra. With fear in his heart, he hurried to meet him halfway. Kirk doubled over, placing his hands on his knees, and drew air to catch his breath. Hugh waited, trying not to let impatience get the best of him. After a moment, Hugh prompted the lad. "So tell me, what happened? Is Tyra all right?"

"Last night Private Truitt tried to attack Tyra." Kirk gasped between heavy breaths. "She fought him. My sister is a fighter."

"What do you mean?" Hugh asked, as shocked anger roiled in him.

"He tried to violate my sister." Kirk took a deep breath, forcing the words out and shaking his head in disbelief. A number of questions burned in his brown eyes. "She prevented him. I never thought a soldier would do somethin' like that."

"Lad, war makes men do things they would never ordinarily do. It changes them." He put a hand on his shoulder. "Now, tell me what else happened—everything."

"He got what he deserved." Kirk's eyes burned with anger. "Tyra kicked 'im in the face. She and Mama strung him up in the barn and left him there all night long. I have never seen Mama so mad."

Hugh had sensed Truitt didn't approve of his leniency with the MacGregors, but this news surprised him. He sighed with relief, thankful she was fine. He rubbed his face, trying to decide what should be done.

"He should have known not to mess with my sister," Kirk said. "Everyone knows she is the War Woman."

"True. Come with me." Hugh had to adjust his long strides so Kirk could keep up. "I will decide what to do about Private Truitt. Since he is under my command, 'twill be my responsibility to see to his punishment. Does Tyra have any injuries?"

"He punched her stomach and her legs. This morning she complained of being sore and limped on her ankle."

Hugh closed his eyes as thoughts flashed through his mind of what Tyra must have endured. The knowledge Truitt had caused her pain angered him until his head seethed with a pounding headache. He guided Kirk down the street and took deep breaths to ease the tension inside.

Even though Hugh was responsible for Truitt, he could not lash out as severe of a punishment as he wanted without Major Craig interfering. Unlike his former commanding officer back in South Carolina, Major Craig cared little about a colonial girl being attacked and nearly raped by a British soldier, especially if she was from a

Patriot family. The only way Truitt could get the kind of sentence he deserved, Hugh would have to prove he had tried to desert the army or disobeyed a direct order.

As Hugh led Kirk down the street toward the Burgwin House, he considered his options. First, he would have to reassign Truitt to another location. Second, he would have to find a way to keep Truitt from talking about the incident or lying about his role. One matter he was certain of, Private Truitt would not like his comrades taunting him for being beaten by a woman—specifically the War Woman. This fact alone might be enough to convince him to keep silent in order to save his ego.

"What will you do, Captain?" Kirk asked.

"I am not sure, yet," Hugh said, patting the lad on the back. The concern in Kirk's voice was understandable and undeniable. Even though Tyra could defend herself, it was clear he still feared for her safety. Hugh wanted to ease his mind. "This I can promise, Truitt will be removed from your house and someone else will take his place. Your mother and sister will be safe from now on."

They lapsed into silence as Kirk accepted him at his word. Hugh's mind drifted through ideas for a solution. Over the past few months, Hugh had come to know the officers under Major Craig's command, as well as the men under his own command. Sergeant McAllister appeared to be fair, trustworthy, and a gentleman. Hugh had witnessed him admonishing one of his own men for teasing a woman who passed by on the street, saying women should be treated with respect. If anyone could be trusted, would it not be a man like McAllister?

Since both Private Truitt and Sergeant McAllister were under Hugh's command, he could put Truitt under McAllister. Then he could be certain Tyra would be safe when he left town to complete his mission in Hillsborough. It would give his mind the peace he needed to concentrate on the campaign to rescue his brother.

Once they reached the Burgwin House, Hugh pointed to the front steps. "Wait right here for me. I need to go inside and speak to someone. I shall return and take you home." Hugh bent toward Kirk's ear. "Do not worry. I have a plan," he whispered, before bounding up the steps and greeting the soldier standing guard. Most likely, McAllister had already arrived and would be breaking his fast. All Hugh had to do was be patient and wait for the right moment to approach him.

⟨℘⟩

Tyra paused the pedal on her spinning wheel to adjust the thread on the spool. The sound of horses outside distracted her. She rose from where she sat at the top of the stairs on the landing by the bay window. It always afforded the most light during the day. Looking through the pane glass, she could see two horses and two men wearing red coats. Kirk slid off the horse behind one of the men, and the tension inside her eased as she recognized Hugh.

She lifted her skirt and rushed down the stairs and into the kitchen where her mother kneaded dough. "Kirk brought Hugh back, and another redcoat is with them."

"I hope it is not Major Craig," Mama said, dusting her hands on her apron. She untied the strings from around her waist and lifted the apron over her head, folding it nice and neat on the table. "I wonder if Kirk will take them to the barn or here."

"I am sure Kirk will take them straight to the barn," Tyra smiled remembering her brother's reaction to how they decided to handle Private Truitt. "He will want them to see what we have done."

"I dare say, the man deserves what he got." Mama stomped out of the room and into the hallway, leaving Tyra to follow. She had always thought her mother a soft, gentle woman who could never harm a soul even to defend herself, but these last few months she had seen more grit and determination in her mother than she ever thought possible. All these years, Tyra assumed she had gotten her iron will from her father, but now she realized it was a combination from both. Her mother had hidden her strong backbone beneath a humbleness

Tyra had misjudged as weakness. She was glad the Lord had shown her the truth and repaired their difficult relationship.

The horses were tied to the fence posts outlining the barnyard. The men were nowhere to be seen as Tyra and her mother made their way across the half-frozen stiff grass. Mama opened the gate to the fence, and it creaked. Tyra set the latch. They approached the wide, arched doorway and stepped inside to the sound of men's voices carrying in laughter.

Hugh's shoulders shook with mirth as he ended up coughing. The other soldier she recognized as Sergeant McAllister. He chuckled with a wide grin and shook his head as he strolled toward Private Truitt, who still hung where she and her mother had left him. His hands were tied above his head on a thick rope hanging from the rafters. The toes of his feet barely touched a wobbly old wooden table. Private Truitt positioned his legs shoulder width apart, balancing himself on the table as if participating in a little dance.

"After what he tried to do to my daughter, we would have stripped his clothing to further humiliate him as he intended to do to her, but we feared the poor man would die from frostbite," Mama said. She crossed her arms and twisted her lips in an angry frown. "I know about men like him. I met dozens of them when I was not much older than my lass."

"Mrs. MacGregor," Hugh said, clearing his throat and standing to his full height. "I realize you may have extreme anger at men after Tyra's last attack in the barn and what Private Truitt tried to do to her, but not all men take advantage of innocent women."

"I know, Captain." Mama walked toward Private Truitt and rocked the corner of the table back and forth. The man gasped, trying to regain his footing. He closed his eyes and gulped in fear. "Ye forget I have a husband and three sons who feel as ye do. However, years ago when we first arrived to the colonies, I was sold as an indentured servant and into slavery at a bordello in Charles Town, but Malcolm MacGregor saved me."

Hugh's gray eyes widened and his mouth opened with no sound. Sergeant McAllister had a similar expression as his gaze shifted to Hugh and then to Tyra. Both men were rendered speechless, unsure of the appropriate response. If the circumstances had been different, Tyra might have found their reaction a bit comical. Instead, she touched her mother's arm in a show of support and comfort.

"Captain, we would like to know what you shall do with him?" Tyra asked. "Will you let him go free?"

"What would you like us to do with him?" Hugh asked, meeting her gaze. "Ordinarily, I would order him whipped, but by the looks of his face, he has already taken quite a beating."

"His face met the bottom of my boot." Tyra pulled her mother back from Private Truitt before she was tempted to do something else. "But I assure you, 'twas only at the provocation of surviving his brutal attack. Otherwise, I would have never considered such desperation. As for what to do with him, I wish to never see him again."

"Indeed, I promise to arrange it for you," Hugh said, glancing up at Private Truitt with a menacing frown. He pressed a finger on his dark goatee beard pondering another thought. "In fact, I have decided to put Private Truitt under Sergeant McAllister's command, which is why he accompanied me here."

"And I will make sure he is so busy with tasks and responsibilities he will never have a spare moment to get out of line again." Sergeant McAllister strolled over to where Private Truitt hung. "Lad, you shall behave yourself like a true soldier of His Majesty's Royal Army or the consequences will be much worse than this, I assure you."

"Please, let me down. The rope is cutting into my wrists, and my arms and shoulders are aching. My joints feel as if they are being disconnected," Private Truitt said through a swollen lip. His bruised jaw looked even darker under the shadow of a few whiskers that had grown overnight. Dried blood from his nose had crusted on his mustache, around his mouth, and dripped onto his shirt.

"I would imagine you prefer us to keep quiet about what happened?" Hugh lifted a dark eyebrow. "Our comrades might think you are a weak man at being bested by a woman. I can hear their teasing jabs now." He glanced over at Sergeant McAllister. "Although it might be a fitting punishment in itself."

"No!" Private Truitt's toes wobbled on the table until he groaned in pain. "'Twill not be necessary. Have I not suffered enough humiliation?"

"Not in my opinion." Hugh crossed his arms and circled around him. "But I shall give you a bit of mercy, if you apologize to Miss MacGregor."

"What? She is naught more than a colonial trollop." Private Truitt gasped as Hugh punched him in the back of his knee. He swung forward, dangling until he could touch his toes upon the tabletop again.

"Now!" Hugh raised his voice.

"I shall not." Truitt gritted his teeth. "We British should never degrade ourselves like that."

"Then I am afraid you shall remain where you are." Hugh turned and walked away, motioning for the rest of them to follow.

"Wait!" Private Truitt called. "Do not leave me like this."

"When you apologize to Miss MacGregor, I want you to look her in the eyes and do it proper."

Cold, dark eyes shifted to Tyra, and her skin crawled as if an army of ants were all over her. The disdain in his expression filled her with discomfort, and she knew he would be a lifelong enemy and a danger as long as he remained in these parts. He took a ragged breath. "Miss MacGregor, I am sorry for what I did."

Knowing his insincerity, she gripped her hands in front of her to keep them from trembling with anger. She would be a better person than he. She took a deep breath. "You are forgiven."

"Cut him down and get him out of here," Hugh ordered. "I dislike the sight of him." He offered Tyra and her mother an arm each. With relief, she gripped him, finally feeling safe—for the moment. She leaned her head on his shoulder, reveling in the musky scent she had come to associate with him. Closing her eyes, Tyra allowed herself to draw strength from Hugh.

The tents were packed, fires put out, and soldiers were lining up in the street. Hugh stood at attention beside Major Craig and Captain Blake. As Lord Cornwallis mounted his white stallion and other officers waited upon their mounts behind him, the drummers began to beat a tune. Cornwallis lifted his hand and saluted them as he rode his horse down the road. His officers followed and the rest of the army was on the move, marching out of town to begin their journey to Richmond, Virginia.

As they made their exit, Hugh wrestled with mixed feelings. The town had suffered from trying to feed and clothe so many men and caring for the wounded. British soldiers had occupied the streets, every public building, even the churches. In spite of the inconveniences, Hugh preferred the leadership of Cornwallis over Major Craig. Cornwallis didn't try to create controversy among his officers, and he didn't show favoritism. Unlike Major Craig, Hugh never witnessed Cornwallis trying to provoke his subordinates. Instead, he asked questions, weighed the consequences and facts before he made decisions. While he was here, Cornwallis had promoted three men and given others chances to prove themselves.

Hugh dreaded the town's occupation being turned back over to Major Craig's control. The man had done little to earn respect among the citizens of Wilmington. Even the Tories questioned his judgment when they asked for Cornelius Harnett to be released so he could die in peace after so much continuous torture. Hugh looked around at the somber faces of the soldiers left behind under Craig's command and the town's citizens now at his mercy, no one looked as happy to see Cornwallis leave as they should have been.

Once the foot soldiers had departed and could no longer be seen, Major Craig rubbed his hands together and grinned. "With things back to normal, I shall be resuming command at the Burgwin House headquarters." Major Craig peered at Captain Blake. "See to having my things moved from the Mitchell House to the Burgwin House."

He whirled toward Hugh. "Time to formulate our strategies for our mission in Hillsborough."

"Yes, sir." Hugh followed Major Craig into the Burgwin House, down the hall, and into the study. "How soon will we be leaving?"

"I would estimate another fortnight," Craig said. "That will give us plenty of time to figure out how much supplies and food we have left, and we will need to reorganize everything back into place."

"Sounds like a good plan, sir." Hugh sat in a chair across from Craig. He crossed his booted foot over his knee and sat back to assess Craig's behavior.

"I want to know how many wounded soldiers were left by Cornwallis," Major Craig said. "Then I want reports on all the activities of the Whig Party and the Patriot families, including the MacGregors."

Hugh tensed, hoping Craig would not notice. After what Tyra had recently endured, the last thing he needed was Craig poking around the MacGregors looking for signs to trap them. While Lord Cornwallis had been here, Craig had been too occupied to worry about Tyra and her family, but now it appeared he would return to his old ways. Why could the man not concentrate on the war at hand like Cornwallis? Why did he feel the need to prey upon innocent women and children?

"Do you believe Miss MacGregor's Indian friends might be of help with your mission in Hillsborough? They obviously know the terrain and the Continentals trust them." Major Craig walked over to a cabinet and pulled out a bottle of port. He poured two glasses and brought it back to Hugh. Even though he didn't ask for it, Hugh accepted it with a nod of thanks. He didn't wish to insult his superior officer, but he wanted to keep his wits about him as he tried to determine Craig's current intentions.

"These particular Indians dislike us British. By the time we actually track them down, time will have passed and then we will spend more time trying to convince them to help us," Hugh said, hoping to deflect him in another direction. "Do we have any soldiers or Tories familiar with the area? It might be more beneficial than trying to convince Indians to cooperate."

"We could use Miss MacGregor as incentive." Major Craig raised a gray eyebrow. "If they believe she is in danger, we might be able to convince them faster."

"We cannot overestimate her value to them." Hugh scratched the side of his temple trying to stamp down his growing concern for Tyra. He pretended to think through the matter as he struggled to steady his racing heart. "After all, she is only a friend. When it comes down to it, Miss MacGregor is not one of them. They will not risk the entire tribe to save the War Woman, especially if they believe she can save herself."

"But we both know the truth, do we not, Captain Morgan?" Craig lifted his glass and took a long sip watching Hugh's reaction. "Although, you make an excellent point about the challenges of the Tuscaroras."

Hugh bit his tongue to hide his disdain for the man. His number one concern was to protect Tyra and her family. "Would you like for me to ask around some of the Tory families to see if anyone has any connections to Hillsborough?" Hugh leaned forward, holding the glass between his knees as he faced Craig. "I am eager to find out what I can and develop a strategic plan for the mission. My brother will be most helpful to you, of that I can promise."

"Helpful in what way?" Major Craig tilted his head as he took another sip of his port. "He did manage to get himself caught. Perhaps he is reckless or impatient in carrying out his missions. How can I be so sure your judgment is not clouded by your loyalty?"

"My brother is neither, I can assure you. I have spent my whole life living in his shadow, so I ought to know all his strengths as annoying as they are."

"A bit of sibling rivalry." Major Craig straightened in his chair, his interest piqued. He lifted a finger and pointed at Hugh with a wide grin. "You know, I do not believe I have ever detected a threat of jealousy in your tone, until now. Tell me more about your brother."

Hugh took a deep breath, wishing they had not ventured down this road. He had never considered himself jealous of his brother, merely annoyed by him. No matter how angry the two of them got at each other, he never doubted Neil's ability to protect him. He would risk everything, even his own life, to protect Hugh. This was his one chance to give something back to his brother for all the things he had done for him over the years. Neil would never let him down, and so failing Neil was not an option.

"You hesitate. I like that. It means you are about to reveal something personal." Major Craig drained the rest of his glass and set it down on a nearby table. He leaned forward with his elbows on his knees. "Tell me about him. Why would I want to risk the lives of other officers and fellow soldiers to save this one man?"

"First of all, you would not just be saving my brother, but other officers as well." Hugh rubbed a sweaty palm on his knee and set his glass down on the floor beside his chair. Unlike Major Craig, he had no nearby table. "Neil always goes after his goals and will not stop until he achieves his purpose. He stays focused and quickly accomplishes tasks. No matter how hard the situation, he will make a decision and never hesitates. He is responsible and willing to carry on more than his share, but he is also a rule follower. If a mistake got them caught, I assure you, it was due to a decision by a superior officer above him, and Neil merely followed orders. When he was taken prisoner, it was only because he refused to desert his men and his superior."

Silence filled the room as Craig stared at him. He scratched his temple. "Tell me, how do you compare to him?"

"I have always strived to be just like him." Hugh cleared his throat feeling extreme discomfort, but he would continue and say whatever was necessary in order to gain permission to lead an expedition to free Neil and his comrades.

"Not like your father?" Major Craig asked, his lips curled in a slight smirk.

"Exactly. Our father was a poor farmer who could not handle his alcohol consumption." The old feelings of inadequacy and judgment rose inside him. He could not continue this discussion. It had to end.

"It is why you always hesitate to drink." Major Craig's dark eyes shifted to the full glass he had set aside.

Hugh didn't answer. He wanted to change the subject. "Sir, do I have your permission to question the Tory families for valuable connections or knowledge of the Hillsborough area? I could begin my inquisition as soon as tomorrow morning."

Major Craig nodded his white head and crossed his legs. "You may, and begin a list of men you would like to take with you on this mission. From what you tell me, I do not want to miss the opportunity to meet Colonel Neil Morgan. You have my complete permission to do what you must to bring your brother home."

"Thank you, sir." Relief filled Hugh as he stood. "I shall get started right away."

15

yra pulled a pan of hot potatoes out of the Dutch oven and set them on the stone hearth to cool. She rubbed her hands on her apron as the front door knocker vibrated through the house.

"I will get it!" Kirk called, his footsteps running to the foyer.

"The lad is full of energy," Mama said, shaking her head as she sliced warm bread. "It does my heart good to know he can still be happy in the midst of a bloody war. 'Tis all he has ever known, when I think about it."

A moment later, Kirk led Captain Morgan into the kitchen. A young man not much older than her brother Scott followed them, wearing a redcoat and carrying a black tricorn hat under his arm. His hair was as fiery red as Tyra's, including his mustache. The rest of his face was clean-shaven and his hair was short compared to most men she knew.

Hugh's gaze fell upon Tyra, and she forgot about their new visitor. Warmth flooded the pit of her stomach like the invasion of a hot July day on the beach. His somber expression eased into a grin, his gray eyes sparked like a smooth shell left by the sea tide. Hugh stood behind a wooden chair and removed his tricorn hat, gripping it in his large hands. He gave her mother a brief nod in greeting.

"I hope I am not interrupting," Hugh said.

"Of course not," Mama said, shaking her head and gesturing to the chair in front of him. "Please, have a seat and join us. We shall be eating the noonday meal soon."

"Something does smell delicious." He sniffed the air, closing his eyes as if savoring the aroma. "Unfortunately, I did not come to eat, but to introduce Private Garrett Stoneman." Hugh gestured to their new visitor, who first nodded at her mother and then her. "He will be taking Private Truitt's place here at The MacGregor Quest. While he is a loyal Tory, he does have family serving on the Patriot side as well. I feel confident he will uphold the regulations set by His Majesty's Army without being overly cruel and unfair. He has a twin sister and will be considerate and respectful to both of you."

"Absolutely, a lady is a lady whether she is a Patriot or a Tory." Private Stoneman said, nodding in agreement. "My mother raised me to be respectful to women. Things are different here in America. I have been here since I was ten, and I understand it, unlike some of my comrades."

"Then we are most grateful to have ye as a guest in our home." Mama gave him a warm smile to welcome him. "We do not have much left after the British raided what we had, but ye're welcome to whatever we prepare. My lad has taken to hunting and fishing with the neighbors. It gets us by, and since all our servants are gone, Tyra and I do all the cooking."

"To tell the truth, I am looking forward to some good home-cooked meals. The army food I have been eating is not all good for my stomach and tastes like uncooked seaweed most of the time." He chuckled with a good-natured shake of his head. "But I try not to complain."

"A good thing," Hugh said. "Or the army cooks might be tempted to sneak in a few splinters of burnt wood."

"Erh!" Kirk wrinkled his smooth face into disgust. "I plan to go deep sea fishing early in the morning with Mr. Simmons. He took me out on his boat one day last week."

"The army has eaten little fish considering we are so close to the sea." Private Stoneman glanced over at Hugh with a questioning look. "Now that I think about it, it seems strange."

"Not considering most of our men are not fishermen." Hugh shrugged as he pulled out a wooden chair. "Besides, Major Craig rarely lets any of the men travel too far. He likes to keep us close in case of unexpected attacks."

"I suppose, but it sure would be nice to have a bit more variety in our diet." Private Stoneman settled into the seat next to Hugh.

"This afternoon, I might go clamming. In the winter, it helps to wear thick leather gloves and some high boots with tough stockings to keep out water. Otherwise, you could freeze to death. The water is always cold this time of year."

"I do not recollect ever eating a clam," Stoneman said.

"Then yer in for a real treat, lad." Mama flipped her dough and continued kneading it with her palms. "For I make a great bread crust to stuff inside them."

"Mmm, 'tis very good." Tyra licked her lips. "You came on a good day."

"Sounds like I might have to stay a little longer myself." Hugh linked his fingers on the tabletop. "I came to impart some more news."

"And what might that be?" Tyra asked, tilting her head as she regarded his handsome profile. He turned to meet her gaze and her pulse quickened like a bird in flight, but the somber expression in his eyes concerned her.

"I shall be going away for a while. I am not at liberty to discuss the details, but I will be leading a group of men on this mission. Private Stoneman has his orders, and while I have no doubt each of you will be in the best capable hands, I have warned him of your tendency to find trouble, Miss MacGregor."

"Are you suggesting I am somehow to blame for what happened?" Shock vibrated through Tyra at the implication, but it quickly faded into painful disappointment, churning into swirling anger. She crossed her arms and narrowed her gaze upon Hugh. "If it is the case, then you are not the man I thought you were."

"You misunderstand me," Hugh said. "What I meant to say is foolish men cannot help themselves around a beautiful woman such as you. Through no fault of your own, they cannot resist temptation." He cleared his throat in obvious discomfort as he shifted in his chair. "But there are to be no disappearing acts in the middle of the night, no attempts to contact the Tuscarora Indians, and no traveling to town without Private Stoneman. Major Craig still questions the fact you may be a spy for the Patriots, and your legend as the War Woman has conjured more mystery about you than I am comfortable with. Men always want to explore a good mystery."

"Captain, your compliments are shrouded in layers of insults— insinuating I am a spy and a War Woman of mystery," she said. "I confess, I am uncertain as to whether I should be flattered or sincerely angry."

"Mrs. MacGregor, may I have a word alone with Miss MacGregor?" Hugh asked.

"No," Tyra said. "Whatever you have to say, may be said in front of everyone else. Unlike the British Army, I have no secrets to hide."

"Mrs. MacGregor? I promise to behave as a gentleman. I hope I have earned your trust by now." Hugh ignored Tyra and kept his gaze upon her mother.

Tyra felt like stomping her foot, but it would be childish, so she managed to refrain. Instead, she crossed her arms and looked down at the floor to calm her temper before she exploded. If he wasn't careful, he might soon encounter the War Woman.

"Indeed, you have, Captain." Mama nodded, reaching over and touching Tyra's arm. Her gentle touch calmed Tyra as she no doubt intended. "Go, and allow him to speak his mind. The captain's mission could be dangerous, and you might regret it later if you do not."

Tyra's heart twisted in fear at the subtle reminder that he could be riding into danger. Her momentary anger faded like a lit match extinguished by a swift breeze. She met his gray eyes and an overwhelming emotion gushed inside her. If anything happened to him, she would be crushed. She wasn't sure how it had happened or when, but she had fallen in love with Captain Donahue Morgan—a man who served her family's enemy.

❦

To Hugh's relief, Tyra finally agreed to put on her cloak and take a stroll outside. He would have to remember to give her mother a special thank-you for encouraging Tyra to give them this private time together. He didn't know why Mrs. MacGregor trusted and accepted him, but he was grateful. The idea of leaving without setting things straight between them left a clump of nerves in his unsettled stomach.

Outside on the porch he offered her his arm. To his surprised delight, she wrapped her arms around his and held him close. She smelled of sweet honey, and he closed his eyes savoring the moment, painting her in his memories. Being next to her like this lifted his spirits.

He led her down the porch steps and onto the path toward the stables. A mixture of white and dark clouds promised afternoon rain.

Tyra sighed. "Tell me, is this mission dangerous?"

"If things do not go as planned, it could be."

"You cannot tell me, because you do not trust me." It was more of a statement than a question, and one he would not argue against. As much as he cared for her and wanted to trust her, he could not.

Too much mystery surrounded her, especially with the Tuscarora Indians, her fighting skills, and the issue of her loyalty to her family. To make matters worse, she believed in the Continental cause, which made her all the more dangerous. As long as she believed they were fighting for freedom, her newfound affection for him may not be strong enough to keep her constant to him.

He had fought for respect among his betters in England, and deep down he knew no matter how hard he fought or how much of a hero he became, the wealthy in society would always see him as a poor man who should stay within his station. At home, he would always be enslaved to his birth status. It was why he also saved for a commission, and how he could even understand the purpose in the colonials' desire for freedom.

His father had always taught him and his brother that a poor man at least could have the honor of his word and the integrity of doing the right thing. Since Hugh had given his word of loyalty to the king, would it not be worth keeping his honor intact? Or would he be subjecting himself to the tyranny of a king who could choose to do as he pleased upon the whim of his will? Did he want to live the poor life his father had lived, never owning his own land or providing better for his future family? In comparison to Tyra's cause, his own reasons for fighting for Britain paled.

"You do not deny it." Her voice fell into a flat, somber tone.

"The less you know, the better off you will be." He covered her hand lying on his arm. It was nice to feel the soft skin of her fingers. The late April air carried a cool breeze, but not so cold she needed gloves. "Major Craig does not trust you, and if I tell you naught, then he cannot blame you if things do not go well. He believes you are a Patriot spy."

"Do you believe I am a spy?" she asked.

"I do not know, and if you are, I do not wish to know." He lifted her cold fingers to his lips and planted a gentle kiss upon her knuckles. "I could not bear the thought of what the British would do to you if they thought you were."

"I know our countries are at war, and I do not wish any harm to come to you." She gripped his arm tighter. Light-hearted warmth pooled in his chest. It was hard to keep his wits about him when she spoke of things he longed to hear. Knowing this moment could be the last time he ever saw or touched her.

"Tyra, I wanted to talk to you privately before I leave, so I could let you know how I feel," he said. "I could never consider you my enemy. You have come to mean a great deal to me. And while I am gone, I want you to know you cannot trust Major Craig. If you feel you are in danger from him, I want you to go into hiding with your Indian friends. The army does not know where they are located, and they may be your only chance at escaping the cruelty of the British."

"You would warn me against your own superior officers and your fellow comrades?" She paused and turned to look up at him. Her green eyes blinked with vivid moisture. Tyra's nose turned pink and her dark lips trembled with emotion. "I thought your loyalty would be to your king and country no matter what."

"Not over the life and safety of the woman I love," he said, gripping her hands in his and lowering his forehead to hers. "Do not misunderstand me. Since I have pledged my loyalty to the king, I still owe my allegiance to my country. I will continue to fight." He gritted his teeth at the internal war inside him and the emotional pain it caused. "But the end of your life will not cause us to win or lose this war, and I would never risk it."

"You love me?" she asked, her breath hitching in her throat as if she held it.

"Yes, I do, Tyra MacGregor." He pulled back and looked into her eyes, brushing her hair from her forehead under her white cap. "I hope the news does not distress you, even though I am a British officer. I believe I started to fall in love with you the day you saved my life."

"If anyone was to find out, you could be accused of consorting with the enemy and punished for treason." She tightened her hold on him, her eyes widening in fear. "Hugh, you must be careful." She stepped closer, lowering her voice to a whisper.

"Do you mean you feel the same way?" He needed to hear her answer. It mattered to him if they had a chance after the war. Once he fulfilled his obligation to king and country, Hugh realized he could live out his days here in the colonies. With no property or other ties to England, he had no real reason to return, but if Tyra loved him, he had every reason to stay.

"Of course, I love you, but my father and brothers will not like it." Tears filled her eyes as she swallowed with difficulty and gulped. "I fear they will believe I betrayed them. And I could never do so. You must understand."

"We shall figure out all the details later. Right now 'tis enough to know you feel the same way." He chuckled as his thumb circled over the top of her hand. "I must warn you. I am a practical man, and not the romantic sort."

"Hush, Captain Donahue Morgan, I know exactly what sort of man you are," she whispered, leaning up on her tiptoes. "I have something I want to give you before you leave, but I must return to my chamber to retrieve it."

"And I want to give you something now." He tilted his head to the right. Hugh lowered his lips to hers in a perfect fit. Her lips were cool and smooth, and she not only smelled of sweet honey, but tasted like it. They belonged like this, together. The knowledge seared his soul, knowing he would have to be separated from her and it could be indefinite. When they broke apart to gasp for air, Hugh wrapped his arms around her, unwilling to part from her sooner than necessary. He squeezed her against him, thanking God for this precious moment. "I am sorry," he said. "All I have to give you right now is the gift of this memory."

$\mathscr{L}$❤

Tyra missed Hugh over the next few weeks as May set in and cold weather melted into warmer temperatures. She wondered if he ever thought about her or if he was too busy on his mission. Often, she prayed for his safe return as she prayed for her father and brothers.

Private Stoneman settled into their home and brought them a bit of humor each night, as well as news from Wilmington on the days he reported to headquarters. Little activity occurred in town. With Cornwallis's troops gone, people settled into their former routines and life grew quiet again.

While Tyra and her mother longed to attend church as before the war, St. James Episcopal church still served as a hospital and the Presbyterian church was filled with Tories who didn't welcome Patriot families. Unlike the MacGregors, most of the Scottish immigrants and descendants were loyal Tories since they had pledged their allegiance to the king after the Scots were subdued during the Jacobite War in Scotland. The Scots started the Presbyterian church in Wilmington and continued to run it.

Her mother held family devotions each Sunday, and Private Stoneman joined them. He prayed and participated in their discussions as if he belonged to the family. At times, he brought a new perspective or insight they had not considered.

One afternoon Tyra went for a stroll through the woods and found the large tree where she left her letters for Red Fox. She crouched down and peered inside the hollow nook where she saw a letter lying under a rock. Her heart thumped with anticipation, wondering what news it may bring.

She grabbed the letter and stood, leaning against the tree. Breaking the seal, she unfolded the letter and another letter fell out. It was addressed to her mother. She tucked it away and concentrated on reading the one addressed to her.

Dear Tyra,

I received your letter of concern. As you have guessed, we were at the Battle of Guilford Courthouse, but please know we are all alive and well. Alec suffered a flesh wound from a bullet that grazed his shoulder. He also suffered a brutal beating from an officer twice his size while in combat, but we are thankful Scott was able to save him.

Callum suffered a bullet in his side, but the surgeon was able to remove it. No vital organs were penetrated. The Quakers at New Garden tended to him while he recovered. Callum was one of the blessed ones with no serious infection. By the time you receive this letter, we will be marching into

South Carolina. We do not know if Callum will be well enough to join us. If he must stay behind with the Quakers, I have every confidence they will give him the best care.

The Battle of Guilford Courthouse was bloody and gruesome. We are blessed to be alive. We lost a lot of good men, including several officers. Therefore, I have been promoted to the rank of Sergeant. Scott and Alec have been assigned to my command.

Please tell Kirk I am proud of him for how well he has provided for you and your mother with his fishing and hunting skills. Thank you for the update you gave us of home. Please give Kirk and your mother all our love.

Da

Tyra closed her eyes and tried to imagine the bloody tumult they must have endured. She wondered if Callum had stayed behind and was now separated from her father and brothers. Should she try to go to him? What if he had not stayed behind? There was no way to know, and she could not keep asking Red Fox and the Tuscaroras to travel such long distances to deliver messages on her behalf.

Perhaps she should write a letter to the Quakers at New Garden if she allowed Private Stoneman to read and approve it. Surely, Major Craig would not have a reason to deny such a simple inquiry? At any rate, it was worth a try.

Tyra pushed herself away from the tree and headed back toward the house. She needed to find a way to get the letters to her mother without Private Stoneman seeing them. The last thing she needed was for him to find out about the secret tree.

As she walked through the forest, the morning sun grew warm and bright. It filtered through tree limbs now full of budding leaves. The temperature grew warmer with each passing hour, and birds sang as they flew above her from branch to branch. Spring was now in full bloom, and she longed to go for a stroll on the beach. Perhaps the next time Kirk went clamming, she would go with him. It would be nice to get out of the house and away from here for a while—to go somewhere peaceful and calm. The sea always made her feel at peace and closer to God.

16

$\mathscr{A}$ slight breeze shifted in the air, cooling the hot sweat dripping down Hugh's neck. All morning the sun beat down, heating the temperature until his redcoat felt more like a cat's claw scratching against his skin. He slapped away a fly buzzing at his ear, wishing the cold weather had lasted a little longer to keep the insects away. He had brought fifty men with him to Hillsborough. Twenty-five waited in the woods on the main road leading into town. The rest were crouched low among tall grass hidden by a row of bushes in a similar position as he.

Last night by the campfire they had discussed the rescue plan in detail. Each man knew his role in the plot. Now, they waited for the right opportunity.

An ache cramped his thigh, and he shifted in discomfort. His hip rolled over on something which felt like a lump. Hugh glanced down to investigate and recognized the brown pouch he had fastened to his side. He pulled it out from under his weight and untied the drawstring. Reaching his finger and thumb inside, Hugh pinched the soft layers of red hair tied by a green ribbon. It was attached to a folded piece of paper. On it, Tyra had written, "Please return to me, my love." This was the gift she had given him before he left. Whenever he could, Hugh took it out and cherished it. He lifted the strands to his nose and sniffed the honey scent still lingering.

Horse hooves approached. On full alert, Hugh shoved Tyra's gift back into the pouch for safekeeping and retied the drawstring as he sat up to peer through the bushes. A young Patriot rode toward them, wearing a complete soldier's uniform, just the thing they needed. He was alone, most likely riding out to deliver a message or scout a nearby area for a planned attack. The lad gave them the perfect opportunity they had been waiting for.

Hugh leaned back and looked at one of his men. He motioned to the lad riding by them and nodded. The British soldier returned the nod in understanding and crawled away through the high grass toward the thick woods where their horses were hidden. He would take the shortcut to where their comrades waited and warn them about the rider's approach so they would know the order to capture the lone Patriot.

The Continentals most likely thought it was safe to send out a lone soldier. Cornwallis had moved into Virginia, and Major Craig had his troops stationed in Wilmington. The only other threat was the British colonel, David Fanning, who had set up camp at Cox Mill on Deep River. While he was closer than the others, he was still a good distance away, and Hugh's scout had witnessed no evidence any of Fanning's men were in the area.

Hugh motioned for his men to stay down and wait. Crickets chirped around them and various birds sang. As long as no snakes showed up, Hugh would be fine staying in the brush. He had heard the North Carolina colony was filled with poisonous copperheads, and since his arrival, he knew the rumor about alligators was certainly true. In his opinion, it was better to be here on dry ground than in the swamps with flesh-eating alligators.

Even though no more than thirty minutes had passed, it seemed like hours before Hugh's soldier returned. He informed Hugh that the Patriot soldier had been captured and a British soldier of the same size had volunteered to put on his clothes and pretend to be a Patriot messenger from another camp.

"Good work, soldier," Hugh said, slapping him on the back.

Hugh turned to the right and then the left to study his men lined up behind the bushes. He whistled to gain their attention. Hugh circled his hand in the air and pointed back to where their horses waited. He set out crawling through the thick grass and weeds, knowing his men would follow his lead.

Once they reached the other men, Hugh learned they had bound, gagged, and tied their prisoner to a tree. The men gathered around Hugh, waiting for further instructions.

"Men, you did well," Hugh said, glancing around at their expectant faces. "We need to wait until tomorrow before we send one of our own as a Patriot messenger. Then, they will be less suspicious anything happened to the man they sent out."

"Who volunteered to be our Patriot messenger?" Hugh asked.

"I did, sir." A young man with brown hair and dark eyes stepped forward from the group of men. He looked no more than ten and six. Hugh met his gaze, a reminder of himself years ago. Most likely, the lad came from a poor family with no future. A military career was his only hope as it had been for Hugh and his brother, Neil.

"Thank you for your bravery." Hugh said, glancing from his worn boots covered in dust, up his stained white breeches, to the faded redcoat hanging from his bony shoulders. Satisfied he would fit the prisoner's clothing, Hugh nodded with an approving grin. "You look about the same size and age." He crossed his arms as he circled around the lad. "You even sound like a colonist. Indeed, you will be most believable." Hugh paused and tilted his head in question. "Where are you from? And what is your name?"

"My name is Private Benjamin Folk, and I was raised in Elizabethtown near Wilmington." The lad straightened to his full height and jutted out his chin as if to say he came from a family worthy enough to do this deed. Hugh cleared his throat, well aware of how it felt to be unworthy in the eyes of others.

"Well, soldier," Hugh said with a grin to put him at ease. "We have a lot to go over. Not only will you be required to don his clothes and ride in as a Patriot soldier with a message, but you will need to know which camp you came from, the names of the commanding officers located there, and specific details in case you are questioned. If they have any soldiers who have been transferred from there, you will need to know enough to keep from raising suspicion."

"Sir, our scouts have returned. I will need to give you a brief report." A soldier stepped forward, a few years older than Private Folk. "They found a local Tory who was able to draw a map of the inside."

"Very well," Hugh said, walking toward a log where he sat. "See that our horses are cared for while I hear the scout's report. By nightfall, I want to have a solid plan in place. We need this mission to be successful with no loss of lives."

✐

It was midmorning as Tyra carried a bucket of ashes to the shed behind the well. The door creaked open where she left it wide to let the light filter inside. She poured the gray matter into the ash hopper and picked up a bucket of water they kept in the shed. Tyra emptied the last of the contents into the ash hopper and checked the lye dribbling into the bottom container. It would take a while for the rest of it to finish making, but she had enough to use for now. She pulled out the container and replaced it with a new one.

Stepping outside, she smelled the fat boiling in a kettle hanging over a fire her mother had built. A mixture of smoke lingered in the air. Tyra carried the lye to her mother, who straightened and watched her approach. She brushed strands of blond hair from her forehead to the side and tucked them behind her ear.

"I have never liked the unpleasant task of soap making." Mama lifted a wooden spoon with her other hand. "Is there enough lye?"

"I think so," Tyra nodded, handing the wooden container over.

Her mother peered at it and stirred the contents with a spoon. She scooped a pile onto the spoon and turned it over, watching it drop. "It seems thick enough. I would test it to see if a potato could float on it, but we do not have any."

"It looks thick enough to float a stone," Tyra said, hoping her mother would be satisfied and not require her to make more lye.

"Indeed, 'twill have to do." Mama nodded and bent to scoop out the lye into the pot. "Now we shall wait for it to come to a boil."

"Mama, redcoats are coming!" Kirk called from where he sat perched in a nearby oak tree. He shielded his eyes with one hand as the bright sun filtered through the leaves.

"Is Hugh with them?" The question slipped out before Tyra could hide her eagerness. Her mother turned a concerned gaze upon her, but to Tyra's relief, she didn't say anything.

"No, but Private Garrett Stoneman is." Kirk scrambled down the trunk of the tree and dropped to the ground, landing with a thud on his feet. He rubbed the remnant of the bark from his hands. "None of them look happy."

Tyra watched as half a dozen redcoats rode toward them, the dust from their horses kicked the air like tiny clouds in their wake. The men charged toward them as she wondered what they could possibly want. Her heart grew heavy and burdened knowing Hugh wasn't among them. A sudden thought struck her. What if Hugh had not survived? Fear lurched in her gut and took her breath away as she waited to find out what they wanted.

They slowed their horses to a halt, and Major Craig speared them with a gaze meant to intimidate them, but his full attention landed on Tyra. "We have had a couple of prisoners escape, and I have reason to believe you might know something about it."

"Who escaped?" Tyra asked.

"Does it matter?" Major Craig asked, his stony expression hardened. "The Tories tell me you are part of the Whig party and have been working as a spy."

"How could she?" Mama asked. "Tyra has been here the whole time. What evidence do you have?" Mama walked toward him with her hands on her hips, her voice full of determination.

"Sir, I knew she would be here just like I told you she would," Private Stoneman said.

"Do not undermine me, Private," Major Craig said, his tone stern like a taskmaster.

"Yes sir." Stoneman hung his head in shame.

"I do not need evidence, all I need is a confession. She knows more than she is telling us. And I intend to get it out of her." Major Craig pointed at Tyra. "Seize her!"

Two redcoats dismounted and headed toward Tyra. Her mother jumped in front of her as Kirk held onto Tyra's arm and gripped her tight. Her brother trembled with fear as his cold fingers curled around her flesh.

"I told you, she has not left this property in months!" Mama's voice rose in a panic. "She has done naught for you to accuse her."

"She is just as guilty for what she knows and does not tell as what she could possibly do," Major Craig said. His gaze shifted to her mother with a wicked stare. "She has no need to leave this property since the Indians come to her and are willing to take and bring messages as she directs them."

"I will not allow you to take her!" Mama said, planting her feet between them.

"You have no choice. How do you expect to stop me?" Major Craig asked, stalking toward Mama as if he would strike her. "Now that Captain Morgan is gone, she has had plenty of time to betray us, especially when Private Stoneman reports to me for duty in town." He pointed over her shoulder at Tyra. "You are coming with us."

"Nay! Ye cannot have her." Mama stood her ground as he came toward her. Major Craig swung his hand across his body until the back of his knuckles slapped her across the face. Her head snapped back, and she staggered to the side.

Tyra gasped and bent to steady her mother, but two of his soldiers grabbed each arm, preventing her. Kirk crouched to catch their mother. The soldiers yanked Tyra and pulled her so hard the muscles in her shoulders locked and strained. She cried out in pain, but her natural reflex would not allow her to remain inhibited. She kicked the man on her left in the crotch. When he bent over in agony, he released her and she swung around and slammed a fist into the gut of the other man holding her. Surprise crossed his expression as his eyes widened. Before he could regain his wits to react, Tyra grabbed the handle at his side and pulled his broad sword from its sheath. Footsteps ran up behind her. She stepped to the side and ducked to miss the swinging fist of another soldier. Tyra swung the sword up to Major Craig's neck.

"Back away or I shall run this blade through him." Tyra glared at the two soldiers who paused to stare at her. Indecision crossed their features as they exchanged glances, uncertain if they believed her. "They do not call me the War Woman for naught. I would have come peaceably with you, but your mistake was hurting my mother."

"Miss MacGregor, a blade is no match for the swiftness of a pistol," said a soldier still sitting atop one of the horses. He aimed a black pistol in the direction of her mother. "I suggest you rethink your position. You may manage to slay Major Craig's neck, but would it be worth the bullet I would put through your mother's head, or the one my comrades will shoot through your brother?"

Tyra's heart sank at the realization of the truth. She had the ability to take down the major, but could she live with the knowledge of risking her mother and brother's life in the process? Never. She would do anything to save them.

"Mama, let me go with them. Remember, Kirk needs you." Tyra relaxed her hold on the sword and allowed Major Craig to take it from her grasp.

"Bind her!" Major Craig grabbed Tyra by the hair until her scalp burned. He shoved her toward his men. "You will pay for that."

"Nay!" Mama screamed as she ran toward Tyra, but Major Craig shoved Tyra toward a soldier and grabbed her mother's wrists and held her tight, pressing her arms behind her.

"Your daughter is right." He shoved her away. She fell backward. "Save the lad's life or lose them both." He shrugged. "I care not."

Tyra's heart pinched as her mother dropped her head in a flood of tears. Kirk bent over her, trying his best to comfort her. A soldier jerked Tyra's hands behind her and tied them with a corded rope that dug into her skin like a blade. Satisfied they were leaving her mother and brother in peace, Tyra held her breath as she was hauled over a redcoat's shoulder and thrown across the lap of another soldier who sat upon a horse. The action crushed the breath from her, and she grunted from the bruising it caused her ribs.

"Subdue her before she causes us anymore trouble." Major Craig's voice came from behind. "I do not trust the little minx."

Something hard, like the hilt of a pistol, cracked the back of her head. Lightning jolted her brain, slicing through the middle as if it was splitting in two, and then an intense throbbing radiated all over. Everything went black, and her hearing faded into blissful silence.

※

Hugh and his men waited in the woods while Private Folk rode into Hillsborough pretending to be a Patriot messenger from another camp. Last night they had gone over the details of what he would say, including the officer names and descriptions of the other camp. Hugh had confidence the lad was ready and could pull this off, but it didn't stop him from pacing back and forth between the trees, wearing a trodden path in the dirt.

One hour turned into two, three, and then four. They had no other choice, but wait. Patience was one virtue Hugh had always struggled to achieve. His brother had always been the one who could wait out anyone—outlast anyone. If a man could survive imprisonment with the Patriots, he knew in his heart it would be his brother, Neil.

The canter of a lone horse drew Hugh's attention. He paused in mid stride and looked up meeting the gazes of his men lounging nearby against tree trunks. Curiosity lingered in their eyes, but not as much as the concern in Hugh's heart.

A soldier hurried toward them, winding around trees and skidding to a halt in front of Hugh. He took a moment to catch his breath as he saluted. "Private Folk is returning, and he looks well," the lad blurted. "No one else appears to be following."

"Excellent." Hugh nodded. "Go back to your station and inform us if aught changes." Hugh saluted him and turned around, his mind already deep in thought, planning their next action.

"If Private Folk succeeded in his mission, then 'tis time to engage in phase two of our plan," Hugh said, using his booted feet to brush away bark and discarded limbs to uncover fresh dirt. He walked over to an oak tree and picked up a sturdy stick that wouldn't break when he pressed it into the ground. His men gathered around the area he had cleared. Hugh drew a long line. "This is the main road leading into Hillsborough." He drew more lines, creating a map.

Private Folk walked his horse toward them, grinning in triumph. "They not only fell for it, but fed me a nice meal and showed me where they are keeping our men in the town jail. I saw a man who resembles you, Captain Morgan. I would wager all I own that he is your brother. He has dark eyes, the same black hair, and walks with an air commanding respect. They have most of our men in a crowded jail cell, but your brother and three other officers are in a different cell together."

Relief and rare sentiment washed through Hugh. An image of his brother came to mind as the two of them enlisted into His Majesty's Royal Army with pride and excitement. After a few weeks they were assigned to separate regiments. Neil received his orders first, to board a ship bound for the Revolutionary War in the American colonies. Hugh had followed six months later. When it came to part ways, Neil had embraced him and slapped him on the back.

"I shall write when I can. Remember, when we both return, we shall be respectable men." His hard brown eyes had pinned Hugh with a stare. "No one will ever think of us as the lads of 'Drunken Morgan' ever again. We shall make our own way in the world." Neil had gripped Hugh's shoulders and shook him for emphasis. "Work hard. Rise through the ranks. Only then, will other men realize the true value and honor in us. We will change the way people see the Morgan name—forever."

Hugh blinked, returning his attention back to the present. He gave Private Folk a level stare, determined to read the truth in his expression, lest he try to ease Hugh's concern. "He is in good health then?"

"Indeed, a little thin and pale, but I suppose it is to be expected." Private Folk nodded with a shrug. "He has a full beard and mustache. I doubt he has seen a bath in a while, but for the most part, he looked well compared to some of the others. He did not have any visible marks to indicate a recent beating. I was told they hoped to exchange our officers for theirs."

Clenching his teeth, Hugh turned from his men and walked away. If Major Craig had not tortured Cornelius Harnett until his death, and now General John Ashe, they could have had leverage to negotiate an exchange of prisoners. Rage rushed through him at the waste of life and the opportunity to avoid risking more lives in a rescue attempt. He rubbed a hand over his face and regrouped his thoughts. It would do him no good to concentrate on what could have been. He needed to work with what he had in his possession. Hugh kneaded the back of his tense neck and turned to face his men.

"If this is the main road into Hillsborough, where is the jail?" Hugh asked, pointing at the line he had drawn with his stick and handing it over to Private Folk.

"The main road becomes Churton Street inside the town." Private Folk drew several squares on both sides of the road and then a rectangle at the end of the road. "Along here are houses. The jail is behind the courthouse on the corner of Churton and Margaret Lane. Eno River runs parallel behind the jail. The woods are on the other side of the bank."

"How many cells do they have on the inside?" Hugh asked.

"Four, with black iron bars. They are on the backside of the building, but the officers are on the left side, here." Private Folk pointed to the side of the rectangle. He drew a square with a steeple. "This is the community church, on the other side across from the courthouse."

"Did you ask them if they had room for a transfer of three more prisoners?" Hugh asked.

"I did." He nodded, leaning on the end of the stick. "They said they could take them in and put them with the officers. They expect the other British prisoners to arrive within two weeks."

"Excellent." Hugh walked around the drawing, considering their options. "How well is the place guarded? Does anyone patrol the back where the river is?"

"Two guards patrol the back, but I was not there long enough to know when they exchange guards. There is a back door. They have two guards at the front entrance of the jail, and there were no side entrances. I noticed three guards at the courthouse, while several were walking up and down the street."

"What about the church?" one of the men asked.

"I saw no one leaving or entering the church, so I am not sure," Private Folk said. "The church or the back might be the best entry points. They do not have as many men as we do in Wilmington. I get the feeling everyone knows each other. A new face would be easily recognized. It would be risky to seize one of their guards and pretend to be one of them."

"Not if we substitute the two guards for two of our men at the back." Hugh pointed at the river. "Once the exchange is made and we have two men on the inside, we could time it so we attack from the front and have twenty-five attack from the woods across the river. Is the river wide and deep?"

"It did not appear to be, but I only saw it from a distance. It looked narrow and dark . . . muddy." Private Folk scratched his temple. "We could wade or swim through it."

"Good. Set a man to watch for the timing of the guard exchange and once we know it, we shall go in."

17

"Tyra MacGregor, wake up!" a man called to her.

A heavy fog clouded her mind into a sea of oblivion. She tried to concentrate on the voice, but couldn't place to whom it belonged. A throbbing pain pierced through the center of her brain, overwhelming her senses and drowning out all awareness.

"Tyra, do you hear me?" The same voice penetrated through her mind again. "You have to wake up."

Something rattled and she jerked, fearing she would be beaten again. Had she been beaten? She couldn't tell. Except for the pain taking over her head and destroying her thoughts, she felt pure numbness everywhere else.

"If Malcolm MacGregor was here, they would not have done this to her." The voice continued to rant. "How dare they leave a woman like Tyra MacGregor down here in the dungeon."

She was in the dungeon? Who was talking? The man obviously knew her father. Could he be trusted? Questions continued to abound in her mind as she fought for coherency. She rolled over on her side and winced as pain sliced through her ribs. Sensations began to seep back into her numb limbs. Her face pressed against the cool floor and uneven bricks lined her body.

With a groan, Tyra set her palms forward and pushed herself upright. She blinked several times, willing her vision to clear from the black abyss claiming her. Instead, her ears picked up on sounds of footsteps and men's voices in the distance. Nearby, she heard scratching and shuffling, followed by the rattle of a chain.

"Good, you are finally coming 'round." The whispered voice coaxed her to fight the sleepiness. "Why are you here? What do they know?"

Tyra tried to swallow, but her dry throat was too parched and swollen, as if someone had gagged her with a linen handkerchief. She blinked again and this time a faint light filtered to her eyes. Thank God she wasn't blind! A whimper of relief escaped her throat.

"'Tis all right," the voice coaxed her. "Never let them see your fear or know the depth of your pain. These animals will prey upon your weakness if they can discover it."

"Mr. Simmons?" Recognition dawned. "Is it you?"

"I knew you would know my voice." Pride beamed in his whispered tone. "Now, tell me how you came to be here. Why would they throw a lady into a dungeon with the likes of us men?"

"Where?" Tyra flinched, pushing herself upright with success this time. She blinked, making out the light from a torch on the wall down a hallway. Horizontal and vertical black bars were before her, confirming she was indeed being confined in a dungeon or something similar. She pulled her knees to her chest and wiped the grime from her palms onto her skirts.

Unbidden panic and fear rose up to her throat until she forced it down with a gulp. More pain sliced through the back of her head, taunting a wave of nausea at the top of her stomach. The stench of urine and rot teased her nose. A queasy sensation engulfed her, pulling Tyra to her knees. She heaved, but her stomach was empty of all contents. The muscles in her middle contracted.

She sat back and closed her eyes on the pain throbbing through her head. Why did her head hurt so much? Reaching up, she touched the swollen spot on the back of her head, and gasped at the sticky dried matter in her hair. Blood. Where had she gotten this wound?

Images of Major Craig flashed through her mind riding toward them with redcoats surrounding him. Her mother and brother had been there. Fear sprung through her as she searched her mind, trying to force herself to remember more details.

"Where are my mother and brother?" The words croaked from her hoarse throat.

"They brought you in alone," Mr. Simmons said. "We were hoping you could tell us what happened."

"We?" Tyra opened her eyes, turned to the right, and winced as another dizzy wave swam through her. Men lurked in the shadows of the cell beside her. She was in a cell all by herself up against the far wall. "Who else is in here?"

"I am General John Ashe." A shadow moved forward, revealing the outline of a man. It was too dim to make out the details of his features, but she recognized the name. He was a well-respected Continental General—someone the redcoats would have taken great pride in capturing.

"The rest of us do not matter," came another Southern drawl from the shadows. "We are all men who have supported the Patriot cause either as Continental soldiers, local volunteers, or political Whigs who helped raise financial support and supplies. Why are you here?"

"I am a Patriot like the rest of you," she said.

"Unlike the rest of us, you are female," General Ashe said with a chuckle. "In case you have not noticed, no other women are among us. You must have done something pretty severe."

"'Tisn't what I have done, but what they suspect me of having done," she mumbled with sarcasm. "They still have no proof, and I have confessed to naught. If I had known I would end up in this nasty place, I would have done plenty to make it count, I assure you."

More laughter erupted. Footsteps sounded down the brick hallway.

"What is all this racket?" a redcoat demanded, his hands on his hips. He turned to Tyra and stalked toward her cell. "So the little miss is awake, is she? I have orders from Major Craig to bring her up as soon as she comes to." He rattled the keys attached to his side, selected one, and slipped it into the lock. It clicked, and he opened the bar door. He pulled out a revolver with his other hand as he grabbed her arm and jerked her to her feet.

"Easy. They warned me about you, War Woman." He laughed. "I would as soon put a bullet through your pretty little head as be bested by the likes of you. If I am ever taken down, 'twill be by a man in battle, not a woman pretending to be a warrior."

Tyra cringed as his grip tightened, but she refused to wince or let him know how much it hurt. Instead, she smiled, determined to inflict as much fear in him as he had tried to do to her. "I am sure it is what the other men thought . . . until I succeeded in putting an end to them."

✑❤

Hugh and his men waited in the woods across the river. Two Continental soldiers patrolled with their rifles over their shoulders. The men started at opposite ends of the building facing each other. They passed by and walked away from each other until they reached the end of the building and turned to repeat the same process.

Motioning for two of his men to move forward, they discarded their redcoats and sank into the water and disappeared beneath the surface. The guards turned and continued their patrol. By the time Hugh's men came back up for air, the guards had turned again. Everything was timed to a perfect schedule. The men waited in the shadows of the bank until the guards turned again. Both slipped from the water, careful not to cause any splashing noises. One hid behind the trunk of a tree, and the other took cover behind a rock.

They waited until the right moment, and when the guards turned again, they ran toward them. With hands covering their mouths, they used their knives and took them down, dragging them behind some nearby bushes. A few moments later, they emerged wearing the Continental uniforms and resumed the guard patrols.

Hugh lifted his hand in the air, waved it to the right and then the left, and gestured his men to move forward. On cue they slipped into the water and waded across. He waited until his men were on the other side and in place before turning to stride away. His horse was tied to a tree and flicked a few flies from his tail. Hugh took the reins and mounted up, urging his horse into a canter.

A few moments later, he reached twenty-five of his men still waiting in the woods outside of town. He maneuvered his horse around and faced them. "Load your weapons." He waited as his men pulled out their powder and poured it into their rifles and loaded the bullets. "Line up! Forward, march."

In unison, they marched on the town, knowing the guard would have changed. The other twenty-five men would have already taken over the jail and started subduing the courthouse. They met little resistance as they marched down Churton Street. Gunfire exploded from the direction of the courthouse and jail.

"Charge!" Hugh raced his horse ahead, leading his men into the skirmish awaiting them. His soldiers on foot broke into a run behind him. A few redcoats were fighting in front of the courthouse as residents rushed inside to take cover. Several peered through windows as they pulled curtains aside.

A child around the age of six clung to a pole in front of a trading post.

"Keep going!" Hugh ordered, swerving his horse in the direction where the child was frozen in fear.

A woman ran outside the building, fear etched across her face as her eyebrows narrowed and dented her forehead. "Johnny!"

"Take him inside so he will not get hurt," Hugh ordered, pointing to her son.

She ran to the child and scooped him into her arms. A moment later, they disappeared inside.

Hugh moved toward the courthouse. Bodies and wounded men were lying in disarray in various places on the street. He rode past the courthouse to the jail. Two more bodies lay on the front steps. One of Hugh's men stood outside with his rifle in his hand.

"We took the town, sir." The soldier nodded toward the jail behind him. "The others are releasing the prisoners now."

"Thank you, private." Hugh dismounted, tied his horse to the front post, and stepped up to the front porch. Inside, three Continentals were locked into a cell. Redcoats were everywhere. Hugh recognized Private Folk and grabbed his arm. "Round up all the Continental soldiers who are not dead or wounded and lock them inside a cell. Throw the key into the river. We do not want the residents to be able to release them any time soon or they can come after us. We need enough time to get away."

"Hugh!" a familiar voice called over all the other conversations and noise. A man came toward him. He had long black hair, a full beard and mustache. "I knew you would come. I never doubted for a moment my little brother would come through." He stepped around people as his pace increased. Hugh looked into the brown eyes he had known growing up—the brother he had always looked up to and strived to be like.

His brother wrapped him in a huge embrace, squeezing the breath out of him. Hugh coughed as Neil stepped back and surveyed him, brushing his knuckles against the stripes of Hugh's rank on his shoulder. "So you are a captain now?"

"I achieved the rank back in South Carolina." Hugh nodded. "My first set of soldiers were attacked by Indians. I was the only survivor, but I made it to Wilmington and where we shall go after today. Major James Craig has taken the city." Hugh gave more orders and slapped his brother on the back. "I hear you are now a colonel?"

"True. I was a captain like you for about a year." Neil gestured around them. "But judging by this expedition, you will soon rise in rank yourself."

Hugh took a deep breath. At one time the idea of rising in rank would have enticed him and made his blood pump with excitement.

Now he had achieved his goal and rescued his brother, the only thing fueling him was the thought of getting back to Tyra MacGregor.

A soldier shoved Tyra into the study where Major Craig waited to interrogate her. She stumbled, but gritted her teeth and regained her balance as she jutted out her chin and squared her shoulders. Tyra met Major Craig's dark gaze as he stood from behind his desk and walked out to meet her. He braced his palm against the corner of his desk with a crooked grin.

"Glad you finally woke. You need to answer a few questions." He reached over and lifted a piece of parchment paper, holding it up by the top corners. "Do you recognize this?"

Tyra leaned forward and pretended to squint. "'Tis a map."

"I know what it is!" He stepped toward her in irritation, shaking the paper in her face. "Have you seen it before? Did you draw this?"

Keeping her attention focused straight ahead, Tyra shrugged. "'Tis hard to say, sir. I have seen plenty of hand-drawn maps of Wilmington and the surrounding area. I cannot remember all of them. 'Twould be an impossible feat."

"Do not be insolent with me." He shook the map in front of her again. "You would remember this one. 'Tis of this very house!" Major Craig pointed to the floor as his face reddened and his temper flared. He stood in front of her, bracing one fist on his hip, and leaned an inch from her nose. "I will ask you one more time. I would advise you to consider and weigh your answer carefully, War Woman. Did you draw this map of the dungeon downstairs leading to a set of underground tunnels beneath the town?"

Tyra jerked her head back with an intriguing gasp and widened her eyes in fake surprise. "So 'tis true? There are underground tunnels beneath the town?" She reached for the map with her bound hands, as if eager to discover the contents of a bag of treats. He yanked the map out of her grasp and turned to walk away. She gasped again.

This time, pretending to be frustrated. "How am I to answer your questions if I cannot see to what you refer?"

Confusion dented his forehead as he stroked his bearded chin in thought. He took a deep breath as he paced toward the far window. "How long has the rumor been around that underground tunnels exist beneath Wilmington?"

"For as long as I can remember—ever since I was a wee lass." Tyra folded her hands in front of her and bit her bottom lip, wondering what he would do next. For the moment, she had succeeded in confusing him enough to save herself another beating, but she had the impression he was not yet convinced of her innocence. "Any native of Wilmington could have drawn the map—providing they knew the details of each tunnel. Some of us have always questioned if the rumor was even true." She shrugged. "Children hear things, but one has no way of knowing what has been embellished for the sake of a good story. I once heard the tunnels were made as an escape route for Blackbeard, the pirate."

"Next, I suppose you will tell me Blackbeard hid his treasure in the tunnels." He whirled, his dark eyes bulging in anger, as he strode toward her. Major Craig reared back and slapped her across the face. The sting continued long after his hand left her cheek. Tyra swallowed the pain as she stood still, waiting for another attack. Instead, he walked away.

"I want facts. For now, I am willing to drop the matter of the map since it is quite possible you may not know about it. There are others who could be tortured into revealing what I need to know about the map . . . like Mr. Simmons."

Tyra stared at the floor, careful to show no reaction. Poor Mr. Simmons. At his age, she doubted the man would last long under such duress. If only she had run Major Craig through with her sword when she had the chance, at least then she would have prevented him from killing more souls like Cornelius Harnett. As soon as the thought crossed her mind, remorse seized her chest.

"How do we know the information you provided to Captain Donahue Morgan was not a trap? You wanted to be rid of him from your home, and once you discovered his brother's capture, you devised a clever plan he would not be able to resist." Major Craig walked behind his desk and set the map under a ledger. He leaned on his palms and met her gaze. "Admit it. You wanted to be free of him so you could resume your spy activities for the Continentals."

"I admit no such thing." Tyra set her jaw at a stubborn angle, determined not to say more than necessary. "I laid no trap for Captain Morgan."

"Fair enough. The safe return of he and his men will determine whether or not you have betrayed him." Major Craig stood and paced again as he shook a finger in the air. "Still, there is the matter of how you managed to smuggle letters to and from your father through the Tuscarora Indians. If you could do so, how do we know you have not provided the Continentals with pertinent information in regard to our activities here in Wilmington?"

"You do not." Tyra kept her tone even. "But I have saved Captain Morgan's life, and you do have evidence I provided your army with accurate information to rescue British officers. The Continental Army could also accuse me of spying for you."

"And why would the War Woman, who has such a formidable reputation, a known Patriot, go against her family, friends, the cause they fight for, and all she believes?" He circled around her, slow and stalking, tracing a finger along the path of her cheek where he had probably left a handprint. "Unless she has developed an attachment to a particular officer on the side of the enemy?" Fear paralyzed Tyra as she met his gaze. "Tell me, do you fancy yourself in love with Captain Donahue Morgan?"

18

*O*ne of the men gave up his horse to Neil since he was weak from food rationings and was also a ranking officer. Hugh rode beside Neil like old times with the exception of the marked changes in Neil. His brother was harder than he remembered, lacking a depth of emotion that concerned him.

As they rode into Wilmington, a feeling of homecoming overwhelmed Hugh. Images of fiery red hair and wide green eyes warmed his heart. Hugh reached down and patted the pouch hanging from his side, content to know Tyra's lock of hair was still with him. Soon he would be able to hold the real woman in his arms, providing he could find a convenient moment away from everyone else.

With the sight of so many redcoats everywhere, he could feel the tension in his soldiers subsiding. They no longer felt the need to keep looking over their shoulders and considering if every nearby noise was a possible movement from the enemy. Conversations increased among the men as they marched down Front Street toward the Burgwin House.

"Halt!" Hugh raised his hand and they all came to a complete stop. He turned to face his men. "You completed a successful mission. You have every reason to be proud of what you have accomplished. We brought back three of our officers and several other prisoners. Take the rest of the night and relax. Report at daybreak on the morrow."

Hugh guided his horse around the house to the back where the stables were kept. Soldiers on duty opened the gate upon their arrival. Hugh and his brother rode through with the others on horseback. The hooves clip-clopped against the graveled dirt.

"Welcome back, sir." one of the soldiers called behind them.

They dismounted and left their animals in the care of the stable lads and entered the house from the back courtyard. Candles were lit on the wall as their footsteps clicked down the hallway. The smell of melting wax and smoking cigars lingered in the air. Voices echoed from the parlor. Hugh followed the sounds knowing his brother and the others would follow.

He paused at the entrance, his gaze searching past Sergeant McAlister and Corporal Jackson on the settee by the window. Captain Gordon and Major Craig were both sitting in wing-backed chairs in front of the fireplace where a small fire blazed. To his relief, no women were present, so they would be able to give their direct report right away. All conversation died as their eyes turned toward him. Hugh stood at attention and saluted his commanding officer.

"Major Craig, we are reporting back from our mission. It was a success, sir." Hugh stepped to the side and allowed his brother and the other two officers to enter the room. "This is Colonel Neil Morgan, Lieutenant Fox, and Second Lieutenant Adams. We brought back twelve other soldiers and sustained no loss of life. Two of our private soldiers have minor injuries."

"Glad to have you back," Major Craig said. "I must admit, I had worried the information Miss MacGregor provided might lead you into an ambush, but I am pleased to know I was wrong."

"I told you I believed she told the truth," Hugh said, wondering why Major Craig would continue to question his judgment. He swallowed and tried to maintain a nonchalant expression. If he showed fear or too much concern, Major Craig would know his vulnerability. He couldn't afford to put Tyra in such a position. He met his superior's dark gaze and recognized an expression of arrogance not present before his departure. "Did something happen while I was away?"

"Only necessary precaution, but rest assured, all is well." Major Craig twisted his lips into a grin. He lifted one side of his gray eyebrow. Hugh had always wondered how he did it without moving the other eyebrow. "I am convinced where you are concerned, the War Woman has a soft spot."

"What do you mean?" Hugh asked.

"Never mind. I think it is more important that you know we had two prisoners escape. Fortunately for us, General Ashe was not one of them. We found a hand-drawn map of several underground tunnels aiding them in the escape. It was in the possession of a Mr. Simmons, a man known to be a Patriot and possibly part of the Whig Party."

"And what did you do?" Hugh walked toward him.

"We have Mr. Simmons in the dungeon below. He has not revealed much information, but he is an elderly man and would not be able to live through too much torture. I have waited to see if he might divulge something to Miss MacGregor."

"How is she part of this? Is she here as well?" Hugh glanced at Sergeant McAlister for a clue. He looked down at the floor, but not before Hugh recognized a moment of guilt in his expression. Fear snaked up Hugh's spine as he thought of the dungeon cells below. He couldn't imagine her being down there with the other prisoners, but he always suspected Major Craig was capable of corrupt things. If Craig already thought an attachment had formed between him and Tyra, he needed to be careful in how he proceeded.

"I am not completely heartless. I put her in a cell by herself next to the others. None of them could lay a hand on her." Major Craig stood and walked past Hugh, brushing his shoulder. He bent over the center table and poured a goblet of port and took a deep swallow. "At first, I thought she might have had something to do with the map." He shrugged. "I thought she might have been working with the Whig Party, but she knew naught, and she has not discussed anything with Mr. Simmons in the cell beside her, as I had hoped."

"Do you mean you believe she is innocent?" Hugh asked, saying a silent prayer for Tyra to have favor.

"For now." Major Craig nodded. He took another swallow from his goblet and grunted. "I suppose you could take her home." He waved a hand in the air.

Hugh turned and strode from the room. His brother sighed in confusion and followed him. Hurrying down the back stairs, Hugh entered the darkness where the cool dampness lurked. His breath came in short gasps, and it felt as if his heart would beat out of his skin. The stench of urine and decay accosted his senses, and he wrinkled his nose. He imagined rats and nasty rodents and grimaced.

"Hugh, slow down! What in the world could be possessing you?" Neil complained behind him.

"Sir, can I help you?" A soldier bounced to his feet. Even in the dim torch light he looked to be no more than ten and six.

"Major Craig is releasing Miss MacGregor. Please get the key," Hugh ordered.

"Yes, sir." He launched into motion at once, rushing over to the last cell by the wall and pulling out the key ring hanging from his side. The man sorted through several keys and inserted it into the lock. He turned until it clicked into place and swung the bar doors open.

To his surprise, Tyra didn't immediately run out to him. Instead, she moved in a slow gait without uttering a sound. Her wild hair was not confined upon her head as usual, but fell around her shoulders in disarray. The torch light revealed dark smudges on her face, but it was to be expected considering where she had been. She stumbled. Hugh bent and swept her in his arms.

"No, consider your reputation," she whispered, pushing him away.

"Nonsense, Major Craig sent me to get you," he whispered back. "I am so sorry."

"'Twas not your fault," she whispered by his ear. Her hot breath brushed his skin, sending unexpected shivers over him.

"The blame is mine to bear just the same," he said. "This would not have happened had I been here."

"What would you have done? Taken on the whole British Army?" She coughed, shaking in his arms.

He pressed his lips to her ear. "If need be."

"Hugh, what is the meaning of this? Have you developed an attachment for some lowly Patriot?" Neil asked, following behind him. "If you have, I will not stand for it. Not after all I have been through."

"Neil, I will explain everything in time, but you must bear in mind people are more than Patriots and Tories."

"Not in our world," came the curt reply.

❦

"I can walk on my own," Tyra said, as Hugh gathered her in his arms and slid down the side of his horse. "I have never been a weak woman. Put me down at once."

"Believe me, no one will ever be able to claim you weak, my dear." Hugh said. His warm breath sent a slight tingle over her body as he gathered her close.

The front door swung open and her mother and Kirk came running out. Private Stoneman followed at a much slower pace.

"Tyra, I have been so worried about ye. I visited every day, but the wretched man would not allow me to see ye." She laid a hand on Hugh's arm and glanced over at Neil in question. "Are ye all right, lass?"

"I am." Tyra nodded, kicking her feet until she caused Hugh to lose control, and she slipped from his arms and landed on her feet. "See? All I have are a few bruises, and I am in need of a bath. I want to be clean. Please . . . I just want a warm bath. The place reeked and was so nasty."

"Of course." Mama wrapped an arm around her and led her toward the house and up the front steps. "I shall heat some water right away." She glanced behind her. "Captain Morgan, would you mind bringing up the tub to Tyra's chamber? You will find it in the chamber where Private Stoneman has been staying."

"Indeed." Hugh nodded. "This is my brother Colonel Neil Morgan. We were able to rescue him from a Continental prison in Hillsborough. He will be staying with us."

"Nice to meet ye, Colonel," Mama said. "Ye're welcome to our home. I made some warm biscuits earlier, and set them out on a plate in the kitchen. Please help yerself, while I tend to Tyra."

"Captain, how did you convince the major to let her go?" Private Stoneman asked. "I tried to tell him she was innocent, but he was determined to take her."

"I know you did your best, Stoneman." Hugh slapped him on the back as he held the door open and they entered the house behind the women. "After questioning her, he realized she was innocent. I merely arrived back in time to bring her home."

"What did they do to you, Tyra?" Kirk followed his mother and sister up the stairs from the foyer. "You have a handprint on the side of your face. No one ever gets away with doing anything to you."

"Kirk, stay down here with the others," Mama said. "Tyra and I need some time alone. Get the soldiers anything they need."

As Tyra climbed the stairs, her arms and legs ached with heaviness. She breathed in the scent of home, baked bread from the kitchen, honey from her room, and the pine floors. Even though she longed to lie down in her cozy bed and sleep the fatigue away, Tyra desired to scrub the filthy grime from her skin even more. Her stomach rumbled as they walked into her chamber. Perhaps afterward, she could eat a warm cooked meal.

"Did anything else happen while I was gone? Did more redcoats come?" Tyra asked as she sank onto her bed. Mama settled beside her.

"Nay, it has been quiet." Her mother reached over and squeezed her in a tight embrace. "I am so glad yer home where ye belong." She took Tyra's hand in her own. "Tell me the truth. Did they violate ye?"

"No, I am so grateful I did not have to endure that. They put me in a dirty cell alone. It reeked of urine and waste. Rats were everywhere. I was afraid to sleep lest I wake up the next morning with my toes missing."

"Kirk is right. Ye have a handprint branded upon yer cheek." Mama cupped her swollen face with the gentleness Tyra had come to know and love about her mother. "How did this happen?" Her voice lowered to a whisper.

"Major Craig slapped me when I gave him an answer he disliked." She took a deep breath. "Mama, I am fine. You will see it when I get ready to bathe, but I have some bruising on my ribs where they shoved me into the brick floor and a painful lump on my head." Tyra lowered her voice to a whisper. "They have Mr. Simmons and found the map of the tunnels. Major Craig is after everyone in the Whig Party. Mr. Simmons is fine for now, but I do not know how long he will last in his condition if they beat him."

"They do not know ye drew it, do they?" Mama asked.

"He suspected me, but I managed to distract him until he gave up or believed I was innocent."

A knock sounded on the door. "I brought the tub." Hugh's voice came through from the other side. Mama went to the door and opened it. Hugh carried the tub inside and set it in the middle of the chamber. He straightened and placed his hands on his hips. "Is there aught else I can do?"

"No." Tyra said. "I am more than grateful you brought me home. I would imagine you need some time to get reacquainted with your brother."

"We had plenty of time to talk from Hillsborough to Wilmington. Right now, I am more concerned with your well-being. Tyra, I should have been here."

"The major was determined, and he had an army. You would not have been able to stop him." Tyra stood and folded her hands in front of her. "If you had tried, things would not have gone well for you, so I am glad you were away."

Hugh walked around the tub and glanced at her mother and back at Tyra. "My brother has changed." He lowered his voice to a whisper.

"Neil developed a severe hatred for colonials while imprisoned. Do not take him into your confidence. And remember, he outranks me."

Tyra gulped. She had endured enough from these tyrannical redcoats. She hoped she would not end up regretting Hugh's success in rescuing his brother.

Hugh stared at the written parchment paper nailed to a tree on Market Street. It was a proclamation from Major James Craig. The order was for all males in the region to give their allegiance to His Royal Majesty or forfeit their property and life by August one, seventeen eighty-one.

Sweat ran between his shoulder blades and down his back as the heat climbed. The summer temperature was just as bad in Wilmington as in Charles Town. He wiped his eyebrows before more sweat could drip into his eyes and sting like the salty sea. Hugh fingered the official seal Major Craig used on his documents.

Was this in retaliation against the two escaped prisoners? If so, Major Craig could be determined to punish all Patriots and Whig members on a personal level. He wanted to take away their property, wealth, security, and crush their spirit. Hugh wished he could keep the residents out of the war, but it was illogical to claim the enemy was not gaining supplies, motivation, and soldiers from the residents.

If they had until August to respond, it meant they had a little over a month to make up their minds. This would give the British plenty of time to harass and bully them into changing their loyalties from the Continentals to the British. The ploy had worked in the past. He shook his head and looked down the street. A soldier was nailing another proclamation to a tree on the other end.

"Good idea." Neil walked up and stood beside him, pointing at the proclamation. "A clever way to call out the traitors to England. I daresay, if measures like this had been taken a long time ago, perhaps this war would have already ended. For myself, I will be glad to return to civilization as soon as possible. 'Twill do me good to wash my hands of these miserable colonies."

"Neil, I am afraid your experience as a Continental prisoner has clouded your judgment on the land as a whole. There is much value and a wonderful future here in resources, wealth, and opportunity. The king sees it and believes in it or he would not be fighting so hard to keep it." Hugh walked away, but Neil kept pace beside him. "Although if I had endured what you did, my viewpoint may not be as bright as it is right now."

"Exactly, I knew you would see things my way." The familiar arrogance Hugh remembered from their past slipped back into Neil's tone. It was a disappointment to Hugh, but he chose to ignore it. "I spoke to Major Craig this morning. He is a likeable fellow and formidable in his policies. I think he was right in bringing Miss MacGregor in for questioning. One can never be too careful, especially in times of war, even where females are concerned."

"He was wrong," Hugh said, clenching his jaw to keep from saying more. The last thing he wanted was to argue with his brother after only being reunited with him for such a short time. This morning Neil had ordered Tyra and her mother about as if they were his personal servants. He needed to make it a priority to remove Neil from The MacGregor Quest. "I have been meaning to mention an idea to you. Major Craig has assigned British officers to live in Patriot homes for dual purposes. One, it gives us a bit more comfort than the tents outside. And two, it affords us the opportunity to witness the behaviors, actions and conversations of the families who would be most likely form a local resistance."

"This is exactly the sort of clever thinking I admire in the man." Neil adjusted his black tricorn hat as he glanced over at Hugh. "How would this arrangement benefit me?"

"Well, with Mr. Simmons imprisoned, there is no one occupying his home. Two of the soldiers who were there before left with Lord Cornwallis. He only has a lad living there. He is the same age as Kirk.

The Simmons are neighbors to the MacGregors, so you would still be close by."

"I see." Neil tugged at his brown goatee beard. "And is this house most agreeable?"

"I have only seen it from the outside, but it appears to be. You could choose a couple of soldiers to occupy it with you. 'Twould give you extra time to investigate the man's study. Perhaps you could learn about his activities in the Whig Party, if he was active at all. As he is getting older, 'tis my understanding he is less sociable."

"And who told you? Miss MacGregor?" Neil's words cut through the air as he slanted his eyes at Hugh. "Allow me to give you a bit of brotherly advice. I know you, Hugh. You favor the girl and spend too much time in her company. In fact, you treat her and her mother as if they were royalty, not the family members of the traitors they are. Major Craig has noticed it or he would not have insisted on taking her and questioning her the way he did. You need to be careful. She is naught but trouble."

"Your brotherly advice is noted." Hugh kept his gaze on the road before them, hoping the anger in his tone wasn't evident. He would not deny the attachment he had already formed to Tyra. Neil did know him, and if he looked into his eyes, he would see the truth. Hugh cared for Tyra . . . loved her. There was not anything he wouldn't do to keep her safe. "If you are agreeable to taking over the Simmons house, let us go submit the idea to Major Craig."

"Indeed, I like the idea." Neil grinned, his brown mustache curled.

Hugh prayed Major Craig approved the idea. It was the best way he could think of to get Neil safely away from the MacGregors without raising further suspicion regarding his feelings for Tyra.

19

$\mathcal{T}$yra waited while her mother broke the seal to the letter just delivered by a messenger. She closed the door and leaned against it, reading the first few lines. Her forehead wrinkled in distress as her free hand flew to her chest. She gripped her shawl. Tyra gulped as her mother slid to her knees. Tears squeezed from her eyes, crawling down her cheeks. A keening cry gushed from her throat and echoed through the foyer.

"Mama, what is it?" She rushed to her mother and crouched by her side. Thoughts of her father and brothers crossed Tyra's mind as fear vibrated through her.

No answer came. Instead, her mother rocked back and forth, groaning as her shoulders shook with grief. Tyra wrapped her arms around her mother and fought the urge to grab the letter and read it for herself. She could only think of a few things to upset her mother this much, and everything that came to mind filled her heart with sorrow.

Mama groaned again, and Tyra's heart ached as she tried to comfort her. Mama sniffled and shoved the letter over her shoulder, pressing it into Tyra's hand. She wiped the tears on her cheeks with the back of her hand, her breaths coming in quick gasps.

Tyra straightened out the wrinkles. She glanced at the scrawled letters and recognized her father's handwriting. The words blurred as tears filled her eyes. She didn't want to read these words, but she had to. Tyra blinked away the tears as they streamed down her cheeks. Her mother settled into silent tears.

Dear Lauren,

I considered not writing this letter, but I gave my word if anything happened to our sons, I would not hide it from you. I regret I must deliver the news this way and cannot be there in person to console you.

Scott was mortally wounded in the Battle at Ninety-Six in South Carolina. I will save you from the details, but I will at least tell you he was shot in the stomach. I know what you are thinking and the questions running through your mind right now. I know you so well. Please know he did not suffer long, and he was not alone. He died in my arms with Callum and Alec on each side of him.

He had enough coherence to ask me to pray the Lord's Prayer with him. He could not say all the words, but his heart was in it, and he prayed what words he could. Lauren, I want you to know his faith was strong until the end. He never doubted what he believed. He asked us to tell you he loves you. His last thought was for you. The lads and I buried him ourselves. Callum made a wooden cross and carved his name into it.

Callum has fully recovered. Alec and I are well. Our hearts are broken with grief as I know yours will be. Break the news to Tyra and Kirk as gently as you can. Comfort each other and know our thoughts will be with you all. I pray this war will be over soon, and we can be reunited again.

With all my love,

Malcolm

Tyra thought of Scott's blue eyes and blond hair as he climbed trees and splashed in the ocean waves as a young lad. Scott was always creative and full of life. He enjoyed teasing them and having fun. Whenever he was around, people smiled. They couldn't help it.

Only ten and eight, and now he was gone. Pain squeezed her heart as she dropped the letter and wrapped her arms around her mother. They wept together until they lost sense of time. Later, the door opened and Kirk walked in, almost stumbling over them.

"What happened?" Kirk bent over them with his hands on his knees. His green eyes widened, and he bit his bottom lip in concern.

Mama sat up on her knees and cupped his right cheek. "There is no easy way to tell ye, son. Scott was killed in battle."

"How?" He rubbed a hand through his red hair as his eyes filled with unshed tears. "What I mean is . . . was he shot, stabbed by a bayonet, or hit by a cannon ball?"

Mama dropped her face in her hands and wept. Tyra rubbed her back in an effort to console her. She wasn't surprised by Kirk's questions, but none of them knew the specific details and their father's letter alluded to the fact there was more. Perhaps it was best they didn't know.

"Go on. Read Da's letter for yourself." Tyra gestured to the parchment paper on the floor. "Right now I need to help Mama to a chair and make us some hot tea."

Kirk bent to retrieve the letter as she and their mother walked down the hallway past the stairs.

"I will be fine," Mama said. "Although a hot cup of tea would be nice. My throat hurts from crying so much." Her voice broke, and she covered her mouth. "I cannot believe I will never see my son again."

"Do not think on it." Tyra gulped back more tears as their footsteps echoed in the hall. "Should I contact Aunt Carleen and Aunt Blair?"

"Aye, I suppose so." Mama nodded. "A letter should do. We will not even be able to have a burial service."

The front door opened, and Tyra glanced back. Hugh and his brother walked in, followed by Private Stoneman. Tyra and her mother kept walking toward the kitchen as Kirk went to meet them and deliver the unfortunate news. A moment later, footsteps hurried down the hall. Hugh appeared at the threshold as Tyra built a new cooking fire.

"Kirk told us what happened," Hugh said, glancing from Tyra to her mother. "Is there aught I can do?"

"Nay." Mama shook her head. "There is naught ye can do or say to bring back my son. I shall be glad when this whole wretched war is over."

"I am sorry," Hugh said, clearing his throat in discomfort.

"Please . . . leave us alone." Tyra poured water into a pot from the water bucket and hung it over the fire. She didn't blame Hugh, but he was part of the army who had killed her brother. Right now, she wanted to spare her mother further pain. The redcoat she and his men wore would be a constant reminder. His gray eyes faltered as he dropped his gaze. Tyra turned from him, hoping he would do as she asked.

Footsteps departed from the kitchen and paused outside in the hallway.

"What are you doing?" Neil asked. "They are the enemy. How can you sympathize with the enemy? As traitors, they got what they deserve."

"'Tis called compassion, Neil," Hugh said, lowering his voice. "What has happened to you? These American colonists are our brothers, most of them are from England. How can you be so indifferent?"

"I have no compassion for traitors!" Neil shouted. "They are lucky we have had mercy not to execute them."

A shuffle followed in the hallway. Tyra rushed to the threshold to see Hugh gripping his brother by the lapels of his jacket and shoving him against the wall. The force of Neil's body thumped. "We will have mercy for women and children."

"Hugh?" Tyra stared at them, fearing what might happen next. "You do not want to fight like this. Believe me, I just lost my brother. Life is too fragile."

"Oh, so she is on a first-name basis with you, now?" Neil threaded his fingers through his dark hair in disgust. He shoved Hugh away. "Major Craig was right. You have developed an affection for a colonial woman . . . our enemy. I have never been more disappointed in you."

❧

Hugh woke at dawn to the smell of coffee and weeping. He sighed, thinking about the MacGregors' grief and the argument Tyra witnessed between him and his brother. Would she hate him now? He wouldn't blame her if she wanted nothing to do with a man who was part of the army who killed her brother. Sorrow grated upon his nerves until he felt raw and exposed.

He sat up, flipped the cover back, and swung his legs over the side. During the night he had sweated in his bed. The heat was almost unbearable at times. He rubbed his face and walked over to the basin where he poured out clean water to wash. Hugh bent over and splashed water on his face, grateful for the cool liquid. He dressed and left his chamber.

The aroma of coffee enticed him to the kitchen. Mrs. MacGregor sat with her arms crossed on the table and her head resting on the crook of her elbow. Her breaths came in an even rhythm as she slept.

"Shush." Tyra pressed a finger to her lips. Dark circles cradled both her green eyes, swollen and bloodshot. Her face was pale and her red hair fell around her shoulders in unruly waves. Had they been here in the kitchen all night?

His chest constricted as he swallowed with difficulty. He nodded in understanding to not wake her mother. Keeping his steps quiet, Hugh walked over to Tyra. "May I have some coffee?" he whispered, leaning toward her ear, wishing he could gather her in his arms and soothe the pain away.

She stepped aside and jerked her head in the opposite direction. The cold snub pierced him, leaving him rooted in the same spot, wondering how to convince her of his innocent sincerity. Perhaps if he remained patient, watched his words, and continued to comfort her as best as he could through her grief, she would stop blaming him. He hated this deep rift between them and wanted things to go back to normal, to how it was before yesterday.

Tyra strode to the cupboard and pulled out a cup. She poured black coffee and carried it to him. As she held it out, she met his gaze. Something in her expression had changed. The warmth he had always cherished in her eyes had vanished, but the tingle shooting up his arm from her fingers when they brushed was still real.

"I am sorry for your loss." Hugh kept his voice low. "Neil left last night and didn't come back. I doubt he will return. I suggested he consider staying at Mr. Simmons's house so he would not be here to taunt and watch your every move. He has changed from the person I remember."

"But what about Darren?" Tyra asked, crossing her arms and rubbing her hands above her elbows as if uncomfortable. "We cannot leave him all alone in the house with your brother. He would consider Darren the enemy since his father is in a British prison and his older brothers are Continental soldiers. Darren is only a lad of ten and four. He lacks maturity and will surely provoke your brother—unknowingly."

"True. I forgot about the lad." Hugh rubbed the back of his knotted neck, swollen from stress and fighting with his brother. He stepped toward Tyra, but she backed away from him. He paused, unsure how to win her trust back. "I will go by there this morning and pick up Darren." He sighed and dropped his gaze from her accusing eyes. "Tyra, I was thinking of you and your family. 'Twas an honest mistake in sending Neil over there with the lad."

Her mother stirred and shifted, but continued to slumber. Hugh hoped Private Stoneman and Kirk would sleep a little longer. He listened for sounds upstairs and in other parts of the house, but all he heard was her mother's even breathing. Several moments passed without a word between them until Tyra took a deep breath.

"Please, bring Darren here. We will take care of him, and he will be more comfortable with Kirk." She brushed a lock of hair from her forehead. "Is there a chance Major Craig will release his father?"

"I doubt it." Hugh shook his head. "I am concerned Mr. Simmons may be used as an example for the Whig Party and other Patriots in a similar way as Cornelius Harnett. I do not recommend giving the lad false hope."

"I understand." Tyra's green eyes filled with tears. "I will prepare something to break your fast before you go."

"I want to go with you." Kirk stood in the doorway with his arms crossed and his lips twisted into a frown. "Darren is my friend. If he is hiding from the British, I will know where to find him."

Hugh started to refuse, but what the lad said made sense. If Darren had hidden from his brother and his men, Kirk could save them time from unnecessary searching. He turned to look at Tyra, but she scowled at her brother in disapproval.

"Absolutely not," she said in a resolute tone, crossing her arms over her chest. "I mean no offense, but I do not trust Colonel Morgan, and he does outrank you. Our family has suffered enough these past few weeks."

"Your sister is right." Hugh nodded, swallowing back the difficult lump rising in the back of this throat. "I shall go for Darren alone, but I would appreciate some tips on where to find him if he is hiding."

⟡

After Hugh left, Tyra convinced her mother to rest in her chamber. Tyra was relieved her mother would now have some solitude, if only for a short while, until she awakened again. Private Stoneman had broken his fast in silence, then disappeared down the hall.

Tyra's eyes were heavy and swollen from a lack of sleep and continuous weeping. Every muscle in her body ached as if she had spent the whole of yesterday working out in the field. She sat at her desk and rolled her neck from shoulder to shoulder. It brought temporary relief as she sighed.

She opened a bottle of ink and took out a piece of parchment paper. She wrote the first letter to her Aunt Blair in Charles Town and the second letter to her Aunt Carleen. The words she penned brought renewed grief to her heart. At one point, she had to turn her head to keep the tears from dripping on the page.

Once she finished the letters, she hurried downstairs and found Private Stoneman in her father's study. He sat behind the desk writing in a journal he used as his report. She cleared her throat, and he looked up in surprise. He paused and sat back in the black chair.

"Come in." He waved her inside. "I am sorry about your brother. Captain Morgan asked me to stay here in his absence. Is there aught I can do for you?"

"Actually, there is." Tyra strolled toward him. "I have written letters to my aunts to inform them of my brother's death. Could you see these letters are delivered?" She handed them over to him.

"Indeed." He accepted the letters and read the inscriptions she had scrawled on the front of each.

"Thank you." She turned and left the study. As she walked through the house, it occurred to her she had not heard from Kirk in a while. She raced upstairs and checked his chamber, but it was empty. A quick search throughout the house proved he must have gone outside.

Tyra stepped out on the front porch and breathed in the heat. She searched the stables, but Kirk wasn't there either. Fear tightened in her throat as memories flashed of her attack in the barn. Taking a deep breath, she headed in that direction.

"Kirk?" Tyra called.

"I am over here." His familiar voice came from the back where something scraped back and forth.

Tyra found him bent over a workbench carving on a slab of wood. Little shavings of splinters lay sprawled all over the dirt floor. Mixed with strands of hay and straw. A lit lantern hung on a peg above his head, casting a contrast of yellow light and dark shadows.

"What are you doing?" Tyra asked.

He sniffed and used the back of his hand to wipe tears from his smooth skin. The color in his face deepened as he looked away in shame. His chin trembled, as he struggled not to cry in front of her. He scratched the side of his left eyebrow as his mouth twisted in emotional agony. Tyra knew the look. Kirk was determined to try and be strong. She waited until he could speak.

"I know Scott is already buried someplace else, but he deserves to be in the family cemetery with the rest of us. Even if his body cannot be here, I want something to mark his memory, so people will not forget him."

Tyra's heart constricted in pain as if someone held it in a fist, twisting it back and forth. She stepped closer, hoping the words she was about to speak connected with Kirk. He needed to know he wasn't alone in his grief. "Kirk, none of us will ever forget him."

"I know, but what about after us? When everyone who knew him is gone?" He held up the slab of wood he had been working on. "I am making this to mark the fact that Scott MacGregor lived on this earth—and he was loved by his family." His voice broke, and he turned away.

"Kirk, unfortunately it happens in every generation, but there is a place where Scott's name is written and will never be forgotten. 'Tis the Book of Life." She leaned forward and touched his arm. "*He that overcometh, the same shall be clothed in white raiment; and I will not blot out his name from the Book of Life, but I will confess his name before my Father and before his angels.*"

Tyra had never been great at remembering Scripture, but she was grateful this verse had come to mind when she needed it. Sensing it would be best to let him contemplate the message she had given him, Tyra gave his arm a gentle squeeze. "I love you." She turned and walked away, praying a silent prayer for God to mend Kirk's young heart and give him peace.

As she walked back to the house, Tyra felt a sudden drain of energy. She had tried to be strong for her mother and brother, but her own grief tugged at her. A moment of weakness, flushed through her tired body and her shoulders might as well have been carrying a cannon ball. The heaviness weighed her down like an anchor lodged deep in the dirt. Loneliness engulfed her until she longed for Hugh's return. How could she be craving the comfort of a man who may one day have to choose between his allegiance to his country and a budding relationship with her?

She shook her head as if ridding herself of the unwanted defect in her heart and closed her eyes. *"Lord, give me strength."*

20

It took a little convincing, but Hugh finally persuaded his brother to allow Darren to come with him. On the way to The MacGregor Quest, Hugh told the lad about Scott MacGregor's death. Darren was quiet for a moment as he looked out over the terrain around them, viewing the flowing Cape Fear River and the pine trees on the other side.

"How is Kirk?" Darren asked.

"He is as well as can be expected under the circumstances." Hugh relaxed his hold on the reins and tried to keep the tension out of his neck and shoulders.

Over the last few months he had come to care a great deal for the MacGregor family, and he did not like seeing them in so much pain. His role as a British soldier in their home had always caused him a bit of discomfort, but now it was worse. "We have not talked much since he discovered the news."

"I know how he feels. I lost my brother two years ago in the war," he said in a somber tone.

"I am hoping you will be able to cheer him up," Hugh said.

"I hope so, too." Darren glanced up at him, his dark eyes wide with questioning. "You are different from Colonel Morgan. I am glad you came. Thank you."

"At one time my brother and I were much the same. We had it hard growing up and as the older one, he always thought it his responsibility to take care of me. Our Father worked all the time, and when he was not working, he drank." Hugh thought back to the small prison cell where his brother had spent the last few months of his life. "Being a prisoner of war has made him hard."

They lapsed into silence as he drove down the lane and The MacGregor Quest came into view. The white house with three pillars on the front porch was a welcome sight. Not only the people here, but the place had grown to his liking as well. The overcrowded streets of London, and the dank smell of the city had transformed into a place representing depression. Here, he enjoyed the wide-open spaces and the fresh air, especially the salt air. The majestic cleansing about it drew him.

Tyra stepped out on the front porch in a blue gown with a grey shawl wrapped around her shoulders. Her red hair slipped out from under her white cap like a halo around her face. Private Stoneman walked the horse from the stables toward her. Tyra must have heard him approaching in the wagon since she looked up with a smile and waved. Private Stoneman followed her gaze and turned. Hugh let the wagon roll to a stop, set the brake, and jumped down. Darren leaped to the ground on the other side and hurried around the front.

"Hello, Darren," Tyra descended the porch steps and strolled to him with a fond smile and a warm expression in her eyes. "I am so glad you could come. Kirk is in the barn making a cross for Scott. I think he could use your company."

"I brought a bag of clothes," Darren lifted a brown bag. "Should I set it inside before I go?"

"I will take it for you," Hugh offered.

Darren handed over the bag before turning to run toward the barn.

"Where are you going?" Hugh looked at Stoneman. He had asked the man to stay here in his absence. He was not pleased to see him leaving.

"I hope you do not mind, but I asked him to deliver two letters for me," Tyra said. "I needed to write my aunts and inform them of Scott's recent death. Kirk is upset, and he wanted to hold a small ceremony in memory of our brother." Guilt kicked him in the gut as her red, swollen eyes filled with new tears and reminded him of her grief and lack of sleep. His anger faded as fast as it had brewed.

"No, of course not." Hugh shook his head and strode to Stoneman, gripping his shoulder. "Thank you for delivering her letters."

"'Tis the least I can do," Private Stoneman said with a brief nod. He grabbed the reins and mounted his horse. Nudging the animal's flanks, he launched in motion, cantering down the lane.

Hugh strolled back to Tyra and stopped before her, an idea forming. "Is there a pastor I could go into town and get for you?"

"No." Her chin trembled as more tears flooded her green eyes, making them look even larger. "We were once part of the small Presbyterian church in Wilmington, but after the war started, we stopped attending. Things changed. People changed."

"What do you mean?" Hugh tilted his head, trying to see her better, but she turned away.

"The Presbyterian church is run by Scotland. Most Scottish families are loyal to the King of England because they took an oath after the Jacobite rebellion. Scots do not break their word once they have given it. Everyone in the whole church are loyalists. When the Revolutionary War began and my father and brothers enlisted with the Continentals, we were told we were no longer welcome."

Hugh stepped closer and touched her arm, but she jerked away. She leaned against a white pillar and took a deep breath, brushing a red curl out of her eye. "I went to church with those people my whole life. I have known them since I was a child. Their betrayal was painful to my mother—to all of us. The one time we needed our friends and their fellowship, none of them were there. I always thought we at least we had our faith in common, but I was wrong. They are hypocrites—all of them."

He stepped closer and placed his knuckled finger under her chin, forcing her to gaze into his eyes. He could tell from her reluctance she had not regained her trust in him. Yet, she didn't flinch or jerk away as she had a moment ago. He sensed she wanted to trust him, as much as he wanted her to. "Do not worry about them. Your faith does not rest in their misguided opinions and crass judgments." He leaned forward and kissed the top of her forehead. "Instead, place your faith in the Lord where it belongs and where it can move mountains—even hardened hearts."

The words he had spoken came from deep inside him. He wasn't sure where he had gotten such wisdom. Was it the Lord whispering to his confused heart? He hoped so, especially since he needed to cling to those words for himself and his brother.

✒

The next morning they held a small service for Scott in the family cemetery on a hill by the main house. The distance was too far for Aunt Blair to travel from Charles Town while expecting. Aunt Carleen and her family arrived in time from the north side of Wilmington. A few families attended from the Whig party, such as Mr. and Mrs. Saunders who owned the boarding house in town. Mrs. Baker came and Tyra had no doubt Mr. Simmons would have been there, if he had not been in prison. None of their friends from church came.

Tyra and her mother had stayed up late mending black gowns for mourning, adding to their already-drained energy. The dim candles had not provided enough light to see by, and Tyra's fingers were sore from several needle pricks. As she stood among her family and close friends, her heavy eyelids drifted closed until she blinked to force them open. She imagined her eyes looked as red and gaunt as her mother's.

While Kirk placed the cross into the ground, Tyra read a passage from 1 Thessalonians, chapter Four. *"For the Lord himself shall descend from heaven with a shout, with the voice of the archangel, and with the trump of God, and the dead in Christ shall rise first: Then we which are alive and remain shall be caught up together with them in the clouds, to meet the Lord in the air: and so shall we ever be with the Lord. Wherefore comfort one another with these words."* Tyra's voice faded as her emotions rose and came close to choking her. She took a moment to compose herself, taking comfort in the words she had read. Once her heart beat with a new peace, she continued. "This is why I know this is not the end. We shall see Scott again—one day in heaven."

The others took turns sharing a memory about Scott, most were funny moments to lighten the mood and lift their hearts. Mama continued mopping at her eyes with her handkerchief. The service was simple and painful, yet it helped to provide a way to say good-bye, even though he could not be buried here. Afterward, Tyra felt a relief she had not expected. She appreciated Kirk suggesting the service. It was a blessing to honor his memory.

Afterward, they strolled back to the main house, doing their best to ignore the hot sun heating their scalps and cooking their red faces. Some of the women beat their fans in front of them. Tyra's mouth watered at the thought of all the food people had brought over to pay their respects. Her stomach churned like a storm at sea, and her parched throat felt scratchy.

Her mother dropped on the settee in the parlor, and Tyra sat beside her, taking her hand in hers. Neither of them spoke, but they drew a quiet strength from each other. They did not have to play the hostesses since Aunt Carleen and her cousin, Rebecca, took on the roles for them.

Tyra and her mother were grateful for their thoughtfulness in serving food and tea to their guests. She appreciated Uncle Ollie for spending time with Kirk and taking his mind off things. Throughout all the activity, Tyra was ever mindful of Hugh's quiet presence lounging in the back of the crowd at the service, almost as if he wasn't sure if he would be welcome. Even now, he stood in the parlor corner giving up a seat to their guests. He did not engage in conversation unless someone approached him first, and to her relief, Uncle Ollie had made an effort to talk to Hugh before heading outside to check on Kirk and Darren.

It would have been easy to blame him since he wore a redcoat and fought for the army who had killed her brother, but in her heart she knew it was no more Hugh's fault than anyone else in her family. Captain Morgan did not kill her brother. He was not responsible for this hideous war. It was not fair to hate him because he was British. Such prejudices had no place in her heart, and she didn't want such feelings to be festering inside her like a disease. Yet, she could not bring herself to let go and trust him with her whole heart.

Right now too much grief consumed her. It took all her will to get through each moment. Sorting through her emotions would have to wait. Her family needed her strength and clarity of mind. She prayed God would give her everything she needed for the days to come.

"Please forgive me, but I believe I need to lie down and rest now." Mama stood as Tyra set her coffee on the table beside her chair. She rose to her feet and took her mother's arm.

"I shall help you," Tyra said.

"Nay," Mama shook her blond head, patting the top of Tyra's hand. "I can take care of myself. Please stay and keep our guests company."

"Will you not eat something before you go?" Tyra wished she could take away all the pain reflecting in her mother's blue eyes, but it would take a miracle. Only the Almighty and time could be a place of refuge and heal her grief. It was bad enough losing a brother, Tyra could not imagine losing a child. "Mama, you have eaten naught all day. You need to keep up your strength. You will need it."

"My stomach is like a rock. I cannot eat. Sleep is what I need." Mama pulled away and strolled from the parlor as her skirts made soft swishing sounds.

Aunt Carleen carried in a new tray of buttered biscuits and paused by Hugh, offering to serve him. Tyra was so thankful for her thoughtfulness, it eased her discomfort for him.

"Have those redcoats not already taken enough?" Miss Baker asked in a disgruntled tone. The lines on her forehead and around her mouth wilted into a frown, making her look every bit of her middle age. "Carleen, I realize you Quakers are neutral in this war, but right now you ought to be thinking about the feelings of your family and the grief they must be going through." She turned away and flipped out her fan, waving it in her face with a vengeance.

"Mrs. Baker, thank you for your concern, but my aunt is doing exactly as we want. While we are grieved by my brother's demise, we are logical enough to realize Captain Morgan is not personally at fault." Tyra glanced in his direction, and the intense focus he gave her almost made her forget what she had planned to say, so she looked back at Mrs. Baker to regain her thoughts. "In fact, he has been most gracious to us compared to how the other British soldiers have treated other Continental families. He has defended us against others in his army, brought us food, and treated us with utmost respect. When Captain Morgan is here, I feel safer than when he is not."

All eyes turned toward Tyra as other conversations in the parlor faded to silence. She could feel her cheeks grow warm, but forced herself to meet the gazes of the others in the room. Rebecca and her aunt wore approving expressions, while others ranged from confusion to surprise. "The MacGregors may not have converted to Quakerism as my aunt and uncle have, but we will not slight anyone in this house for having a difference in opinion or where they come from. We have been the victims of such behavior from people we thought were our friends. We shall not do the same to someone who has shown us naught but kindness." Tyra stood and folded her hands in front of her. "Please excuse me. I believe we need another pot of tea."

As Hugh stood in the parlor and listened to Tyra defend him to all her friends, he realized she was the most honorable woman he had ever known. It angered him at how people from her church had treated Tyra and her family. Their actions reminded him of the way people had treated him and his family back home, and all because of his family's poor status.

Such inequality had existed for centuries in England, and the reason in the ideals of the American colonists now appealed to him. Being here on the other side of the world in the midst of a war and all the controversy gave him a different perspective than he had grown up believing. Without knowing it, Tyra had challenged him to examine his own ideals, and when he compared his to hers, his came up lacking.

The next few weeks passed in silent solitude around the MacGregor house. Darren and Kirk spent their time hunting game and fishing. Due to their diligence, none of them went hungry. Preparing the meals kept Tyra and her mother busy so they did not concentrate as heavily upon their grief. Uncle Ollie and Aunt Carleen stayed an extra week to help out and keep them company. Rebecca was a great comfort to Tyra, as was her mother to Mrs. MacGregor. After their departure, letters arrived often from them throughout the rest of the month.

At the end of July, Hugh arrived home from a long day in Wilmington with news he dreaded to impart. As he rode by the vegetable garden Tyra and her mother had planted, pride swelled inside him. Their garden was filled with life, growth, and abundance just like the MacGregors. These women were survivors and regardless of what they had faced, they found ways to keep going. Rather than be defeated, or fall victim to the pieces life left after tragedy, they still rose each morning to embrace life. So many women in London had given up and allowed unfortunate circumstances to dictate their low station in life. The MacGregor women lived by the faith they believed, unbound by the traditions of society, and unlimited by one's station.

Hugh dismounted from his horse and guided the animal into the back stall where he unsaddled and fed him, and poured a bucket of water in the trough. He pulled the brush from a nail on the wall and brushed him down before heading to the main house. Voices reached his ears as he walked through the front door and closed it behind him.

"You are just in time for dinner," Private Stoneman walked toward him from the parlor, a welcoming grin crossed his features and his dark eyes brightened. "Kirk and Darren brought home some trout and crab meat earlier. I must say, I am quite looking forward to a good morsel myself."

"Mama and I picked a basket full of vegetables, and we have prepared them. We even had enough from the herb garden to create some new spices." Tyra smiled as she strolled toward them and placed her hands against the side of her face, lowering her voice to a whisper. "Mama received a letter from Aunt Blair. There are some complications with her delicate condition, and she is no longer allowed to leave her chamber. Mama is worried and would like to go to her, but Private Stoneman advised against it."

"Although I am sorry for your aunt's situation, I approve of his advice." Hugh gave Private Stoneman a nod of appreciation. "I would have told her the same thing." Hugh extended his arm in a gesture indicating they head down the hallway. "I have some news myself, but let us eat, and I shall tell it to all of you at once."

Tyra stepped to his side and surprised him by taking his arm and leading him forward. Private Stoneman followed, their heels clicking against the wood floor. As they approached the kitchen, animated chatter between Darren and Kirk grew more distinct. Mrs. MacGregor chuckled at something one of them said. It was good to hear her lively voice again. They entered the kitchen, and all eyes turned toward them at the entrance. Smiles of welcoming recognition landed on Hugh first, then shifted to the others. Relief washed over him, thankful his presence would not cause them further pain.

When they were seated around the table with plates piled high, Mrs. MacGregor held out her hands on each side of her and met their gazes around the table. Her blue eyes were still bloodshot and framed by dark circles, but they were not as swollen as before. A smile curled her lips, and he knew it was in an effort for Tyra and Kirk.

"Let us pray," Mrs. MacGregor said, bowing her head. Hugh exchanged a quick glance with Tyra before they bowed their heads and closed their eyes. "Lord, thank you for your blessings. I pray you will keep Malcolm, Callum, and Alec safe during the rest of this war. Please bring an end to all the killing as soon as possible." Mrs. MacGregor's voice broke into a whisper and tears lingered in her tone. She cleared her throat and forced herself to continue. "I thank you Scott is now in a better place. I will do my best to trust you. Thank you for your provision and please bless the food we have prepared. Amen."

Mrs. MacGregor sighed and wiped a stray tear from her cheek. She picked up her fork and waved her other hand in the air. "Let us eat."

Hugh stared at the long crab legs lying across his plate over green leafy vegetables of spinach, buttered potatoes, and yellow corn on the cob. Hugh never had corn before coming to the colonies. While he didn't mind the taste of it, he disliked the way it lodged in his teeth. He hoped he would not offend them if he chose not to eat it.

"I have never had crab legs before," Hugh said, picking up the hard shell between his finger and thumb. "How does one eat it?"

"'Tis easy," Kirk gripped a crab leg in both hands and cracked it into pieces. He pulled out the soft meat, plunged it into his mouth, and chewed with a satisfied grin.

"It can be quite messy." Tyra held up a silver nutcracker. "Mama and I like to use nutcrackers to snap our crab legs."

"Well, I dare say, it is quite clever," Private Stoneman said with a nod.

Kirk and Darren launched into a snapping contest to see who could eat the most crab legs. While they bantered back and forth, Tyra turned to Hugh.

"I believe you have some news for us?" Tyra lifted red eyebrows.

"Well, in a few days the deadline of August first will be upon us." Blank stares blinked at him from around the table. "If you recall, Major Craig had posted a proclamation all over Wilmington demanding allegiance to the king. Tomorrow he will be leaving for New Bern where he will begin to implement the proclamation. Those who will not give their allegiance to the king and promise they will no longer help the Continental Army will forfeit their lands and all their property. They will be seized and taken to prison. If they resist, they will be shot."

Momentary silence carried new tension in the room. Tyra straightened her shoulders and set her chin at an angle. "Why not start here in Wilmington?"

"We have heard certain reports indicating there may be a possible uprising there," Hugh said.

"Will you be going with them?" Kirk asked.

"No, my brother and the other officers will be leaving with Major Craig. I have been left in charge. Private Stoneman will continue to stay here while I am at the Burgwin House." He shoved a spoonful of potatoes into his mouth. They were seasoned with something he could not name, but the heightened flavor was pleasing on his tongue. "Mmm, this is very good."

"Thank you," Mrs. MacGregor said.

"Will you let the prisoners go?" Tyra asked.

He braced himself for the onslaught of her anger and swallowed half his water. Setting his cup down, he met her gaze, giving her his full attention. "You know well I cannot. 'Twould be disobedient to a direct order from my superior officer." He sat back in his chair with a sigh. "But what I can do is give them better treatment than they have been receiving." He reached over his plate for another biscuit in the bread basket. "I give you my word."

"So if I was rotting in prison as I was before, you would do naught to help?" Disbelief threaded her voice.

"That was a different situation," he said, wishing the conversation had never gone in this direction.

"How is it any different?" Her liquid eyes sparkled like emeralds, and her lips tightened into a thin line.

"Because it is." Hugh risked a quick glance across the table. "You are an innocent woman."

"They are innocent." The words tumbled from her tongue as if she forced them. She pressed her lips together and threw down her napkin. Tyra scooted her chair back.

Did she expect him to admit his love in front of Private Stoneman? While he was willing to risk the consequences of a beating for her sake, he was not yet willing to do so for her imprisoned friends.

She stood to her feet.

"Where are you going?" he asked, his heart raced in concern, but he swallowed back the fear lurking at his throat.

She did not answer as she turned and strode from the room. Hugh looked around at the surprised expressions on the lads' faces and the disapproving expressions from Mrs. MacGregor and Private Stoneman.

"What does she want from me?" He lifted his palms in confusion, exasperated that matters between him and Tyra always turned into a cloudy mess.

"Something you cannot give her," Mrs. MacGregor said. "A miracle."

21

It had been a week since Tyra last saw Hugh. He had departed the next morning after she left the dinner table in anger without her having a chance to say good-bye. Her anger cooled a little more with each passing day until she began to wonder how he was doing. Private Stoneman gave her no information when she inquired about Hugh. The man was most disappointing. She decided she would have to devise a reason to go into town and take matters into her own hands. Since Major Craig had left town with half his army, the roads should be safe to travel for an afternoon visit with their cousins. Her mother agreed, and Kirk and Darren were more than eager for a venture into town.

Tyra rode in back of the wagon with Darren, while her mother sat in front on the bench with Kirk as he drove. Over the past hour, Tyra suspected her brother hit every rock and crevice in the road on purpose. He enjoyed swinging them from one way to the other like it was a game. The wagon wheel dipped into another hole, snapping Tyra's neck back against her shoulders.

"Kirk, if you keep doing that, I promise you will walk home." Tyra gripped the side and hoped she would not suffer any blisters on her palms. She groaned in frustration as the wagon jostled her again, shaking her insides.

Darren chuckled as he rested his arms over his knees and linked his hands in the middle. He shook his head with a twisted grin. "You make it too easy for him to enjoy aggravating you. If you ignore him and stop complaining, he will grow bored of his antics. I promise."

"He would only find something else to annoy me with." Tyra said.

"I declare this day to be peaceful among my children," Mama said, glancing over her shoulder.

While there was no reproach in her tone, an image of Scott came to mind. Remorse filled her with a deep ache, and suddenly Kirk's behavior no longer seemed so frustrating. She glanced up at the back of his head and smiled at the brown hair hanging down his neck from under his hat. He straightened his shoulders and braced his posture as if proud to be escorting them into town. Her youngest brother had grown up witnessing the war. It wasn't fair his childhood should be cut so short. It would not hurt to allow him to enjoy a little fun, no matter how silly.

"Indeed, we shall be on our best behavior for the day," Tyra said. "'Twill be our gift to you, Mama."

As they arrived in Wilmington and traveled down Front Street, they witnessed few redcoats walking along the streets. Tyra caught sight of a little wooden building on the other side of the street. The white paint now peeled with a splintered sign reading, *Cape Fear Mercury*. Her heart quickened at the thought of learning updated news on the war. They spent so much time in seclusion at The MacGregor Quest they knew little about the world and what was going on around them.

"Mama, could we stop and get a newspaper?" Tyra asked, leaning up on her knees and gripping the back of the bench between where her mother and Kirk sat.

"Yes, could we?" Kirk glanced in their mother's direction. The wagon jolted them and Tyra stumbled, but she gritted her teeth and kept silent. At least this time, Kirk did not cause it on purpose.

"I suppose so," Mama said, glancing up at the building ahead of them. "Truth be told, I am curious as to the latest news myself.

Perhaps we shall have some news to share with your cousins when we arrive."

Kirk pulled over to the side of the road in front of the newspaper shop.

"Wait here, and I shall go purchase the latest paper," Tyra said. She crawled to the back gate. As her knees caught in the fabric of her skirts, she made an awkward mess of things and lost her balance.

"Allow me to help you," Darren said, as he knelt toward her and held out his hand.

"Thank you, but I am fine." Tyra jerked away and continued in her impatient flight. She fidgeted with the lock. Once it released, she pushed the gate down where it rocked in the hinges. Tyra scooted to the edge and leaped to the ground. She brushed the dust from her dark blue linen skirts.

"Tyra, please remember to behave like a lady. Never hasten when it is not necessary or reject a gallant offer of assistance when it is appropriate." Mama shifted her gaze toward Darren's crestfallen expression and shook her head in disappointment, as if she had told Tyra these things time and again.

"I am sorry, Darren." Tyra met his gaze. He watched her with curious confusion as his face darkened. Feeling chastised, she looked away in discomfort and pretended to adjust her straw hat at an angle to keep her eyes shaded. The blue ribbon attached to the flat brim shifted in the breeze as a passing horse cantered by. No matter how hard she tried, Tyra often forgot herself and her manners.

"'Tis all right. I did not want you to ruin your dress." Darren waved a hand in the air to dismiss the subject. "Off with you, now."

With a deep breath, Tyra squared her shoulders and marched forward. She stomped up the wooden steps and swung the front door wide open. As she stepped inside, the door slammed behind her, rattling. Three surprised faces turned in her direction, but she only recognized one. Mr. Hawkins, the editor, frowned at the interruption but quickly forced a rigid smile.

"Miss MacGregor, I have not seen you in a while," Mr. Hawkins said, his gray mustache curled up with his smiling lips framed by a full beard. The gray hair on his head curled in every direction. "What can we do for you?"

"'Tis good to see you as well," Tyra gave him a polite nod and acknowledged the other two men with a slight incline of her head. "I apologize for barging in like this, but I came to buy the latest addition of your paper."

"Ah, so glad you decided to drop by. Do not worry about the door. It often causes people problems." He pointed in the direction of a shelf on the far gray wall, containing a stack full of folded papers. "Johnny, please assist Miss MacGregor."

A lad about Kirk's age rushed over, lifted the top paper, and carried it to her. "'Twill be two pence, Miss." His voice cracked between low and high pitches as his wide brown eyes stared up at her. Tyra knew he was probably shocked by her height.

"Two pence?" Tyra glanced over at Mr. Hawkins, lifting an eyebrow. "Last time I bought a paper from you, 'twas only one pence."

"Indeed, the war has increased the demand for news an' I can hardly keep up with all the expenses." He nodded so hard his round cheeks jiggled. He linked his fingers across his bowl belly. "Ink an' paper does have its cost, ya know. An' I have to pay these fine lads, I do."

Tyra dug into her change purse and pulled out the required coins. It did not seem fair Mr. Hawkins would up his prices knowing the fine folks of Wilmington had most all of their belongings and supplies stolen by the British. Too many families no longer had men at home to farm the land or servants to keep the plantations going. All of them had suffered financial loss, why did Mr. Hawkins feel the need to take further advantage of them?

Tyra paid for the newspaper, gave a brief curtsy, and stepped outside into the sunshine. She climbed up onto the wagon and closed the gate. The latch clicked in place. With as much diplomacy as possible, she crawled back into her spot and fanned her skirts around her legs to cover herself. Unfolding the newspaper, she spread it wide and skimmed the headlines, one stood out in bold letters, "Patriots Defeated at Rockfish Creek." Tyra pulled the paper closer and read the rest of the passage aloud. "Brave militiamen under Colonel Kenan tried to hold Rockfish Creek in Duplin County. They had no ammunition against British Major Craig who had a force of over four hundred men and light artillery. They drove the Patriots from the area and took twenty to thirty men as prisoners. Major Craig then marched from Duplin to New Bern being cruel and causing the inhabitants more distress than General Cornwallis. He plundered the town, destroyed the public stores, and is now heading back to Wilmington."

How could Hugh align his loyalties to such a man? Anger roared inside her like a lion on the prowl. She closed the paper and shoved it aside. "Kirk, take me to the Burgwin House!"

"Now?" He glanced over his shoulder in confusion. "But I thought we were going to Aunt Carleen's."

"First, I want to see Captain Morgan. I intend to confront him before Major Craig returns to town."

❦

As soon as Hugh learned Tyra had come to visit, the nerves in his stomach knotted and burned. He set the quill down, closed the ledger book, and stood at his desk. He linked his hands behind his back and walked to the window where he stared out at the street and watched a carriage and horseman pass by. Two ladies were taking a leisurely stroll in the other direction with their parasols covering their heads in the shade.

Although he could not release the Patriot prisoners, Hugh had kept his word to Tyra and managed to treat the prisoners better than Major Craig. Knowing he could not give her what she wanted, he had felt it would be best to leave without risking another face-to-face argument they would both regret. Over the past week, she had been constant in his thoughts, and Private Stoneman had kept him informed of her well-being. It pleased Hugh she had asked about him. It gave him hope she had not forgotten him, and perhaps a reconciliation was still in their future.

Footsteps sounded down the hall, one set a steady gate, the other a stampede he could only assume belonged to Tyra. The pace of his heart increased at the thought of seeing her again, but he took a deep breath and forced his mind to stay coherent. He had no way of knowing if this visit was a friendly or negative attempt to berate him into taking advantage of the fact Craig was gone.

One of his soldiers led her into the study. Tyra wore a flat straw hat with a blue ribbon and white blouse over a royal blue skirt. Her fiery red hair brought color into the room. With the side strands pinned up, the rest fell in a mixture of waves and curls around her shoulders and down her back. The scent of honey lingered in her presence and brought parts of him back to life he had not realized lay dormant since his departure of The MacGregor Quest.

In spite of his enthusiasm to see her, the passionate anger burning in her green eyes and the twisted frown on her lips no longer left him in doubt as to the nature of her visit. Was she still angry about the same thing or had something else upset her? Either way, Hugh intended to see if he could somehow bridge the distance between them.

"I would like to see you . . . alone." Tyra said.

Hugh glanced at the soldier still standing behind her and gave him a brief nod. "Please close the door and see that no one disturbs us."

After the man departed, Tyra strode over and slammed the newspaper on the desk. She jabbed her finger at a bold headline. "How could you serve a man like this?" Tears welled in her eyes like pools of painted green glass. His heart ached in reaction, and he longed to go to her and wrap her in his arms. She didn't wait for his response. Instead, she drew a deep breath and continued on. "Major Craig is deplorable, and he has no regard for human life whatsoever. He is marching through the country plundering people's homes and whole towns, and depriving them of all they need to survive. These are innocent civilians, farmers, women, children, poor servants and none of them are soldiers in the Continental Army nor have they signed up with the Patriot militia."

Hugh closed his eyes and rubbed the headache beginning around his temples and across his forehead. How could he make her understand without angering her further? He had to try and calm her before she did something to jeopardize her life.

"Tyra, I do not always agree with the methods Major Craig chooses to carry out his mission, but it does not mean I should break my loyalty to king and country." She started to interrupt, but he lifted his palm to stop her. "Allow me to finish speaking. Even if the Continentals succeeded in creating a new country, even among your own people there will be the contrast of good and evil. I cannot abandon my integrity and break my word to the king."

"What about the right of freedom?" she demanded. "The king believes nobility is born to rule over other men, women, and children. By birthright, he intends to enforce these thoughts and ideas. Here in the American colonies, we believe leaders should earn the right to lead others in action, deeds, and integrity. As you have already pointed out, some are born good and others are born evil, including kings and the precious nobility."

The woman ought to write speeches. The passionate way she said her words with such conviction spoke to a man's heart. How could he argue against her logic? He knew her words to be true. Had he not lived the downtrodden past the king and society had stamped upon him? Fighting for the British made a mockery of him. Yet, he had given his allegiance, if he was to go back on his word, it would make a liar of him. He had always taken pride that he was a man of principle, trustworthy, and truthful.

Hugh clutched his hands behind him and paced across the room. "It seems I can never win an argument with you."

"Why must there be an argument between us? Once you learned of this treachery, I had hoped we could come to an agreement." Tyra walked toward him and laid her hand on his arm. Her close presence brought a welcoming warmth he had missed all week. He closed his eyes, savoring the moment as he placed his hand over hers, unable to resist touching her hand. "Something must be done."

"And what would you have me do?" He glanced down at her upturned face, so close to his he longed to taste the smooth warmth of her lips once again.

He traced the smooth skin from her temple down the side of her cheek. "Would you have me, a lone man, go up against the whole British Army?"

"Of course not!" Tyra's eyes widened as she stepped back. "It would be suicide. And I could not bear it if something were to happen to you." Tears pooled in her eyes.

"Tyra, you will have to accept that I am a soldier in His Majesty's army. I am sorry this fact causes you so much pain. I wish I could change things, but I cannot."

"Can you not?" Clear liquid tears spilled over her lashes and crawled down her white cheeks. "Men leave the service and sell their commission for all sorts of reasons. 'Twould not be any different for you, except your reason would be more noble. You have had a change of heart."

"It feels like betrayal." He pressed his fingers against the knotted muscles in the back of his neck as he paced to the window and back. "My commission is not over for another year."

"In the meantime, you will be killing more innocent people. You will continue taking orders from a superior officer who is evil and supports the king of tyranny." Tyra straightened into a rigid posture and lifted her chin in defiance. "I love you, Captain Donahue Morgan, but if you do not have the courage to do the right thing and stand with me, then you are not the right man for me." Tyra turned and strode out the door, leaving him with a burdened heart clawing and digging deep until he bled inside.

Tyra bent over her garden as her knees pressed into the soft dirt where she had dug out some weeds between her red geraniums and white lilies. Even though the sun had dropped behind looming gray clouds, the heat still prevailed and perspiration dripped from her forehead. She reached up and wiped her brow on the sleeve of her blouse.

Thunder rumbled in the distance, and Tyra sat back with a heavy sigh. Two days had passed since she last saw Hugh, and the words she shot at him still haunted her. No matter how much it pained her, she would have to stick by what she said. How would her father and brothers feel if they returned to discover she had developed affection for a man who was part of the enemy, especially after Scott's death?

Tears stung her eyes as she weighed all the circumstances. What did she know of Hugh? He had told her little about his family and life back in England. The only knowledge she had was of his elder brother, Colonel Neil Morgan, a man who had made it clear of his hatred for the colonials, especially the Patriot families like the MacGregors. She wished she had asked Hugh more about his life before the war. What were his future goals and dreams?

The wind swept her hair over her shoulders and brushed against her like a wave from the sea. Her flowers bent over until they hung to the ground like a sad case of drooping depression. Footsteps approached from behind, and Tyra turned to see Kirk and Darren striding toward her, a frown of concern on her brother's young face.

"We have secured all the livestock missed by the redcoats in the far fields. You must come in, Tyra. The storm will soon be upon us." Kirk held out his hand. "'Tisn't safe out here. Come in with us, so Mama will not worry."

Lightning streaked the sky in a white jagged shape flashing across the landscape, revealing crevices and shadows across the land. She stood and dusted her hands, grimacing at the dirt caked on her skin and under her nails. "I shall wash first."

"Do not take long." Kirk glanced behind him beyond the dirt road to the other side where the Cape Fear River flowed like rapids. Usually this part of the river was calm, but not today. "I hope it does not flood. Do you think it is another hurricane?" He asked, glancing up at the dark clouds swirling above them.

"I hope not. The rice fields barely survived the last one." These were the moments when she missed her father the most.

"Looks like another one to me." Darren stepped back with his fists on his hips and surveyed the sky. Concern darkened his tense expression.

Thunder exploded, lightning sparked, and massive wind swept through the air and snapped several tree limbs. A large branch broke and flew across the yard, tumbling like a weed. Fear twisted through her stirring a wave of panic. Tyra gulped, remembering how several years ago a huge hurricane came through. Their father had boarded up the windows to protect the glass. What if the branch had burst through the front window of the house?

"Kirk, run to the barn and get those flat wooden boards Da keeps in the loft." She pointed in the direction of the red barn as her skirts danced in the wind. "We are going to board up the windows. We do not have much time. 'Twill soon be upon us."

"You think the storm will be that bad?" Kirk asked, his dark eyebrows lifting.

"We should not take a chance. This is what Da would do if he was here." Tyra turned and ran to the well. She cranked the handle to lower the bucket and pulled it back up. More thunder cracked the sky, causing her to jump. She found the lye soap on the side of the well and scrubbed the dirt from her hands. Fat raindrops began to pour. Within seconds, it had soaked her white cap to her head in a flat mess. She kept blinking the rain from her eyes, but it pounded harder, like tiny bullets on the top of her head and along the skin of her hands and arms.

She ran to the side door and paused inside, not wanting to leave a trail of water as it dripped on the floor. "Mama?" She called through the house. "Would you bring the hammer and nails? We need to board up the windows."

"I will be right there." Mama's voice sounded strained in the distance. Thunder rumbled over the house like something scraping the roof. Footsteps carried down the hall. A thump sounded then something slammed before more footsteps came toward her. Mama appeared with two hammers and a container of nails.

"I had nearly forgotten where Malcolm kept these." She lifted the container of nails in one hand and two hammers in the other. "Thank the good Lord, my senses finally returned to me." Her gaze slid over Tyra to the puddle of water on the floor. "Goodness, lass, at least ye had the good sense to enter by the side door. The brick floor will handle the mess ye've made much better than the pine floor at the front door."

"Come, Mama, we do not have much time. The storm is already raging." Tyra stepped forward and took the tools from her mother.

By the time they reached the front of the house, Kirk and Darren had managed to carry several boards from the barn. They took turns holding the boards against the windows and hammering the nails into the wooden shutters.

"How will we manage the second story windows?" Kirk called over the howling wind. "None of us would be able to stay on a ladder long enough."

"Who would be riding out to our place in this terrible storm?" Mama looked down at the drive.

"It could be Private Stoneman. He left earlier to give his report." Tyra followed her gaze to see the shadow of a lone rider approaching them. The dark clouds and pelting rain kept the man's identity hidden. Whoever he was, his horse galloped at great speed, fighting against the wind to progress toward them. As he drew closer, Tyra recognized a redcoat and the familiar posture of Hugh. Her heart quickened, and her throat tightened.

"I declare, I believe 'tis Captain Morgan!" Mama threw a hand on her hip and squinted, blinking against the rain falling in her face.

Tyra paused holding her end of the next board they planned to mount. She almost dropped it as she strained to see the rider.

"Come on, Tyra," Kirk said, groaning under the pressure. "This is the last one. Let us get it over with."

"I got it." Darren grabbed the opposite end of the board and groaned under the pressure.

Tyra launched into action, guiding them to the next window on the side of the house. The rider came to a halt and dismounted without tethering his horse. Footsteps ran over to them.

"Mrs. MacGregor! Please, go inside before you catch your death in this ghastly weather." He grabbed their mother's arm and pulled her away, taking her place beside Tyra. "Go on." He nodded toward the house.

"I shall make you all some warm tea and 'twill be waiting when you finish and come inside," Mama said, waving Tyra toward her.

"What are you doing here?" Tyra asked, ignoring her mother's gesture.

"Did you honestly believe I would leave you here alone in such a terrible storm?" He grabbed a hammer and banged the nail into the top left corner of the board over the window. "In spite of what you might think of me, Miss MacGregor, you and your family have come to mean much more to me than you realize."

Tyra had no chance to reply. Her mother grabbed her elbow and pulled Tyra away. "Come. Allow the men to finish this."

22

*H*ugh assisted Kirk and Darren with boarding up the last window and ushered the lads inside as the wind grew. As promised, Mrs. MacGregor boiled a pot of water for some warm tea, while Tyra waited for them in the foyer.

"Come and stand on this rug. 'Twill soak the excess water dripping from your clothes." Tyra had hauled a thick rug from a back room. She grabbed a bundle of clothes she had draped over the stair rail and brought them to Kirk and Darren. "Here is something dry to change into."

The lads unbuttoned their wet shirts, as they shivered in a soggy state. Hugh stepped onto the rug, grimacing at the puddle he had left on their good floor. "I am sorry, I shall clean up the mess I made, if you have a towel available?"

"Never mind," Tyra said, handing him a set of dry clothes. "Put these on."

"What is this?" Hugh asked, meeting her hesitant gaze. Her wet hair hung in matted strands down her back and around her shoulders, making it look darker. Today there was an uninhibited presence about her—almost a vulnerability he had not noticed before.

"These belonged to Scott." Pain filled her green eyes as she blinked back tears and swallowed. They locked gazes.

"I cannot accept these." Hugh shook his head and shoved them back at her as if they were on fire. If wearing her dead brother's clothes brought her further grief, he could not in good conscience do it. The guilt of being regarded as an enemy to her family already weighed heavy upon him. The idea of adding to their burden was more than he could bear.

"Indeed, you can." She shoved them back at him with more force than he anticipated. "Besides, he has no more need of them and you do." She leaned forward and blinked back tears. "I am glad you came back. I missed you," she whispered in his ear.

Tyra stepped away and glanced from Hugh to Kirk and Darren. "Mama and I will wait in the kitchen for you to finish dressing. By then, a cup of warm tea should be ready for all of you." She turned and strode down the hall. Hugh watched her disappear in the shadows as words faded into a mass of confusion clouding his brain.

"My sister can be stubborn," Kirk said, as he stepped into a pair of brown breeches and buttoned them. "And she is right. Scott has no need of his possessions now."

"I know you may feel strange," Darren said, buttoning his own new breeches. "But she is right. You need something dry and comfortable to wear."

"What about you? Will it bother you if I wear your brother's clothes?" Hugh glanced at Kirk as he pulled off the heavy redcoat that once represented a sense of pride to him. Of late, he was almost embarrassed to wear it in the presence of the MacGregor family, especially in front of a pair of green eyes. He waited, assessing the lad as he set his boots on a corner of the rug and stepped to the side where he sat on the floor to pull on a pair of socks to warm his feet.

"I feel the same as Tyra, and I am certain our mother does as well." He took a deep breath and paused looking down at the floor. "I do not know if my father or my other two brothers will ever return home before this war is over. For all I know, I have seen them for the last time."

"Do not talk like that," Darren said, buttoning his shirt.

Hugh started to speak as well, but Kirk lifted a hand. "Things changed after Scott died. I began to see the world in a different way. His death is painful, but it has also brought a reality of death I did not understand before. Other than clinging to my faith, all I know is the moment. Even if I never get a chance to see the others again, you must know I am thankful you came into our lives, Captain Morgan. The British Army could have sent other men with questionable character, but I believe God sent you."

Hugh blinked back sudden moisture in his eyes. The war had robbed the lad of his innocence, but it would have happened sooner or later. He was destined to become a man, and based on what he had just heard, Kirk MacGregor would be an honorable man of good character.

An image of Tyra came to mind. When the war finally ended, he would never see her again. His heart constricted at the thought. It pained him more than never returning home to England. No one other than his mother cared what he managed to achieve here. While it saddened him to part from his brother, they were already divided by principle. They no longer viewed life or this war in the same way. He longed to spend the rest of his life with Tyra. In truth, the only ones whose opinions mattered were the Almighty and Tyra.

"Thank you, Kirk. It means a great deal to me to hear you say so, lad." Hugh hurried out of his wet clothes and donned the new ones while Kirk and Darren waited, now fully dressed. If Mrs. MacGregor and Kirk had come to accept him, would it be unreasonable to assume her father and brothers might as well?

More thunder boomed across the sky as lightning flashed through the upstairs windows and a loud crash struck the back of the house. "Kirk, see if your mother and sister are all right. Bring them to the front parlor. 'Tis safer where no trees are likely to crash through the ceiling and injure someone."

Kirk nodded and hurried down the hallway, while Hugh finished dressing and Darren waited with him. By the time they reappeared, Hugh was wearing Scott's clothes. The garments were a perfect fit.

He was relieved to see both women were fine. Mrs. MacGregor carried a tray with a pot of tea and cups, while Tyra carried a plate of bread slices.

Once they were all settled and the storm continued to rage around them, Tyra glanced at Hugh and his pulse pounded. "What brought you here in the middle of such a catastrophe? I thought you were commanded to stay at the headquarters at Burgwin House?"

"I was, but Major Craig returned late last night, and I was free to come once I discovered the oncoming storm. I did not want to leave you here alone. Private Stoneman elected to stay in town where it is safer from flooding."

"We thank ye, Captain." Mrs. MacGregor poured a cup of tea and handed it to him. "Ye've always done more on our behalf than was ever expected."

"Did you find out the extent of the damage Major Craig caused in his travels?" Tyra's voice took on a hard edge as she watched him closely.

"I did." Hugh sighed, taking a sip of the warm tea, allowing it to soothe his dry throat. "You are bound to hear about it, so I might as well tell you what I know." He took a deep breath and set his cup on its saucer as he took a moment to meet each of their gazes. "Major Craig met up with Colonel David Fanning. They burned the plantation homes of Captain Thomas Robeson and Colonel Peter Robeson, as well as Captain James Gillespie. They captured Campbelltown."

"'Tis no surprise to us, Captain. I was once a Campbell myself. Most of the people there are Tories," Mrs. MacGregor said. "Many of them are distant relations to my father and would not have put up much resistance."

"I see," Hugh said, surprised by this news. Did this mean she and Malcolm MacGregor's union was once opposed by their families? Hope lifted inside him as he risked a glance in Tyra's direction. She poured a cup of tea and handed it to Kirk. "Many of the men are afraid of losing everything. Some have already enlisted with the British. It seems the Whigs are losing support."

"Cowards," Tyra said. "What good are such possessions if one loses them to high taxes anyway? I pray General Washington has a plan to turn this war around. Freedom must prevail."

For once, Hugh agreed, but he refrained from saying so. He merely picked up his tea and drank it.

⌇❦

A few days later, Tyra answered the front door. Colonel Neil Morgan stood facing her with almost twenty men in redcoats waiting on horses in front of their house. Fear spiraled through her like a spring in her abdomen. The last time this many redcoats came, she ended up being carted off to prison. She searched for Hugh, but didn't see him among them. To her relief, Major Craig was not among them either.

Summoning her courage, she looked into Colonel Morgan's dark brown eyes and read the contempt in them. She clenched her jaw, saying nothing in greeting. Instead, she would wait for him to deliver the horrible news, for it could be nothing but bad, whatever it was. She gripped the door handle tight, but did not widen it to welcome him in.

"I assume you have seen or heard of the proclamation Major Craig has posted in Wilmington and the surrounding area?" His harsh tone was demanding, almost as if he dared her to deny it.

"I have." Tyra offered no more information. Anything she said could be twisted against her or her family. They were looking for any excuse to harass them.

"And no one has complied with the terms from The MacGregor Quest. Are you prepared to denounce your allegiance to the Continentals and pledge your loyalty to king and country?" He lifted a dark brow and twisted his mouth. "You will, of course, be required to give your word you will never again take up arms against England and His Majesty's Royal Army."

"I have not taken up arms against England."

"And in order to maintain your property, no one in this house may do so." He pressed his palm against the door. "It is my understanding your father and brothers have done so. Do you deny it?"

Knowing he would send her back to prison or kick them out of their home, Tyra set her chin and gave him a defiant glare. "I do not."

"Then you and anyone here must vacate the premises immediately." He shoved the door open, scraping the corner against her arm as she lost her grip on the knob. Tyra whirled and shoved her hips against the door, trying to close it on him. Colonel Morgan used his weight to push the door against her, forcing his way inside. The blunt impact caused Tyra to lose her balance, and she stumbled backward.

In a rage of anger, Tyra ran at him. He braced his arms as if he intended to grab her by the shoulders to stop her, but Tyra ducked and kicked, bringing him down to his knees. Her plan worked, and he hit the floor in a thump, but her skirt kept her from having the momentum she wanted. Instead of dislocating his kneecap, she only managed to take him off guard for a few moments. Tyra pushed him with her other foot, hoping to nudge him away from the threshold so she could close the door. Colonel Morgan proved to be too heavy, and she only managed to slide him a couple of inches.

"I said get out of my house!" Tyra stood and used her back to try to force the door closed, but Colonel Morgan recovered himself and prevented her.

"You are going to regret this," he said between groans, slamming his body against the other side of the door.

Two more soldiers joined him. Her strength gave out against all of them. They crashed through the entrance, and Tyra went sprawling to the floor. Colonel Morgan gripped her hair through her cap and jerked her head back. "If it were not for my brother, I would kill you for your insolence."

"If it were not for your brother, I would have already killed you," she gritted through her teeth.

He slammed a fist into her jaw. Her vision went black as pain vibrated through her head. She blinked as her blurry vision returned. Her jaw throbbed, and she feared he might have broken it.

"Do you know what happens to people who resist a British officer, or worse, attack a British officer?" His voice was a low dangerous pitch. When she didn't answer, he tightened his grip, burning her scalp as if it was on fire. "Do you?"

"What is going on?" Her mother's voice came from above where she descended the staircase. "Let go of my daughter at once!"

In her predicament, Tyra could not turn and look at her mother, but the worry and anger in her voice was evident.

"I checked out the side and back doors," Kirk said. "And they have soldiers everywhere." His young voice cracked from the hallway. Darren stood behind him, looking just as pale.

"You are in no position to make demands." Colonel Morgan let go of Tyra's head, and she breathed a sigh of relief. His booted feet stepped over her as if she were a rodent on the floor. "We are confiscating this house and property for His Majesty. You may gather what you can carry and leave at once. Your daughter made the unfortunate mistake of defying me. I suggest not doing the same thing."

"Ye dare to hurt an innocent woman?" Mama asked.

"She is not innocent. In fact, she attacked me first."

"She was protecting our home!"

"Which belongs to the king!"

"Ye cannot take our home from us." Mama gripped her long brown skirts and hurried down the remaining steps. "We purchased this land with our own money, and we have built everything on it with our bare hands. This is our property. Ye do not have the right."

"That is the trouble with you colonials, you fail to recognize the king has the right to do as he pleases. And right now his army is taking all of your property. Be thankful you still have your lives." He rubbed his hands together as if dusting them. "In fact, I suggest you get your things quickly before I change my mind."

"Where is Captain Morgan?" Kirk asked, as Tyra pushed to her knees and staggered to her feet. Her aching side and bruised knee rebelled in protest, but her jaw was worse, like a swollen boulder.

"I thought I would save him the trouble of having to do this. So I volunteered to take care of it myself." Colonel Morgan pointed to the outdoors. "You will not be allowed to take a horse or wagon. You will only be allowed to take what you can carry."

"Come on, Kirk and Darren," Tyra said, waving her brother toward her. She was forced to talk out of one side of her mouth. Without a word, both lads came forward, giving the soldiers a hesitant glance, as if they didn't trust them. Tyra bent to Kirk's ear. "Two pairs of socks, breeches, shirts, and underclothes. Only one blanket for each of you."

The four of them climbed the stairs in silence. Once they reached the landing, Kirk and Darren went to Kirk's room. Tyra turned to her mother. "We cannot sneak a rifle by their notice," Tyra said. "But we could possibly get away with a pistol. I will get the one father left me and some ammunition, but we will need to put it in your bundle. They would not suspect you of carrying a weapon, but they would have no doubt about me."

Her mother reached up and wiped blood from the corner of Tyra's mouth with her sleeve. Tears sprang to her eyes. "Yer a brave lass, but ye might be bruised and sore for a wee while."

"True." Tyra gripped her hand. "We must hurry."

In her chamber, Tyra hated leaving behind her best gowns, but it could not be helped. She needed sturdy and sensible clothing to survive the harsh reality of travel and treacherous weather. She scrounged through her trunk and chose a suitable blue gown, as well as a green flannel dress with a stitched floral print. She selected a basic change of undergarments, two white caps, a brush, a few hair combs, and rolled up the blanket from her bed. The last item she grabbed was the pistol and the ammunition.

Tyra hurried to her mother. She had been staying in Callum's chamber since the British had taken over the master bedchamber downstairs. She laid the weaponry on the small table by the bed. "I will go downstairs and try to convince them to allow us some food and water from the kitchen."

"Good idea, lass," Mama grabbed the pistol. "And Tyra?" She paused in the doorway. "Do not do or say naught to provoke them further."

"I will behave," she promised, gripping the threshold frame. *What if they provoke me?*

When she arrived downstairs, Colonel Morgan waited with his arms crossed over his chest. His lips turned into a satisfied grin and his dark eyes watched her as he strolled to the bottom step to meet her. It was clear he thoroughly enjoyed his orders to remove them from their home. Did Hugh know? Had he chosen to stay away because it would be easier? Anger and betrayal simmered inside, but she swallowed it back, determined to keep her promise to her mother.

"Would you permit us to gather some food and water from the kitchen?" Tyra's stomach churned at the thought of having to ask this man for anything, but she set aside her pride and did it for her family. She had no idea what awaited them in the next few days and weeks. For now, they needed food to survive.

"Are you hard of hearing?" Colonel Morgan asked, twisting his head at an angle. He stared at her with a disgruntled expression. "I told you to carry whatever you could."

Tyra ground her teeth and stepped around him, resisting the urge to plunge her fist into his stomach. Instead, she held her head high, her shoulders straight, and walked down the hall to the kitchen.

She grabbed a loaf of bread her mother had made earlier. Securing a block of cheese, she listened to the sounds of her mother and the lads descending the stairs. Tyra gathered several slices of beef jerky and raisin cakes. Next, she grabbed three empty canteens from the cabinet cupboard and poured water in each of them. A moment later, she joined the rest of her family outside in front of the house.

The redcoats stepped aside giving them a wide path to walk through. They carried their belongings on foot, she and her brother on each side of her mother with Darren on the other side of Kirk.

Once they were out of the redcoat's hearing, Tyra noticed silent tears crawling down her mother's face, but she kept her chin at a determined angle.

"Will we go to Aunt Carleen's?" Kirk asked.

"Nay," Mama shook her head. "They will not sign a proclamation either. Quakers will not give their allegiance or bow to any human king. They will be forced out as well. 'Tis why they came to the colonies in the first place."

"Then what shall we do?" Kirk asked.

"We will go to the Tuscaroras," Tyra said. "'Tis what Da told me to do if things got worse."

*

Hugh was at the crossroad where Front and Church Streets intersected. It reminded him of a similar crossroad of where he stood in his own life. He had some serious decisions to make. All day he had carried out orders to evict families from their homes if they would not comply with Major Craig's proclamation. He had watched as families refused to give up their convictions to sign a proclamation they didn't believe in. Women and children cried in fear and grief over losing their homes.

Witnessing one family in particular would stay with him for the rest of his days. They were the Bates family, and he feared Tyra would never forgive him for what he did to her aunt and uncle. As he carried out his orders, they had looked at him with such disappointment and betrayal. Shame ate at Hugh like termites on a piece of wood.

Even though they were losing all they had worked for, Mrs. Bates had asked if the same thing was happening to the MacGregors. He could not give her the assurance she wanted, but he could tell her their names were not on the list he had seen.

Now the day was done, he could either enjoy a nice hot meal at the Burgwin House with the other officers or go to the MacGregors and confess what he had done to their cousins. As much as he dreaded the deed, Hugh did not want to shirk his responsibilities. He would tell them the truth. They deserved as much. In the meantime, he would pray they would give him understanding and forgiveness. These days he prayed more often.

"There you are!" His brother rode toward him and pulled to a stop beside him. "I was hoping you would come back and take dinner with the rest of us."

"I was contemplating it, but I thought I would go out to the MacGregors and give them the bad news of what happened to their cousins today." Hugh leaned forward on the pommel of his saddle.

Neil looked away, cleared his throat in discomfort, and adjusted his tricorn hat as if it didn't fit right. He recognized the signs, the same actions Neil had always shown when he was trying to protect Hugh from something. Dread pooled in his stomach like a brewing storm.

"Neil? What are you not telling me?"

"I know how fond you are of the MacGregor family," Neil said, scratching the side of his temple. "They were on Major Craig's list, and I offered to handle it. I knew it would be hard for you, and I figured you would refuse. The punishment for disobeying a direct order could get you imprisoned, beaten, or court-martialed. I did not want to see it happen."

"'Tisn't your place to make that decision for me," Hugh snapped, anger burrowing deep inside him. "You cannot always protect me like you did when we were young." Hugh pointed his thumb at his own chest. "I have grown up, Neil. I no longer think and want the same things as I did when we were lads in England determined to prove our worth to the world and all the people who had turned their noses at us. I no longer care about those people. They mean naught to me."

It was true. Everything that mattered to him was right here in the colonies. Why did he not see it before? Tyra MacGregor was worth more than a lifetime career in His Majesty's Royal Army. A hundred times more. What a fool he had been, hesitating and waiting. Now it could be too late.

"Where did the MacGregors go?" Hugh asked, gripping the reins tight in his fist.

"How am I supposed to know?" Neil demanded, his tone scratchy and irritated. "All I know is they packed their things and took off down the road. We secured the property, and I left a few men there to keep the place from looters and habitable."

Frustration pumped through Hugh's veins like dynamite ready to explode. Somehow, he managed to keep his temper in check. Even after being separated and at war for the past two years, his brother knew him too well.

"Did you overhear them say where they might go?" he asked.

"No, and I do not care. I think it is best they are gone." He jabbed a finger toward Hugh. "You were getting too attached to the girl. You may not realize it now, but I did you a favor."

"You fool yourself, brother." Hugh maneuvered his horse toward Neil. "'Tis I who did you a favor. I organized your escape from prison, while you have only caused a rift between us."

"Come Hugh, what is the meaning of this?" Neil slapped his thigh in anger and threw his fist on his hip while holding the reins with his other hand. "We have never kept score for favors in the past, and I do not intend to start now. You are my brother and that is the end of it."

"The favor I would ask of you is to let me go. I never intend to return to England. I dislike their high-handed ways, and there is naught there I wish to return to. My future is here in the colonies where a man can choose to be himself and make the most of his life through his skills, a trade in business, and where new money is every bit as good as old money."

"You speak treason!" Neil lowered his angered tone to a whisper. "I will not hear any more of this nonsense. Say you manage to escape the British Army, once we win the war, what then? You will be an outlaw, a criminal. Do you want that?"

"I do not want *this*!" Hugh jerked on the sleeve of his redcoat. "When I gave my allegiance to the king, I had no idea it would include removing innocent women and children from their homes, and depriving thriving communities of their basic freedoms, or how the tyranny people had claimed to suffer could be so bold in the face of my existence and contribution toward it."

"I knew you had become too enthralled with the wench!" Neil leaned forward as venom spewed from his mouth. "She has cast some spell over you. I have never heard you talk with so much confusion in all my life. You are lucky most people have gone inside and only I have heard you speak such betrayal. I wish I could say you are too deep into your cups, but alas, I cannot even give you that much credit to this absurdity of which you speak."

"At least her words have more clarity than yours do at this moment." Hugh shook his head with a scoffing chuckle. "I am going after her, and I will find her. You can be sure of it."

"I will not allow it!" Neil struck Hugh with a solid punch, but the swift action spooked Hugh's horse and he reared up. It gave him the right momentum he needed to lunge at his brother. They both flew over the animal and landed with a thump onto the hard ground. Neil's body hit first, cushioning Hugh's landing.

Neil's words echoed in Hugh's head, igniting the fury of his anger all over. Rage spurred him to his knees, and he pounded his fists into Neil's face, determined to teach him a lesson. Neil turned his head and lifted his elbows to block the onslaught.

A wad of gritty sand flew into Hugh's face, blinding and stinging him. He jumped up and staggered back, blinking as tears poured. Hugh hoped the sand would wash out before his brother came at him again. He had inhaled enough sand as it choked him and caused him to sneeze.

A disgruntled groan reached his ears, as movement followed. "I think you broke my nose!"

"You deserved it for what you did to Tyra and her family."

Hugh longed to rub his eyes, but he feared he would make things worse. He kept blinking and hoping his tears would wash out the sand. "We are finished Neil. After today, I want naught to do with you."

"You will change your mind once you realize the chit is not worth all you are giving up." Neil sputtered through the blood pouring from his nose and lip as he sat up.

"I cannot believe you would continue to call her such names." Hugh shook his head in disbelief. "You are not worth me wasting any more time on you."

Hugh found his horse a few feet away and mounted up. He took the reins, turned his horse, and broke into a canter.

While Hugh knew Tyra and her family were no longer at The MacGregor Quest, it was where her unwanted journey had started. He hoped he could find some clues or tracks to trace them. Where would they have gone? Since the Bates family had been evicted from their property as well, the MacGregors could not have gone there. Mrs. MacGregor had a pregnant sister in Charles Town. Would they have tried to travel so far on foot? Panic squeezed his heart. Whatever he did, he would have to hurry since the British Army would soon be after him.

"Lord, I realize I have not turned to you for guidance often in my life, but right now I need your help. Lead me to Tyra and her family. Please help me find them. And give me wisdom in how to protect them. Amen."

If he was going to start living a free life, he wanted to start it out right. Besides, after what he had just done, he was in jeopardy of being pursued and killed by both the British and the Continentals. The number of days he had left could be short indeed. With the increased chances of him departing this world, he wanted to be on better terms with his Maker. Everything was so clear. Why had he not seen the sorry state of his life before now? Perhaps he had, and he had chosen to ignore it, as his brother continued to do.

He approached The MacGregor Quest as darkness cascaded the landscape into a canvas of black. Where could they have gone? There was the sea on one side and nothing but swamp land behind them and on the other side. In front of them was the barrier of the Cape Fear River. They had not returned to Wilmington on the main road, the only other answer was the nasty swamp. He loathed the idea of going back to the place. Alligators and other unknown creatures lurked in the swamp—among the Tuscaroras.

Hugh's thoughts halted. When he had met her, she had saved his life from the Tuscaroras. When she wanted answers about her father and brothers and Neil, she had gone to the Tuscaroras. Had he not confined her in solitude for three days for venturing out into the swamps to find the Indians? They had come to her aid time after time. She trusted them, and it was obvious they were loyal to her. It made sense she would go to them now. Hugh glanced up to peer into the darkness surrounding him. But how would he find her?

23

Tyra woke with a start as a wagon rolled over the wooden bridge above them. Since she had not been able to follow the trails on her own property, she was not sure how to find the Tuscaroras. Her only hope was to circle back around from the other side of the woods and hope she could get close enough to the Tuscaroras to find them.

She stretched and yawned, rubbing her back from where she had been leaning against the wooden post beneath the bridge. It did not help to know her sordid sleeping arrangements would now increase the pain Colonel Morgan had inflicted upon her body yesterday. Tyra glanced over at her mother and the lads still sleeping. Their situation through the night had been no better. Like herself, Kirk and Darren were young and would recover quickly, but she was more concerned about their mother, even though she was in good health.

The wagon above them now rolled beyond the bridge and down the dirt road. Tyra wondered if they were friend or foe. Perhaps they could hitch a ride in the back of their wagon. She jumped to her feet and hurried up the embankment to the road where the wagon rolled at a slow pace. Only a few bags were in the bed of the wagon littered with a layer of hay. An elderly couple sat on the bench dressed in simple attire.

"Wait!" Tyra headed toward them, waving in the hope of getting their attention. The woman glanced over her shoulder with a curious expression, and her mouth dropped open. Gray curls crept out from her white mob cap. She turned and tapped her husband's arm and leaned over to whisper in his ear.

He glanced over his shoulder and pulled the reins to stop the wagon. They waited as Tyra reached them. The woman folded her hands in her plump lap and leaned forward. "My dear, are you out here all alone?" Her gaze traveled from the top of Tyra's head down to her dirty and wrinkled dress and the dust covering her black boots. "What happened to ya?"

Tyra decided they didn't have much more to lose, so she would tell the truth and risk the chance that they could be Tories. "Our home and property were confiscated by the British due to the Proclamation. We slept under the bridge last night, because we had nowhere else to go. If you happen to be going the same way as us, I was hoping you would allow us to ride in your wagon for a little ways?"

"Ah, the Proclamation, yes we have been the victim of the beast ourselves." The woman bobbed her head and clicked her tongue. "Those redcoats are an evil bunch, they are."

"We are headed to Elizabethtown," The man leaned forward placing his elbows on his knees. "How many of you are there?"

"Just myself, my brother, his friend, and my mother," Tyra said.

Her heart raced with anticipation. The idea of being able to sit for a while on a soft bed of hay was enticing.

After a moment, the man touched his fingers to the brim of his bicorn hat. "I reckon it will be all right," he said. "The good Lord knows we all need to help each other right now."

"Thank you, we are very grateful." Tyra shoved her thumb over her shoulder. "I will go get them, and we shall be right back."

By the time she made it to where she had left them under the bridge, both her mother and Kirk were awake. Her mother gave her a suspicious look and crossed her arms. "What are ye doing, lass?"

"Hurry!" Tyra pointed to their blankets. "Pack your things. An elderly couple agreed to give us a ride on their wagon."

"Get up!" Kirk shook Darren, who rolled over and grumbled as if he relished sleeping in a comfortable bed rather than the hard ground.

"How do we know we can trust them?" Mama asked. "How do we know they are safe?"

"Mama, our predicament is not ideal," Tyra said, rolling up her blanket. "In order to survive, we will need to trust strangers. My goal was to save our feet and legs from as much walking as possible, because in the coming days, I fear we will be walking much more than any of us are used to."

"Besides, did you not say they were an elderly couple?" Kirk asked. "I would think the three of us could handle an old couple."

"Of course we can." Darren rubbed his face as he sat up.

Tyra chuckled as she slung her bag over her back and waited for them to finish readying themselves.

Kirk helped Darren pack his things.

"True," Mama said with a grin. She gathered her bag in her arms and straightened. "Let us go."

The couple introduced themselves as Mr. and Mrs. Jeter. Once they were all settled in the back of the wagon, Mr. Jeter flipped the reins, and they launched the wagon in motion.

"How did you get to keep your wagon?" Kirk asked.

Tyra elbowed Kirk for asking such personal questions, but truth be known, she had wondered the same thing.

"Actually, they took everything from us except for the few clothes we could carry and a little bit of food. They did not allow us to keep our wagon either," Mr. Jeter said. "I waited until we reached a family outside of Wilmington and negotiated the purchase of this particular wagon."

"They must have been Tories," Kirk said with disgust. "Other than the British, the Tories are the only ones allowed to keep anything."

"He was my cousin," Mr. Jeter said. "He is not a Tory, but he gave in and signed the Proclamation."

"Do either of you know if all the Patriots in Wilmington were put out of their homes?" Mama asked.

Tyra knew her mother was wondering about Aunt Carleen and Uncle Ollie. If they had some way of reaching them, then perhaps they could join them.

"Indeed, our neighbors were put out of their home as well, but they went to Charles Town to be with family." Mrs. Jeter twisted around so she could see them.

"I have a sister in Charles Town as well," Mama said. "And the thought to go there did cross my mind, but I keep hoping this is only temporary, and we will soon be able to go back home."

"My dear, we are all hoping for it," Mrs. Jeter said.

"May I ask why you are heading to Elizabethtown?" Tyra asked. "Is it safer for Patriots there?"

"Before the British came to our house, we learned from a friend over sixty farmers got together joining the Patriot cause near Elizabethtown." Mr. Jeter said. "They took the bridge crossing the Cape Fear River and drove over three hundred Tories to the Tory Hole."

"And the good part is a woman helped them do it," Mrs. Jeter said, her brown eyes lit with excitement as thin lines formed around her eyes and mouth. "A woman by the name of Sally Salter served as a spy carrying a basket of baked goods into the enemy camp."

"Really?" Tyra asked.

"She sure did," Mr. Jeter said. "She was able to take information she had learned about the camp back to the Patriots. 'Twas valuable."

Tyra exchanged a knowing look with her mother. If they were not successful at finding the Tuscarora Indians, then they could possibly go to Elizabethtown and be safe.

"I must say, you all were blessed by the good Lord. 'Tis not yet cold outside or you might have frozen last night."

"True. August passed by so fast," Mama said. "So far, September is going by just as quickly."

They talked for another half hour until they came to a field Tyra recognized. She asked them to pause so they could get off the wagon. Tyra and her mother thanked them and said their good-byes. They waded through tall grass in the field as she led her mother and the lads to the woods where she knew the swamp would be.

"Tyra, I am not afraid of the swamp, but I do fear alligators," Mama said. "Is there some way to keep those wretched creatures away from us? 'Twas my only concern when yer father decided to settle here an' years later I still feel the same way about them."

"Just keep your eyes open and stay away from them. For the most part, they will not bother us as long as we do not bother them." Tyra laughed. "At least, that is what Da always told me."

They walked for several more hours, their boots sank into thick mud and mush. Kirk complained of hunger, so they stopped to eat some raisin cake and drink water from their canteens. A few moments later, they were back on the move.

The sound of twigs snapped several feet to the right.

"Did you hear?" Darren asked.

Tyra met her mother's worried gaze. If they all heard it, then it couldn't be her imagination. Could it be an animal? Something moved, and she saw the color red. What animal was red? Fear pumped through her veins like a tidal wave as she realized what they had seen was not an animal, but a person.

✐❦

Hugh's throat was dry as he swallowed and struggled to open his eyes. The room felt warm and cozy. In fact, it was the best sleep he had experienced in a long time. Whispering voices spoke a language he didn't understand. Who was in his room? Alarm shot through him as he summoned the courage to force his stubborn eyes open. A hazy glow greeted him, but he still couldn't make out the shapes of what he saw.

"Who is here . . . in my chamber?" His hoarse voice squeaked past his throat.

"My name is White Cloud." A female voice penetrated through his mind, but she didn't sound like Tyra or her mother. White Cloud? What did she mean?

"Where is Tyra MacGregor?" he asked, hoping for some good news. The last thing he remembered was looking for her as he thrashed through the woods in the dark. He couldn't see anything, but he kept remembering back to when he had last found her in the swamp and she had led him home through the woods behind her house. Before losing consciousness he had heard a noise, followed it, and stumbled over a root and hit his head against something—probably a tree trunk.

"Red Fox and his brothers look for her." The same soft voice spoke closer to him.

Hugh rubbed his face and blinked several times until a woman appeared in front of him. She had long black hair braided over her shoulders and a warm smile welcoming him. Her dark eyes narrowed as if she assessed him. She had such dark skin. Realization dawned and his eyes popped wide open. He jerked up to a sitting position and realized he had been sleeping on a fur mat.

"You are Tuscarora?" The spontaneous question came out like an accusation. To keep her from thinking the worst of him, he said, "Tyra told me about you. The British Army made her family leave their home. It was wrong and unfair. I hoped she might have come here."

"My husband a good tracker. They find her." She nodded, trying to encourage him.

He glanced around the room. They were in a long house with wooden beams across the top and poles holding up the place. A small fire burned in the center and the smoke floated up through an opening like a unique chimney. Two children were eating porridge by the fire, or at least, it looked like porridge.

"How did I get here?" he asked.

"You hurt head." She pointed to the side of his head. Hugh reached up and felt material wrapped around his head. At least the pain had dulled to a complete numbness. He wasn't sure if it was a good or bad sign. His black boots had been removed and placed against the wall. He still wore his white breeches and his white shirt hung loosely around him, but his redcoat was gone.

"Where is my red coat?" He pointed both hands to each shoulder.

"My brother liked it." She grinned as if it was perfectly acceptable for her brother to take something that did not belong to him. He decided it would be in his best interest to let the matter go. Besides, it wasn't as if he had need of it now that he had left the British Army to join the Continental forces—if they would have him.

"How did you know I was a good redcoat?" he asked, not understanding why they would risk helping him without knowing him.

"War Woman trust you." White Cloud shrugged as if it answered everything. "You not stay in her home, if she not trust you."

Hugh wanted to laugh at the concept but managed to refrain. If only they knew the politics of the British Army and how the MacGregors were not given a choice. Tyra had put up with his constant presence to keep the wrath and suspicion of Major Craig from her family.

Would she blame him since it was his brother who had evicted them with so little empathy? He prayed the Lord would bring forgiveness to her heart. To prove his sincere loyalty to the Continental cause and in the hope of winning over her father and brothers, he intended to enlist as soon as possible—after seeing to her safety.

Hugh sniffed the aroma of coffee mixed with the smell of burning wood from the small fire. A blue pot simmered on a hot rock. They lacked the convenience of modern furniture, solid wood walls, paintings and candelabras used to decorate most homes here in the colonies, but a coffee pot was not something he would have expected in such a primitive place either. Bows and arrows with handmade spears were in the far corner. Furs were draped over the walls constructed of rocks and red clay mud. Wooden utensils and clay pots and bowls were stacked on one side. A pile of chopped wood was on the other side.

"You like coffee?" White Cloud asked with a gentle smile.

"Yes." Hugh nodded, looking forward to the warm brew jolting him awake and stimulating his dormant senses. Since being with the MacGregors, he had developed a taste for the dark brew.

He spent the rest of the morning in White Cloud's pleasant company and with her two children. Hugh fought the urge not to go out on his own and search for Tyra. The only thing keeping him around the longhouse was the fact he would get lost in the swamp.

A crowd of voices grew louder outside and came closer. White Cloud looked up with a startled expression, but at the sound of more conversation, a slow smile drifted to her face. Female voices joined the others, and Hugh recognized Tyra and Mrs. MacGregor. "Red Fox found them," the words tumbled from his mouth as he stood and strode outside with White Cloud. Her children followed.

Shielding his eyes from the bright sun, Hugh squinted to see them. They looked tired and dirty, but well. Relief poured through him as Tyra's green eyes settled on him. Her smile faded as she crossed her arms and glared at him. Concern ate at the frayed edges of his nerves, but he continued striding toward her, ready to face whatever was his due. He glanced at Mrs. MacGregor and then at Kirk and Darren, but they only gave him wary looks, not the cold anger he sensed from Tyra.

"What are you doing here?" Tyra asked, pausing in front of him.

"I quit the British Army. I could no longer abide by the decisions being made," Hugh said. "I am sorry, Tyra. Sorry for what happened to The MacGregor Quest, and sorry for not leaving sooner. But most of all, I am thankful all of you are safe now."

"You quit?" she asked, eyeing him with hesitant suspicion as she tilted her head.

"Indeed, as I intend to join the Continentals as soon as I am able."

The news Hugh just delivered was not what Tyra expected. The wind whipped her hair into her eyes, and she brushed it behind her ear. It was rare for Hugh not to wear his red coat, instead he wore a white buttoned shirt with blooming sleeves down to his wrists.

"Is it why you gave Howling Wolf your red coat?" Tyra asked, glancing over at Red Fox's brother in the offending garment. It was the first thing she had seen flashing through the woods when the Tuscaroras had found them yesterday evening. Nightfall hit before they could return, and they ended up camping in a dry space. It was too dangerous to travel through the swamp in the dark.

Hugh cleared his throat in discomfort as he gave a quick glance in Howling Wolf's direction. "I did not exactly give it to him, but he is welcome to it. I have no further need of it."

"Will the British not come for you?" she asked, trying to imagine if he would have to spend the rest of his days hiding in the swamp until the end of the war.

"They are probably looking for me right now," he said. "Tyra, I had to do this. I left the British Army because I no longer agree with their policies or with the king."

"Fine, I believe you, and I agree with you. In fact, I am proud of the decision you have made." She pressed the heel of her hand to her forehead and looked away shaking her head. "I fear for your life. I understand why you left the army, but I do not understand why you feel the need to join the Patriots. Why can you not take a break from the war?"

"Right now I am a wanted man by both the British and the Continentals. I need to make peace with one side or the other, and I have made my decision."

"What decision?" she asked, tears springing into her eyes. "I do not want you to go back to war. Every day I live in fear I will receive more dreadful news about my father or one of my brothers. I do not want to feel the same way about you, as well."

"Tyra, you need to listen to me." Hugh grabbed her shoulders in a firm, but gentle grip. "The decision I have made is I want to spend ·

the rest of my life loving you. I never want to return to England. I want to stay here in the colonies with you and your family. I want us to wed, have children, and build our home here. But I cannot expect to do so if I do not earn the trust and approval of your father and brothers."

He leaned forward and kissed the top of her forehead. She smelled the scent of leather and coffee and savored the moment. Tyra closed her eyes as the tears spilled over onto her cheeks. "I am going back to war and will sign up with the Patriots, so our family will be at peace in the future. I do not want to give your father and brothers more reason to resent me." He cupped her cheeks, tilted her face up, and lowered his voice to a whisper. "I have to do this."

Her throat ached and her heart trembled with fear. Now that he had finally made the decision to leave the British as she had hoped, once again she could lose him to this blasted war. As much as she wanted to beg and plead with him, she also recognized the determination in his eyes and knew her efforts would be fruitless. Right now, they needed to make the most of the time they had left before his departure.

She took a deep breath and almost choked.

"Was this your way of proposing to me?" she asked, placing her hand against her heart as if to calm the rapid beating against her ribcage. Conversations started around them, most of what she heard was in the Tuscarora language, but Hugh remained silent. Just as she feared she had been mistaken in what she heard, he lowered his head and pressed his lips to hers. His kiss was as soft as a whisper of breath. When he pulled back, the Tuscarora men yelled their approval. Heat flooded her neck and face until she looked away and stared at her toes.

"It is." He took her hand and lifted it to his lips for another brief kiss. "But I have no ring to present to you, and I wish to have your father's consent. 'Twill wait until I return after the war." Hugh sighed. "This way you shall not be burdened with a particular understanding if I do not return whole or not at all."

"I would never turn my back on you if injured, but 'tis why I wish you would not enlist again," she said.

"And I would want the approval of your mother as well." Hugh gestured to Mama with an elegant bow and a handsome grin charming her straight through to the heart.

"Captain Morgan, my husband has not had the benefit of knowing ye as I have. If he had, I have no doubt he would be as pleased as I am." She wagged a finger at him with a sincere smile. "Although, I must say shedding the red coat will give ye favor with my Malcolm, it will."

"Then I am glad I did it." Hugh offered his right arm to Mrs. MacGregor and his left arm to Tyra. They both accepted him and headed toward the longhouse with everyone else following.

"When and where shall you enlist?" Tyra asked.

"In a few days, I shall travel to Elizabethtown, but for now, let us enjoy the refuge your Tuscarora friends have given us."

24

The next week passed by in a blur, and Tyra could not remember being happier. They spent their days living with the Tuscarora Indians and learning from them. While she and Hugh had an understanding, they set no wedding date and decided not to write her father and brothers of their engagement. She enjoyed their long walks and the freedom to hold hands without societal rules languishing between them.

Red Fox gave Tyra a bow and arrow so she and the lads could hunt their own food. Tyra gave Kirk and Hugh shooting lessons with the bow. To her amusement, Kirk turned out to be a fast learner. Hugh was too awkward with the bow and kept popping the string, sending the arrow into the ground instead of the intended target.

Now that the day had come for Hugh to leave for Elizabethtown, Tyra and her mother insisted on going with him. While her mother was grateful for the Tuscaroras' assistance, she longed to be among civilized society where she had a real roof over her head, a fireplace with a rock chimney to lessen the risk of fire, wood floors instead of dirt, and a bed not part of the hard ground. She had not learned the Tuscarora language and could not communicate with them. Tyra longed to make things easier on her and agreed to convince Hugh to take them along.

Since Hugh only had one horse, Tyra and her mother took turns riding, while he, Kirk, and Darren walked. Red Fox escorted them through the swamp to the main road heading west. As they traveled down the dirt road, Tyra prayed they would not come across any redcoats or Tories.

Too much of the war-torn world seemed to be in total chaos. The futility of societal rules seemed absurd compared to the need for survival. While on the road to Elizabethtown, they had come across entire families who were now homeless, many had split up among relatives and friends. Food was scarce. Horses, wagons, and carriages were a luxury. Ammunition for hunting rifles was nonexistent.

After traveling two days, they arrived in Elizabethtown on a bleak afternoon with the sky shrouded in white clouds. The temperature had dropped. Tyra guessed it was sometime near the end of September. Tree leaves had started changing to yellow, orange, and red, while some stubborn leaves remained summer green.

The town was much smaller than Wilmington. A mixture of homes and merchants lined the streets. The steeple of a church rose above all the other roofs, but it was the soldiers who caught her attention. They wore dirty and torn clothes. None of them had any consistent uniforms.

"Excuse me, sir!" Hugh called to a man coming toward them on foot. He carried a rifle over his shoulder and wore a black tricorn hat. A scruffy brown beard and mustache covered half his face. The man paused and gave Hugh a brief nod in greeting. He took his hat off as he turned to Tyra and her mother and bowed in greeting. Hugh realized the fellow was much younger than he originally thought, no more than a score of years.

"You look new to town," the lad said, tilting his head to the side and assessing them.

"I was wondering where I could enlist with the Patriots?" Hugh asked.

"Our militia took over the courthouse down the street on the right in the brick building." The lad pointed in the direction where they were already heading.

"Would there happen to be an inn or a boarding house for the ladies?" Hugh nodded toward Tyra and her mother. "They need a decent place to spend the night until I can make permanent arrangements for them on the morrow."

"We do not have an inn here, but Mrs. Wakefield lets out a couple of her bedchambers. 'Tis a respectable place." He settled his hat back on his head and adjusted it. "'Tis a small house, and she does not put out a sign to indicate it is a boarding house. You already passed it. 'Tis the gray house with the large porch and the fancy flowers out front."

"I saw it," Tyra said, remembering the geraniums and white lilies.

"We are much obliged, Sir," Hugh said, sticking out his hand. The man gripped him in a bold handshake.

"My name is Larson Gray if you need anything else," he said.

"Do you have any news on the war?" Kirk asked.

"Indeed, it is what I want to know," Darren said.

"As a matter of fact, I might," he rubbed his bearded chin as he gave the lads a teasing grin. "Have you heard the British took Hillsborough?" At the shake of their heads, he continued. "Patriot Governor Thomas Burke was captured."

"How terrible," Mama said, shaking her head in disbelief and disappointment. "I had hoped this war would soon come to an end."

Tyra stepped closer to the horse where her mother sat and reached up to take her hand in a show of support. "'Twill not be long, Mama. Let us keep praying. We cannot give up hope."

"'Tis nice to meet you." His gaze slid to Mama. "I have heard your sentiments expressed by several others of late. Unfortunately, there is no sign either side is winning the war. Your daughter is right and wise. We must not lose heart."

"Thank ye." Mama offered a smile that Tyra knew was forced. "I do not mean to sound downtrodden, but most recently, I have lost a son to the Patriot cause. I cannot help fearing I could lose my husband and two more sons."

"I understand your dilemma." He tipped his fingers to his hat in a farewell. "I must be on my way, but if any of you need anything, I am stationed at the courthouse with most of the other men in the militia."

As Mr. Gray walked away, Hugh looked over at Tyra and her mother and shrugged. "Shall we continue to the courthouse since we have already passed the boarding house?"

"Nay, I believe we should split up." Mama dismounted Hugh's horse and handed the reins to him. "You head over to the courthouse, while we go find lodgings at the boarding house."

"Nonsense, the courthouse can wait," Hugh said. "As long as I am here, 'tis my duty to see you, Tyra, and the lads settled and cared for. Besides, I intended to pay your rent. I know the British stripped you of everything. 'Tis the least I can do."

"Lad, ye forget I am a Scotswoman," Mrs. MacGregor said, reaching up and patting him on the cheek as if he was Kirk.

✍

It took some convincing, but Hugh finally convinced Mrs. MacGregor to allow him to pay the rent for the first two months. He argued there was no telling how long he would be away, as well as her husband and sons. In the meantime, she would need what savings she had in order to provide food and necessary items for herself and her children.

He left them to get settled and headed down Main Street toward the courthouse. The slight breeze brushed against his face, as a man passed by on horseback. When Hugh drew closer to the courthouse, he realized the building was not made of brick, but merely painted the color of brick. The front entrance was level with the street, and the wooden door was propped open with a rock. Hugh stepped inside and walked over to a soldier writing at his desk.

"Pardon me, sir," he said. "We have recently arrived from Wilmington, and I would like to enlist."

The soldier looked up and trained his dark blue eyes on Hugh, assessing him. Unlike the other soldiers he had seen on the street, this man wore a blue uniform coat and a white wig tied by a blue ribbon at the nape. With a lift of his brown eyebrows, he set his quill in the holder and placed his elbows on the desk before his fingers.

"My name is Captain Longstreet. I take it the Tories have forced you out of your home? Yours is not the first family to arrive here in the last fortnight, although I must say, few of them have the distinct English accent that you have."

"True, I was born in East London. In the short time I have been here in the colonies, I have enjoyed my freedom, and I have come to respect the Patriot cause. I wish to marry and make my life here."

Captain Longstreet pulled out a book, opened it to an empty page, and pointed to the first line. "Please sign your name here." He sat back in his chair and surveyed Hugh for another moment. "Just how long have you been here in the colonies?"

"Three years," he said, signing his name in bold strokes in oblong curves and loops.

"And we have been at war with England much longer. How have you managed to avoid enlisting before now?" Captain Longstreet tilted his head in question.

"I did not." Hugh stepped back and dropped his hands at his side as he met Captain Longstreet's gaze. "I served under Major James Craig in Wilmington, and before him General Lord Cornwallis in the British Army."

The captain sat in silence, while Hugh waited to see if he would be carted off to prison or laughed at and rejected. Captain Longstreet took a deep breath. "I have lost count of the number of men who have defected from British forces or to the British forces. In the last month alone, we have lost hundreds of men on the East Coast due to Major Craig's Proclamation. I must say, you are the first to defect to our side during this time."

"I have witnessed enough treachery against the innocent civilians of Wilmington and the surrounding areas. I will not serve under a leadership who mistreat women and children and makes them homeless."

"You say you want to wed here, I take it the woman is a colonial?" He linked his hands behind his head and waited for an answer. His lips twisted in a mischievous grin. "There is naught better than a pretty face to change a man's heart."

Hugh did not deny it. Instead, he straightened and met the man's gaze. "What are my orders?"

"You have no orders as yet," Captain Longstreet said. "First, you must meet with Colonel Robeson. He will determine your fate." He scooted his chair back and stood to his feet. Captain Longstreet strode out to the hallway and disappeared, leaving Hugh to wonder what would happen next.

A few moments later, Hugh was taken back to a small office where he met another man wearing a blue coat uniform and a white wig. Captain Longstreet introduced him to Colonel Robeson. The man looked to be in his early forties and had a deep voice ringing with authority. On first impression, Hugh liked him much better than Major Craig.

Over the next hour, Hugh was drilled on his knowledge about the British forces. They asked numerous questions about the headquarters in Wilmington, those who were prisoners, and if the community still supported the Tories. On that score, Hugh had to give them the unfortunate truth—most all were Tories.

Hugh sat in an uncomfortable wooden chair creaking with every move he made. He tried to remain still, but his muscles and joints ached sitting in one position for so long. The other two men sat in similar chairs across the oak table, facing him.

"Mr. Morgan, how do we know you are trustworthy?" Colonel Robeson asked. "We intend to lead a charge to free Governor Thomas Burke, and for all we know, you could lead us into an ambush."

"Colonel, you have a valid concern." Hugh crossed his booted foot over his knee and rested his elbows on the arms of the chair. "I cannot give you evidence of my new loyalty to the Patriot cause. You will have to decide if you want to step out in faith and trust me."

"Unfortunately, you speak the truth," Colonel Robeson said with a sigh. "The day after the governor was captured, a force of three hundred left Hillsborough to try and take him back. Over two hundred men were wounded or killed. The attempt was not successful. Yet, the attack left the British vulnerable. I have heard a report Colonel David Fanning was shot in the arm and shoulder. If ever there was a chance to rescue Governor Burke, now would be the time."

"I did not know about the rescue attempt," Hugh said, as he scratched his bearded chin weighing all the possibilities. "From what you have told me, I would agree. I have met Colonel Fanning, and he is a ruthless man, much like Major James Craig himself."

"We leave in two hours, and you may go with us, but you will be under Captain Longstreet's command." Colonel Robeson nodded in the direction of the captain. "Your skills and experience as an officer will have to suffice at the rank of a private until we know you can be trusted."

"Meet us in front of the courthouse in two hours. Then I will give you a rifle and ammunition, and you shall receive your marching orders," Captain Longstreet said. "In the meantime, I suggest you eat a hearty meal and bring what food you can. Dismissed."

⦆

Tyra surveyed their rented chamber in somber silence. It was not what they had hoped for, but it would have to do. The bed was pressed against the wall with a narrow table holding a wash basin beside it. There was not enough space to afford an extra chair for a visitor or a looking glass. She feared the tiny fireplace could not hold a fire brave enough to warm the chamber. No mantle graced the bare wall. The only other piece of furniture in the room was a simple pine carved wardrobe standing against the far wall.

Mama sat down on the bed with a huge sigh and brushed her blonde hair from her forehead. She glanced around the chamber, shaking her head in disbelief. "Do ye believe the two of us can manage in this wee chamber?"

"We must," Tyra said. "Do you not believe this is better than sleeping on a dirt floor with the Tuscarora Indians?"

"I do." Mama nodded. "But I do not like being separated from the lads with so many strangers in the house."

"I know, but they are together and will be fine." Tyra wrapped an arm around her mother's shoulder and squeezed her in a tight hug. "Da will be so proud of Kirk when he returns. He has stopped complaining of not being in the war and has greatly matured since we learned of Scott's passing. If it were not for Kirk, we would not have had so many fine meals this past year. The lad has taken excellent care of us."

"Indeed, he has. I intend to go inspect his and Darren's makeshift chamber to be sure 'tis suitable." Mama chuckled as she stood to her feet. "I must admit, they are most pleased to be sharing the basement quarters with Mr. Morgan." She lifted her finger for emphasis. "Now there is a man of contrast, if I ever did know one. Even when he was on the wrong side, one could not help liking him."

"I keep finding it difficult to call him Mr. instead of Captain." Tyra gripped her knees as she met her mother's deep blue-eyed gaze. "Do you think he will come to regret his decision? He has lost his rank, the respect of his friends and family, and his country. I do not wish him to come to resent me."

"Do ye love him, lass?" Mama asked, settling her hands on her hips with a lift of her eyebrow.

"Of course I do, but is it enough?" She waved a hand in the air. "What if he changes his mind and comes to fancy some petite beauty who is not a giant like me? Someone who sews and cooks better and says all the right things around his friends and acquaintances. Someone who does not embarrass him."

"Then I daresay, 'twas not true love that established the bond between ye. What is all this nonsense talk anyway? Ye do not sound like the bold and defiant lass I know I raised." Mama stepped closer and leaned forward to better inspect Tyra in the lantern light. "Of all the people I have known, ye've never been one to second guess yerself. Ye knew yer own mind afore ye was two years."

Tyra swallowed with difficulty under her mother's scrutinizing gaze, and her breath caught. A heavy burden tugged at her heart as she tried to muster enough faith to trust God and let go. She never questioned her family's love and devotion. She had been born among them and always felt loved by them. Donahue Morgan was the first person she had ever come to love so deeply outside of her family who did not actually have to return her love. What if he only thought he loved her and later changed his mind?

"I know my mind. 'Tisn't my mind I am worried about." Tyra wrung her hands in discomfort and stood, ready to end this discussion. "I shall go with you to inspect their new chamber."

"Lass, do not allow fear to control yer heart. Every man and woman must take a risk in loving each other. 'Tis the way it is." Mama gripped her shoulders, not allowing her to escape. She gave Tyra a gentle shake. "But if the two of ye also love each other through the eyes of Christ, yer love shall be perfect and 'twill endure." She reached up and laid a comforting palm on Tyra's cheek. "Remember, lass, in First John it says, *there is no fear in love; but perfect love casteth out fear; because fear hath torment. He that feareth is not made perfect in love.*" She turned and walked toward the door. "Now let us go down to the basement."

Tyra followed her mother in silence, pondering what she had said. It sounded simple enough, but it didn't feel like it. The stairs were narrow and shrouded in darkness with walls on each side. As they reached the bottom, cool air breezed over the exposed skin on their hands, face and neck. It felt refreshing, and Tyra forgot her worries as she focused in the dim lantern light. The walls were made of rock and clay mud, and it smelled of damp earth. Her skin crawled with the fear that snakes and other creatures could be lurking down here. She wanted to inspect the corners for nasty spiders and rid her brother of their troublesome presence.

"'Tis great," Kirk said with a wide grin. He raised his arms and turned around in a circle, while Darren leaned against the wall and crossed his arms. "Feels like I am living in a cave." His voice took on the tone of a storyteller filled with adventure and imagination. "I can pretend to be an ancient caveman who hunts and lives off the land with naught but my wits and knowledge. And I am already prepared." He pointed to the bow and arrows lying by his bed against the wall. Tyra recognized the set Red Fox had given them.

"It does resemble a cave," Darren said with a grin.

"How would ye like to make a cedar trunk to hold yer clothes and personal items?" Mama asked. "I think 'twould be good for ye to learn a new trade. A woodworker down the street might like to take on an apprentice. He had a sign in his window looking for one. I believe ye're ready, son."

"Really?" Kirk beamed with excitement as his eyes grew wide in surprise. "I will check with him first thing on the morrow."

"What about me?" Darren asked.

"We shall find something for you as well," Mama said.

"Tyra?" Hugh's deep voice carried from above. Footsteps came down the stairs toward them. "I have some news."

He had returned sooner than she anticipated. Tyra strode toward the stairs and met him. He grabbed her hand and lifted it to his lips, and she could feel herself blush. Thankful the light was dim, Tyra pulled him toward her mother and brother in the center of the room. "We were just inspecting your new quarters."

"I will not have a chance to stay the night as I had hoped. The Patriots have accepted me as a private until I have proven myself and I can be trusted. They are pleased to use my knowledge of the British Army."

"But why will you not be allowed to stay the night here? Have they put you up someplace else?" Tyra asked.

"No, we leave in less than two hours to go on a campaign to try and free Governor Burke from the clutches of the British." She gripped his hand tighter, and he patted the top of her smooth skin in an attempt to comfort her. "I have been advised to eat a warm, hearty meal before I go. I spoke to Mrs. Wakefield before I came down, and she has agreed to make us such a meal. Apparently, there are three other soldiers who have rented rooms from her, and she would like to send us off with full bellies."

Tyra bit her lip in disappointment. He was leaving her much too soon. *God, please bring him back to me safe and whole.*

25

*H*ugh loaded his gun and set his powder back in the container hanging from his belt. He hoped it wouldn't get wet in the rain pouring down around them. While gray clouds had filled the sky all day, by evening dark clouds rolled in, and with it came the wind and rain. Water poured off his tricorn hat onto the worn brown coat another soldier had loaned him. There were no more blue uniforms and all he owned was what the British Army had provided. Right now he didn't care for his new comrades to know he had fought for the enemy, and he hoped his superior officers wouldn't tell them.

They marched four men abreast against the roaring wind. At times it sounded like lonely wolves howling in the distance. Only the officers had horses. Hugh had left his own horse in the livery stable for Tyra and her mother in case they had need of it. He paid for the animal's care so they would not be burdened. Reaching for the container with Tyra's lock of hair, Hugh gripped it in his palm thinking of the tears she tried to hide from him when she had kissed him good-bye. His heart ached being separated from her, but it was filled with love and gratitude in knowing she would be waiting for him when he returned.

Only sixty men were well enough to travel on this campaign. Hugh knew his superior officers were counting on the British being too wounded to put up much of a resistance. This strategy would only work if their reports were accurate. Colonel Fanning had far more soldiers than their sixty.

He splashed through several mud puddles and hoped his old boots would hold up through the harsh conditions. As they marched on, the sound of the rain pounding the trees and earth grew louder. Glimpses of the Cape Fear River through the woods proved it now flowed over the bank at a rapid pace. Flooding would soon be a problem if the storm continued at this rate. It reminded him of the last storm they endured at The MacGregor Quest. At least this time, Tyra and her family were out of harm's way at the boarding house. The river would have to flood a great distance to reach them, and it was unlikely.

Thunder cracked through the sky with a flash of lightning. It struck a tree above them and snapped the trunk. It swayed and tee-tered until it crashed over into another tree, smashing into various limbs and bringing a load down toward them.

"Watch out!" one of the soldiers from the back called.

Men scattered in different directions, but two were not fast enough. Both men were hit. One received a blow to the head, while the other was trapped beneath the larger half of the branch. Something snapped, and Hugh prayed it wasn't his leg bone.

"Argh!" The agonizing cry ripped through the air, piercing one's gut like a lance.

Hugh and the others rushed to pull the heavy limb off him. It took three of them as they bent to help and their voices were lost in another rumble of thunder.

"On three," Hugh said. "One, two, three!" They strained as one unit, lifting the offending piece of wood as two others pulled the wounded soldier free. The man cried out in pain. Hugh glanced down and saw his bone protruding through his bleeding skin. The rain washed over it as fast as the blood continued to surface. Hugh glanced away and fought a rising tide of nausea. He feared the leg would have to be amputated.

Captain Longstreet rode over to the men bending over the uncon-scious soldier, while Colonel Robeson came to where Hugh and the other men tended to the soldier with the broken leg. He dismounted, peered at the injury, and shook his head. More lightning lit up the world around them.

"You four will stay behind." Colonel Robeson pointed to a group of soldiers behind Hugh. "Take these two injured men back to Elizabethtown and find a doctor. Let them know the river is flooding the area and they may need to send rescuers to the local farms." He stood to his full height and swung his arm around in a circle above his head. "The rest of you march forward!"

As ordered, Hugh stepped back in line and marched on. Over the next three hours they continued to persevere through the storm. His clothes were now so wet they clung to him like matted dirt. If they came across the British, he couldn't imagine being able to shoot a target or reload a gun in the onslaught of this weather.

Colonel Robeson and Captain Longstreet rode their horses up front. Two other officers rode at the end of the marching soldiers, while two others flanked the sides in the middle. A blister on his right heel began to nag at him since water had managed to seep into his boots. The temperature continued to drop as he shivered in the cold rain.

"Halt!" Colonel Robeson lifted his palm, and everyone rolled to a stop.

Hugh strained to see over the shoulders of the men in front of him, but the pouring rain and dark clouds made it impossible. Conversations grew louder among the soldiers at the front and some pointed at something.

"What is it?" Hugh asked aloud to no one in particular.

"The river has flooded across the road." One of the soldiers turned to answer.

The captain and colonel continued to discuss what to do, or at least it is what Hugh assumed they were doing. A crashing and splashing sound broke through the woods. Captain Longstreet and Colonel Robeson turned their mounts and yelled commands as they rode by the line of men. Their words consumed by the noise and rumbling thunder around them. Soldiers from the front ran toward them. They were swallowed by the rushing wave crashing over them and destroying everything in its path. Hugh turned to run, but he feared it was too late.

⟡

Tyra woke with a terrible headache from a restless night of sleep. Not only did it storm most of the night, but she and her mother had so little space that Tyra fell off the edge of the bed and spent the rest of the night on the floor. Her back was sore and her eyes felt heavy, but she went ahead and dressed, trying to stay as quiet as possible without waking her mother.

She tiptoed past the kitchen where Mrs. Wakefield was already cooking bacon and eggs. The aroma drifted into the hallway and teased her nose until her stomach rumbled. She clenched her jaw, determined to go for a walk before taking the time to break her fast. Last night she had dreamed of floods and tidal waves—crazy things leaving her feeling uncomfortable and insecure. Tyra hoped the walk in the fresh air would help clear her mind.

Outside, the sunrise painted the sky into a mixture of pink and orange. It was gorgeous, and she wished she had the talent to capture it onto a canvas. The entire world was wet from the storm and puddles were everywhere in the street. She kept stepping right and then left to avoid them. Before she knew it, she had passed the livery stable, the church, and the courthouse. On the other side, she noticed a small brick building. A dim light shone through the front window, Tyra paused, staring inside. A man stood at a large iron printing machine. She wondered if he had news on the war. Without thinking about it, she wandered inside.

The elderly man looked up in surprise. He pressed his wire spectacles up on his nose and rubbed his fingers through his gray hair. Tilting his head, he blinked in confusion. He was so thin his bony shoulders hunched over through his wrinkled shirt. Black ink covered the tips of his fingers. "We are not yet open. I am still working on the morning edition of the news."

"Do you need any assistance?" Tyra asked. "I write well and could help you with your stories."

"I have never hired a woman before." He chuckled as if the notion were insane. "I lost my apprentice when he decided to join the war. I have been on my own ever since."

"Do you have any news about the war?" she asked.

"If I did, I would not tell you." He went back to placing his block letters on the metal plate. "'Twould be hard for me to sell newspapers."

"If I can read and write, what should it matter if I am a woman?" Tyra shrugged, determined to press the matter since she needed a job and could not think of anything else she could do. She was not an excellent cook or seamstress, at least not for pay. Her skills in shooting a gun, wielding a sword, or shooting archery were not in high demand for women, and most men did not want to be taught by a woman.

"Men do not want to read about business, war, or politics written by a woman. The fact you can read and write does not mean you have a good understanding of the topic, or that you should." He turned his back on her and kept working. "Now, if you will pardon me, I have work to do."

"How do you compete with the newspaper in Wilmington since it is not far from here?" Tyra walked toward him, trying to think of something to prove he needed her without offending him with the idea that his newspaper lacked something. "They cover both local and regional news, especially about the war."

"I cannot afford to send reporters about the country to bring back news from other places." He sighed, taking off his spectacles and pinching the bridge of his nose. "Since it is just myself, I cannot afford to leave the office unmanaged. I have an arrangement with the Wilmington editor. I buy a certain number of copies in exchange for the ability to reprint some of his news. Otherwise, I rely on letters from residents and friends elsewhere, and I mostly report on the town news here."

"If you allow me to work as your assistant in the office, you would be able to travel to other places and report the news yourself."

"I am too old." He shook his head and plopped his spectacles back on his nose. "I like my current arrangement."

"If you change your mind, I am staying at Mrs. Wakefield's." Disappointment filled her. She would probably end up cleaning people's laundry for meager change. "Are you certain you do not have any news about the war? I have not heard from my father and brothers in a long time, not since one of my brothers was killed."

"I am sorry about your brother." He turned back to placing his letters again. "It may be because they are stuck in Yorktown, Virginia, on the battlefield."

"In Yorktown? What do you mean?" Tyra asked, trying to remember where Yorktown was in Virginia. Her mind went blank, and she longed for a map. Lately, her sense of direction seemed impaired, much like the chaos in the world around them. The colonies had been at war for so long she had forgotten what life was like before the fighting began.

"I do not want you spreading this news on the street, but the latest is General George Washington has General Lord Cornwallis trapped in Yorktown. The British have nowhere else to turn. Washington is besieging them on one side, and there is naught but the sea on the other." He turned and gave her a meaningful glance. "The war may soon be over."

"The door burst open and a young man hurried in breathing hard. "Some soldiers returned wounded. The Cape Fear River has overflowed!"

☙✦

The water flipped Hugh's feet from under him and the force of the impact took his breath away, especially the cold temperature.

Something slammed into his side, and it felt like someone's boot kicked him in the head. He fought to stay conscious as the current dragged him under. He kicked to the surface and broke through to gasp for air. It was too dark to see anything, and the clouds hid the light of the moon and stars. Just as he caught his breath again, the water slammed him into a tree.

Hugh wrapped his arms around the trunk, clawing at the bark until he grasped a sturdy limb and hung on. The water kept climbing. He took a few moments to catch his breath before reaching for another sturdy branch above him and forced himself up. At times, the tree swayed in the wind and from the impact of the current and other objects hitting it. He listened as men screamed and cried out for help, and there was nothing he could do but survive.

After what seemed like hours, the cries stopped, the storm calmed, and the water reached a steady level, but never to the height where he had climbed. His muscles ached as he hung on in one position. Throughout the night he talked to himself and sang songs to stay awake, and when his patience was near an end, he talked to his Maker. He talked for so long he began to feel as if he wasn't alone— as if God was right beside him—listening to everything. It gave him comfort, something he desperately needed when his arms were so weary he could no longer feel them.

The words, *I will never leave thee, nor forsake thee* kept repeating in his mind. He was not like Tyra and had never memorized Bible Scriptures, so he hoped his mind was not playing tricks on him. He wanted to believe those words. As the voices of his comrades had long faded into darkness, Hugh did not want to be alone. He had a feeling this was going to be the longest night of his life.

Dawn finally came and with it the long awaited sunlight he had prayed for. Somehow he had finally fallen asleep and managed to keep himself positioned in the tree where he had taken refuge. He glanced down and realized the water had receded several feet. He wondered if anyone else had survived. His fingers were stiff and almost frozen to the tree. He made a fist and pressed his fingers out like a fan and repeated the process to get his blood pumping to his fingertips. With slow precision, Hugh began to move each part of his body until he thought he could manage to climb down the tree and swim. More than anything, he dreaded lowering himself back into the freezing water, but he couldn't remain here forever, so it had to be done.

He feared pneumonia would overtake him as he plunged into the water. Hugh swung his arms and kicked his legs, determined he would not freeze to death before he found another resting place or someone came to his rescue. His lungs burned, and his head pained him with fatigue. After a while, numbness set in, and he feared the worst. "Lord . . . please . . . help me . . . keep going."

"There is someone!" a voice said in the distance, but Hugh was too weak and numb to respond. Even though he could no longer feel his body, he willed his arms and legs to keep moving. "Hurry! He is in trouble."

A rowboat appeared beside him. Voices kept talking to him, but he could not understand what they were saying. He knew they spoke English, at least he thought they did, but his mind was so foggy. He continued to shiver as he tried to speak and his lips trembled. "Cold."

"Yes, I know," the voice said. It sounded like Tyra, but he could not be sure. Perhaps his mind had conjured her up in a dream.

"Kirk, help me get this wet coat off him." It was Tyra. Relief swept through him, and he knew he would be warmed and cared for.

People kept moving him around. He didn't mind. It meant he was still alive and had survived the ordeal.

"Private Morgan, I know you are having trouble concentrating, but was there anyone else out there?" a man's voice asked.

Hugh tried to open his eyes, but they refused to cooperate. Instead, he shook his head and the world spun out of control. He coughed and took a moment to recover. "Voices screamed, but they faded."

Something dry wrapped around him as soft hands cradled his head.

"Let us get him back to town. He needs dry clothes and a warm fire," a female voice said.

"Tyra?"

"Yes, my love." Warm lips kissed his forehead. "'Tis me. I am here."

Hugh continued to fade in and out of consciousness. Each time he woke, Tyra was there to comfort him. At times, he recognized her mother and brother. At other moments, it sounded as if a doctor was poking and prodding him, or talking over him as if he wasn't present.

At one point, he woke to see a chamber with four walls and a fire blazing in the hearth. The heat felt so wonderful. Hugh did not recognize the chamber, but he only wanted to hear Tyra's voice. He kept calling for her. Finally, she appeared over him with a relieved smile.

"You are awake," she said.

"I am." He tried to sit up, but his head pounded with a heaviness he could not endure. "Where am I?"

"You are in a chamber at Mrs. Wakefield's. She gave up her own chamber for you." Tyra lifted his hand to her lips and kissed it.

"Who survived?" he asked.

"So you remember what happened?"

"Unfortunately, most of it." Hugh lifted his free hand to his forehead, wishing the aching pain would go away. "It feels good to finally be warm again."

"Oh, thank God." Tears sprang to her eyes. "The doctor said you suffered hypothermia and could have brain damage. The fact you remember everything means you will be fine."

"I should hope so." He took a deep breath and swallowed, realizing how thirsty he felt. "I need water."

"I will get it for him," Mrs. MacGregor said, standing at the foot of his bed.

"Colonel Robeson survived, but Captain Longstreet did not." Tyra reached for his hand and leaned close.

"What about the others?" he asked.

"'Tis my understanding that sixty went out on the campaign and only fifteen have survived." Tyra bent forward and kissed his forehead as her red hair spilled over her shoulders and around his face. The scent of honey breathed new life into him. His stomach rumbled.

"I am hungry."

"Oh, Hugh." She pressed her warm lips against his and leaned back all too soon. "I have so much to tell you."

26

$\mathcal{A}$ week passed before Hugh was back to himself again. For once, Elizabethtown had the exclusive story that Wilmington wanted. Hugh's survival story was one many wanted to hear, but he would only grant Tyra the opportunity to write it. By mid-October, she finally had her name in print. The story ran in the Elizabethtown newspaper, as well as in the *Cape Fear Mercury* of Wilmington. The other great breaking news in the headlines was General Lord Cornwallis had surrendered to General George Washington. The colonists had created history in beating the greatest army in Europe. They had actually won their freedom from England and folks celebrated the news all over town.

Tyra prayed her father and brothers would soon return home. Most everyone was in great spirits these days, even her mother and Kirk. Darren had discovered an aunt who had fled to Elizabethtown and decided to stay with her. Hugh continued to mend, and his full recovery looked optimistic. October flew in and out of their lives like a whirlwind.

One November afternoon, Tyra read in the newspaper John Ashe had contracted smallpox and had been released from the Wilmington prison. He had died on his way home to Sampson County. Knowing Cornwallis had surrendered and Major Craig would soon be forced to give up Wilmington, Tyra and her mother wanted to return home.

Hugh refused to let them go. He wanted to give the smallpox epidemic more time to leave Wilmington. They ended up spending Thanksgiving at Mrs. Wakefield's house. A week later news reached them that Major James Craig had abandoned Wilmington and his destination was Nova Scotia. It was time to return home.

Hugh rented a wagon for them and hitched his horse. Colonel Robeson granted him a few days leave to escort them. Tyra rode in back of the wagon bed with Kirk, while her mother rode up front on the bench with Hugh driving. They huddled under a quilt with a warm brick as their only heat.

"I do not want to sound ungrateful," Tyra said through chattering teeth. "But I am glad we will not have to spend another holiday away from home. Christmas would not feel the same if we were not at The MacGregor Quest."

"'Tis still three weeks away," Kirk said. "Do you think Da, Callum, and Alec will have enough time to return home?"

"I am certain they will do their best," Mama said, with a quick glance over her shoulder. "Still, I think we should not get our hopes up." Sadness lingered in her tone, and Tyra knew she was thinking of Scott. It would be their first Christmas without him, and even if the others made it home safely, nothing would change the fact that he would never again be with them.

Her mother had carried on for her and Kirk's sake, but Tyra had heard the weeping at night when her mother thought she was asleep. It carried on for several months, and Tyra would lay still as silent tears crawled down her face. For herself, she had come to terms with Scott's passing, but she grieved for her mother's pain. It was hard enough losing a brother, but even though she was not yet a mother herself, she sensed there was no comparison. In truth, she never wanted to know the feeling of losing a child.

They traveled for most of the day and arrived home late in the afternoon. Daylight still lingered, and they would have a chance to see in what condition the British had left their beloved home. As they drove down the dirt road, the Cape Fear River sparkled in the sun's remaining rays. Excitement built inside her as the white two-story house came in view up on the hill. At least from this distance, it looked as beautiful as she remembered. The British had burned so many homes throughout the colonies. She closed her eyes and whispered a prayer of thanks that The MacGregor Quest still stood as tall as the day her father had built it. At least, their father and brothers would have a home to come back to after years of marching on foot and living in makeshift tents and temporary shelters.

"Mama and Kirk, we are home!" Tyra's heart pounded as they pulled up the circular drive, and she rose up on her knees. She never wanted to leave this blessed place again. Once they slowed to a stop, Tyra scrambled to the edge and leaped down.

Hugh hurried around to help her mother descend, while Kirk jumped out behind Tyra. She gripped her mother's arm, and Kirk took their mother's other arm. They climbed the porch steps as one. The oak wood on the front door looked weathered and scarred from where Neil had kicked it during their struggle. Inside, the foyer and hall was littered with broken pieces of furniture and a combination of empty liquor bottles and jugs of rum. Paintings had been slashed and the walls were scarred and scratched, but the overall structure looked intact.

Mama clutched a hand to her stomach and covered her mouth with the other. Tears filled her eyes as she looked at Tyra. "'Twill be all right. God has preserved our home!"

Tyra embraced her as Kirk wrapped strong arms around them both. Over the last year he had grown into a tall tree of a man. He now equaled Tyra's height, and his shoulders and back were almost as broad as her Da and Callum. She wondered if Alec had grown as well.

"We should probably inspect the rest of the house," Hugh said as he walked into the parlor.

It looked much the same. The keys on the piano were destroyed. Someone had taken an object and hammered them to pieces. The kitchen had been raided of all its contents. In each room, soot from the fireplaces had been dumped into the floor. Someone had taken a sword and slashed the beds to shreds.

"Unfortunately, I was most definitely looking forward to sleeping in the comfort of my bed again." Tyra dropped her hands to her waist as she stared at what was once her bed. "I suppose a good night's rest will still have to wait."

"I am so sorry, my love." Hugh walked over and wrapped an arm around her shoulders and kissed the top of her head. "What they did was useless and cruel, but your mother is right. At least they did not burn the place."

"I know." She nodded, trying not to let the despondency seep into her heart. "Did you see my wardrobe? All my clothes were slashed as well."

"'Twill be replaced. I promise," he said, lifting her hand and sealing his promise with a kiss on top of her knuckles.

"Now, I will not need to feel guilty for buying new material for the latest fashion." She sighed and folded her arms. "When next I can afford it."

"Tyra!" Mama called. She could tell something had distressed her. Tyra rushed to the door and down the hall to Scott's chamber. Her mother stood in the middle of the chamber, slowly turning in a circle.

"They touched naught in this chamber." Fresh tears filled her eyes. "Why everything else except this room?"

"I do not know," Tyra said, shaking her head. It was true. Everything was just as Scott had left it. A quilt lay stretched across the bed with his pillow lying in place. The desk and chair were against the far wall with his ink and quill, as well as blank parchment paper. His wardrobe still held his clothes, and the chest at the foot of his bed contained his personal items.

Mama sank to her knees and burst into tears. She shook her head. "I do not understand it."

"Perhaps they were called away before they could get to this chamber," Hugh said, shrugging his shoulders in the same bewilderment.

"Still, I find it strange as well," Tyra said, meeting his gaze. "We shall never know why."

The next few weeks they worked hard to clean up The MacGregor Quest. The project became much easier when Colonel Robeson promoted Hugh to the rank of captain and stationed him over troops of men in Wilmington. He no longer had to travel to and from Elizabethtown. His orders were to establish Patriot control over the city and make sure the Tories were subdued since there had been so many loyalists in the area.

He had Tyra make a list of all the known Whigs in town and called on them for support. Many were more than eager to help. The rest of his time was spent assessing homes destroyed or wrecked by the British before they left. People who had fled slowly returned as news spread the Continentals had won.

As Christmas drew near, soldiers made their way home. Many passed through Wilmington on their way to Charles Town. They brought news and stories of what they witnessed and what it was like in the war. The fighting had been brutal, and the accounts of Yorktown were beyond belief. When Hugh learned Cornwallis had been too proud to meet General Washington on the field and sent his second-in-command to surrender for him, Hugh's decision to fight for the Continentals was once again validated. The British had marched off the field with their musicians playing the tune *The World Turned Upside Down*.

Once Mrs. Wakefield learned of what had happened to the MacGregor home, she donated two chairs and a sofa. Hugh and Tyra sat on the sofa in the parlor. He had asked her to join him this morning so he could share his plans with her. Taking Tyra's hand in his, he looked into her wide green eyes.

"Tyra, I have taken a room at Mr. and Mrs. Saunders's boarding house."

"But why?" She gestured around them. "I realize we do not have much to offer, but you are welcome to stay here. Mama said so."

"Yes, I know, and I am grateful to her." He tightened his grip on her hands. Over the last couple of weeks, she had developed calluses from working so hard to restore their home. "Now that so many soldiers are starting to return, I anticipate the arrival of your father and brothers. 'Twould not be appropriate for me to be staying here. The last thing I need is to evoke your father's wrath before I have a chance to win his approval."

"My noble Hugh," she said, cupping his cheek and peering into his eyes. "Always determined to do the right thing no matter the consequence or how hard it might be." She shook her head, but her eyes were lit with fondness. "'Twill seem strange to have you staying elsewhere."

"It may seem like it at first, but when your father and brothers return, I doubt it will seem so strange." He chuckled. "I cannot ever remember being so nervous to meet someone or so eager to gain a person's approval." He covered her hand with his and circled his thumb over her wrist.

"He will love you once he comes to know you." She linked her fingers through his in an attempt to encourage him. "You worry too much, Captain Donahue Morgan."

"With good reason." Hugh took a deep breath and tried not to think of all the stories Kirk had told Hugh about his father's prowess and feats. "I want to marry Malcolm MacGregor's only daughter."

"True." She nodded as a slow smile curled her pink lips. "He will probably draw his broadsword on you rather than his revolver."

Hugh gulped.

"'Tis a joke." Tyra laughed, shoving her knuckles into his arm. "You should relax. My da is a fair and honorable man."

"Well, if he does not draw a weapon on me for wanting to wed his only daughter, he might once he learns I was a British officer who fought against them for several years, the same army who took his son's life."

This time, Tyra didn't respond. Instead, she looked away. Hugh's gut clenched in reaction. Now he knew what he ought to be worried about.

The sound of horses rode up the lane. Tyra jumped up and rushed to the window. She paused as she squinted and tilted her head. Her breath caught as she covered her mouth. "'Tis them." Tears filled her eyes and her voice. "Mama! They are here! Da and the lads have come home!"

✍❦

Hugh stayed inside and watched the MacGregor family rejoin each other. Now he knew where Tyra had gotten her height. The MacGregor men were huge. He imagined they would have been a formidable force in battle. In spite of the cold weather, his hands began to sweat and he wiped them on his breeches. If it would not hurt Tyra's feelings, he would have slipped out the back door unnoticed to give them time to enjoy each other's company and get reacquainted without the immediate need to explain his identity and connection to the family.

Instead, he waited. They walked toward the house. His heart raced. The initial reunion was over, and now they would learn of all the changes which took place in their absence. It was the opening he needed to tell Tyra goodbye and make his escape. He stepped outside onto the porch. Malcolm and his sons paused to stare at him in curious surprise.

"Who are you?" Malcolm asked, lifting a suspicious eyebrow. He had long russet-colored hair with gray at the temples and a full beard and mustache of the same color. He matched Hugh's height, but was much broader. He wore a blue coat as part of his uniform, but it was worn at the elbows and over the right shoulder. The stripes on his arm showed the rank of captain. Hugh stood at attention and saluted him.

"I am Captain Donahue Morgan," Hugh said. "Colonel Robeson of Elizabethtown set me in charge of Wilmington after the British retreated. 'Tis an honor to meet you, sir."

"Aye, but what are ye doing at my house?" Malcolm asked, crossing his muscled arms. His deep voice held the same Scottish brogue as his wife.

"Da, he is my fiancé." Tyra stepped forward and gripped Hugh's arm. "We have much to tell you since you have been away."

"Fiancé?" He balled his fists and planted them on his hips. "What is the meaning o'this?"

"Tyra, they have only just returned." Hugh patted her hand on his arm. "There will be plenty of time for discussion later. Right now, enjoy getting reacquainted with them. I will return in a few days." Hugh saluted her father and brothers. He hurried down the porch steps and strode toward his horse tethered to a nearby tree. *"Lord, please convince her father to give us his blessing."*

The whispered prayer wasn't loud enough for the others to hear, but he intended to repeat the prayer until he knew the Almighty at least heard him.

☙❧

For a week Tyra waited on Hugh to call again. She kept busy listening to her brothers tell stories of the war and tease her with tales, but even they could not lift her spirits after what she suspected her father had done. He had drilled her and Mama with questions about Hugh and demanded to know how they met. When he discovered Hugh had been a British soldier, he ranted about how a double-minded man could not be trusted. Not even Mama could calm his temper.

The next day Da took himself off saying he intended to visit Hugh and speak to him man to man. He returned in a somber mood, saying no more about Hugh. Tyra had questioned her mother, but her father had told her nothing and refused to speak about the matter.

Tyra knew she would have to confront him sooner or later, but she dreaded it. For years, she had longed for her father and brothers to return home and the war to be over, and now that her prayers were finally answered, this rift between them ripped her heart to shreds.

Christmas morning she woke with a heavy heart and stared outside her window at the rising sun sparkling on the surface of the frostbitten grass and bare tree limbs. A year ago, her family had feasted together—all of them—but this year Scott would not be among them. Now it appeared Hugh would not be with them either. She took a deep breath and dressed in her dark green gown, a new gown her father had a seamstress from town to make for her. Tyra twisted her hair up in a couple of combs upon the crown of her head.

She had made up her mind. Since her father refused to accept Hugh, she would spend this last Christmas with her family and then she intended to elope with Hugh if he would still have her. Hugh was an honorable man. If her father had forbidden him from seeing her, he would stay away in order to do the right thing. It would be up to her to go to him. She had to try.

By the time she arrived downstairs, her mother was already in the kitchen cooking. Tyra went in and pulled an apron off the peg and tied it around her. "What can I do to help?" she asked.

"Ye can stop moping around," Mama said, punching a fist in a ball of dough. "I do not like seeing ye so unhappy, lass."

"I am sorry, and since it is Christmas, I will try to make an extra effort to be happy today."

"Ye make happiness sound like a burden." Mama glanced at her with a lift of her blond eyebrow. "I realize ye're disappointed in yer Da, but we are so blessed to have him and yer brothers home—especially at Christmas."

As they worked on the Christmas feast over the next hour, Alec and Callum joined them, while Kirk and Da went on an errand. Tyra wasn't fooled. The two of them were looking for opportunities to sneak a bite here and there and it made her love them all the more.

Alec's brown eyes were still the same, but other things had changed about him. Like Kirk, he had grown taller and broader. He looked more like Callum than before. Their dark hair was now the same brown shade and they wore it at a similar length. Scott was the only one who had favored their mother with blond hair and blue eyes. It felt like a hole would forever be in her heart each time he crossed her mind. She gulped and tried to turn her thoughts in a different direction.

The front door swung open and Kirk called to them. "Alec and Callum, come help us!"

"What is going on?" Tyra looked over at her mother who looked up with the same surprise Tyra felt. Mama shrugged as she wiped her hands on her apron and followed her sons out the kitchen and down the hall. Tyra sighed and followed her, the last to step out onto the porch.

Her father and brothers were helping Hugh unload a carved dining table. She gasped in joyous surprise. "Hugh, what are you doing here?"

"What? Do you not want me here?" He glanced up at her with a grin as he jumped down from the wagon beside Callum and they both lifted a corner of the table.

"Of course I do, but I have not heard from you in over a week." She crossed her arms and walked to the edge of the porch, refraining from the urge to demand an explanation in front of her family.

"I invited him here," Da said, carrying his corner of the table to the end of the wagon bed. "The two of us have talked, and we have come to an understanding when I visited him last week."

"Where did this beautiful oak table come from?" Mama asked.

"'Tis a Christmas gift from me," Hugh said. "I thought your family could use it for your Christmas feast since the other one was destroyed." He glanced over at Tyra and winked. "I had to go all the way to Campbellton to get it. 'Tis why you have not heard from me."

"What understanding? Da, did you know about this table?" she asked, unable to stop the grin lurking at the corners of her mouth.

"Not about the table." Da shook his head and grunted as they hoisted the table up and climbed the porch steps. They paused on the porch landing. "I merely grew tired of watching ye mope around the house as if yer life was at an end, so Kirk and I left this morn to collect Captain Morgan."

"Tyra, would you stop distracting him so we can get this inside?" Alec gave her an irritated look as he rolled his eyes heavenward and shook his head.

The men lifted the table and angled it sideways to carry it across the threshold. Once they were through, Mama raced inside to check on the food. With a little more maneuvering, they managed to set it down in the same place where the other one used to be.

"Now we need to bring in the chairs." Kirk waved his brothers outside. They all filed out the door again.

Her father stayed inside, no doubt, to chaperone her and Hugh. The two men stood in silence until Tyra grew uncomfortable. She moved closer to Hugh and grabbed his arm. "Da when you went to visit Hugh and speak to him, you gave the impression you intended to forbid him to marry me."

"I did." He nodded and crossed his arms as he set his chin at a stubborn angle.

"Did Hugh say or do something to displease you?" she asked.

"He did not." He shook his head.

"Did he explain to you why he enlisted in the British Army and why he changed his mind and joined the Patriot cause?" she asked, trying to understand what was happening with her father.

"He did."

"Well, could you not understand why he enlisted in the British Army hoping to improve his station and circumstances in life? Surely, as a poor lad in Scotland, you could identify with his reasons. And as a man of principle, you can also understand why he came to the colonies, saw a different way of life, one of opportunity and freedom."

"I know, Tyra." He scratched his gray temple and looked down at the floor as if to escape her scrutinizing gaze. As her brothers carried in the chairs, he turned toward them. "Kirk, would you tell your mother I would like her presence in the dining room?"

Her brothers set all the chairs at the table and stood back as if waiting to see what would happen next. Her mother arrived and joined her father's side. He looked at Tyra and then at Hugh. "I have thought about my conduct upon hearing of yer engagement. I have considered everyone's point of view, especially yer mother's." Da stopped to glance at Mama and gave her a charming grin. "I have prayed long and hard 'bout this. I realized after being away at war for six years, I feel as if I missed seeing ye grow up, lass. Ye were twelve when I left and now yer ten and eight." Tears filled his eyes, and he paused to collect his emotions as his nose turned red. "Tyra, ye grew up without me, and my visits were so few and short during that time. I was not expecting to come home and lose ye just when I had gotten ye back."

"Da, you will not be losing me. I promise." Tears sprang to Tyra's eyes. It was rare to see her father cry, and this was not what she expected. His temper was something she had anticipated, not an emotional explanation to touch her heart like this.

"My Christmas gift to ye both is my blessing," Da said. "Once he faced me like a man and asked for yer hand in marriage, I knew what the right answer should be."

Her brothers cheered and roared with excitement. Her mother gasped and leaned over to kiss her father's cheek. Tyra squealed with delight and turned to Hugh. He engulfed her in a warm embrace. "I love you, Tyra MacGregor," he whispered in her ear.

"I love you, too," she whispered back.

"All right, you two, that is good enough." Her father pulled on her arm. "There will always be a chaperone with you until the day of the wedding."

Tyra exchanged a happy grin with her husband to be. Perhaps the wedding date should be very soon!

Discussion Questions

1. Tyra MacGregor mentions that people in her church were friends she had grown up with and known all her life, but the moment the Revolutionary War broke out and the MacGregors became Continentals, they were not welcome at church. How realistic is this to modern-day church splits, human nature, and other divisions?

2. Captain Donahue Morgan thought he knew what he wanted out of life until he met Tyra and she helped him see things differently. What events or books have made you open your mind to ideas you were once closed-minded about?

3. There were several real-life events and people used in *For Love or Country* regarding the Revolutionary War. What events surprised you most? What historical myths were dispelled?

4. Tyra was put into a self-defense position of killing someone to save herself. Even though she feels like she did what she had to do, she still wrestles with guilt and fears it happening again. There were some Scriptures that comforted her, but what other biblical Scriptures could have worked as well? What would you have done in her shoes?

5. Captain Donahue Morgan came to a deciding factor when he had to choose between serving the British Army or choosing Tyra and the Continentals. Other than his love for Tyra, what other significant things impacted his decision?

6. At times Hugh didn't agree with Major James Craig and how he abused his power, but Hugh was limited being under his command. Have you ever been under someone who consistently abused their power and authority? How did you handle it? What were some other choices that Hugh might have had?

7. The story begins at Christmas and ends a year later at Christmas, but so much has changed. How did this make

you feel in the passage of time? Have you ever had your life change so drastically in only a year?

8. The MacGregors live so differently from the Tuscarora Indians, yet they were able to trust them and maintain a friendship with them through the worst. By all appearances, one would think the MacGregors had more in common with their Tory friends who betrayed them. What does this say about true friendship and trust?

Want to learn more about author
Jennifer Hudson Taylor and check out other great
fiction from Abingdon Press?

Check out
www.AbingdonPress.com
to read interviews with your favorite authors, find tips
for starting a reading group, and stay posted on what
new titles are on the horizon.

Be sure to visit Jennifer online!

http://jenniferswriting.blogspot.com/.com
http://jenniferhudsontaylorsbooks.blogspot.com/
https://www.facebook.com/JenniferHudsonTaylor
http://carolinascots-irish.blogspot.com/

We hope you enjoyed Jennifer Hudson Taylor's *For Love or Country*, the second book in her MacGregor Legacy series. We hope you will be inspired to check out the next book of the series, *For Love or Liberty*. Here's chapter one, which sets the stage for a romance set against the dramatic events of the War of 1812.

ℒ♥

1

*C*harlotte stood in the sand as waves washed over her bare feet, burying her heels and toes like an anchor holding her captive in time. The cool sea water receded from her skin leaving a mist of white foam layered with broken shells along the shore—much like the residue of the broken pieces of her life.

Her grieving heart threatened to succumb to the pain engulfing her, but the glistening colors of the scattered shells across the wet sand painted a brilliant scene of hope. If she could still see something beautiful through the dark clouds residing in her heart, it was a tiny reminder that the Lord had not forsaken her. Even though Emily was gone, her twin sister had left behind two precious children for her to love and help raise. She clung to that thought with resolve, especially since it was Emily's last request of her.

Charlotte covered her heavy chest with a trembling hand and released the aching sob she had held throughout the funeral. Here . . . alone . . . with the wide ocean as comfort, she could finally let out the pain. She wept until her empty stomach rolled and tears choked her. Charlotte's eyes and nose swelled and breathing grew difficult as the inside of her head swirled like a monsoon attacking her brain.

Charlotte lost track of time and dropped to her knees. Oncoming waves swept her black gown into a floating parasol around her legs.

The sound of the rolling ocean managed to console her as she lifted her face to the warm sun. From her earliest memories, the sea had always comforted her in times of distress.

An aggressive wave tumbled over Charlotte, knocking her off balance and onto her side. Her head plunged under and her eyes burned from the saltwater. Once the wave passed, Charlotte sputtered and gasped for air, rubbing at her eyes.

"Charlotte! What are you doing?" A man's voice carried through the breeze and over the splashing waves.

She groaned at the idea of Conrad Deaton finding her in such a predicament. Why did he always have the habit of catching her at her worst? Ignoring the broken shells beneath her feet, Charlotte scrambled to regain her balance before he reached her. She winced as a sharp edge sliced through the bottom of her heel. She grabbed her foot as another wave slammed her under a second time. Charlotte splashed her arms and legs, determined to land on her feet before the next wave hit.

Strong hands grabbed her around the waist and pulled her out of the water. Charlotte gasped as cold air hit her wet skin and she could breathe again. Propelled against the warmth of a solid chest with a fast beating heart, she clutched at his shirt.

"What are you trying to do? Drown yourself?" Conrad asked, his voice like a commanding officer.

Well, she wasn't one of his sailors to be commanded. Charlotte pushed against him and kicked in an attempt to be free. A lock of sandy brown hair fell across his forehead as he gripped her tight and grinned. His mustache moved with his mouth, revealing a row of healthy teeth in spite of his time commanding *The Victorious* at sea. His hazel eyes lit in challenge, and a hint of his boyish freckles peeked across his nose in the bright sun. Something in her chest skipped with light-hearted joy at seeing him in a different light, but she swallowed back the temptation to let down her guard. This was Conrad, the man who had tried to sabotage his brother's courtship with her sister and would have succeeded had it not been for her wise intervention in distracting him.

Everyone saw him as a sea loving adventurer who lived for the thrill of exciting heroism, but she knew him for what he was. Captain Conrad Deaton was a man bent on destroying true love because he could never give up his beloved freedom and adventures at sea. Marriage imprisoned men with responsibilities and trials. He had begged his brother to avoid it. Charlotte feared that while the rest of them grieved, he secretly viewed her sister's death as a way out for his younger brother, David.

He had shed his Navy coat and wore a white buttoned shirt with blooming sleeves, navy pants, and black boots that sloshed in the water and crunched seashells beneath his heels. Conrad smelled of leather and musk from a fresh shave and bath, having made a special attempt to look his best for her sister's funeral that morning. Charlotte closed her eyes and breathed in the scent of him. It had an unexpected calming effect on her. She rested her aching head against him, knowing her struggles would be futile against his strength.

"I realize you are grieving for your sister, but I am NOT about to sit back and watch you drown yourself over it." Conrad clenched his jaw as he tightened his hold on her and concentrated on a targeted spot in the sand. "Do you not think the family has been through enough these last few days?"

"It is true that I am deeply grieved over the loss of my sister, but contrary to your belief, I was not about to drown myself." Charlotte sighed in exasperation and shook her head. "I only needed a moment alone, to grieve freely without anyone watching and waiting for me to fall apart. Besides, I would never think of relieving you of my presence so easily. Whether you like it or not, I made a promise to help raise our niece and nephew, and I aim to do it."

Conrad blew out a deep breath as he set her down on a mound of dry sand near his discarded coat. The rank of captain displayed in bold yellow threads on the shoulders. He settled beside her, propping his knees up and linking his hands between them. Conrad gave her a sideways glance, a look of determination crossing his expression. "Likewise, my dear, I am afraid you will have to put up with me as well. I have no intention of neglecting my brother in his time of need. I, too, intend to be part of my niece and nephew's life."

"We shall see about that." She shrugged and looked away, wiping wet strands of hair from her eyes. "I doubt you could stay in one place long enough to be much of an influence on anyone." Charlotte lifted her hand and gestured to the ocean. "The sea will call you back before little Davie turns six and Ashlynn is a year old."

"Actually, the Navy has already tried to lure me away. I received word yesterday that I am being transferred to the war on the Great Lakes. They need a captain to command one of their new ships on Lake Erie. I shall be stationed in Cleaveland." He leaned closer, brushing her hair down the side of her face and behind her ear. "I suppose you shall get your wish. You shall be rid of me within the fortnight."

"What happened to not abandoning your brother in his time of need?" Charlotte jerked away from his touch, glaring at him with contempt.

"Which is why I requested David to be transferred under my command, so I can look out for him. Do not be so quick to judge me." He reached for her again, but she slapped his hand away and scooted out of reach. Charlotte dug her palms into the thick sand for leverage and pushed her wet body to her feet.

"You would have him abandon his children after only a few days of losing their mother?" Her voice rose as the waves crashed behind her. She shoved her fists on her hips and stared down at him in disbelief. "You are insufferable!"

"There you go again, assuming the worst about me." He pointed at her as he stood. Conrad frowned and turned to wipe the sand from his backside. "We are taking the children with us. Your father has agreed to help us find a nursemaid for Ashlynn. I am not as insensitive and uncaring you like to think."

"Indeed you are." She stepped closer, ignoring the ache in her neck from staring up at him. "My sister knew what she was doing in asking me to help raise her children. She knew David would be too weak to deal with the likes of you and your meddling." She poked his chest. "You will not take those children across the country in this war."

"No, their father is and there is naught you can do about it." He crossed his arms.

"We shall see about that." She turned on her heel and stomped through the sand.

Conrad groaned as Charlotte rushed from him. He bent to retrieve his coat and realized a trail of red stains followed her footprints in the sand. Was it blood? Concerned, he ran after her.

"Charlotte, wait!" He caught up to her, grabbing her arm. "Your foot is bleeding."

"Let go of me!" She jerked away and stumbled. Wincing, she reached for her heel. "I shall be fine."

"Not if you get sand in the wound and end up with an infection." Conrad reached for her again, but she averted him. Tired of arguing with her, he strode after Charlotte and gathered her around the waist. He ignored her surprised gasp and lifted her up, tossing her over his shoulder. "I will not have the family blaming me for allowing you to be so foolish."

"Oh, so I am another one of your heroic deeds, am I?" She beat upon his back. "Put me down. You have no right."

Conrad pivoted around and carried her back to the sea. Charlotte continued to hurl insults at him, but he paid her no heed. He waded into the water at a foot deep and bent to one knee. Maneuvering Charlotte from his shoulder and settling her on his bent knee, Conrad dipped her injured foot into the water to wash off the gritty wound.

She stopped her complaints long enough to bite her bottom lip in obvious discomfort. It was all the confirmation he needed to know he had done the right thing. The blood washed away, and he could see a half circle cut, but it wasn't too deep. If she would stay off it a couple of days, stitches wouldn't be necessary nor would she risk an infection.

"At least this nasty gash is on your heel and not the tender part of your foot." Unable to resist, Conrad lightly trailed a fingertip along the inside of her foot, tickling her. She kicked in reaction and jerked back with enough force to send him on his backside. With a chuckle, Conrad managed to keep her in his grasp and took the full brunt of the fall. His breeches were thick enough to protect his flesh from the shells, but not enough to keep from bruising his hide.

"That is completely inappropriate," she said, her green eyes blazing like fire. Charlotte's pink lips twisted into a frown, and her wet blond hair tangled around her face and shoulders. Even now she looked beautiful in spite of her disheveled state. The fact that she glared at him as if she wished she had a pitchfork in her hand did not even discourage him in the least.

Another wave rushed at them. Conrad gathered her tight in his arms and stood to his feet in time to avoid it. Breathing a sigh of relief, he glanced down at her. "We had better get you back, but I must say, I have quite enjoyed the fun." A grin tugged at his mouth. He could never resist teasing her. She made the temptation too enjoyable.

"Fun . . . indeed." She turned and motioned to an object lying in the sand. "Do not forget my slippers."

"Would never think of it." Conrad carried her over to them. "Step down on your good foot and I shall retrieve them for you."

For once she obeyed, leaning on his arm for support as he bent to grab her brown slippers. He dumped out sand that had blown into them. She couldn't put them back on and risk getting sand in the wound. He held them out and met her gaze. She grinned. "You could rinse the sand out of them and then I could wear them again."

"And I could just carry you."

"All the way back to the house?" She lifted a golden eyebrow, her expression suggested he had gone daft.

"No, back to my horse." He bent and swept her up before she could protest. "Your mother asked me to find you. She was worried since you disappeared right after we arrived home from your sister's funeral. The longer it takes me to get you back, the longer she will continue to worry."

At the mention of the funeral, Charlotte's expression fell into a pensive frown. "I have been thinking, it would have been harder if Emma had not already married your brother and moved from home." Charlotte surprised him by lying her head against his shoulder. "Now I am used to having my own chamber and being alone. Still, the aching pain lingers and deepens."

"I know we have had our differences, but I am sorry you are going through this." Conrad wanted to comfort her, but he wasn't sure if she would allow it. Instead, he kept silent as he carried her to where he had left his horse tethered to a nearby tree. Once he settled her in the saddle, he took the reins and mounted up behind her. Now that they were away from the water, the humid heat made his lungs feel like they were suffocating, and the discomfort of his wet clothes and soggy boots scratched at his skin.

Conrad smelled the salty sea in her wet hair brushing against his chin. His arms pressed against hers as he guided the reins. Rather than increasing his discomfort, having her near brought a measure of satisfaction he had not anticipated. He wondered if she felt the same. Was it a bond between them or attraction? Charlotte had a way of confusing him like no other, but she also infuriated him quicker than anyone. He used to think his brother had that distinctive honor, and then he had met Charlotte.

They arrived at the two-story brick home half an hour later. As he rode up to the front porch, Charlotte sighed. "Now we will have to explain why we look so disheveled."

"Do not worry, I am sure they are used to it by now. Since the day my brother and I met you and your sister six years ago, you have been headstrong and in constant trouble." He didn't say it, but he had always thought that Emma was her voice of reason, keeping Charlotte from straying too far. With the passing of her twin, he feared Charlotte's behavior would stretch beyond the limits of what was considered proper. Her grief alone could launch her in any direction. The way the family watched her, and the comments they made, told him he wasn't alone in his concern.

The front door opened and her mother rushed out wringing her hands and worry in her wrinkled brow. She was tall for a woman. He guessed nearly six feet, but she remained thin and healthy for one nearing fifty. Her hair was swept up on her head in a mixture of red and gray locks. She wore a black gown, but had removed the black hat she had worn to the funeral.

Conrad helped Charlotte dismount as her father and brothers followed her mother out onto the porch with marked concern on their stern faces. A moment later her brothers' wives and children appeared, flanking around them and shielding their eyes from the sun.

"Charlotte, you have been worrying your mother—today of all days." Her father crossed his arms and shook his gray head in disappointment. He stroked his full beard in thought as if pondering how best to handle the situation. He wore a black suit and his gray eyes flickered as he assessed their rumpled attire and wayward hair. Unsure of how Captain Donahue Morgan would react, Conrad remained silent. Charlotte leaned into him, as if seeking his support to face them all. He swept her into his arms and carried her to toward the house.

Mrs. Tyra Morgan breathed deeply as tears filled her eyes, but she took a defiant step forward and shoved her hands on her hips. "What have you gone and done now, Charlotte? Why can you not walk?"

"Where did you find her?" Charlotte's father's asked, stepping forward to take her.

"In the ocean." Conrad handed her over to her father, knowing the man was still in fine health and could handle her weight. "She has cut her foot on a shell and we needed to clean sand out of it. I think she will be fine."

"Hugh, take her in and set her on the couch so I can see if she needs stitching," Mrs. Morgan said.

"Thank you," Hugh said, his gray eyes meeting Conrad's. "Is there anything else we should know? Other injuries?"

"No, I am fine," Charlotte said. "I am sorry, I did not mean to worry everyone. I only needed to be alone. You all know how I find solace at the sea."

"Since we just buried Emma this morning, it would help if you would think of someone else besides yourself once in a while." Scott, her oldest brother scolded her.

Someone cleared her throat and the whole family parted, creating an aisle for Charlotte's grandmother. She walked forward, leaning on a cane, as she approached Charlotte. Unlike the others, a smile lit her wrinkled face, but moisture gathered in her blue eyes as she reached over and cupped Charlotte's cheek.

"Lass, ye remind me so much of yer mother when she was yer age, strong-willed and stubborn. And Emma was more like me when I came from Scotland." She turned and stared up at Mr. and Mrs. Morgan. "This family has had enough sadness for one day. There is no place for anger in a grieving family. 'Tisn't unusual for Charlotte to go running off. She is back now. Let us take comfort in that and in each other. Right now, there is much to be decided for Emma's children."

$\mathscr{L}$

Charlotte sat on the couch in the parlor and listened to her family's chastisement for disappearing after Emma's funeral. Painful memories flashed through her mind. Staring down at her twin's cold, empty body, felt like she stared at herself in that coffin. As identical twins, she and Emma shared more than their looks, a bond that was beyond anything she could ever hope to explain. The moment she held her sister's hand and watched her breathe her last, something inside her snapped and a deep loneliness engulfed her. She had forced herself to endure the funeral, including all the nods and condolences of their friends, but afterwards, she could no longer cope and fled.

Little Davie came over and crawled onto her lap. At five years old, she could only imagine what must be going through his mind. While he seemed to understand that his mother had died and would never come back, did he really comprehend death when Charlotte continued to struggle with it at a score and three years? Did he feel like his mother had abandoned him?

"Auntie, I thought you left like Mama." Davie swung his tiny arms around her neck and squeezed so tight that he cut off her breath.

"No, I only went for a walk to the ocean." She hugged him back, resting her chin on his brown head. Not once had it occurred to her that he might think of her dying as well. The idea of hurting him was more than she could bear. The muscles in her chest closed in on her lungs, nearly suffocating her. She closed her eyes as she kissed the top of his head. Fresh tears squeezed past her eyelids and crawled down her face as the ache in her heart and chest deepened.

David couldn't take the children away. At less than a week old, Ashlynn wouldn't know any better, but Davie would. His reaction to her brief disappearance proved it. Besides, she had made a promise to her sister, and as she had told Conrad, she intended to keep it.

"While I am still living and breathing, I will never leave you. I promise." Charlotte stroked the back of Davie's head. His wide hazel eyes blinked up at her as a slow grin spread across his face.

"I love you, Auntie!" Satisfied and reassured, he gave her another big hug and scooted off her lap to go play.

Charlotte took a deep breath and used the back of her hand to wipe the tears from her face. She glanced over at Grandma Lauren rocking little Ashlynn to sleep in a wooden rocker that Grandpa had made her before his death two years ago. Grandma understood her grief. She once told Charlotte that everything reminded her of Grandpa Malcolm. Now, everything would remind Charlotte of

Emma. There was a childhood memory lurking in each room, lingering in every corner, all the places in town would haunt her, even her own face each time she looked in the mirror.

Throughout the afternoon families dropped by to express their condolences and brought dishes of food and baked desserts. While it was a strain on her family to keep up the fake smiles, the trivial conversations, and their true feelings at bay, it was expected. Their distant cousins from the Baker family were the last to leave.

Charlotte's father closed the front door in the foyer. A moment later he walked back into the living room and paused to clear his throat. "David, it is my understanding from your brother that you are being transferred to the Great Lakes. I would like to know what you have decided to do about the children. Who will care for them during the long months that you will be serving aboard a naval ship?"

Silence filled the room as the air thickened with anticipation. Like the rest of her family, Charlotte watched David's reaction, hoping he would be willing to let the children stay where she could better care for them. They were familiar with their home here, their grandparent's home, and the city of Wilmington. Here, familiar faces surrounded them in love, comfort, and security.

Fear clutched her heart as she glanced around the somber room. The bottom half of the walls were made of dark paneling encased in carved squares and thick molding, while the upper half of the walls were painted beige. As the sun's light diminished through the windows, someone lit candles around the room.

Charlotte's mother sat on the couch beside her, mopping at her damp face with the handkerchief her father had given her. Melanie, her older sister at a score and five years sat on Charlotte's other side, no doubt charged with the responsibility of watching over her in case Charlotte decided to disappear again. She favored their mother with fiery red hair and green eyes. Her Husband, Rob McCauley, was outside with their toddler son, making sure the older children behaved. He claimed to be out there to watch the kids, but Charlotte knew it was because he smoked his pipe.

Her oldest brother Scott and his wife Caroline sat on the settee by the window. He was named for their uncle, Scott MacGregor, who had fought and died in the War of Independence. At the age of three score, her brother now had four children, who all chased lightning bugs outside with their cousins. Like Emma and her, he had blond hair favoring their Grandma Lauren, but unlike them, he had the same deep blue eyes as their grandmother.

Her brother Duncan stood beside his wife, Elizabeth, seated in a wood chair by the pianoforte. Duncan was named for their great-grandfather from Argyll, Scotland. At a score and seven years, he was the second oldest with dark brown eyes and black hair like their father. During their seven year marriage, they had a six year old son and a three year old daughter.

"David, we know you do not feel like discussing these decisions right now, but we have to find a permanent nursemaid for Ashlynn." Uncle Callum's deep voice carried across the room as he walked to stand beside Charlotte's father. After Grandpa Malcolm passed away, he now ran The MacGregor Quest estate and took over as the patriarch of the MacGregor family. "Mrs. Brown has agreed to come over and feed her for the night, but only this one night. We need to hear your plans so we can help you, lad."

David stared at the wood floor where he sat in a chair in a dark corner. His eyes were red and swollen with shadows beneath them testifying to his lack of sleep. He had not shaved, so brown whiskers now graced his face and neck. Kneeling forward, he placed his elbows on his knees and rubbed his chin with a weary sigh.

"I promised Emma that I would be a good father, and I cannot do that if I abandon my children and leave them here. They have already lost their Mama. I cannot allow them to lose their daddy, too." His voice broke and he looked away at the wall.

Charlotte closed her eyes as familiar pain sliced through her chest. Even though Conrad had already told her their plans, a small part of her still hoped David would change his mind. She glanced over at Conrad leaning against the wall near his brother. His warm hazel eyes locked with hers as he remained silent. Doubt flickered in his eyes. Did he doubt his brother's decision, but felt honor-bound to stand by him? Her unease grew.

"But David, have you considered how dangerous it would be to travel with a newborn infant?" Mama asked, disbelief thickening her tone.

"I have already spoken to the doctor and will wait a fortnight as he suggested before we leave." David brushed his hand through his hair leaving a small gap on the side. "Once we arrive and get settled in Cleaveland, Ohio, I plan to hire a nursemaid to stay with the children."

"A complete stranger?" Mama pressed the heel of her hand against her forehead. "I cannot believe this. Besides, you will need a nurse-maid for the journey. You cannot wait until you arrive."

"I am sorry, Mrs. Morgan," David blinked back tears. "But I am their father, and war or no war, I will not abandon my children. My mind is made up. They are coming with me."

"It will be hard finding a nursemaid who is willing and able to travel with you." Charlotte's father crossed his arms with a frown wrinkling his forehead. "However, I shall endeavor to do my best to find someone."

"Hugh! You cannot be serious?" Mama scooted to the edge of the couch, ready to battle all of them for the care and safety of her grand-children. "The country is at war with England once again. And dare I suggest the worst? David will be fighting on a battleship. What if he cannot return to them? The children will be all alone in a strange place."

"I made a promise to my twin." Charlotte stood, her chin trem-bled and tears threatened to choke her, but she swallowed them back. "For as long as they need me, wherever they go, I will go. Unlike the rest of you, I have no husband, no children, and I am available."

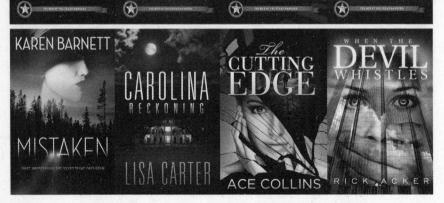

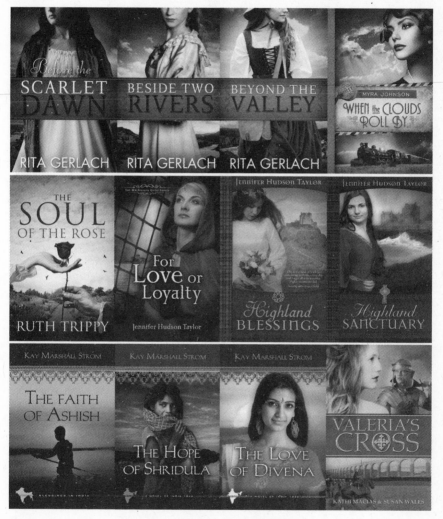